ZERO KILL

ALSO BY M.K. HILL

Two O'Clock Boy
It Was Her
One Bad Thing

Sasha Dawson Series
The Bad Place
The Woman in the Wood

ZERO KILL

M. K. HILL

An Aries Book

First published in the UK in 2023 by Head of Zeus,
part of Bloomsbury Publishing Plc

9 7 5 3 1 2 4 6 8

A catalogue record for this book is available from the British Library.

ISBN (HB): 9781804549193
ISBN (XTPB): 9781804549216
ISBN (E): 9781804549230

Cover design: Ben Prior

Typeset by Siliconchips Services Ltd UK

Printed and bound in Great Britain by
CPI Group (UK) Ltd, Croydon CR0 4YY

Head of Zeus
First Floor East
5–8 Hardwick Street
London EC1R 4RG

WWW.HEADOFZEUS.COM

For Laurence

1

Date Night was going pretty well, until the clock struck midnight and everything went to shit.

Joel did his best to make it a night to remember. There'd be no kids to spoil the romantic mood, he told her. 'I'm going to treat you like a queen.'

Which didn't sound too bad to Elsa's ears. He took her to a posh restaurant off the King's Road, one of those trendy places you have to book months in advance, thinking she'd be impressed. What he didn't know was that back in her old life, the one he had no idea about, Elsa was familiar with places like this, and it was just the kind of snooty chophouse that bored her senseless.

But Joel was like a puppy desperate to please, and kept telling her about the strings he pulled to get them in the door, so she offered up a couple of appreciative remarks to make him feel good. Despite the fact the menu was pretentious, the waiters walked around with their noses in the air, and there was nowhere to place her elbows on the table because there was cutlery everywhere.

Plus, the price of the wine was fucking ridiculous.

'A small glass,' Elsa told him when he implored her to choose anything she wanted. You didn't reach the fitness levels of an elite athlete – 15 per cent body fat; VO_2max of 40 per cent; optimal bone density and muscle mass – by drinking alcohol. But he insisted on buying a bottle with a long unpronounceable name and longer price tag, just to show off. It would be pathetic, really, if she didn't find his eagerness to please such a turn-on.

Joel looked handsome and relaxed in a casual suit, the stiff cuffs of his pink shirt peeking jauntily at the sleeves, but then he liked to dress smartly. Elsa, who spent every day in sweat tops, leggings and trainers, felt uncomfortable and foolish in towering heels and a tight red dress that clenched her torso, from her broad shoulders to her flat stomach, before running out of fabric halfway down her long thighs. Thanks to the plunging neckline, she spent most of the night trying to cover her tits.

'Just for the record.' He watched her pluck at the elastic. 'You look magnificent.'

'I feel like an idiot.' She eyed the other diners. 'And everybody's staring.'

He laughed. 'Because you're a goddess.'

When they had eaten – the food was delicious, but Elsa picked at it, as usual – she looked around the high-ceilinged room, still packed late on a Thursday night. People chatted loudly and brayed with laughter, pleased with themselves for being there. Champagne corks popped; sizzling dishes were delivered to tables. When she caught a fat guy across the room ogling her, her stare made him quickly look away.

'We should have stayed home with a takeaway and a movie.'

'We can do that any night. It's healthy to get out occasionally, just the two of us.' Joel lifted an eyebrow. 'So I can treat the woman I love the way she deserves.'

'You don't have to lay it on thick, I was planning on fucking you tonight.'

She said it just as a waiter arrived at the table, making Joel blush. Elsa nodded at her empty glass. 'I asked for sparkling water.'

'I'm sorry, madam,' said the waiter. 'I'll get it as soon as I can.'

She gave him a terse smile. 'Now, please.'

He blinked. 'Of course, madam.'

'I'm sorry,' Joel apologized as the guy left, and he shook his head ruefully at Elsa. 'You could start a fight in an empty room.'

'Ready when you are.' She pouted. 'I'm never going to be nicey-nicey.'

'I love your sharp edges, and wouldn't have you any other way.'

'I told you already, I'll let you have me tonight.'

'But, also—'

She rolled her eyes. 'Here it comes.'

'The waiter is rushed off his feet and doing his best, so maybe… you could consider apologizing.'

She raised her glass, with its dribble of wine at the bottom. 'Here's to us.'

'Now you're just trying to shut me up.' They clinked. 'To my fierce and unpredictable girlfriend, who I love.'

'To my oh-so *predictable* boyfriend.'

Joel's fingers drummed the table anxiously. 'There's something I wanted to… there's no easy way to…'

'Just tell me.' She'd had a dread feeling that something like this was going to happen, and Joel was making it all super awkward. He reached into his jacket and took out a ring. It was the most beautiful thing Elsa had ever seen, a thin band with a precise glittering point at its centre; a diamond, no doubt.

He slipped out of his chair and dropped to one knee, holding the ring above his head like an offering to the gods. 'Elsa, will you do me—'

'Get up,' she hissed. 'You're making a fool of yourself.'

Slipping back into his chair, Joel said, 'Elsa, will you marry me?'

She shifted uncomfortably in her seat, because everyone was watching them.

Maybe he wasn't The One, because she had only ever loved one man and had no plans ever to fall in love again, but she had to admit that he was kind and attentive – and it was undeniable that the kids adored him. Her relationship with her own parents was so poor that maybe a dull, dependable father figure was just what they needed in their lives. Joel felt like the guy to fill that elusive role.

He looked positively ill as he waited for her to answer, so she said, 'I guess we could give it a go.'

'So…' Joel frowned. 'Is that…?'

'Sure.' She shrugged. 'Why not?'

'She said yes!' Joel told the room, and there was a smattering of applause as he reached across the ocean of cutlery to slip the ring onto the third finger of her left hand.

Elsa admired the ring. 'It's gorgeous,' she admitted.

'It's eighteen carats,' he told her proudly. 'Only the best for you. Because I love you.'

She opened her mouth to reply, the *word* on the tip of her tongue – but nothing came out.

'For a moment, I almost thought you were going to

return the compliment.' He leaned forward. 'You know you want to.'

Elsa plonked down her glass. 'It's hard.'

'Not if you mean it. If it's what you feel, it's the most natural thing in the world.'

'Thank you.' She presented her long fingers across the table, showing him the ring, and he tried to hide his disappointment with a smile.

'We should go.' Slipping one foot out of its shoe, she touched her toes to his groin beneath the table. 'Or maybe you would rather have dessert first?'

'Now you're trying to distract me.' His voice rose an octave as her toes pressed harder. 'But it's true I've gone off the idea of dessert.'

The moment the clock on the wall chimed midnight, Joel's phone rang in his pocket.

'Is it Stacey?' Elsa asked, because it might be the babysitter. She cursed herself again for forgetting her phone. They'd been late getting here. Elsa had occasion to apply make-up approximately once every three years, and had spent such a long time trying to remember how to put it on her face that in the rush to leave she'd left her mobile at home. 'Has something happened?'

Joel stared at the screen, then pulled back his chair. 'I'm sorry, I'm going to have to take this.'

'Not fair!' She threw up her hands. 'I don't even have my phone to stare at when you're gone.'

He smiled weakly as he walked towards the reception. The nature of his job – he was something dull in shipping – meant he received calls day and night.

The waiter hurried over with a bottle of sparkling water.

They didn't need it now. Elsa was about to shoo him away, but thought of what Joel had said earlier. When Elsa took his wrist, the man flinched, and she realized she'd grabbed him more forcefully than intended.

'I just wanted to say...' She wasn't used to apologizing, but would prove Joel wrong and show him that she could be... pleasant. 'I was abrupt with you earlier, rude, I guess. What I'm trying to say is...' She blurted it out. 'I suppose I'm sorry.'

Her apology wasn't hugely convincing, even to her own ears, but she had done it and felt pretty good about herself.

The waiter pulled his wrist free. 'Would you like anything else?'

'Just the bill.'

Rolling the warm metal ring on her finger, Elsa felt her life was at a tipping point. She was going to marry; she would have a proper family. The idea of spending the rest of her life with the same person, day in, day out, felt strange, but Joel deserved more for his patience and persistence. She decided to get it over with: she'd tell him she loved him as soon as he got back. The little white lie would make him feel better, and maybe one day it might even come true.

She plucked at the elasticated fabric of the dress squeezed tightly across her stomach – it was like being crushed by some medieval torture machine – but it snapped back into place. Elsa couldn't wait to get back home and throw the dress and heels in the wardrobe. The kids would be asleep, so she and Joel could party.

But he was taking an age.

When a woman walked past, Elsa asked, 'What's the time?'

'It's gone midnight.'

The fact that Joel went outside to take the call bothered her. Maybe something had happened at home and he didn't want to worry her. Waiters bustled around the room, carrying dishes, pouring wine.

Catching the fat guy sneak another look, Elsa decided that if he did it one more time, she'd pour soup over his head.

Sick of waiting, she tossed the napkin from her lap, slipped her feet into the heels, and went to reception to see what the problem was.

Joel was turned away, his head lowered over the phone.

'Hey,' she asked. 'What's going on?'

When he turned, his face was wretched: sad, resigned.

'Elsa,' he whispered, 'I'm so sorry.'

She frowned. 'What are you talking about?'

And then he spun into the air, swinging one leg at dizzying speed to kick her viciously in the side of the head.

2

Joel kept coming, delivering blows all over her body. Jumping and kicking, landing on the balls of his feet with the precision of a ballet dancer and leaping again; legs thrashing like pistons, smashing into her, sending her staggering back.

Punches, devastating chops – in her ribs and face, her shoulders and sides – made her stumble; each attack focused, targeted. He pressed forward relentlessly until she was pinned against a wall.

Shaken, bewildered, Elsa cringed under the tsunami of painful blows. 'Wait! Stop! No!'

Her words were lost in the relentless attack. Her head slammed against the wall by a juddering punch; her mind fogged. She could barely see because of the hair in her eyes. Something warm and sticky was running down her face – blood! Pressed against the wall, there was no escape. She couldn't move, let alone run, and her ankles kept bending in those fucking heels.

A sluggish thought came to her: *He's going to kill me.*

Muscle memory kicking in, she began to defend herself. Lifting her arms to block Joel's attacks, mirroring his lunges, trying to find a fluidity in her own movement, she let instinct take over – muscle slammed into muscle; bone crashed painfully against bone – then started probing for weaknesses, for a way to fight back.

Spinning away from the wall, Elsa brought her legs up hard, one after the other, flicking her feet to launch the shoes like missiles at his face. He swiped one away with his arm, ducked to avoid the other.

But it gave her time to vault the reception desk – the woman cowering behind it ran away screaming; Elsa was vaguely aware of pandemonium all around them – and drop into a crouch behind it, searching quickly for a weapon. And when Joel slid over the counter, arms already raised, she came up with a landline telephone, a heavy Bakelite thing that signified the restaurant's retro class, and slammed it as hard as she could into his nose.

He jerked back, disorientated, blood exploding every which way across his face. Elsa grabbed his hair and smashed his head into the wall once, twice, three times, making plaster crack around it in a jagged halo. When his head lolled back, she wrapped the telephone cord around his neck and yanked.

'Stop, Joel!' She stood behind him, knee pressed into his lower spine, tightening the cord. Unable to breathe, lips glistening with blood, Joel's mouth gaped. 'Just stop! Talk to me!'

The more Joel's fingers plucked frantically at the cord cutting into his throat, the more she pulled it taut.

'I don't want to hurt you!' Elsa hissed, still unable to make sense of what was happening. She couldn't comprehend the enormity of it; the insanity.

Joel wanted to kill her.

And then her anger surged, erupting quick and hot, burning her cheeks.

Only minutes ago, she'd almost said those three precious words. Had almost said, *I love you.* Offered them to him, to *him*, on a silver platter, and now look!

She'd allowed this man into her life, into her home, into her bed. She'd believed he was a dependable man who might prove a decent father to Harley and India.

She'd let him near her kids!

Just the thought of it made her instinctively tighten the cord. Joel's face was turning purple; his eyes bulged in their sockets. Little *ack ack* sounds were coming from his mouth. It didn't take long to make someone unconscious by strangling – less than a minute – but she needed him to explain.

'Get away!' she screamed when some idiot with a death wish came near, and then hissed into Joel's ear, 'I'm going to let you breathe, but let me down and I'll snap your neck.'

Ack, he said. *Ack ack*.

Joel squirmed, not getting the message, and she twisted the cord tight; the plastic wire dug into her palms, the tendons in her long arms stretched taut. *Ack ack*. Joel's eyes fluttered into his skull, and he went limp.

Alarmed, she slackened the cord – she needed information – what a Date Night this had turned out to be! – and fell for the oldest trick in the book.

His elbow pumped back into her gut and she doubled over, gasping. Joel let out a howling gasp as he scrabbled at his windpipe, untangling the cord, swinging the telephone around his head and launching it at her.

When she ducked, he came at her. The heel of his right hand snapped up beneath her chin, sending her careening over a food trolley. She hit the floor in a noisy clatter of greasy plates and dishes.

He lifted his leg to stomp on her head, heel first. She rolled, jumping to her feet, feeling all the old moves coming back, better late than never, and snatched up a metal tray, smashing it into the back of his head with a reverberating bong.

'Stop!' she shouted, but he kept coming.

Arms moving like pistons, chopping and pumping. Elsa blocked his attacks with the tray – his fists crashed against the metal, the sound like crashing cymbals, until it was so bent out of shape it could be worn as a hat – then with her bare arms and legs. Intercepting his strikes, soaking up the shrieking pain in lean muscle and bone. When his left arm went high, her right forearm met it; when his right leg whistled past her nose, she swung away, retreating into the dining area.

A kick to her shoulder sent her flying. She hardly heard the screams of the fleeing customers. She rolled across the floor and came up as Joel flew at her with a skewer, a greasy cuttlefish still impaled on it. Elsa ducked low, grabbing his outstretched arm and twisting, using his momentum to spin him over her shoulders. He landed like a starfish on a table. China, glass, stainless steel crashed everywhere.

'Enough!' Elsa held up a warning hand, but Joel sucked a pair of serving knives from a joint of fatty meat and leaped.

She lifted a chopping board in front of her face. The

knives embedded deep. She threw the board aside as he lunged again.

'The police are coming!' someone screeched as Elsa and Joel crashed together through the swing doors to the kitchen in a deadly dance. Shards of glass embedded in her soles, the tiled floor slid beneath her bloodied feet. Later – if she managed to survive this – they'd hurt like hell. But right now, adrenaline and a single, instinctive focus, *stay the fuck alive*, kept her moving, kept her fighting.

She ducked when Joel swung a frying pan that sizzled with fat – it flew above her head in a whistling arc – and dodged when it returned backhanded. Droplets of hot oil scalded her cheeks.

Reaching a hob, she picked up a pan of boiling water and threw it at Joel, who turned away just in time. His back arched when it hit his suit jacket, neck and shoulders. His fists clenched in agony, his lips curled over grinding teeth, and it gave her time to lash out with a leg. Her heel smashed into his lower back, sending him crashing across a counter.

When he leaped back over, pink skin was peeling down his neck. Swinging low, he scooped a kitchen knife off the floor with a metallic scrape, and came at her.

The blade danced inches from her eyes. Stabbing high and low, swooping backwards and forwards. Joel dropped suddenly to slash at her stomach. But tiring now, his movements imprecise, grimacing face a mess of blood and sweat, the final lunge was clumsy. Elsa grabbed his wrist and pulled. But she didn't see the shattered stem of a wine glass in his other hand, which he plunged into her collarbone and twisted. It sank into the flesh like a knife into soft butter.

She roared, harnessing all her pain and fury – her kids! – to lift him across her body, grabbing the back of his neck to push his face onto a griddle. He shrieked in a plume of smoke and sparks. The air filled with the smell of burning flesh as his left cheek sizzled greedily on the red-hot plate.

Panting, Elsa stepped back, her buttocks bumping up against a work surface, blood blooming around the flimsy shoulder strap of her dress. Joel staggered to a window and leaned wearily against the pane, fingers lifted to his molten, bubbling cheek.

She pointed at the broken glass in his hand. 'That's enough.'

He dropped it and laughed.

Incredulous, she asked, 'What's so funny?'

'I still love you.'

People were edging back into the kitchen – staff and customers – armed with various kitchen implements, but Elsa ignored them.

She needed to know. '*Why?*'

'You know how it works.' She realized he was speaking in an American accent. 'I just do as I'm told.'

'I trusted you,' she spat. 'I let you into my life.'

She and Joel had been together for a year. She had convinced herself that he was the man who would finally allow her to leave the past behind, that she could heal with him – she'd believed they had a future together. They'd be a family.

Truth was, she never knew him at all.

'Admit it.' The curdling flesh on his face gave his rueful smile a hideous aspect. 'I know how to show you a good time.'

The last few minutes had been a surreal nightmare:

obscene, cruel. But Elsa sensed her troubles were only just beginning.

Her heart leaped when she thought of Harley and India at home.

'Guess what, Joel,' she told him. 'The engagement's off!'

Then she jumped up to grab with both hands the steel rail above her head that held all the kitchen's pots and pans, and swung her legs to hit him square in the chest.

Joel crashed backwards out of the window. Elsa dropped to the floor and grabbed the biggest knife she could find, and because they were in a professional kitchen there were some very big knives. At the window, she saw broken glass in the alley outside – but no sign of Joel.

Elsa padded through the kitchen, people backing away warily as she passed. Through the swing doors back into the restaurant, past the chaos of upturned tables, broken glass and smashed china. The room looked like a bomb had hit it.

Most customers had fled, but a small number huddled together, watching her fearfully. When Elsa glanced in a full-length mirror, she saw her dress was slashed, her abs visible through the torn fabric, her limbs red and bruised. Shiny sweat mingled with the blood smeared across her face, obliterating the make-up she'd spent so long trying to get right for Joel.

She looked on the floor. 'I can't find my bag.'

A waitress picked up a small clutch. 'Is it this one?'

Elsa snatched it and went through it with trembling fingers, looking for her phone, but remembered she hadn't brought it. Dropping the bag, she eyed the customers, who pressed back against the wall as if she were a dangerous animal.

They had no idea.

She pointed at the fat guy who had ogled her, and he gulped like a toad. 'Give me your phone.'

He fumbled in his jacket and handed her his mobile. She suddenly grabbed him by the back of his neck and pulled him close, making him whimper. Holding the phone to his face, activating the facial recognition security, and unlocking the device.

'Enjoy the rest of your evening,' she told everyone.

3

When she ran outside, an ambulance was already parked at the kerb. Two green-uniformed paramedics rushed towards her.

'Miss,' said the woman paramedic urgently. 'You need treatment.'

With blood streaming down her shoulder, and all the other angry cuts and abrasions on her arms and legs, it was probably a good idea, but Elsa wasn't going to spend hours waiting in a hospital A & E. She had to get home to her children. Sirens wailed in the distance.

'Not now.' She waved them off. 'Not tonight.'

'This way.' The woman tried to pull her towards the ambulance, its back doors gaping wide. 'Let's get you fixed up.'

Elsa backed away, still getting her breath back after the life-and-death struggle with her devoted fiancé.

'That wound looks nasty,' insisted the paramedic. 'You need to come with us.'

The sirens were getting closer. In Elsa's shock and bewilderment, it hadn't occurred to her that this ambulance was already parked outside the restaurant.

Shit, where was the other paramedic?

Arms grabbed her from behind, clamping around

her chest, pinning her left arm to her side. The woman paramedic rushed at her with a mask attached to a canister. Elsa heard its sinister gaseous hiss.

'Hold her tight!'

Elsa instinctively lifted her free arm, which still held the phone, to stop the whispering mask being placed over her mouth and nose. If that happened, she knew, she would quickly become unconscious – or even dead. She knocked it away, and the mask skittered to the floor.

Elsa scraped her bare feet into the pavement, bloody heels stinging on the concrete, and heaved herself against the man holding her, pushing him backwards. Picking up momentum, they crunched hard onto the bonnet of a parked sports car. The man grunted as his spine slammed against the metal. The shrill alarm of the car erupted; its security lights flashed crazily.

'Hold her,' shouted the woman, and she scooped up the mask, scurrying forward. But Elsa elbowed the man behind her in the face three times, and when he finally let go with a groan, she kicked out a long leg, bringing the top of her foot up into the woman's throat, sending her flying.

And then she was running.

Blood flying off her, her ruined dress bunched high up her legs so she could sprint barefoot along the King's Road, oblivious of the looks and stares of startled passers-by. Behind her, she glimpsed a flurry of flashing blue lights, as patrol cars and vans skidded to a stop outside the restaurant.

'That's her!' someone shouted. 'She's the one!'

Arms and legs pumping, Elsa ran into oncoming traffic, leaping across the bonnet of one moving car to jump to the pavement on the other side and get off the busy road, with its crowds and brightly lit shopfronts, into a neat square of tall Edwardian homes.

Racing along a connecting street, she became conscious of excruciating pain in her feet and legs. She had no idea what Stacey's mobile number was, so she called her own home number, thinking it hopeless – nobody in their right mind answered a landline gone midnight.

To her astonishment, a voice answered. 'Hello?'

'Stacey!' Flying around a corner, Elsa nearly collided with a startled man and his barking dog.

'Hi, Mrs Zee,' said Stacey brightly. 'How was Date Night? Give me all the gory details!'

She shouted, 'Where are the kids?'

'They're in bed.' The girl stuttered, maybe because the notoriously terse Elsa Zero was being even more brusque than usual and panting into the phone. 'Is anything wrong?'

Elsa couldn't explain, what the hell could she tell the girl, the whole situation was mad.

'Listen to me and don't interrupt,' Elsa gasped, trying to keep up her breakneck speed while she spoke.

Shooting pains crackled up and down her body; her shoulder felt numb. Her only priority was to get home fast and grab the kids. They'd go abroad. Somewhere far away – a remote beach, a mountain hideaway – where they would never be found. She'd stashed a bunch of passports using different identities for just this kind of eventuality, but had never in a million years believed it would ever happen. Not after all this time.

'Hang on, Stacey.' A BMW was coming down the street towards her and she ran in front of it – it screeched to a halt – to smash her fists hard on the bonnet. Inside, a middle-aged couple stared at her in shock. It didn't even occur to Elsa what she must look like. A six-foot-something madwoman: barefoot; hair a towering, swaying mess; her dress bloodied and tattered. She rapped her knuckles on the driver's side window.

'Are you okay, miss?' asked the man, as the window lowered.

'Out!' she told him.

'What are you doi—'

Elsa opened the door and dragged him out, so that he fell in a heap on the road. When she climbed into his warm seat, the woman beside her gaped in horror.

'What did I just tell you?' Elsa snarled, in no mood to argue, and the woman scrambled out. Elsa dropped the phone onto the passenger seat and hit the speaker. She floored the accelerator and the car surged. 'Stacey, are you still there?'

'Yes,' said the girl, confused. 'I'm here.'

'Lock all the doors and windows, and turn out all the lights. Don't answer the door to anyone.'

The girl sounded scared. 'Shall I call the police?'

'No!' Elsa shot a red light. 'I'm on my way!'

'You're frightening me.'

'I'll be back soon,' Elsa shouted above the roar of the engine. She took a corner hard. The car skidded, wheels bumping onto the kerb. Trying to get her bearings, calculate the quickest route, she was desperate to shave critical seconds from her journey, but couldn't afford to become embroiled in a high-speed police chase. 'Just don't answer the door to anybody but me.'

'When will you and Joel be home?' asked Stacey.

At the mention of his name, Elsa sucked down a breath.

'Make sure you put the latch on.' As if that would do any good. 'And if Joel turns up, don't let him in.'

'I think I should probably go home,' said Stacey anxiously.

'I'm only a few minutes away. Don't leave the kids,' Elsa said, and tossed the phone out the window.

She gunned the BMW through the streets of South London as fast as she dared. Speeding across junctions, ignoring speed limits, jumping a central reservation to make a U-turn. The accelerator pedal was slick with blood by the time she swung the car to the kerb a block from her house in Clapham.

She banged on the front door, yelling to be let in, carefully watching the row of small terraced houses. Elsa had lived here for years, but always had mixed feelings about it. She was never a good fit for a life in the suburbs, where the neighbours knew each other's business, took in each other's parcels, baked each other cakes, and held a street party every year that Elsa felt compelled to attend. Her attempt at living such a life had ended in disaster, as deep down she had always suspected it would. That so-called normal life, that fantasy, was dead in the water.

Stacey unlocked the door. She gawped when she saw the state of Elsa. The way her hair flew every which way on her head, the bloody mess of the dress bunched up to her knickers.

'Mrs Zee, what's happening?'

She slipped inside.

'Go.' The girl stared, and Elsa realized she wanted to get paid. But Elsa didn't have money on her, and no time to find any, so she took Stacey's coat from the banister and shoved it at her, pushed her out the door. 'Get out.'

Her eight-year-old twins, Harley and India, stood sleepily in their PJs at the top of the stairs, and she bounded up towards them. Took them in her arms and held them tight, inhaled the smell of shampoo and sleep on the top of their heads. Her relief was overwhelming. Before she was a mother, Elsa had no idea her love for two other human beings could be so total, so complete. So perfect.

But there was no time.

'Get dressed, it's night-time so make sure you wrap up warm, and get your rucksacks.' She led them towards their room. 'Fill them with clothes, a toothbrush and anything else you need.'

'A toy?' asked India.

'Whatever.'

Wide-eyed, Harley looked his mum up and down. 'Have you been in an accident?'

Elsa hoped the dim landing light would obscure most of the blood. 'A tiny one.'

'Are you hurt?'

'No – yes – a bit.'

India poked her finger into one of the slashes in her dress. 'You have holes.'

'I fell into a hedge.' Elsa opened the wardrobe in their room. 'Get your stuff together.'

'Is Joel here?' asked Harley.

'Not tonight.' Elsa kneeled, pulling her kids closer to her. 'I'll explain later. We're leaving asap.'

'What's asap?'

'As soon as possible.'

'It's very late,' India informed her gravely.

'Yeah, it is.' She was a great mum, her kids were everything to her, but she had never been the most imaginative of parents, never very good at those creative flights of fancy with which people were meant to indulge their kids. Playing dress-up, writing to Santa, making shit up on the spot. Reading books at bedtime, night after night, bored her. She'd hurry through make-believe stories about wizards, talking animals, an endless parade of naughty children who saved the world or learned an important life lesson. Elsa found it all dull and patronizing.

Back in her former life, the only lesson she had ever needed to learn was how to stay alive from one day to the next; and that wasn't something she ever wanted to have to teach her own kids.

'Slow down, you're spoiling it!' they'd whine when she turned the pages too quickly, or tell her she wasn't doing the voices properly.

But they'd ask to hear the very same story again the following night, and then the next and next, and it drove Elsa crazy. When Joel came over, Harley and India insisted he read instead, and he really got into it; he took his time with the story and did all the silly voices and sound effects. But now... now Joel was gone.

And she had to try to make something up.

'We're going on a trip, far away,' she told them. 'It's going to be an adventure.'

'Where?' asked Harley.

'That would spoil the surprise, right?'

India made a face. 'I'm tired, can we go in the morning?'

Elsa was getting impatient with all the questions. 'We'll play a game. Let's see who can get dressed the quickest!'

'What do we win?' asked Harley, excited.

'Just do as I tell you,' she snapped, and shoved rucksacks at them. 'Chop chop!'

Then Elsa ran into her bedroom, where she had spent many exciting nights with Joel, and where he hadn't tried to smash her brains out. They'd been together for a year, which meant she had broken the record for her longest relationship by about eleven months. She'd been totally taken in by him, and cursed herself again for being so foolish, so naïve, to think she could have escaped the past. To believe she could just leave her old life behind, all the bad things she had done – even after all these years.

She used scissors to slice off the dress, careful not to irritate the throbbing wound below her collarbone, or any of the many other cuts and lesions, and tossed it; stripped off her bra and knickers. She snatched up her phone, which she'd left beside the bed, and went into the bathroom.

There, beneath the harsh light, she studied her own naked body, letting her fingers roam up and down her arms and legs, checking her ribs and stomach, feeling carefully for fractures, breaks and other internal injuries. One livid purple bruise bloomed down the left side of her body like the map of Chile, but considering the ferocity of Joel's attack, she'd had a lucky escape.

Tipping gauze and bandages and creams and painkillers from the cabinet into the sink, she went to work on the bloody gouge in her shoulder. Checking for fragments of glass; sponging the wound with wet cotton wool; grimacing as she dabbed it with rubbing alcohol and petroleum jelly;

dressing and bandaging it. She cleaned the worst of the other cuts and abrasions as quickly as she could. Swinging her gashed feet beneath the cold tap in the bath to wash off the blood, she called a number on her phone.

A voice she didn't recognize said, 'Westwood Club.'

'Where's Panda?' said Elsa.

'Who is this, please?'

'It's Elsa Zero.'

She didn't appreciate the long, tense pause on the other end – when Elsa phoned Panda, she expected to be put straight through – and it didn't bode well.

'I'm sorry,' said the voice finally. 'Panda is out of the country.'

'Don't be daft, Panda hasn't left the club in three hundred years.' Sitting on the toilet seat, Elsa used tweezers to pick fragments of glass from the soles of her feet, dropping them into the bath. 'Put him on, it's urgent.'

'I'm afraid that's not going to be poss—'

'What's your name?' she interrupted.

'I don't have a name,' said the voice.

'Mummy?' called Harley from down the hall. 'Shall I wear my hoodie or a T-shirt?'

'Both!' Elsa shouted and said quietly into the phone, 'What you mean is, you don't want to give me your name, which is different, and right at this moment, a very wise decision. Make up a name, so I can call you something.'

'Megatron.'

'Seriously?' She frowned. 'Is that the best you can do?'

'Off the top of my head,' said the voice defensively.

'Mummy.'

India stood at the bathroom door and Elsa pressed the phone to her chest. 'Yes, baby.'

'I can't find my ballet shoes.'

'You're not going to need your ballet shoes where we're going.'

'But I won't be able to practise.'

'Ballet practice is cancelled for the time being.'

'Yessss!' Her daughter pumped the air with her fist and left.

'Well, *Megatron*,' Elsa said into the phone. 'I don't know what Panda is playing at, but tell him I'm coming to visit, whether he likes it or not.'

She threw the phone across the bathroom, had no intention of ever using it again, and finished dressing and bandaging her feet. Palming a couple of ibuprofen, she hunched at the sink to swallow them down with water from the tap. When she lifted her hand to pull back her hair in the mirror, the diamond ring glinted on her finger.

She twisted it once, and then took it off.

Dropped it in the toilet, flushed it away.

Walking into the bedroom, Elsa climbed into knickers and a sports bra. Pulled on a pair of leggings, a T-shirt and hoodie, forced her bandaged feet into a pair of trainers and laced them up.

She pulled a rucksack from the top shelf of the wardrobe and stuffed it with clothes. She threw in the bottle of ibuprofen and a first-aid bag. Then helped her kids fill their backpacks, ignoring the endless questions they fired at her as they haphazardly continued to dress. If she told them to hurry up once, she told them a hundred times.

Moments later, she pulled down the ladder to the attic. Harley appeared on the landing when she was halfway up. 'Where are you going?'

'Show me your teeth,' she commanded him and inspected his grotesque chimp smile. 'Go brush them.'

'I've brushed them already tonight.'

'Go and do it again, and tell your sister to clean hers. I don't want your stinky breath in the car.'

When he ran off, Elsa lifted herself into the attic and tugged the pull cord to turn on the naked bulb that dangled from the low roof. She walked in a crouch across the central beam in the sallow light, negotiating the piles of junk stored up there – the furniture and broken toys and decorating materials, all the normal stuff so beloved of normal people – to squat at the far end of the roof space. There, under a piece of lagging, was a bag she had hidden because – you know, old habits die hard.

She took out an envelope that should have contained twenty thousand in cash, but was empty. The stash of passports and various ID cards for her and the kids was also gone. Taking out a small rectangular case and opening it, she found her SIG Sauer P365 pistol missing from its neoprene lining, along with the box of ammo.

She hadn't been up here for years, more fool her, because at some point Joel had found the bag and emptied its contents. Had he done it as a precaution, or because he knew something like tonight would happen sooner or later?

Her world fell apart at the stroke of midnight.

When the clock struck twelve, even Cinderella wasn't forced to fight for her life against Prince Charming.

Elsa ground her teeth in anger for letting that snake Joel into her life.

But there was a burner phone still in the bag, she saw. A Nokia 8800, a simple graphite rectangle, the charger cable wrapped tightly around it. The plastic phone felt light and insubstantial in her hand. Elsa struggled to remember anything about it, until she recalled how Max Saint had insisted years ago that she take it.

'What's this about?' she had asked him.

'Every sinner needs a Saint.' He tapped the side of his nose. 'You ever need me, Elsie, give me a bell.'

Elsa inspected the phone closely, wondering if Joel had left it behind because he believed it was old and useless, or if he had fitted a tracker inside it. The moulding was smooth and didn't look like it had been tampered with, so she put it in the rucksack, just as Harley's head appeared at the top of the ladder.

'What are you doing?' he asked.

'Did you clean your teeth?' she demanded.

He gave her another hideous grin to prove it. 'Where are we going?'

Coming towards the ladder, she said, 'Never you mind.'

Truth was, she didn't have a clue.

4

She needed to park the kids for an hour, until she could think of somewhere safe to take them, a long way from whatever horror show was unfurling.

Nowhere sprang to mind. There were associates from her old life who could provide secure mansions filled with private muscle, steel shutters that covered the windows in a split second, panic rooms; all kinds of state-of-the-art security. But they weren't the kind of people Elsa would trust to protect a packet of Percy Pigs if there was money to be earned, let alone her kids. And she didn't want to drive around in search of refuge, activating every single ANPR and face-recognition camera in the city.

'Come on.' Pulling a baseball cap low over her face, she hurried her children outside.

'Where are we going?' asked India.

There was no point in locking up – a heavily armed team of Kevlar-wearing thugs would soon take their size twelves to the front door – and they ran across the street.

She hoped the plan she had come up with was counterintuitive. Nobody would believe she'd leave her children so close to her own house. They, whoever *they* were, would think she was on her way to a seaport, a secluded airstrip or a safe house, and that's what she would probably have to do soon enough. But her immediate priority was to get a handle on what was happening; try to find out why her life had suddenly been torn apart.

Rushing the twins across the street beneath the orange spray of the streetlamps, Elsa swallowed down the anger she felt at Joel's betrayal. If she survived the night, maybe there'd be time to contemplate the bitter fact that their whole relationship – all the fun and intimacy and laughs, all those accumulated moments of shared experience – was a treacherous lie; their imagined future together a ridiculous fantasy.

The joke was on her, and Elsa didn't like being made fun of. She intended to catch up with him – and kill him.

'Hurry up, guys.' With the clock edging towards one in the morning, the South London street was empty. There was no late-night traffic, no pedestrians, just cars parked bumper to bumper at each kerb.

India let out a yawn. 'Where are we going?'

Elsa hadn't made many friends in her life; she could probably count them all on the fingers of both hands. Of those, at least three were dead, two had vanished in mysterious circumstances, one was serving time in a supermax, and the others were flung across the globe.

Fact was, she found other people hard to trust, hardly surprising considering her former line of work, and it was wearying to keep so many secrets when they got too close. She had learned to keep a distance – her own nutcase parents had given her a head start in that regard – and maintain a healthy paranoia. Which is why it hurt, it really fucking hurt, that she had dropped her guard and allowed Joel within touching distance of her heart.

'I said, where are we going?'

'We're going to Miriam's.' She pushed them through the gate leading to the house opposite her own.

Miriam was one of the few neighbours that Elsa had any time for. She was a lonely middle-aged woman who spent her days baking cakes and doing errands for vulnerable people. Elsa couldn't remember how they'd got talking a few months back; it certainly wouldn't have been Elsa's choice to strike up conversation. But all her attempts to stonewall Miriam by glaring at her, which usually worked a treat with the mums at the school gates, delivery people, tradesmen, and everyone else, came to nothing. Miriam was one of those people who didn't get the message when you ignored them in the street, and she insisted on chatting whether Elsa liked it or not. Eventually, Elsa allowed Miriam to make flapjacks for the kids, and she had even on occasion babysat the twins. Thank God, Elsa had never got around to mentioning her neighbour to Joel.

Elsa banged on Miriam's front door, anxious to get off the street. Joel had answered his phone at the stroke of midnight, when some kind of kill order had been activated; it would have become clear very quickly to whoever sent that order that Elsa wasn't dead. They could be on the way to her house right now.

'She won't hear you, she's asleep,' said Harley.

'Then let's get her up,' said Elsa, as if it was a funny game, and she placed her finger on the bell and kept it there. The last thing she needed was to wake the neighbourhood, but she didn't have any choice. When a car turned into the street, she pulled her kids into the shadow of the porch, but the vehicle went past without slowing.

Then the hallway light went on and Elsa saw Miriam's blurred figure shuffle to the door, pulling a dressing gown around her. After spending a lot of time fiddling with locks and latches, she finally cracked the door and peered out, bleary-eyed, hair sticking up every which way.

'Elsa?' Miriam said in surprise. 'Is that you?'

'Hi, Miriam.' Elsa took a deep breath and tried a smile on for size. The last thing she needed was for Miriam, as nice as she was, to refuse to help. 'I'm so sorry, but I wonder if you could look after the kids for a couple of hours. I'd be terribly grateful.'

'Do you know the—'

'Yes, it's very late,' she said impatiently. 'But it's an emergency. I really need to—' *find out what the fuck is going on* '—see someone as a matter of urgency. And obviously I can't leave Harley and India alone.'

'Oh dear, not bad news, I hope?' asked Miriam, interested in the way Elsa glanced up and down the street.

'No, everything's fine, really fine. Lovely!' Elsa grinned. 'But I wouldn't ask you if it wasn't important.'

Miriam opened the door wide for the kids. 'Well, you munchkins had better come in!'

'Thanks, Mir,' said Elsa. 'I owe you one.'

When Harley and India ran inside, Miriam said quietly to Elsa, 'Why don't you come in for a cup of tea? If there's a problem—'

'Why would there be a problem?' snapped Elsa.

Miriam looked carefully at the cuts on Elsa's face, the cap pulled low over her unruly hair; at her leggings, hoodie and rucksack. 'Because you're dropping the children off at my house in the middle of the night.'

'Oh.' Elsa rooted in the bag for the mobile she'd found in the attic. 'Do you mind charging this for me?'

Miriam took it, bewildered.

'One more thing.' She didn't want to take her own car because the number plate would be identified as soon as it turned onto the high street, and the police – and her mystery assailants – could already be looking for the BMW she'd carjacked. 'I need your car.'

Miriam looked concerned. 'I'm worried about you.'

If only you knew, thought Elsa.

'It's really nothing, I'll explain when I get back.' There were two lies in that short sentence. 'But I need to borrow your car.' She winced at having to say the word… 'Please.'

The kids were running around in Miriam's kitchen at the rear. Excited by the unexpected late-night adventure, they weren't going to sleep any time soon. Miriam sighed, then fished in a coat hanging from the banister. Took out her car keys.

'Thanks.' Elsa reached for them. 'I'll be an hour or so. But if I don't come back—'

'Why wouldn't you come back?' Miriam pulled the keys out of her reach, and Elsa knew she'd said too much.

She smiled sweetly. 'Of course I'll be back.'

And snatched the car keys.

5

Elsa drove Miriam's Renault Clio into the West End. Across Chelsea Bridge, up through Victoria, skirting the edge of Hyde Park to turn onto Park Lane, beneath a silver moon the size of a dinner plate. Traffic was light: minicabs, mostly, and night buses cruising the near-empty streets, carrying home the last dregs of the Thursday night crowd.

She drove as fast as she dared, conscious of the many cameras lining the route, trying to work out who had targeted her and why. Elsa Zero had learned to live with the paranoid possibility that retribution would one day come her way as an unexpectedly bitter taste in her morning coffee, a fatal collision on the street, a pinprick in Waitrose, but she was still bewildered and angry that it had been Joel who had attacked her.

She only had herself to blame for hooking up with him in the first place. Elsa never had any intention of starting a relationship. But tired of being alone, vaguely hoping that one day a suitable co-parent for her kids may come along, she'd let down her guard and flirted with a charming, good-looking stranger in a café.

It was a slippery slope, and like most relationships full of unexpected twists and turns. One moment he was buying her a chai latte, the next asking for her telephone number, insinuating himself into her life, winning her trust and the devotion of her children, then lunging at her throat with a pair of greasy kebab skewers.

Elsa had genuinely believed Joel was a normal middle-management guy. Sensible, dependable, maybe a little on the dull side. She had met his 'friends', she had met his 'family', she had given him a spare key to her house. Sometimes when she got home he'd be there, jiggling about to Smooth Radio as he made dinner.

Joel had loved her, or so he had said – and she'd almost, *almost*, told him the same thing. Seconds later, they were fighting to the death, which was a brutal and unexpected way for a relationship to end, even by her own low standards.

Furious with herself, disgusted at her own weakness, Elsa lifted her fists high and smashed them down on the steering wheel again and again, screaming in fury with each blow.

She didn't believe that Joel had planned earlier in the evening to kill her, or he wouldn't have smiled so easily, or flirted so much; he wouldn't have asked for her hand in marriage seconds before that phone call. His face when he looked up from his mobile – resigned, sad – said it all. The kill order had been given – and he struck. Judging by his fighting prowess, Joel was trained to use lethal force, but he could have done the job anytime. Snapped her neck when she was turned away, in the toilets, in the cab, back at her place. She wouldn't have felt a thing.

Her instinct was that Joel had been placed in her life as a deep cover operative, but he'd gone way too deep and fallen for her, and when the clock struck twelve and he was ordered to kill her, he'd panicked. Which may just have given her the edge she needed.

But if he had been ordered to kill her, who were the jokers who had tried to bundle her into the fake ambulance outside the restaurant?

Elsa parked Miriam's car in Mayfair. In the early hours, this part of the West End, one of the most expensive areas in the world, was deserted. Moonlight reflected off the upper windows of the tall, imposing apartment blocks. But there was life even in this sleepy place, and Elsa knew exactly where to find it. Walking a couple of streets to a parade of shuttered shops and luxury boutiques, she found a queue of people standing at a velvet rope.

Men and women dressed in suits and slinky dresses waited in a noxious cloud of perfume and vape to be let into Panda's club, ready to party till dawn. Elsa swung a leg over the rope, ignoring complaints from the people behind her. A massive bouncer stood in front of a blue door, his hands folded demurely in front of his groin.

'Hello, Terry.'

Elsa was tall, but Terry was a giant, and used his height and bulk – like most doormen, he looked like he knew his way around a string of sausages – to intimidate.

He looked genuinely happy to see her. 'Long time no see, Elsa.'

'Is it?' she asked, but he was right, because she'd had scant reason to visit Panda in the last few years.

'You're looking great, my darling.' He grinned from ear to ear. 'You know how much I love you.'

She ignored the scowls and comments coming from the people queuing. 'I've come to see Panda.'

'Here's the thing.' Terry led her away from the camera above the door. 'I've been told not to let you in.'

'Get to the back of the queue!' shouted a woman, who shivered in a ridiculously short skirt and crop top.

Elsa pointed at a sign beside the door: Strictly Smart Dress. 'Is it because of what I'm wearing?'

'I think you're bloody lovely whatever you wear.' Terry raised his voice so the woman in the skirt could hear. 'Not like mutton dressed as lamb.'

'Go on, Tel.' She pressed a finger against his massive arm. 'Let me in.'

He looked genuinely sad. 'Really wish I could, Elsa, but no can do.' When she gave him an evaluating look, he gestured behind him. 'Even if you knock me cold, they'll never open the door.'

Elsa looked at the solid door to the club – with no outside handle, it could only be opened from the inside – and up at the black bulb of the video camera above it.

'Is Panda inside?' she asked quietly.

'No, love,' Terry told her loudly, but a miniscule nod of the head indicated otherwise.

'I'd better go, then.'

'Sure, my lovely, you have a good evening.'

'Terry.' Elsa looked back as she pushed past the queue of people. 'A word of advice: don't come inside.'

'No chance of that.' He gestured at the line of disgruntled punters. 'Got my hands full with this bunch of losers, don't I?'

Someone in the line called him out on the comment and Terry jabbed a finger. 'Shut it!'

Elsa walked around the corner to find another way in. Because that was what she used to do for a living: get into places. Halfway down the street was a tall gate that led to a courtyard behind the club, and she climbed over it. Cameras would cover every angle, she knew that. Someone like Panda, who had his fat fingers in a lot of pies, would have security everywhere. Someone sitting in a dark room in front of a bank of screens had no doubt watched her jump the gate and already picked up a phone.

There was no point in trying to get in via the basement, there would be a steel door and all manner of sophisticated locks and security devices, so she'd have to go all the way up.

Elsa rocked back on her heels like an Olympic sprinter and ran across the courtyard, pumping her arms. There was a window with a security grille straight ahead and she leaped at it, climbing the bars, ignoring her shrieking shoulder and hurty feet, using all her strength to heave herself to a first-floor sill, straddling it, then leaping to a drainpipe. Sweating even in the chill of the night, she shimmied up, wedging her toes into the rusty brackets attaching the pipe to the wall.

Distant traffic noise, sirens and horns, the electric hum of the city, became more pronounced the higher she climbed. Elsa thought she heard voices inside the building, frantic footsteps.

She should be lying in bed dreaming of an exotic honeymoon, but here she was in the early hours, dragging herself floor by floor, inch by painful inch, up the side of a building. One of the brackets popped out of the brick, she heard it clink against a dustbin way below, and the drainpipe shifted slightly away from the wall. It would be a bad idea to look down, disorientating and gut-fluttering – Elsa had fallen off a building before, and didn't recommend it – but she couldn't help but peek at the concrete courtyard from seven floors up.

When she reached the roof, she heaved herself over the guttering, barely pausing to appreciate the Mary Poppins skyline. Towering chimney stacks and wonky roofs, silhouetted against racing silver cloud. She ran up the steep incline to a skylight, slate tiles clicking beneath her feet, and wrenched it open – the lock on the sill was old and flimsy because nobody had been to the top of this building in years – and dropped into the dark.

She was eight floors above the club. Panda's goons were already coming up the stairs, she heard their pounding steps, but there was a lot of helpful junk in the attic space. She picked up a metal chair leg gathering dust under the eaves, flipping it in her fingers to get a sense of its weight and balance, and as soon as the door slammed open and the first gentleman came in, she swung it into his head. He was still spinning when Elsa dropped to one knee in the darkness. The hollow pipe whistled through the air as she brought it up behind the knees of the second guy. Dust flew up in a cloud when he hit the floor.

Elsa found the main stairway, which descended around a central caged lift shaft, and ran down. Seven floors and counting.

On the sixth floor, another of Panda's men appeared in the stairwell and they grappled. Spinning, gripping each other tight, lifting each other off the floor, taking it in turns to slam the other against the wall, both of them somehow managing to keep their footing on the faded carpet as momentum pulled them down to the fifth.

Elsa finally managed to overpower him with a succession

of Krav Maga elbow and knee strikes to his throat and kidneys, and he dropped to the floor, just as another guy came hurtling through the door on the fourth. Elsa saw the glint of a handgun, and when she upended him in a single, fluid movement, she heard it clatter down the central shaft.

On the third, more footsteps approached along the corridor. Elsa tucked in behind the fire door. When the first man came through, she gave him a helpful kick down the stairs, took the second thug's head in her hands and jumped. Her knee whipped up to meet his nose cartilage. He rebounded off the metal mesh of the lift shaft and crumpled to the floor.

Elsa skipped lightly over the guy, down to the second floor, where a man swung an extendable baton back and forth in front of her face, the metal rod clanging against the handrail and the lift shaft. When it hit the shaft, she jabbed the heel of a palm against the rod so it became stuck in the grille, then lifted an old fire extinguisher off the wall and spun it by the hose, first high, cracking a bone in the man's wrist; low, to splinter a shin; high again into the side of his head.

On the first, three men hurried up the stairs towards her. Elsa slid down the banister, accelerating, jumping off behind them, bringing the heel of her left foot down on the back of the calf of the nearest guy. There was a sickening snap and he howled. Grabbing the arm of one of the others, twisting it, causing his body to jerk stiff as an ironing board, she slammed him into the wall. She should have done it harder, but the guy clearly wasn't up for a fight; he made a pathetic little noise and fell in a heap, pretending to be unconscious.

The last man came at her, fists clenched like he'd watched too many MMA bouts, hopping from foot to foot, making snorting piston noises every time he jabbed. One of his punches connected with her injured shoulder, and it *hurt*; her eyes stung. Elsa was sick of getting punched and kicked, and when the man overreached with his next lumbering jab, she moved in low, grabbing his chest with one hand and his groin with the other, using all her momentum and balance to dump him on his head.

By the time she reached the ground floor, Elsa was aching and sweating hard. Her hair was plastered to her forehead. She walked through the office area of the club, flicking a bank of light switches to bring up the house lights, and onto the dance floor, discreetly adjusting her twisted leggings because all the exertion had given her a camel toe.

Afraid of the havoc Elsa would cause in his precious club, Panda had already told everyone to leave. The DJ was placing his vinyl away in record boxes; disgruntled punters made their way out. Elsa walked through the crowd of smartly dressed people. Terry had been brought inside and he shouted for everyone to collect their stuff from the cloakroom. He winked at her as she passed. With all the main lights on, the inside of the sophisticated Mayfair club looked tawdry, and badly in need of updating.

Panda was sitting in his usual place on a stool at the end of the bar, watching her approach. She was about to speak, but he held up a finger, *wait*, and sipped serenely from a rum and Coke. When the room finally emptied, Panda climbed off his stool to go behind the curved bar, with its shelves of bottles backlit by colourful lights.

'Would you like a drink, Elsa?'

'No, thanks.' She watched him scoop ice from a bucket. 'Wouldn't it have been easier to just let me in?'

'I see that now.' Panda chuckled ruefully. 'But you'll forgive me for not encouraging your presence here right now, not in the circumstances.'

'And what exactly are those circumstances?'

There wasn't much that Panda, who provided intel for sundry parties on all sides of the law – crime gangs, mercenary groups, military departments, global corporations, private security companies, dictators, and billionaires – didn't know about.

'My people picked up international chatter earlier this evening that suggested your life was about to become very difficult.'

'From who?'

He poured bourbon into a tumbler, placed a coaster beneath it and pushed it in front of her. 'Your name appeared in encrypted communications between a number of intelligence agencies, in which you have been classified as a very dangerous and expendable individual. Congratulations, Elsa, you're a top-level threat.'

She stared in disbelief. 'Why?'

'The source of the original communication can't be verified at this time, even by my people. It could have come from a particular agency or somewhere else entirely.'

'What the actual fu—'

'Washington, London, Moscow, Beijing – all the big boys and girls have got their knickers in a twist about you, Elsa.'

'Someone tried to kill me tonight.'

He smiled sympathetically. 'I'd get used to it.'

Elsa had always been cautious about her own safety and that of her children. She stayed alert, which was only sensible considering the great number of enemies she had made in her life, but it had been nine years since she had left the business. And much of her work as a deep cover agent for the private security agency RedQueen – all the incursions, along with the extractions, assassinations and kidnappings – had remained highly classified. Her own identity had always been kept top secret, known only by a small and dwindling number of people.

'Why?'

'I was hoping you would tell me.' Panda nodded at the glass in front of her. 'Have a drink, you look like you need it.'

She pulled it towards her. 'I've been out of the business for years.'

Panda propped his elbows on the bar to cradle his chin in his upturned hands. 'Your name still pops up on security channels, did you know that? Even after all these years, the agencies still share information about you. They keep tabs on your whereabouts, what you're up to. These discussions occur on quite a regular basis. Once, twice, sometimes three times a year. You are still a person of great interest to high-level sections of the intelligence community.'

Elsa felt like she was falling down a rabbit hole, as if the ground was dropping away beneath her. She lifted the bourbon to her lips, but placed the glass back down without taking a sip.

'I don't understand.'

She'd been retired for years now, had lived a life of obscurity in a terraced street in South London, along with all the other nobodies. Bringing up her kids, setting up a business as a fitness trainer; getting all the accreditation, passing the exams. She'd almost come to believe her old life, with its constant threat of violence and betrayal – both real and imagined – was long behind her.

'You've never been trusted,' said Panda. 'Maybe not since Buenos Aires.'

When she looked at him sharply, he smiled because he knew he'd hit a nerve.

'I was nearly killed in Buenos Aires.' She thought of the phone Saint gave her when she had finally recovered and returned to the UK, the one charging in Miriam's kitchen. 'Tell me.'

'That's all I know, I'm afraid. I've seen comms that have mentioned you in the context of Buenos Aires. The mission was code-named Pilot Fish, I believe.' He shrugged. 'Alas, these days I'm very much on the outside of the goldfish bowl looking in, much like you.'

Except Panda – for whom signals intelligence, the interception of electronic communications, was something of an obsession – still made stealing the seemingly impregnable encrypted comms of SIS, the CIA, GRU, MSS and other agencies very much his business. Elsa knew he had cryptanalysis teams working 24/7 in numerous locations around the world.

'Who is Joel Harris?' she asked him.

He frowned. 'I've no idea.'

'He was my boyfriend up until a couple of hours ago, and my fiancé for several seconds, until he attempted to kill me. I'm very keen to speak to him.'

'I don't believe you ever introduced us. You don't come

to see me any more, Elsa, and I'm very hurt about it. It's almost as if you're ashamed of our previous association.' Panda looked sad. 'What will you do?'

She didn't have the faintest idea. Her first priority was to get Harley and India somewhere safe, if such a place even existed.

Panda placed the bottle of bourbon back on the shelf. 'Come on, drink up. No offence, but I don't want you here a moment longer.'

She could do with a drink right then, one little sip wouldn't hurt; it might even numb her aching wounds. She was in shock, in pain, already tired of fighting the world.

Elsa lifted the glass to her mouth and Panda raised his own tumbler in salute. She smelled the pungent spirit – and stopped.

She'd known Panda for many years; he'd helped her several times in the past, as she had given him assistance in various matters. But if her death was such a priority for numerous unknown parties, then there was good money to be earned from it. And Elsa knew that more than anything, certainly much more than friendship and loyalty, Panda loved money. He also knew Elsa had serious trust issues, and was sly enough to know that the most effective way to persuade her to come inside was by trying to keep her out. There were very few people Elsa trusted in this world, the list was getting more miniscule by the hour, but in all honesty… Panda never made the cut.

'Tell you what.' She slid the glass across the bar towards him, cowboy style. 'You drink it.'

He looked at the glass for a long moment, then shook his head. 'Alas, I'm not a bourbon man.'

Was there something in that glass? A poison or sedative? Panda stood to earn a big payday if he delivered Elsa – dead or alive – to whoever had given the order to have her killed.

'Well.' He poured her drink into a sink behind the bar. 'If you don't want it, you had better go.'

Elsa climbed off the stool and turned to see Panda's sore and injured men standing behind her, some of them bent crooked. At the entrance, Terry opened the front door with a flourish, and she walked out into the empty night.

'Night, Tel.'

'Night, love.' He waved, as she trudged off, like an exhausted clubber who'd been partying all night. 'You take care.'

Buenos Aires, she thought. *What the actual.*

6

Nine years earlier

Thin light ignited faintly across the horizon at dawn, revealing the cold plains of Uruguay as the Bell 212 flew at low altitude towards the brown mass of the Rio de la Plata.

Sitting in the rear cabin, Elsa watched the last of the dark scrub blur past below the open hatch as they approached the river's edge.

Beside her, Max Saint's right heel beat an anxious rhythm against the metal floor. Saint simply couldn't keep still. His scarred face twitched, his tongue probed constantly over his gums, his neck rolled on his shoulders.

Finally, he asked Camille Archard over the headset, 'What's it all about?'

'How would I know? Your guess is as good as mine.'

He grinned. 'Thought you'd have the inside track.'

Opposite, Camille's face was a blank mask, her pale grey eyes hidden behind mirrored aviator sunglasses so it was impossible to tell who she was looking at. But Elsa couldn't shake the feeling Camille was staring at her.

'He doesn't tell me anything,' she answered finally.

When Saint began to sing loudly to himself, oblivious that his amplified dirge was being broadcast into the ears of the other two passengers on the transport, Camille leaned forward to ask Elsa, 'He's like this the whole time?'

'Oh yeah.' Elsa shrugged. 'You get used to it.'

Saint whooped into his mic, 'One of a kind, baby!'

He lifted a hip flask and took a swift, unobtrusive swig. When he caught Elsa watching, he held it out, *want some?*

She gave him a flat smile. 'Too early for me.'

'It's always the right time somewhere in the world,' he said with a wink.

The helicopter dropped steeply to avoid radar detection, the brown water below writhing beneath the downwash of the blades, and then banked sharply. Elsa felt her stomach flutter, bracing her hands on the sides of the seat to stop herself getting thrown into Saint's lap. Opposite, Camille sat composed with her hands on her knees, as if her slim, muscular frame was weighted by some super-heavy interior force – Elsa marvelled at her core control – except for the icy blonde hair that was whipped frenziedly around her face by the blast of cold air rushing through the open hatch, and which even occasionally lifted the severe geometric fringe that bladed high across her forehead. Her face was serene, despite the turbulence and noise.

As the Bell approached the Argentine coast, the pilot's voice crackled, 'Ten minutes.'

This part of the shore was full of deserted petrochemical refineries. Hulking ugly gunmetal structures, cylindrical tanks and seared flare stacks, huge industrial complexes abandoned for many years and left to rust. They were flying towards a crumbling helipad beside one of the buildings.

'One for the road!' Saint took out the flask and, pressing himself almost horizontal against the fuselage, tipped the dregs into his mouth. When he threw the flask out of the hatch, something flew out of one of his pockets and skittered around the cabin, until Elsa trapped it beneath her foot. She picked up the scrap of paper and unfolded it. It was a faded image of a clapboard shack beside a white beach and a sea of vivid blue.

'What's this?' she asked.

'My future home.' He held out his hand. 'When I'm finally done with all this shit.'

'Looks nice.' Elsa gave it back, and Saint carefully replaced it in his pocket, making sure it was sealed inside. 'Where is it?'

'No idea, I tore it from a magazine.' Saint turned back to the window. 'But I'll find it one day.'

The Bell circled the helipad, with its faded white painted 'H', its downwash sending leaves skittering across the concrete. The skids touched down; its three-tonne weight settled.

'It's here.' Camille nodded at an SUV approaching in a cloud of billowing dust. Elsa grabbed her tactical backpack and jumped out of the cabin. When they were clear of the whirling rotors, the Bell lifted into the sky, returning to Uruguay.

Elsa didn't want to sit beside Camille on the long drive into Buenos Aires, had been avoiding her as much as possible, and to her relief her friend climbed into the front of the SUV. Saint climbed in beside her in the back, folding a stick of gum into his mouth.

The drive into the centre of the city took a couple of hours. With its eclectic mix of low-rise buildings and skyscrapers, there was an almost European vibe to Buenos Aires, Elsa thought. Particularly when they reached the expensive neighbourhood of Recoleta, with its French-style apartment blocks, plazas, street markets, and bustling cafés and bars, which were opening for the day.

'Hey, mate.' As they neared the centre of the city's cultural district, Saint leaned forward to the driver. 'Deténgase aquí, sí?'

Their destination was an abandoned apartment building on a street that had been temporarily closed for repair. The building ran half the length of the block. Its masonry was covered in grime; the tall windows had been boarded up. But despite its obvious decrepitude, the building still retained a faded majesty. Long stone balconies swept its length, from where Elsa imagined Juan and Eva Perón once upon a time waved at adoring crowds.

The ornate stone surround of the entrance had been fitted with heavy steel doors to keep out squatters. Exposed wiring exploded from a rusted metal box at the side. Camille pressed the naked tips of two of the wires together and waited. Moments later, one of the doors unlocked with a buzz and the three of them slipped inside. As soon as it clanged shut, booming around the squalid reception, the ambient noise of the city – roaring traffic, blaring horns, sirens, the chatter of pneumatic drills – ceased immediately.

Dank and shabby, the reception still held echoes of its former grandeur: art deco mouldings, stained glass, iron banisters. Hidden behind sheets of plasterboard was a disused cage lift, its dirty metal grille disappearing into the ceiling. In the early part of the last century, this space represented the epitome of sophisticated city living, but it was now a decayed husk, awaiting demolition.

Camille led Saint and Elsa up the sweeping staircase, crunching over fallen masonry and soggy cardboard. It felt like they were the only people who had been here for years, but Elsa knew that their progress was being carefully watched.

'Classy,' said Saint, stepping over a dead pigeon.

On the second floor, Camille rapped on an apartment door, which was opened by a mountain of a man.

Camille immediately flung herself at him, snapping her legs around his waist, her arms around his shoulders. Elsa and Saint waited uncomfortably while her hands moved hungrily up and down the man's handsome face, her fingers yanking at his hair, nails digging into his temples. Her mouth writhed against his.

'Missed you, baby,' she hissed into his ear.

The man finally pulled Camille off him and nodded for the others to come inside.

'Where's my snog?' Max Saint asked as he walked past.

Steve Carragher clapped him on the back. 'Good to see you, Saint.'

He nodded at Elsa; they made eye contact for a brief moment.

'Hey,' he said.

'Hey.'

Camille couldn't keep her hands off her husband as he led them along the wide central corridor of the apartment. Behind them, Saint nudged Elsa, and leered.

'What are you, five years old?' she whispered.

The apartment was absolutely huge but, like the rest of the building, in terrible disrepair. Fragments of damp plaster had fallen from the wall to rot on the floor. Wallpaper drooped, exposing stains. The door to a vast kitchen hung off its hinges, revealing broken furniture, splintered floorboards and smashed fittings. A pair of porcelain sinks lay shattered on the floor. There were mouse droppings everywhere; piles of foetid rubbish, shredded by pests, could have been there decades.

But there was power, at least. Wall sconces gave off a sallow orange light that threw long dark shadows.

'I'll show you where you're sleeping,' Carragher said.

He swung open a door to reveal an enormous room that was empty except for a camp bed. 'Saint, you're in here.'

Max Saint frowned. 'I expressly stipulated an en suite.'

'And Elsa...' Carragher opened another door. 'This is yours.'

She stood in the doorway beside him, conscious of the warmth of his upper arm brushing against hers, the sound of his breathing, and looked inside. It was large and gloomy. Rectangular patches tattooed the bare walls, the ghosts of paintings and mirrors that long ago hung there. Where there had once been a sumptuous carpet was now just floorboards. A threadbare rug beside another camp bed had been decimated by moths. The windows in the room were boarded up; the only light came from an electric lamp.

Elsa walked inside, just to get some distance from

Carragher, and dropped her backpack. She hated herself for wondering where he was sleeping – didn't have to wait long to find out.

'We're in here, yes?' Camille opened a door directly opposite. It was empty like all the others, except for a mattress. Camille slammed herself against Carragher. 'I can't wait to try it out.'

He took her rucksack, tossed it in the room and closed the door.

'Come with me,' he told the three of them.

When Elsa came out of her own doorway, Camille, her eyes still hidden behind the mirrored shades, held out her hand, *after you*.

'There's not much hot water,' Carragher said over his shoulder. 'And there are six of us now, so we wash on alternate days, and take turns to cook.'

'We passed some nice restaurants on the way,' said Saint, winking at Elsa.

'I'm going to presume that was a joke, but in case it wasn't, nobody leaves this building unless I say so.'

'How long will we be here?' Elsa asked.

'As long as it takes.'

None of them knew why they were there, and Elsa knew it was fruitless to press him on it. They'd find out soon enough.

Carragher led them into a giant living room.

Decades ago, the split-level space – steps a third of the way into the room led down into a wider area – would have been sumptuous. You'd fit in a grand piano, easy – hell, there was space for a whole orchestra – but now the room was a characterless shell, stinking of damp and decay. As elsewhere, the tall windows overlooking the street had been boarded up. Low-wattage bulbs in two battery-operated lamps barely lit half of the space, the rest of which lay in cold shadow, despite the bright, warm morning outside.

There were three hardback chairs, and sheets of foam folded up against walls, so it was possible to sit.

'Love what you've done with the place,' said Saint.

The other two members of the team sat at a folding table in front of a pair of laptops. Both men had been here several days already with Carragher.

Elsa hadn't met either Gert Klimt or Paulson Antovic, had never heard of either of them before today. But they had no doubt been recruited like the rest of the team – with the exception of Steve Carragher – by the shadowy private security agency RedQueen.

Elsa saw at a glance that Klimt and Antovic were also Special Forces veterans. Klimt was a hulking Hungarian whose thin lips pursed in an arrogant pout. He kept himself to himself and disappeared regularly to his room, where they could hear him grunt his way through endless repetitions of push-ups and crunches. A fluent Spanish speaker, Klimt was the only team member Carragher allowed to leave the apartment. He had already acquired much of the equipment they needed for the mission, including clothes, audio-visual apparatus and, apparently, a vehicle.

Antovic, the Croatian, was even less of a conversationalist; maybe because he was self-conscious about opening his mouth, which was crowded with large, untidy teeth. He had a ruddy, pockmarked face, and odd whirls of smoothness on his shaved head suggested alopecia. Sat in front of the laptops 24/7, Elsa couldn't recall him saying more than a dozen words to anyone except Carragher, whom he updated regularly about what he saw on the multiple video images on both screens.

As soon as Carragher had made the introductions, he turned one of the laptops so everyone could see it. It showed various live feeds, in and around an apartment block identical to the one they were standing in, but which was still used as a residential building.

The tidy, well-to-do streets surrounding the building were quiet. An occasional car drove past, or someone walked with their dog; the dark alleyway behind it was empty. There was an interior feed of the busy ground-floor reception. The same shape and size as the reception downstairs, it was still a bright and glamorous place; its beautiful art deco stylings remained intact, along with the polished iron and wood cage lift.

There was also a live feed – from a camera embedded in a window frame on the landing; placed there by Antovic, Elsa later learned, when he temporarily joined a team of window cleaners who serviced the building – of the door of an apartment on the second floor.

'This is why we're here.' Carragher pointed at the laptop. 'To get inside Apartment 7b.'

The derelict apartment they were standing in now was huge. Elsa could only imagine how much it would cost to own property in the upscale building in the expensive neighbourhood they saw on the screen.

'An incursion,' said Saint. 'Colour me shocked.'

'The target apartment is exactly the same as the one we're standing in, and in the same position in the building, the east side of the second floor. There have been no major structural alterations to either the apartment or the building that change the layout from this one. No walls have been moved, no corridors rerouted, or extra rooms added. Which is why we're going to spend the next two weeks committing every room and corridor in this apartment to memory, so that when we go in there...' He tapped the building on the screen. 'We'll know every single inch of it.'

'Two weeks? Seriously?' Saint made a face. 'How hard can it be to remember where the bathroom is?'

'We'll have four or five minutes max to get in and out of that building, so we'll go inside when, and only when, I'm satisfied we're ready. This mission is too important, so we won't be taking any silly risks.'

Saint nodded at the boarded-up window. 'Will we be getting any sunlight at all in the next couple of weeks, because I suffer from a vitamin D deficiency.'

Camille snapped, 'Pay attention to Steve.'

Elsa had been recruited to take part in this top-secret mission only days before – by Carragher himself. Usually, the agencies who employed RedQueen to do their dirty work made sure to keep a distance from the company's anonymous contractors, so that they could disavow any mission that was compromised. But Carragher worked for the Secret Intelligence Service. The fact that he was leading the operation himself meant that whatever they intended to do, it was a high priority.

'I need the best, Elsa,' he'd told her as they lay together in a bed in Geneva. 'And that means you.'

But he'd never mentioned then that his wife would be on the team, too.

If they were going into that apartment, it would be to kill somebody, or extract someone, steal something or destroy it, and then get the hell out. What that something or someone was, Elsa had no idea. And, clearly, neither did any of the others.

'Hard to say no to a good-looking fella like Steve, right?' Saint whispered in her ear.

Carragher looked up from the laptop. 'Are you still with us, Saint?'

'Sure, chief.' Saint gave him an ironic salute.

'So, I repeat, we don't leave here until I'm satisfied we're ready, is that understood?'

He looked at each of them in turn.

'Understood,' said Klimt.

Antovic nodded, and Elsa, too.

'Yes,' answered Camille fiercely.

Saint scratched his chin. 'We've got plenty of deodorant in, right? Because I've been trapped with Elsie before, and it can get kind of ripe.'

Elsa ignored him, and because nobody had asked the question they all wanted answered, said, 'What is it we're going to do?'

Carragher folded his arms. 'We're going to destroy something.'

Everybody waited for him to continue.

'Okay, fine, I'll ask.' Saint sighed. 'What is it?'

'You don't need to know what it is,' Carragher said. 'In fact, the less you all know the better. The only thing you need to know is that inside that apartment there's a vault, and inside the vault is something that we're going to blow into a million fucking pieces, and that there'll be people in that apartment who'll try to stop us.'

'How many?' asked Camille.

'There are never less than seven men there at any time, but never more than ten,' said Klimt.

'And whose apartment is it?' Elsa asked.

'That's classified information.' Carragher's gaze barely made contact with hers.

'He knows, but he ain't letting on.' Saint wagged a finger. 'He's a sneaky bugger.'

'All you have to do is get the job done and then in two weeks forget it ever happened, same as always.'

Saint shook his head in exasperation. 'We don't need to be stuck here practising the big moment for a fortnight, it's three or four days' preparation, tops.'

'Max,' snapped Camille, who didn't like her husband's commands being questioned.

'Because believe it or not...' Saint moved around the room restlessly. 'This ain't my first rodeo.'

'We're still building a clear picture of the movements of the security detail in that apartment. Who goes in and out, and when. The security is small and relatively discreet, the building is in a busy residential hub, after all, but they'll more than likely be heavily armed. However, they shouldn't give us much trouble *if* we're properly prepared.'

'And who's going inside?' asked Elsa.

'You, me, Saint.' Standing in that dark, damp-smelling room, as the city came to life outside beneath a bright, blistering sun, Carragher looked at them all in turn. 'We go in, we destroy the target, we leave.'

'Sounds like fun.' Saint nodded. 'Let's do it.'

7

Elsa expected her street to be crawling with police, intelligence agents and military – assassins, too, probably – so she parked the car round the corner and made her way to Miriam's. She didn't see anything suspicious as she slipped into the narrow alley behind the house and ran up the path of the neat garden.

Miriam was sitting tensely in her kitchen, staring at a mobile phone. When Elsa rapped on the back door, her neighbour nearly jumped out of her skin.

'Where are they?' said Elsa when Miriam let her inside.

'Watching a film,' Miriam said. 'It's *Frozen*, I hope you think it's age-appropriate.'

'Thanks, Mir. We'll get out of your way.'

Elsa walked into the living room to find her kids gawping at a stupid-looking snowman prancing about on the TV. Harley and India barely lifted their tired, glassy eyes from the screen as she peeked through the closed curtains at her own home opposite. The house was completely dark; the windows black. When she returned to the kitchen, Miriam pointed at the old Nokia and said, 'It's charged.'

Elsa picked it up and turned it on. A single number had been programmed into it. Taking the phone, she walked towards the stairs. 'I need to use your toilet.'

'No! It's a mess upstairs, use this one.' Elsa considered Miriam curiously as she opened a door under the stairs and tugged a pull cord to turn on the light in a tiny triangular room with a steeply sloping ceiling. 'That's much more cosy.'

Shutting the door, Elsa hunched her tall frame in the cramped space, pulled down her leggings and knickers, and sat on the toilet. An extractor fan rattled noisily above her head. The toxic stench of an air freshener was overpowering in the tiny room. Folded over the phone, she thumbed the call button, listened to it connect. But it rang and rang – nobody answered. Which was just as well, because the extractor was as loud as a jet engine above her head.

When the call went to voicemail, she left a message.

'Saint, this is Elsa Zero. I know it's been a long time, but you said to ring if I needed your help. Well, I'm in trouble, Saint. Ring me.'

She killed the call and considered how much she required Saint's expertise and extensive network of contacts right now. She may not be able to trust her own connections, but he knew people who knew people, and would help her get a new identity; arrange for her to slip out of the country with her kids.

Elsa remembered Saint as a loose cannon, a man battling with his own demons – but someone you could rely on in a fix. He'd already saved her life once. She remembered his hand gripping hers as they flew high above Buenos Aires, wind lashing her fevered face as blood emptied from her body.

Elsa prayed Saint hadn't forgotten he'd given her the phone. But she didn't have time to wait for him to reply, she had to get her kids to safety. She pulled up her knickers and leggings and flushed the toilet, cracking her funny bone on the wall in the confined space, which was typical of the night she was having.

When she walked back into the kitchen, Miriam was turned away, whispering.

'Miriam?'

At the sound of Elsa's voice, her neighbour turned in fright and said quickly into her mobile, 'Sorry, Auntie, got to go!' She dropped the phone in her dressing-gown pocket, clapped her hands together. 'Let's have a lovely cup of tea and then we can talk!'

Elsa nodded at the pocket. 'Who was on the phone, Miriam?'

'Just Auntie,' she said in a strained sing-song. 'She's always up with the larks.'

It was two o'clock in the morning; the larks were definitely still dozing.

'It's the middle of the night.' When Elsa moved slowly around the kitchen table, Miriam made sure to keep on the other side. When Elsa turned in the opposite direction, Miriam went the other way, so that the table was always between them. 'Who calls their auntie at 2 a.m.?'

'She's got insomnia,' stammered Miriam. Elsa got bored of circling the table and headed to the door.

'Wait,' said Miriam. 'Where are you going?'

She climbed the stairs, taking three at a time, and Miriam followed her, frantically calling, 'You can't go up there, that's private.'

Elsa went into the front bedroom, which looked across to her own house opposite. It was a completely normal bedroom – with a double bed, a wardrobe, a dresser

– except for the trestle table at the bay window laden with state-of-the-art surveillance equipment. A video camera on a tripod was pointed at her house; a laptop, digital cameras, headphones and lenses, leads and power adaptors were stashed neatly in boxes beneath the table.

'You a keen birdwatcher, Miriam?' Elsa asked.

'That equipment isn't mine,' said Miriam at the door. 'I'm keeping it for someone.'

'Miriam!' Elsa's bark made her flinch. 'I've had a shitty night already, please don't make things worse.'

'I don't have a proper income and my mum needs care,' Miriam blurted out. Elsa spun a finger in irritation, *hurry up*. 'They came to me and told me they needed to watch your house.'

'Who came to you?'

'I don't know, the police, or the spy people, they never said. They told me I had a duty to my country. A pair of them come every few weeks to watch your house, it's different people every time. And they listen, too. They have microphones in your house, I think, maybe cameras.' As Elsa moved closer, Miriam spoke faster and faster. 'I have to let them know if you do anything out of the ordinary.'

'You've been spying on me.'

'Not me, no – I would never!' Miriam swallowed. 'But they – the spy people – they ask me questions about who you're with, and who comes to the house.'

'Nobody,' said Elsa, outraged. 'Nobody comes to see me.'

'That's what I said, it's not like you have a different man here every week, not now you have a boyfriend, and I told them you don't have friends. I'm so sorry, Elsa, but they paid me.' Tears bulged in Miriam's eyes. 'Mum's care is so expensive. I had no choice.'

'How long?'

'A year or two… or maybe more. Time flies, doesn't it?'

'Who did you phone downstairs?'

'They gave me a number for emergencies. I told them you were here – and that you were leaving. I didn't do it earlier because I was torn, confused. I like you, Elsa.'

Elsa nodded at the phone. 'How long do I have?'

'They told me to lock myself in the bathroom and ring them back.'

'Oh, Miriam,' said Elsa, with genuine sadness. Her neighbour had been sweet to her. Running errands, baking brownies, babysitting Harley and India. She was a kind soul, really, if you turned a blind eye to the snooping spies in her house. It was all very disappointing.

'Give me the phone.'

Miriam took it from her pocket and handed it over. Then Elsa's arm lashed out and Miriam fell unconscious to the floor.

'Hey, kids.' Elsa ran downstairs into the living room. 'Time to go!'

'But the film isn't finished,' said India, her eyes snapping open.

Elsa looked through the curtains. The street was seemingly deserted.

'You've seen that movie a billion times,' she said, switching it off. 'Let it go.'

Her daughter, who always wanted the last word, told her, 'You always say to never be a quitter.'

'Last one to the car gets nits.' Elsa pulled the kids off the sofa and picked up their bags. She didn't have to tell them twice, they both raced to the front door. 'Not that way, it's too easy. Out the back!'

Together, they ran up the garden in the dark. At the end of the alley behind Miriam's house, Elsa held Harley and India in the shadows while she peeked back at her street. She saw a parked van with its lights off; men in Kevlar with automatic weapons kneeled in position behind it.

'Come on.' She lifted the kids and carried them to Miriam's car two streets away. 'It's a dead heat!'

When she had clicked their seat belts into place in the back, she closed the door and crouch-ran to a parked car from behind which she could watch her own street. She called the number on Miriam's phone, and as soon as it connected, whispered, 'I'm safe.'

Moments later, the van's headlights flashed on, the engine roared into life. It accelerated up the road, with the armed unit running behind it. She heard other vehicles coming from the opposite direction, converging on Miriam's house. She heard shouts and a bang as the front door was kicked in. Elsa crunched Miriam's phone under her heel and ran back to the car.

'Let the adventure begin,' she said, climbing into the car. When neither Harley nor India replied, she saw they were both slumped in the back, asleep.

She lifted the Nokia from the rucksack pocket and thought again about Saint. They had been team members on the ill-fated mission nine years previous that somehow held the key to what was happening to her now. Which meant, if she was looking for him, others would be, too.

If that was the case, Saint – an experienced ghost – may already have vanished off-grid.

Elsa had to decide where to go next. It wouldn't take long for whoever was after her to discover she was using Miriam's car. London was the most heavily surveilled city in the world, with hundreds of thousands of CCTV cameras, and countless face-recognition and ANPR systems. The first thing she needed to do was find another vehicle. She knew where to get one.

And then what?

She had to take her kids to safety somewhere. Had to make a quick decision. There was only one place she could think to take them.

Her last resort.

She turned the ignition.

8

Elsa cursed herself for not having some sort of safe house for just this kind of emergency. An empty flat or lock-up, a secret lair where she stored equipment and supplies: food, tech, a chunky bag of automatic weapons she could fling over her shoulder. But how was she meant to afford it on her income? So she drove to a house, owned by one of her personal training clients, that she knew was currently empty.

She was running for her life, so she wasn't going to feel guilty about a little bit of breaking and entering. Besides, it wasn't like she was going to be taking anything from the house. Except the car – sure, she was going to take that, but she intended to bring it back, or leave it where it could be found, so in a way it didn't count – and technically speaking, it wasn't even like she was doing much in the way of breaking in.

The seven-bedroom house, in an expensive neighbourhood in Chiswick, was owned by an overweight investment banker called Douglas Heston. Dougie had been given an ultimatum by his wife, Roberta, lose the pounds or lose me, and so he'd installed gleaming new gym apparatus in the basement – because it was that kind of house.

Elsa went there twice a week to put Dougie through his

paces, although he spent most of the sessions bragging to Elsa about all the money he'd made, his holiday home in Portugal and time-share in Ibiza, his financial portfolio, cellar of expensive wines, and his cars; and sneaking glances at Elsa's body when he thought she wasn't looking. With his bulging belly and impressive collection of chins, Dougie made heavy weather of the very basic exercises Elsa made him do. At the end of each hour, sweat pouring off him, he punched the air, as if he had survived fifteen rounds in the ring with Rocky Balboa.

Dougie and Roberta's home was palatial compared to Elsa's small terraced house. As well as the gym, there was a home cinema, a games room, a hot tub in the garden, and a double garage big enough to hide Miriam's car. At the end of their most recent session, Dougie had explained to Elsa's tits that he and his wife were off to Portugal for a couple of weeks.

But Dougie wasn't the only person with a wandering eye. Elsa saw where he kept a spare key to the rear sliding doors – in a fake stone in the Zen rockery – and memorized the alarm security code Dougie keyed in. Because: old habits.

Leaving the kids asleep in Miriam's car, she climbed over the fence into the garden under cover of darkness, and found the fake stone. She unlocked the sliding doors, slipped into the vast white kitchen and disarmed the alarm.

Another noise momentarily confused her until she realized it was coming from her pocket. The old Nokia was ringing. She took it out and hit the green button. 'Saint?'

'Uh.' The voice on the other end was uncertain. 'Who is this?'

'It's Elsa Zero.' She heard him grunt. 'You gave me a phone, Saint, and told me to call you.'

'Did I? When was this?'

'Nine years ago.'

'Woah, okay.'

'I need to see you, I need your help.'

'Not a problem. Saint's always happy to help.' He coughed violently for nearly a minute. 'Who did you say you were again?'

This wasn't the way she'd expected the conversation to go. 'It's Elsa, Saint. Elsa Zero.'

'Sure.' There was a thick silence. She could practically hear the cogs grinding in Saint's head, and then he barked, 'Elsie, it's you! Jeez, long time no see! Yeah, whatever you need, luv. Although if it's money you're after, you're bang out of luck.'

'When can we meet?'

His laugh disintegrated into another phlegmy cough. 'You must be in trouble if you need my help. Hold on, what time is it? It's dark out.'

'It can't wait,' she told him.

'Been a long night, Elsie, and I'm cream-crackered.' He yawned. 'Let's catch up tomorrow afternoon. I'll call you, I promise.'

'Saint, it's urgent.'

'Yeah, sure, we'll meet later.'

'Where?'

'Here,' he said.

'Where's here?' she asked impatiently.

'Uh. I'm at…' He mumbled to himself, trying to recall, and then said in a slur, 'I'm at the shelter in Somers Town.'

'A shelter?' She was confused, but didn't have time to think about that. 'I'll be there at eight.'

'Sure thing.' He didn't sound keen. 'Make it nine, yeah? I'm a bit shitfaced, and need some kip. Be nice to catch up, Elsie. Bring a bottle, we can celebrate.'

'Saint—' She wanted to impress on him to be careful, particularly if what was happening was connected to the ill-fated Buenos Aires mission code-named Pilot Fish, but he'd hung up. When she tried to ring him back, his phone was switched off.

Elsa went into the spacious garage connected to the house, where Dougie's flash Audi was parked, and hit the switch to open the door. She drove Miriam's car inside. It would be a massive mistake to presume she could stay indefinitely at this house. Spooks would more than likely already have access to the contacts on her phone, her diary in the cloud, and would be poring over the data; identifying contacts, making connections. Dougie's details would come to their attention soon enough. However, the place would be a useful sanctuary for maybe another twenty-four hours.

She found the keys to Dougie's car in a Faraday packet in a kitchen drawer, transferred her sleeping children from Miriam's car to his, and drove out of the garage.

Out of the city.

9

She drove up the M4 to Burnham Beeches in Buckinghamshire. Her exhausted kids sleeping in the back, she kept to a steady speed, careful not to go over the limit. Elsa felt herself becoming more tense – if that was even possible after the events of the night – the nearer she got to her destination.

Finally, she pulled off a country lane and down a rutted dirt road. Past all the *Keep Out! Private Property! Turn Around! This Is Your Last Chance!* signs, one every couple of yards, just in case anyone unfortunate enough to find their suspension bouncing violently on the narrow, potholed track didn't get the message.

The car crunched over churned ridges of mud between scrubby bushes that scratched at the doors, and finally emerged into open space, a large field where cows and horses grazed. Elsa felt a familiar disgust when she saw the dilapidated farmhouse ahead – it looked almost derelict – the skeletal chassis of an ancient John Deere tractor, and the piles of scrap metal and junk that filled the yard. Beyond the farmhouse and a disintegrating barn were more fields and woods.

Standing waiting with shotguns raised, and with two

large Alsatian dogs sitting alert on either side of them, were her parents.

The car crashed into a last pothole. One of the many chickens that clucked around the muddy yard took flight over the bonnet. As Elsa pulled up, Howard Zero rapped his knuckles on the driver's side window.

'Can't you read, this is private property?'

Elsa lowered the window. 'It's me, Dad.'

Howard was joined at the window by his wife, Greta, and together they stared grimly at their daughter. Greta pointed at a space beside a heap of scrap in front of the barn, as if Elsa was a visiting tradesman. 'Park over there.'

Elsa hadn't even got out of the car and already regretted coming. She should have just kept travelling north, as far from the city as possible; tried to catch a ferry somewhere, or stolen a boat to get to the continent. She certainly shouldn't have come back to this unhappy place, where her parents hid from the human race.

But she did as she was told. Killed the engine and got out. It had been nearly twenty years since she'd last seen them, and with the both of them in their early eighties, their faces were etched with deep creases. Howard had let his thick, snowy white hair grow madly to his shoulders, but Greta had the same severe short back and sides she had always worn, now flecked with grey. Despite their age, they stood ramrod straight in Barbour jackets and Hunters, radiating the same stubborn, indestructible energy they always had. Elsa felt a sense of angry failure at having to come back to this godforsaken place.

It was the unbending military bearing, the cold, harsh

attitude of Howard and Greta that had made Elsa submerge her emotions as a child. They had taught her to distrust everything and everyone, and the intense paranoia that had made the Zeros reject the rest of the world and become reclusive on this farm had inevitably left them estranged from their own daughter.

Howard Zero was a former Royal Marine, and Greta – God knows what she had got up to as a young woman; Elsa was forbidden to ask about it. No wonder Elsa had been unable to say 'I love you' to anybody, because she never once heard those words as a child.

In the end, after endless conflict, she had washed her hands of them, and they of her. But as is often the case with antagonistic relationships, she had followed in their footsteps, forging a military career; and then a shadowy life where her own secretive, paranoid nature had kept her alive – up until the present moment, at least.

Greta and Howard came over, the dogs trotting beside them, to look in the back of the car.

'We've converted your bedroom into a workshop,' Greta said.

'Don't worry.' Elsa slammed the car door. 'I'm not staying.'

'Well, then.' When Greta Zero scowled, the deep lines in her face almost obliterated her brown eyes. She wore glasses now, Elsa was surprised to see. At least her parents were still alive; she had half expected to arrive to discover them both gone and the farmland developed into four hundred homes. When one of them keeled over, the other was sure to follow soon after, she was convinced of that. 'I suppose you had better come in.'

Elsa hesitated – the kids were still asleep in the back.

'Leave them there,' said Howard. At a click of his fingers, the Alsatians curled up by the car.

Elsa followed her parents into the dingy farmhouse. Howard replaced the shotguns with the other guns in a cabinet in the cluttered, musty-smelling living room, and locked it. The kitchen was the same squalid room she remembered, full of salvaged furniture and boxes of junk – if anything, there was much more of it – a cracked porcelain sink, leaking pipes, a boiler as loud as a jackhammer, and the same grimy net curtains. Her parents stood together, as cold and hostile as the last time they had spoken, two decades ago.

'What?' she asked sarcastically. 'Aren't you going to offer me tea?'

'No,' Greta told her.

'I'll come straight to the point, then. I need you to look after my kids.'

'The ones in the back of the car,' said Howard.

'No,' snapped Elsa. 'There are some more in the boot.'

Greta nodded. 'You turn up here, after twenty years, and ask us to babysit children we have never met, nor even been told about.'

Elsa blinked. 'It's complicated.'

'You're in trouble,' said Howard.

'Yes.' Exhausted and desperate, Elsa forced down a surge of angry emotion. Now wasn't the time to reopen old wounds; her children's safety was everything. 'You understand I wouldn't have come here if I had any other choice.'

Howard glanced at his wife. 'That's perfectly clear, isn't it, Greta?'

'What is happening?' Peering at the cuts and bruises on Elsa's face, her mother spoke in that curious, uninflected way of hers. 'What is going on?'

'I don't know. I'm trying to find out, and when I do, and when the problem is solved, I'll come back.'

'And if someone comes for the children?' said Greta, who perfectly understood the situation. 'What do we do?'

'You don't let them take them,' Elsa told her.

Greta and Howard shared a look, coming to silent agreement. Her parents spent every waking minute together, had done so for decades, and knew instinctively what the other was thinking.

'And if you don't come back, what happens then?' asked Greta.

Elsa didn't want to think about the consequences, said instead, 'They're your grandchildren, don't you want to know their names?'

'That would be a good idea, I suppose,' said Howard, bristling at her tone. 'Let's go and see them.'

As they walked back to the car, he asked her, 'Do either of them like Tolstoy?'

At a gesture from Greta, the dogs moved away from the car and Elsa woke the kids.

'Harley and India, these are your grandparents.'

Greta raised an eyebrow. 'Those are regarded as acceptable names in this day and age, are they?'

The kids were tired and bewildered, but seemed to take the new people, and their strange new surroundings, in their stride.

'You're going to stay with them here for a couple of days.'

Elsa waited for the inevitable flood of questions, but none

came. Standing in the yard, Harley and India evaluated Howard and Greta, and Howard and Greta considered them in return.

'Are we on holiday already?' India asked Elsa.

Howard told them, 'There are rules you'll have to obey while you're guests in our house. We run a very tight ship here.'

'Do you have a swimming pool?' asked India.

'We have a septic tank.'

'Do you have a PlayStation?' said Harley.

Howard and Greta narrowed their eyes. 'We don't know what that is.'

'Can we watch television?'

'We don't have a television, or computer, or smartphone,' Greta told the children, who looked shocked. 'Because of the low-frequency transmissions. It's how the general population is enslaved by the lies and propaganda of the controlling liberal elite.'

Elsa bit her lip.

'Do you have any jigsaws or games?' asked India.

'Do you play chess?'

The kids shook their heads, but they'd heard of it.

'Chess is a fine game.' Howard's chin jutted as he warmed to his theme. 'It will teach you about life, and survival. About how to anticipate the moves of your opponent. How to turn solid defence into devastating attack and mercilessly crush your adversary.' Howard clenched a fist for emphasis. 'Lessons that will stand you in good stead in life.'

'Can I pet your dogs?' asked Harley.

'You may,' Howard said. He gestured at the dogs, which stepped forward to allow themselves to be stroked.

'What are they called?'

'Churchill and Montgomery,' said Howard.

'They're very friendly,' said Harley.

'At a single word from me, they would rip your throats out.'

'Howard!' snapped Elsa.

India pointed into the field. 'Are those horses?'

'Yes,' said Greta.

'Do they have names?'

'Yes,' said Greta.

There was an awkward silence while everyone looked at the grazing horses, and Howard said finally, 'Would you like to meet them?'

The kids followed him across the muddy field towards the animals.

'I'm going to have to go,' said Elsa.

'We'll cope,' said Greta.

She didn't want to leave Harley and India without saying goodbye, but knew that they would only get upset, as she was now. A quick getaway, a clean break, while they were looking at the horses, was the best thing. But the reality of the situation hit her – it may be the last time she ever saw them. Elsa clenched her teeth, determined not to shed tears in the presence of her mother, who would regard her emotion as weak and shameful. It shouldn't matter, she shouldn't give a shit about what Greta and Howard thought, but she also needed to stay focused.

'Thanks for this,' Elsa mumbled. Throwing the kids' bags onto the packed mud of the yard, she climbed behind the wheel of Dougie's car. When she slammed the door, Greta Zero rapped on the window, and Elsa lowered it.

'Make sure you come back,' Greta said sharply, and Elsa thought she sensed something almost like concern in her mother's tone. But then the old woman added, 'We don't want them here too long.'

'I'll do my best,' Elsa told her, and started the engine.

10

Zoe Castle's mum was insistent. 'Stand up.'

'I'm not going to do that, Mum.' Zoe rolled her eyes, indignant, and stood.

'Now give us a twirl.' On the other side of the world, her mother's face loomed close to the screen as Zoe dutifully turned 360 in front of the laptop's judgmental lens. 'Oh, love, you've really let yourself go.'

Zoe took a steadying breath to stop herself slamming shut the lid of her laptop.

It was true she had put on quite a bit of weight, mostly around the tummy and hips. She was a middle-aged woman who worked in an intense environment and who kept emergency biscuits in the top drawer, but her mum never missed an opportunity to get in a little dig. It wasn't Zoe's fault she didn't have the slim body shape and fierce metabolism of her sisters. She wished she had never got up early for this Zoom call.

'Take yourself out for a jog, is my advice.'

Zoe worked hard at her part-time job, and also volunteered a couple of mornings for the local foodbank, so she liked to spend as much time as possible at the weekends with Jim and Charlie. She enjoyed cooking and baking – nobody got happy eating a salad, after all – and frankly didn't fancy huffing and puffing around the park for the sake of losing a couple of kilos. Where exercise was concerned, taking the dog for a walk was about as far as she got. She didn't need to validate herself by trying to be someone she wasn't. Besides, Jim liked her curves.

Zoe was trying to think of a good excuse to end the call – they'd been chatting for an hour before the conversation turned inevitably to her weight, and she wasn't in the mood to listen to her mother's dietary advice, or her usual monologue about the healthy lifestyle she enjoyed since emigrating to Melbourne – when her mobile rang.

While her mum was talking, she picked it up. 'Hello?'

'Zoe Castle?'

'Speaking.'

'You need to come in,' the voice told her.

Because there was no caller ID, it took her a moment to realize it was someone from work. She heard frantic chatter in the background. Zoe's reduced hours could be unpredictable, that was the nature of the job, but she didn't usually work Fridays – and a call at daybreak was unprecedented.

'There's a car outside your house.'

She went to the window to see a black SUV with tinted windows parked opposite. Zoe wondered whether someone in HR had made a mistake. It wasn't like she was full-time any more, and besides, she had never been senior enough to have a car sent for her. On the rare occasions she was called in to work at short notice, she had been expected to make her own way there. But she knew better than to ask questions over the phone.

'Give me five minutes,' she said.

'You have two,' said the voice, and the line went dead.

At the laptop, Zoe told her mum that she had to go and promised to call her again next week. Closed the lid with a click. In the hallway, she pulled on her shoes and picked up her bag.

'Jim,' she called upstairs. 'I have to go to work.'

Her husband came to the top of the landing, wearing a T-shirt and pyjama bottoms, his hair mussed up from sleep. 'How long will you be?'

She shrugged. *Search me.*

Moments later, she was being driven from her home in Acton into the centre of London. There was no file to read in the back of the car, no tablet, nothing to explain what was happening, and the driver made no attempt to speak.

Zoe had worked as an analyst at SIS, the British foreign intelligence service also known as MI6, full-time for sixteen years, part-time for four, and nothing like this had ever happened. Worried she had somehow fouled up, she bit her nails and gazed out of the window, watching the joggers, dog walkers and cyclists, the people heading to work or to pick up breakfast, as the early morning came to life.

When she was finally dropped off at the SIS Building at Vauxhall Cross on the Albert Embankment and walked into reception, there was nobody to meet her, so she took the lift up to the office on the fifth floor where she hot-desked, and waited. When nobody came to find her, she made a coffee in the kitchen.

There was constant activity in the corridor. The lifts kept disgorging important people, who hurried towards the conference room in a tense huddle of assistants and analysts. Sipping her coffee, Zoe watched government ministers, section chiefs, judges, scientists and senior members of the security establishment stride past.

Accompanying one senior spook was one of the lead intelligence officers at SIS, Nigel Plowright. A man with round wire glasses, floppy hair and a pinched face, he was so thin and insubstantial in his creased suit and tie, and wore such a harried expression, that he looked like he was being taken to the back of the bike sheds to be given a good kicking.

Plowright glanced at Zoe as he hurried past. She had never worked with him, never even spoken to him – about which she was glad, because his reputation wasn't the best – but she saw a flicker of recognition in his eyes.

The minutes she sat there, catching up on some work, online shopping at ASOS, arranging a home delivery from Tesco, turned into an hour, and then two. Finally, during her umpteenth game of Candy Crush on her phone, Zoe heard footsteps come back down the corridor. Plowright opened the door of the office and impatiently crooked a finger. *Follow me*. Zoe jumped to her feet.

'All we need you to do is answer a few questions.' He strode quickly towards the conference room. 'As succinctly as you can.'

'I don't know what this is about,' Zoe said, trying to keep up. 'Nobody's explained anything.'

'You don't need to know what it's about, all you need to do is answer the questions asked of you.' Plowright reached the conference room door and gripped the handle. He looked her up and down, taking in her scruffy blouse, faded denim skirt and old ballet pumps, and she sensed he didn't much like what he saw. 'Don't offer any observations that aren't solicited, and never refer to anybody in the room by name.'

The door swung open and an intelligence officer pushed past. Zoe glimpsed a dark room full of people, heard vigorous discussion.

'What's happening?' she asked Plowright, desperate for answers.

'What's happening?' he replied tersely. 'An enormous clusterfuck of unimaginable proportions, that's what's happening.'

Zoe followed him into the room where a long conference table was lined with people, and the walls illuminated by video screens. Many of the men and women squeezed around the table she knew from the intelligence service and government: civil service mandarins, judges, ministers, medical advisors. Backlit by the electronic light from the screens, ghoulish shadows dropped down their faces. On the screens were dignitaries who presumably couldn't get to the meeting in person. Plowright pointed to a chair inside the door and Zoe sat, listening to the urgent conversation.

A senior spook at the far end of the table peered over the top of his bifocals at a tablet as he spoke. 'GCHQ has picked up ominous chatter suggesting that numerous agents from our counterpart agencies are en route to London. We're trying to reach out to our friends to assure them the situation is under control, but it appears they're taking measures, nonetheless.'

'Taking measures, that's a good way of putting it.' A distinguished-looking man midway along the table snorted mirthlessly. 'You're telling us the city is going to be crawling with assassins.'

The spook whipped off his glasses and tossed them on files in front of him.

'And it's also safe to presume that a number of hostile parties, Moscow and Beijing among them, will attempt to take advantage of the situation and intercept Miss Zero and whisk her out of the country at the earliest opportunity.' Zoe tensed at the mention of the name. 'I don't need to remind any of you ladies and gentlemen of the gravity of the situation should that happen.'

On a screen, a government minister sat on a sunny veranda, a beach of blistering white sand behind him. 'Washington doesn't have faith that we can handle the situation?'

A woman Zoe recognized as a strategic security officer shook her head. 'Can you blame them? The situation is unprecedented. It's been nearly seven hours since the attempt on Elsa Zero's life and we're still struggling to get a handle on everything. The entire global intelligence community appears to be one step ahead of us. All our usual channels have let us down.'

Plowright walked over to the distinguished-looking man and whispered into his ear, and the man glanced over at Zoe. He cleared his throat sharply, as if to say, *let's stop the conversation.*

'I understand that Zoe Castle here is an intelligence officer who has worked closely with Zero on a number of highly classified operations.' The man looked at her expectantly. 'Can you tell us more about her, Mrs Castle?'

Zoe sat gawping, but when Plowright glared, she stood quickly.

'I'm not a...' Everyone looked at her closely and she

blushed. 'I'm not an intelligence officer, I'm just a data analyst.'

The man asked, 'We've been misinformed?'

She blinked at Plowright, who stepped quickly from the wall.

'I'm afraid Mrs Castle is the only person who has had personal contact with Zero that we can find this morning,' he said. 'Zero's other contacts within the department have all dispersed in the intervening years, and we've had trouble locating them at such short notice. I regret to say our databases need overhauling.'

There was a tense silence in the room. The strategic security lady said, 'Well, you're here now. What can you tell us about Elsa Zero?'

Zoe wracked her brains, not wanting to stammer or stumble in front of the packed room of very important people. 'I, uh, worked with Elsa… with Zero on two or three occasions, but it was a long time ago, this was in twenty—'

'Do you have any idea why SIS would contract a private security agency to engage in clandestine operations on foreign soil?' On a screen, a man sitting in a library of leather-bound books and dark wood glared into the camera. 'People with seemingly no loyalty to this country?'

'Mrs Castle is a data analyst, Henry,' said the spook lady with an exasperated sigh. 'I don't believe the question is within her purview. Please, Mrs Castle, tell us about Zero. She was a deep cover agent?'

'Deep cover, yes. She specialized in incursions.'

'What does that mean, exactly?'

'Elsa Zero was employed to access forbidden domains

– high-security offices, homes, compounds, vaults – either covertly or by force.'

The distinguished man frowned. 'To do what?'

'Whatever we wanted her to do,' interrupted Plowright.

'I only worked with her on a couple of simple surveillance operations, more than a decade ago now, so my memory may not be the best,' said Zoe. 'But I remember she was extraordinarily good at her job.'

'We are all abundantly aware of her skills, Mrs Castle,' said the distinguished-looking man. 'But what was she like as a person?'

Zoe was surprised by the question. 'Like many operatives, she was a difficult person to get to know. She was guarded... perhaps not the easiest person to get on with. I found her impatient, headstrong, confident in her skill set. She was very guarded, and could be curt and dismissive – but deep cover agents are secretive by nature and not the most sociable of people.'

'Did you work with RedQueen on a black-ops incursion...' The minister looked up from a file. '... Code-named Pilot Fish?'

From the way a number of people stiffened, Zoe guessed he'd said something that wasn't intended for her ears. 'I don't—'

'I'm afraid Mrs Castle doesn't have the necessary clearance where the most classified missions are concerned,' Plowright said quickly. 'She's worked mostly on low-level operations.'

'Then why is she here?' Behind the minister, a flamingo flew across the surf. 'She clearly can't provide vital tactical knowledge or psychological insights that will help us find the woman.'

'Is there anything, anything at all, that you think may be of any help to us, Mrs Castle?' asked the strategic lady.

Zoe squirmed, trying to think of something to tell them.

'It was a long time ago, and as I say, she was never very talkative, but...' Something occurred to her, the only thing she had. 'I remember I had to rush home one day because my son was ill. She asked me questions about him, and my home life, it was the only time she showed any interest at all in me, and I got the impression she was... envious.'

The senior spook clasped his hands. 'About what?'

'That I had a family, a home.'

Nobody in the room seemed much impressed with her observation.

'Did you like her?' asked an older man at the other end of the room, and the way he looked at her – with a sharp, questioning intelligence – made Zoe think he was some kind of judge. 'Elsa Zero?'

'Yes, despite everything, I think I did.' She couldn't help but ask, 'Is she... in trouble?'

'What is her weakness, do you think?' asked the spook lady.

'That's pretty obvious, isn't it?' said the minister. 'We get her children, we get her.'

'Thank you, Zoe, for coming in at such short notice,' said the distinguished gentleman quickly. 'I'm sure you understand that everything you heard in this room must be kept strictly confidential.'

It was clear the meeting wouldn't continue until she left,

but Zoe hesitated at the door, and turned to the assembled faces. 'If Elsa's in trouble, I'd like to help bring her in.'

There was an embarrassed silence, and then the judge said, 'I'm sure someone will organize a car to get you home.'

Plowright bundled her out of the door, hissing, 'What did I tell you? Don't speak unless you're spoken to.'

'Tell me what's going on,' Zoe said, trying to keep up as he led her towards the lift.

He barked with bitter laughter. 'I'm afraid it's way above your pay grade.'

'She's running, isn't she?'

'There'll be a car waiting downstairs,' he told her.

'Let me help. I don't know her well, hardly at all, really... but I'm sure I can be useful.'

Plowright glanced back towards the conference room, where assistants went in and out with regular updates, then pulled her into an office, closing the door.

'Someone tried to kill Elsa Zero last night. In a crowded restaurant on the King's Road. They tore the place apart. Both parties left the scene, bloodied but alive, and by the time we were alerted and got to her home, she and her kids had fled.' Plowright pushed his round glasses up his sharp nose. 'But there's nowhere she can go, because every intelligence agency on Earth is looking for her.'

'But why?' asked Zoe, bewildered.

Plowright's mouth twisted as he pondered how much to tell her. 'SIS has been keeping Zero under observation for some time. We suspect she's a key player in a major global conspiracy, and chatter we picked up last night seems to confirm it.'

She had heard Zero retired years ago – deep cover agents burned out quickly – and what Plowright told her didn't make any sense.

'Then let me help bring her in.'

'Zero is a target,' he told her.

'Who wants to kill her?'

'Everyone.'

'Why?' asked Zoe in shock.

'Why?' There was no humour in Plowright's bitter laugh. 'Because right now Elsa Zero is the most dangerous person on the planet.'

11

When she got back to London, Elsa parked Dougie's car near Russell Square and made her way to the shelter in Somers Town, skirting as best she could the numerous CCTV cameras around Euston Station. Meaning to reconnoitre the shelter, she was surprised to see Saint on the pavement outside.

Standing smoking a cigarette with a group of other men, he looked terrible. Once upon a time Max Saint had been cocksure and confident, and with good reason, but he was a shadow of the handsome, super-fit athlete Elsa once knew.

They were roughly the same age, but you'd never know it. His hair, once cropped in a military cut, fell lankly to his shoulders. His thin, blotched face was etched with deep creases, and ravaged by mysterious sores and blemishes; his eyes, once a dazzling blue, were puffy and bloodshot. A beard covered his jaw as best it could over skin interrupted by raised cords of scar tissue. Bundled in layers of filthy clothing, it was obvious that Max Saint had been living on the streets.

But he seemed animated enough as he stood with the other men, arms waving wildly, tall frame in constant, nervous motion, joking and chatting. His laugh exploded into a crackly cough as he swigged from a half-bottle of rum.

Elsa came out of her hiding place and walked quickly up behind him. 'Saint.'

At the surprise mention of his name, he turned slowly; the wary Saint of old would have had her in a headlock instantly. A roll-up trembling between his chapped lips, his tired eyes finally managed to focus.

'Elsie?' He smiled, revealing green teeth, livid red gums and unsightly gaps. 'Lads, it's Elsie Zero!'

Moving in for a hug, he enveloped her in a smelly cloud of alcohol, body odour and a musky stink she didn't even want to contemplate the nature of.

Saint turned to the other guys, homeless men with equally careworn faces, broken smiles and shattered lives. They clutched filthy bedding and plastic bags, carried tattered rucksacks containing everything they owned.

'Lads, this lovely lady is a good friend of mine, Elsie Zero.' The last thing she needed was for Saint to keep shouting her name on a busy London street. 'What are you doing here?'

One of the men, who had a little dog on a piece of string, grinned, displaying a solitary tooth. 'How you doing, lass?'

'We spoke last night.'

Saint's eyes blinked slowly as he tried to remember, and she realized he was just as pissed this morning. 'Did we?'

'I need to speak to you inside,' Elsa told him, in no mood to chitchat with his mates.

'I was just telling the lads about the SAS.' Saint placed a hand to his stomach and grimaced; his guts were probably in a right state. 'Those were happy days, they really was.'

Elsa felt paranoid and vulnerable standing on the busy street, with its constant stream of traffic and passers-by. 'Now, Saint.'

'Sure.' He held up his fag. 'Let me just finish this, doll.'

'I'll have it, if the young lady wants to speak to you,' suggested one of the other gentlemen.

Saint must have clocked her uneasiness because she saw a glimmer of understanding in his eyes.

'Sure, I remember now.' He gave the roll-up to one of the other guys, tapped him lightly on the cheek. 'You owe me one, sport.'

Saint, who had once triumphantly smashed Special Forces endurance training by carrying seventy pounds of equipment across miles of scorched desert in blistering temperatures, limped unsteadily alongside her in his dirty, bloated trainers. She wondered how long he'd been living like this.

Walking into a small common area, Saint asked, 'Beverage, Elsie?'

'No time for that.' She eyed the men and women hunched over plastic cups. 'We need to talk.'

'Hey, Saint,' someone shouted. 'You've pulled!'

Saint gave him the finger and everyone roared.

A staff member pointed at Elsa. 'She can't be here.'

'She ain't my dealer; Elsie's an old friend.' He placed his hands together, as if in humble prayer. 'You know me, fella. Saint by name, Saint by nature.'

'Two minutes,' said the man.

When they went into a long corridor, Elsa couldn't help but ask, 'What happened to you, Saint?'

'It's a sad story. Things didn't turn out the way I imagined, life took a few wonky turns.' He nodded amiably to everyone who passed them. 'Ain't no big deal; it's happened to better people than me.'

Elsa had heard years ago that he was struggling. PTSD,

they'd said, from all the things he'd seen and done as a mercenary.

Elite soldiers for hire like Saint moved from one war zone to another, selling their expertise to the highest bidder, leaving family and friends in the past, never putting down roots. These stateless warriors lived out of backpacks, staying in camps and field tents, becoming ever more estranged from conventional forms of living. They became addicted to conflict, craving risk and danger, using drink and drugs to make the periods in between tolerable.

Finally, too damaged and paranoid, and often hunted by vengeful adversaries, many ended up living off the grid altogether. When they struggled with mental health problems and addiction, there was no safety net to catch them, and they plummeted quickly through the cracks of a society they'd never felt a part of in the first place.

All the signs were there, Elsa supposed. Back in the day, she had more than once hit the town with Saint after completing a job. In the early hours she'd call it a night, but he'd disappear in search of chemical adventure to fill his noisy head. She'd later find out Saint's bender lasted days or even weeks. When she'd heard of his struggles, Elsa had tried to locate him – after all, she owed him her life – but none of their mutual contacts knew where he was. She'd completely forgotten about the Nokia he'd given her.

'It's a hard life, Elsie,' Saint told her with a drunken smirk. 'But I'm a hard man.'

'They're after us, Saint.' In his state, he'd be a sitting duck.

He shifted his body weight, and she saw he was sweating. 'Yeah, who's that?'

'Years ago, you gave me a phone. After Buenos Aires, after I—'

'Yeah, I thought we'd lost you…' Wincing, he clutched his side.

'Are you all right?'

'Just a twinge.' He dug a phone from his pocket, identical to the one she had, a Nokia 8800. It was covered in lint, and sticky with tissue and mysterious blobs of God-knows-what. He must have been carrying it around for years. 'Always kept it charged; guess I knew you'd call sooner or later.'

'Why did you give me the phone, Saint?'

'I just knew that… How you doing, Pat, all right?' He winked at an old guy who shuffled past, and then whispered, 'I knew that wasn't the end of it, and that fucking disaster of a job would come back to haunt us, it was nailed on.'

'Someone tried to kill me last night.'

'Yeah?' Leaning heavily against an office door, he grimaced in pain.

'And if it's got anything to do with Buenos Aires, they may try to do the same to you.'

'Gotcha.' Nodding, he took the bottle from his pocket and swigged. 'Now it all makes sense.'

'What does?'

Saint flung the door open to reveal a small office where two men were tied to chairs with duct tape, heads slumped on their chests. Elsa went inside to check their pulses, which were slow and steady.

'What happened?'

'I was in here minding my own business, filling out benefit forms – you wouldn't believe what you have to go through,

Elsie, to get state assistance; it's criminal after all the things I've done in the service of this country – when they came in and tried to drag me out.' Saint made a face. 'And I weren't having that, no way. So there was handbags.'

Slumping wearily against a wall, he lifted layers of stained clothes to reveal a wound in the side of his stomach.

'I popped outside to have a fag and then I was going to come back and find out what they wanted.'

'You're injured,' she said.

'Got stabbed with my own knife.' He swigged the rum. 'Just a scratch, but a tad embarrassing.'

'When did this happen?'

'Just before you came,' he said. 'About five minutes ago.'

The small room was a mess. There was a broken table, an overturned cabinet. Saint had fought a life-and-death struggle with these two men and then calmly gone outside for a cigarette. Even in bad shape, he was more than a match for them.

Saint nodded at the earpieces the intruders wore. 'Spooks, defo.'

She pushed him towards the door. If they were secret service, more would be coming at any moment.

'We have to get out of here.'

'We should probably kill these two first,' he suggested.

Elsa shoved him into the corridor.

12

Plowright put down the phone and demanded of his team, 'Where is she?'

Deep in the heart of the most restricted area in the SIS building at Vauxhall Cross, he paced across an ops room. With its technicians hunched over monitors, and its three walls of screens showing constantly changing camera feeds of the streets of London, it looked more like the command hub of a battleship, or a TV production gallery.

He rubbed his hands – his slim limbs were prone to cold and the air conditioning in the room was chill – as he anxiously searched the screens for Elsa Zero, watching as face-recognition software triangulated on the faces of the thousands of people captured on CCTV on nearby streets. Citizens hurrying along pavements, across roads, standing on Tube platforms, crowds pouring in and out of Euston Station; a surging tide of workers, shoppers and tourists.

Digital grids shimmered and shifted across their features. Biometric algorithms scanned faces and compared them almost instantaneously to photographs lifted from numerous databases, the information processing at a bewildering rate. A constant thread of information dropped down the side of the screens, too fast for the human eye to read.

'We've got them,' called one of the techs, and CCTV footage immediately appeared on the huge central screen.

Plowright and his team, including his deputy officer, Justine Vydelingum, watched Elsa Zero and a scruffy individual flee the shelter in Somers Town and race into the warren of streets north of Euston Road. Agents were closing in, converging from different directions in two SUVs. On a monitor, the vehicles were represented as red GPS dots on a street map.

Plowright clenched his fists. A tall, slim woman in a hoodie, her long legs taking big, easy strides, headed along a street towards Somers Town. Behind her, a limping, lopsided figure, swathed in a bundle of clothes, struggled to keep up. If the shambling figure was Max Saint, as Plowright strongly suspected, he must have been catastrophically hot in all the layers he wore: at least two body warmers over a padded sports jacket, a sweatshirt, maybe more under that; tracksuit bottoms that flapped at his ankles; a battered pair of trainers.

'Confirmation, please!'

'It's them.' Justine repeatedly clicked a pen top in a manner he found highly irritating. 'I can feel it.'

Pressing the bridge of his glasses up his nose, he watched the figures run below the camera on Chalton Street. 'I need confirmation before I commit both teams. How far away are those vehicles?'

'Thirty seconds,' said a tech. 'They'll have a visual any moment.'

'Is that Max Saint?' Suspecting a decoy, Plowright jabbed a finger at the screen. 'Someone, anyone, identify that individual.'

The aim had been to bring Max Saint in for questioning. Plowright's superiors had worried that sending a full assault team to the shelter would create unnecessary noise and visibility. He was an alcoholic druggie with mental health problems, but what they hadn't factored into their thinking was that Saint was also a former captain in the SAS, a notorious mercenary and a veteran of numerous black ops missions.

Against his own better judgement, Plowright had been ordered to keep Saint's arrest low-key by sending in a single pair of agents – with whom they had immediately lost contact.

But that's what happened when you tried to run a delicate operation like this by committee: you were asking for trouble. Finally, the penny had dropped with his superiors. After last night's debacle when an assault team arrived in Zero's street and found her gone, and now the obvious conclusion that the agents had failed to apprehend Saint, Plowright had moments ago been given sole responsibility to hunt Zero.

He didn't want the job, it was a poisoned chalice, but if he could take down Elsa Zero, he might just avoid the inevitable fallout from this absolute shitshow; he was damned if he was going to be made a scapegoat if she was allowed to evade capture again.

All was not yet lost. Plowright couldn't see their faces, but that was Zero and Saint running on the screen, he was sure of it.

'Where's that bird I asked for?' he demanded.

'Helicopter's en route,' someone told him.

A voice dulled by engine roar came over the speaker: the

lead officer in one of the SUVs. 'We're turning into Chalton Street. Do we commit? Please advise.'

'Let's see their dashboard cam.' Plowright loomed over the technician, the fingers of his left hand twitching – if he knew which button to press on the keyboard, he'd do it himself – but the feed changed almost immediately to the view from inside the vehicle as it accelerated up the street. He couldn't see them yet, but it would be any moment now. There were four officers in that car, and four in the other vehicle.

'Let me speak.' Plowright snatched up a headset so that he could be heard clearly in the car. 'You're almost on them. Use any measures necessary to bring them down. I repeat, *any* measures necessary.'

On another screen, the running figures ran past a street camera, and then something unexpected happened. Elsa Zero came back, pulling down her hood to reveal her face as she trotted closer, while the other figure shuffled around a corner ahead.

From the POV of the dashboard camera in the SUV, Zero could be seen in the distance. They were almost on her. 'We've got a visual!' said the lead officer in the SUV.

'What on earth is she doing?' asked Justine.

Incredulous, Plowright pushed his glasses up his nose. Zero came to a stop beneath the CCTV camera and looked directly into its lens, mouthed something up at it.

'Is there sound on that thing?' Plowright said, and when nobody answered, he shouted, 'Will someone tell me?'

'No, sir,' said one of the flustered techs.

Then she was sprinting away again, following the other

figure around the corner; disappearing off the dashboard cam as it roared towards her.

'They've turned onto Polygon Road,' Plowright told the officers in the car, which was approaching the turn. 'You're almost on them.'

The dash camera jerked as the car took the junction too fast, crunching up onto the pavement, sending a bin spinning, but when it turned onto the adjacent street there was no sign of Zero or Saint.

'Is there another camera nearby?' Plowright asked the room. But he knew there wasn't, that would be just too fucking convenient.

'There's no sign,' said the lead officer in the SUV, which braked hard. 'We're going to search by foot.'

Plowright heard doors slam. The officers jumped from the car, handguns held discreetly at their sides. But Plowright knew Zero and Saint had escaped into one of the many buildings along the route, and that there wasn't a hope in hell they'd pick them up on camera again.

'What do we do next?' asked Justine, clicking the pen top. Plowright's gaze moved to the central screen, where he could see the officers trotting along the street from directly above, the helicopter having moved into position. But the thermal imaging camera on board wouldn't be able to penetrate any of the buildings. He listened to the officers on the ground as they searched the area.

After twenty minutes, with every search option exhausted and Zero and Saint vanished, his attention turned to why she had so brazenly approached that camera.

They watched the footage several times. Elsa Zero stood

beneath the camera, her bright eyes gazing coolly into the lens: challenging, defiant. Her mouth moved again and again, soundlessly repeating the same two words.

'Shall we get a lip reader?' Justine asked.

'No.' Plowright waved her off. 'I know exactly what she's saying.'

13

Zoe Castle was still in the building, Plowright learned. Sitting at her desk in the hope she'd be needed again. He didn't know whether to be impressed or to fire her for insubordination.

'You can't fire her,' Justine told him. 'HR would be on you like a shot.'

'It was a joke,' Plowright snapped, picking up the phone in his office. 'Just get her in here.'

He was making calls, giving his superiors updates on his progress – or lack of it – in finding and terminating Elsa Zero, when Zoe knocked on his door.

Plowright gestured for her to sit while he finished the last one, nodding tensely as he was shouted at. Zoe sat looking around the office, pretending not to hear the murmur of the angry voice bleeding from the earpiece. Not that there was a lot to see. Senior intelligence officers never remained long in the job. Many burned out from the stress and pressure of running networks of agents and assets and numerous covert counter-terrorism operations; or were offered up as sacrificial lambs when things went spectacularly wrong, as they often did. There was little point in adding homely touches to an office you would in all likelihood be vacating within months.

'I told you to go home, Mrs Castle,' Plowright said, slamming down the phone.

'I thought I might be of assistance.'

He folded his hands and considered her. 'As it turns out, you could be. This morning, Elsa Zero approached a CCTV camera in central London, as bold as brass, and said something into it.'

When he didn't elaborate, Zoe had to ask, 'What did she say?'

'She said your name. She said, *Zoe Castle*. Which is a bit of a turn-up for the books, wouldn't you say?'

Zoe blinked in shock.

'Just to give you some background on this, Zero is a cross-agency priority. Pilot Fish was our cock-up, so SIS is taking the lead, but both arms of British intelligence – MI5 and MI6 – are working closely to find and eliminate her with the utmost urgency. Zero represents not only a very serious domestic threat, but also an international one.' Plowright stood to pace the small room. 'We believe she may be working, or intending to work, with any number of hostile nations. Elsa Zero has quite the reputation. She was – most likely still is – a first-class operative, with a close association to the private security agency RedQueen and, through that, loose affiliations to many foreign intelligence agencies that we know of, and very probably a fair number that we don't. I'm afraid to say she was employed by RedQueen to execute several highly classified operations abroad on behalf of British intelligence.'

'Years ago,' said Zoe.

'All before my time, of course. If I'd had anything to do

with it, I wouldn't have let her, or any cowboy private agency, anywhere near the building, let alone operations of the most secret and sensitive kind.' Sitting back down, Plowright rested his elbows on the armrests of his ergonomic chair to steeple his fingers. 'But it also begs the question, why on earth she has brought you – with the utmost respect, an undistinguished part-time data analyst – into this situation.'

Zoe's eyes lifted to the ceiling, trying to make sense of it; only one explanation came to mind. 'I'm the one person she can trust.'

Plowright frowned. 'And why would she think that?'

'Because if I was Elsa Zero right now, and someone was trying to kill me, but I didn't know who, I'd reach out to someone way down the chain of command. Someone unambitious, and yes, undistinguished, who I wouldn't consider an immediate threat.'

Plowright pressed his fingers together. 'Go on.'

'Elsa knows I'm a lifer here; I'll potter about in the building till I finally retire and receive a meagre civil service pension. She knows the kind of person I am. I've no allies, but no enemies either, so I'm not a threat to her. I think she wants to come in.'

He shook his head. 'The kill order is active.'

'If she thinks it's a trap, or that I'll betray her, she'll run. She'll use all her contacts and resources to go underground, and you'll lose her.' Plowright tapped his fingers together, thinking about it. 'Why is she a target?'

'She is…' Plowright's mouth crimped as he evaluated how much to tell her. 'A critical player in a global conspiracy.'

'If that's the case, and hostile nations and God knows

who else are after her, then the longer she manages to stay alive, the longer she's out there alone in the wild, the greater the chance she'll be captured or ally herself to antagonistic forces. If she hasn't already.' She sighed. 'But you know all this.'

Plowright gazed at her for a long moment. 'Okay, Mrs Castle, we'll bring her in, and you'll help us do it.'

'If the intention is to kill her, I want nothing to do with it.'

He shook his head. 'They won't go for it upstairs. You have no idea of the threat level we're dealing with here.'

'I need you to guarantee her safety.'

'Even if I could give it to you, and the last time I looked you were just a data analyst without the authority to ask me for fuck all, my guarantee wouldn't be worth the paper it's written on.'

'I've never worked with you, Mr Plowright, but I know your reputation. They say you're an irritable bully and an arrogant tosspot.'

'Who says that?'

'Everyone, mostly.'

Plowright pressed a finger under his glasses to rub his eye. 'Flattery will get you everywhere.'

'But you also have a reputation as a man who always does the right thing by his agents in the field.'

'Zero's not our agent, and never has been.' She looked steadily at him, and he sighed. 'Okay, Zoe Castle, I'll give you a window. I'll speak to upstairs about getting the kill order... temporarily suspended. But first I should tell you what this is about, so you understand just what we're dealing with here.'

'And then what?'

'And then you go home.' When she looked aghast, he added, 'Because there's not a hope in hell Elsa Zero is going to call our switchboard.'

14

Elsa took Saint to Dougie's, getting him to lie flat on the back seat as she drove along the expensive Chiswick street.

'What,' he asked, 'is it cos you're ashamed of me?'

A dog walker peered at the car as it approached the house, and Elsa hoped they didn't see her. She pressed the remote to open the garage door and swung the vehicle in; remained at the wheel till the door had lowered to the floor behind them.

Saint shuffled into the large, airy house; walked around the spotless state-of-the-art kitchen, with its smooth, clean lines, graphite tiles and the numerous gadgets on the epic granite surfaces, as if he was having a religious experience. Moving from room to room, whooping and yelling, he was oblivious of the pain he was in, or the blood he smeared on every surface. Elsa saw him disappear through a door and clatter downstairs into a cellar, heard his roar of triumph. When he returned, he had a bottle of wine in each fist, and a pair of bottles sticking out of each pocket.

'I've died and gone to heaven. There's a whole cellar full of wine, Elsie. Walls of it!'

She took the bottles from his hands and pockets, before

they fell and smashed, and placed them on the counter. 'We're not on holiday, Saint.'

He flung open kitchen drawers, looking for a bottle opener. 'Bastards are trying to kill me. The wine in that cellar is probably the last I'll ever get to drink!'

The doorbell rang and they stared at each other. Elsa peeked down the long, wide hallway. A blurred figure stood behind the stained glass of the front door. If it was the man who saw them on the street, they could be in trouble. But a package came through the letterbox and plopped to the mat, and the postman walked away. Elsa felt some of the tension ease from her shoulders. But on a street like this, with Neighbourhood Watch stickers in every window, they couldn't stay for long. If Elsa's plan to bring them both in from the cold worked, they wouldn't have to.

Saint was opening a bottle of red, his shaking hands working feverishly at the neck. 'Who uses bloody corks, these days?'

Elsa didn't know much about wine, but could see from the label that it was old and expensive. When he got it open, he didn't bother with a glass, just gulped it from the bottle, his Adam's apple pulsing as he glugged, the red liquid dribbling into his straggly beard.

'Meant to leave it to breathe,' Saint said when he finally came up for air. 'But who's got time for that?'

Intrigued by the fine layer of dust on the bottle, Elsa couldn't help but ask, 'What's it like?'

He shrugged. 'Like wine.'

While he sat drinking on a stool at the central island, Elsa searched for a first-aid kit; found one in a utility room off the kitchen. She told him to take off his stinking body warmers, hoodies and vests, which he managed to do without once putting down the bottle. Trying not to breathe in the stench of his BO, Elsa went about cleaning and treating the wound on his stomach.

'What's our next move, anyway?'

'We can't run forever,' she told him.

She missed Harley and India already, and prayed Howard and Greta would keep them safe.

As she was still swabbing his wound, Saint stood and headed into a massive living room, which ended in an enormous conservatory with glass on three sides, and threw himself on a long grey L-shaped sofa. Lifting his legs onto a heavy glass coffee table and crossing his ankles, he grabbed the TV remote.

The seventy-foot landscaped garden was surrounded by a tall fence – when the weather was good, Elsa and Dougie did fitness sessions on the patio – but it was still possible to see into the house from the top floors of the homes opposite. Elsa palmed a switch on the wall, and blinds dropped slowly down each wall of glass to conceal the room.

Saint rested his head wearily against the back of the sofa and gazed blankly at a cartoon on the television. His eyes were moist and unfocused; face pale and blotched. She sat beside him to patch up his stomach as best she could.

'We know people with jets and private airstrips, yeah? We could get out of the country.'

Elsa shook her head. 'Panda said there's a kill order out on me, and I need to find out why, or I'll never be safe. There's been some kind of misunderstanding or miscommunication

– or I've been set up. I've been accused of something, implicated in a conspiracy, and I have no idea what it is.'

He raised the bottle in a drunken salute. 'Good luck to you, madam.'

'What made you give me that phone?' she asked. 'After Buenos Aires.'

He wiped the back of his hand across his mouth. 'Because we walked into a trap, that's as clear as day. We were never meant to survive that mission, Elsie, none of us. SIS wanted whatever was in that apartment destroyed and us dead, and everything wrapped up in a cute little bow, that's what I reckon. And if they were prepared to kill us then, Elsie, what's to stop them trying again?'

'But it was nine years ago,' said Elsa. 'Sit up.'

She helped lift Saint forward, and he swigged from the bottle while she wound a bandage around his middle, trying not to get too close to his stinking body.

'We lost half the team, and we nearly lost you. Carragher never got stuff wrong, Elsie. You know how prepared he always was, he was a professional. He was set up; we were set up.'

She hadn't thought about that mission for a long time.

Lying on board a helicopter as a slick of her blood cools and trembles on the diamond plate metal floor beneath her.

Saint shouting in her face, trying to keep her awake, his words obliterated by the noisy thrum of the rotors.

The wind chilling her hot, fevered face.

The sky twists and turns below her, the sprawling city recedes above her head. Barely conscious, she feels a faint pressure on her ice-cold hand.

Camille squeezes it.

She thinks, I'm dying. This is what it's like to die.

But she clung to life, thanks to a massive blood transfusion as she slipped in and out of consciousness at a secret medical facility.

Officially, the mission was deemed a success. The contents of the vault in the apartment, that mysterious glowing box, were destroyed. During her long and intense debrief by SIS agents in London, Elsa was questioned repeatedly about what happened. She recounted everything she remembered about the incursion, but she could never shake the feeling that she had somehow been blamed for the debacle.

And she never worked for RedQueen, or with British intelligence, again.

Elsa left her old life, with its constant threat of sudden violent death, behind. She was a mum now, and a businesswoman, just another face in the crowd.

Or so she thought.

'Set up? By who?'

'Someone in British intelligence, I guess, or one of the deep state American agencies. Carragher was in charge of some kind of ultra-secret task force, those were the rumours. And that glowing box was the endgame.' Saint's eyes blazed with righteous energy. 'Someone betrayed us, Elsie, someone tried to send us all to our deaths, and now they want to finish the job.'

But that scenario didn't make sense. On the way back to the house, Saint had talked about his vulnerable existence in the years since she'd last seen him. He'd had spells in rehab and prison, had even been locked up in a secure hospital, a maximum-security institution where he was given strong medication. Nobody would have batted an eyelid if he hadn't come out of any of those places alive. And he'd been on the streets a long time, a dangerous place full of casual, sudden violence. If there was ever a plan to liquidate Saint, there had been plenty of opportunity in the preceding years to get it done.

They weren't after Saint; it was Elsa they wanted.

Every single intelligence agency wanted her dead.

But why?

'Saint,' she asked, when his attention drifted back to the TV, 'where's Camille now?'

He didn't take his eyes off the screen. 'No idea.'

'Is she still with RedQueen?'

'Ain't seen Camille for years. Could be dead for all I know.'

Elsa recalled again that rectangular box in the vault, with its band of pulsing blue light. 'Do you have any idea what we destroyed in that apartment?'

'Some kind of hard drive, right?' He shrugged. 'I think Carragher had an inkling there was a chance that mission was going to get messy; why else go to the trouble of setting up a field hospital? Nah, I'm telling you, something about that mission stank.'

Elsa wasn't going to get answers on the run; the best she could hope for was to not get killed. And every hour she was hunted, the harder that was going to be.

'The only way to survive is to give ourselves up,' she told him. 'Get back inside the machine.'

She expected him to challenge her, but he shrugged. 'You want me to help?'

The truth was that the presence of Saint – slow, injured,

inebriated – wasn't going to simplify a dangerous situation. 'Stay here, keep your head down, *don't* answer the door. When I've made contact with SIS, I'll arrange to bring you in safely. And Saint…'

His attention snapped from the TV to her. 'Yes, boss?'

'Try not to break anything, don't drink all the wine, and don't piss on the toilet seat.'

'Can I have a shower?'

'Please, *please*, take a shower.'

He put down the bottle on the edge of the glass coffee table, but it tipped over. Red wine glugged onto the expensive pale carpet. Elsa picked the bottle up quickly.

'I'm going to need your phone.'

'Yeah, of course.' Saint had closed his eyes, and his breathing had slowed. 'Just going to have a kip first.'

'Saint, I need it now.'

Without opening his eyes, he fished in the pocket of his tracky bottoms and slapped the ancient phone into her hand.

15

Nine years earlier

They planned and practised the incursion for ten days.

Carragher, Elsa and Saint moved through the empty reception of the building, up the stairs and into the apartment, wearing Kevlar vests and pointing unloaded Heckler & Koch HK416 carbines.

Moving as a unit along the corridor, committing every step and turn to muscle memory, securing each room against hypothetical assailants. Sometimes they did it blindfolded, so that whatever the conditions in Apartment 7b, even if the interior was obscured by smoke or cloaked in darkness, they would be able to move fluidly, instinctively anticipating walls and doorways, openings and corners. They each took turns to take point, moving in a triangular combat formation towards their objective at the far end of the apartment. They did it twenty, thirty, forty times a day.

'Assailant to your left,' Camille would say as she followed them with a stopwatch, and Carragher would swing round to take him down.

'Hostile straight ahead!'

Saint dropped to his knee and aimed. 'Boom!'

'On your right!' Anticipating the threat, Elsa twisted and pulled the trigger.

On the afternoon of the tenth day, Camille thumbed her stopwatch. 'Two seconds longer than the previous time.'

Carragher took off his blindfold. 'Let's go again.'

'Fuck this shit.' Saint had lost count of the number of times they had done it already that day, and it was barely two o'clock. 'We've got it, we know how to climb a set of fucking stairs, because we're professionals, it's what we do.'

He pressed two fingers of his left hand together and mimed blowing his own brains out.

'We go again,' Carragher told him.

'Ten minutes.' Saint threw his carbine to the floor and shrugged off his vest. 'I need a slash.'

Carragher picked up the weapon and shoved it against Saint's chest. 'Again.'

Saint's eyes flashed in fury and for a tense moment Elsa thought the two men were going to come to blows.

'Gentlemen,' said Camille softly. 'Let's go one more time, then I suggest we eat.'

Saint snatched up the vest and rifle and walked towards the entrance. Carragher grimly watched him go, and Elsa knew he suspected the same thing she did: that Saint was drinking in his room of a night.

Saint's attitude was becoming a problem. Elsa had worked with him several times before. He was a conceited big mouth, and invariably got shitfaced at the end of a job, but he'd always been utterly professional. But during their time holed up in the apartment, he'd been distracted and abrasive. When the three of them went into Apartment 7b, it was critical they could trust each other with their lives.

'Come on,' Saint said at the front door. 'Let's get this over with before I piss myself.'

'Once more with feeling,' said Elsa, trying to break the tension. Carragher nodded, but didn't look at her. She could count on one hand the number of times he'd managed to look her in the eye, and she was just as bad.

In the evening, Carragher once again briefed Camille, Klimt and Antovic on their own roles, before the team ate together – Klimt prepared the food on a portable stove in the derelict kitchen – and everyone retired to their rooms. Some evenings, Elsa lay in her camp bed listening to Camille and Carragher having noisy sex in the room opposite.

Elsa wanted to talk to Carragher about what had happened between them, but there was nowhere they could get any privacy, even if Carragher had been willing to communicate. When they weren't training during the day, he avoided her – and Camille never strayed far from his side. If he didn't want Elsa here, why had he even asked her to join the team?

Antovic spent all day and long into the night watching the live laptop images of the target apartment door, the building's reception, and the street outside. When he saw any activity of interest, he'd log it. Elsa had tried more than once to engage him in conversation, but his monosyllabic replies and dead-eyed stare didn't fascinate, and she gave up.

Checking and counter-checking the real-time feeds with online databases and regional facial recognition systems, he built up a detailed picture of all the people who lived in, worked in, and visited the building on a regular basis. He knew the resident of each apartment: how long they had owned the property, how often they were in residence, and when.

When pressed on the identity of the owner of Apartment 7b, Carragher said the precise ownership of the apartment was shielded behind a complicated trail of proxy owners and shell companies, which bounced across the world several times. In other words, if he knew he wasn't going to say.

As the days stretched deep into the second week, the operation was imminent. And on the evening of the twelfth day, Elsa heard Carragher tell Camille, 'Get everyone together.'

There was a rap on the door of her room, and Camille poked her head in. 'Hey.'

'I heard,' Elsa said, and Camille raised an eyebrow, as if to say, *this is it, then.*

When Elsa followed Camille into the living room, Carragher was there with Klimt and Antovic – but Saint was missing.

'Where is he?' Carragher asked impatiently.

'He's not in his room,' Camille said.

'He left.' Antovic turned from his precious laptops. 'Said he needed a walk.'

Saint had complained about being trapped in the apartment since the first day. 'It ain't right, being imprisoned here,' he'd said. 'It's criminal in a party town like this!'

Carragher had never been the kind of man to let his emotions show; his cool demeanour was one of the reasons Elsa was attracted to him. His expression didn't change when Antovic spoke, but she saw rage flare behind his eyes.

'Everybody wait here.' He walked to the door. 'I'll find him.'

Camille followed. 'I'll come with you.'

'No,' he snapped, and pointed at Elsa. 'You.'

Elsa avoided Camille's surprised look. By the time she closed the steel door to the street, he was already moving quickly along the *vereda* – the sidewalk – heading towards the centre of bustling Recoleta.

She sensed the fury pouring off him, saw it in the way he moved quickly, with big, rolling strides, arms swinging purposefully below his wide shoulders. There was a solidity to Carragher, such power in his body, which was all muscle and hardened scar tissue, that Elsa imagined that anything unfortunate enough to get in his way, a bike, a car, a tank, would be torn apart on impact.

People swarmed about them as they approached the main tourist drag. The warm, twinkling lights of the many bars and restaurants were inviting in the dwindling light. They both knew Saint would be attracted to this neighbourhood like a moth to a lamp.

'Steve.' Elsa struggled to catch up with him. 'Hold on.'

But he didn't slow his relentless pace. After nearly two weeks of being treated like shit, she was tired of playing games.

'For fuck's sake!' she shouted. 'Stop!'

Carragher lifted his eyes to the sky, and spun on his heels to face her.

'I'm struggling to understand what's going on here.'

'We have to find him,' Carragher said. 'Before he opens his big mouth to the wrong person.'

'Not Saint,' she said. 'You know what I'm talking about.'

Hands on his hips, he stared at her accusingly. 'Were you going to tell me? You thought I'd never find out?'

'What are you...?' But it was obvious what he was talking about. 'How do you know?'

'Oh, come on, Elsa, I probably knew before you did.' He had access to the computer system of the clinic she'd gone to, or a contact; he'd been tracking her movements; he was spying on her. 'Is it mine?'

Standing in the middle of the crowded drag, people flowing past on either side of them, they couldn't be more conspicuous if they tried: a man and woman, both as tall as the Eiffel Tower, dressed in camos and armless vests, like they had both just dropped out of the back of a transport plane. Carragher was breaking all his own strict rules about keeping a low profile.

There was anger in his voice. 'Are you pregnant with my kid?'

She didn't know how to answer. Part of her had always intended to tell him. But not when his head was full of the mission, and certainly not while his wife was hanging off his arm. Maybe when they had flown home, in a few weeks, or at the end of the first trimester, when she was sure that everything was going to be okay. She didn't know when, hadn't planned that far in the future. Or maybe, she swallowed down the truth, she never planned to tell him at all.

'What does it matter?' she asked. Elsa was the one who had to listen to him and Camille having sex nearly every night, and who only ever got to see him sporadically in various crappy hotels and safe houses across the world when their schedules converged.

'Because if it is, then...'

'Then what, Steve?' she demanded. 'What will you do?'

'I'll leave Camille. We can be together, the three of us.'

She smiled sadly. 'That's not going to happen.'

'I want to be with you,' he told her grimly.

'You've got a funny way of showing it,' she said. It was no fun having to listen to Camille's nocturnal moans and screams.

He shook his head. 'That's Camille, not me.'

'Come on, Steve, it takes two to tango.'

'Once this mission is over…' He came close, keeping his voice low. 'We'll bring up the child, *our* child, together.'

He'd made the exact same promise before, that he was going to leave Camille, more than once. He'd told her in Geneva and in Naypyidaw and in Paris; he swore the same thing as they hung out the back of a C-5 Galaxy flying low over the South China Sea. But nothing ever came of his promises, and she saw no reason to believe him now.

They had been seeing each other on and off for a year. If they found themselves in the same city, in Detroit, Tokyo or Kuala Lumpur, they'd hook up, two lonely travellers. But as they discovered more about each other, the relationship had developed into something more intense and intimate – to Elsa's shock, because both of them were withdrawn, inaccessible personalities – until it became difficult for her to deny her deep feelings for him.

The affair left her bewildered and emotionally adrift, she'd never felt this way about anyone in her life, but she never expected it to last. It was a ridiculous notion that she and Carragher could ever be together. They both lived dangerous lives. Either of them could be killed at any moment, or disappear off the face of the Earth. Just vanish – killed on a mission, or more likely abducted by an antagonist and never seen again. In their game, you had to grab happy moments by the throat.

Elsa had found out she was pregnant three weeks ago, when she missed her period. She was terrified by the prospect, but recognized immediately that having a kid was the catalyst for the change she craved. If she couldn't love another adult properly, maybe she'd be better as a mother; she certainly couldn't do the parenting thing worse than her own mum and dad.

'I love you,' Carragher said.

She'd always been quick to end relationships with the handful of men and women with whom she'd been intimate before any of them ever uttered those words. Maybe the reason she hooked up with Steve Carragher was that she had always believed he would never in a million years dare to love her; she felt her world tilt sideways at his declaration. She opened her mouth to speak, but he pulled his hands down her arms.

'As soon as this is over, I'm telling Camille it's finished.'

Elsa knew just how crazy Camille was about her husband. She'd be devastated, insane with anger; she'd want revenge.

'But Camille—'

'Fuck Camille,' he said. 'It's you I want.'

'When this is over, I'm getting out.'

Carragher nodded. 'I'm with you. This mission is the end of a long, difficult road for me. We'll go far away, bring up our family in peace. We'll have the best life.' His hand reached for her flat stomach, but she edged away. 'How long?'

'You tell me, Steve. You seem to know more about my pregnancy than I do.' But she relented. 'Paris.'

The last time she'd seen him. They'd spent four days in a hotel room. It had only been four weeks ago, and she hadn't expected to see him again for months. But then he contacted her again to recruit her for Pilot Fish, and days later she arrived in Argentina.

'Why is Camille even here?' she wanted to know. 'You told me she wouldn't be involved. There must be someone else you could have used?'

'A team member dropped out at the last minute and I needed a replacement. Camille's RedQueen like you, and damned good at what she does. I can trust her to get the job done. But there's nothing more important than us, Elsa. We *will* be together. If that's what you want, too...'

She knew he wanted her to say those three words back to him, but she had never said it to another living person.

'It doesn't matter.' He scowled and looked away.

'No.' She took his face in her fingers to force his gaze back to hers. 'I want to say it. I...' Elsa had abseiled down skyscrapers, HALO jumped, broken into impregnable buildings and out of impregnable buildings, she had been airlifted onto nuclear submarines, but telling him how she felt was the hardest thing she had ever done. She didn't know if she could say the words. Her heart pounded, her nerves crackled.

But to her own surprise, she found they came easily. 'I love you, too.'

Carragher nodded gravely.

'I'm pregnant with your child,' she told him. 'So I mean it, Steve, about RedQueen and the business, I'm getting out.'

'We both are,' he told her.

They stood in a sea of people, the evening crowd surging

around them, both of them a little bit stunned, because they knew there was no going back.

Elsa didn't know if their proposed life together was feasible. They both carted around so many secrets, and they had both survived for so long in the constant shadow of violence and treachery. Maybe stripped of their adrenaline lives, they'd find they had nothing in common. But she didn't think so, and she sensed that Carragher had also tired of the strain of a dangerous life. Elsa didn't have the faintest clue about how to live like an ordinary citizen; maybe it would be the hardest lesson of all.

They kissed hard in the middle of the pavement, oblivious of the crowd – but then Carragher stepped back.

'What is it?' Elsa heard an altercation close by, and a familiar voice.

She followed Carragher into the gloomy interior of a bar. Saint was standing at the counter, arguing loudly with a couple of men. There was a tall beer glass beside him, a row of shot glasses filled with bourbon. He jabbed a finger at the men, using his height and build to intimidate.

'Maradona? Big fucking cheat. Hand of God, my arse!'

'Sal de aquí!' One of the men gestured at the door. 'No eres bienvenido!'

'Come on, then.' Saint fluttered his fingers in an aggressive *make me* gesture. 'No? Didn't think so.'

He plopped one of the shot glasses into his beer, tipped back his head and downed it in one. Slammed his palm onto the surface of the bar twice.

'Another one over here, señor!' He nodded at the glass, but the guy behind the bar waved his arms low across his stomach, telling Saint that wasn't going to happen. 'Give me a break, it's these dudes who're making trouble, I'm trying to mind my own business.'

Carragher came up behind Saint and hissed, 'Get outside. *Now.*'

'Hey, man.' Saint turned, grinning drunkenly. 'It's my old mates Steve and Elsie. Stay and have a drink, and buy one for me – no, wait, two for me – cos it don't look like my credit's good here.'

Carragher told him with quiet menace, 'I said, outside.'

Saint didn't look intimidated in the slightest, and stepped forward. The two men once again stood nose to nose, eyeball to eyeball. Saint's manic, glassy expression suggested that a confrontation – a brawl, fistfight, or fight to the death – would be just the thing to clear the air, if that's what Carragher wanted.

But Saint was drunk, his reactions compromised, and somewhere in the small cave at the back of his mind where he was still able to think logically, he must have realized he didn't stand a chance in his current condition, not against Carragher.

But he didn't step back, lower his gaze, or show any kind of weakness. Instead, he laughed, and swiped his hand across the counter, sending the beer and shot glasses smashing to the floor.

Saint told the bartender, 'Your beer is overpriced.'

Then he walked outside.

'What the hell do you think you're doing?' said Carragher, following him out. 'You've put everyone at risk!'

'No harm done.' Saint loped down the street, as if he didn't have a care in the world. 'Just a bit of handbags.'

'Which part of *stay in the apartment* don't you understand?'

'Being trapped in that rotten place was doing my head in.'

'Look at the state of you.' Carragher grabbed him by the shoulders.

'Careful, Steve.' Saint smirked. 'People are looking.'

'You're no good to us, you're no good to anybody. You're going home.'

Saint blinked. 'I can do the job.'

'You're a drunk.' Carragher looked disgusted. 'And a liability.'

Saint's fists balled at his side, and Elsa thought he was going to take a swing, but instead he winked. 'I'm just a sociable person, chief.'

'You're out, I'm putting you on a flight home.'

Carragher pushed him away and began striding back to the apartment building.

Saint tried to keep up. 'You need me.'

'You're muscle, that's all you are, and I've got plenty of that already. One of the others will take your place.'

'He can still do a job,' insisted Elsa, trying to calm the tension.

Carragher didn't look at her. 'You're sticking up for him?'

'Yeah.' She made a face at Saint, *don't let me down*. 'He's going back to the apartment to sober up, he'll be good to go tomorrow.'

'Sure I will.' Saint made the sign of the cross on his chest. 'Won't touch another drop, I promise.'

Carragher stopped walking and turned to Saint. The

others waited tensely for him to speak. 'I'm putting you on the roof.'

Saint grimaced. 'But all the training we've put in!'

'You follow my commands, or you go home.'

Pressing his lips together to stop himself saying anything he'd regret, Saint gave a tiny nod of acknowledgement.

'And after it's over, you're finished, I'll make sure everyone knows that.' Carragher snapped a glance at Elsa as he walked away. 'Make sure he sobers up. The incursion happens tomorrow.'

16

The kitchen was an absolute tip when Zoe got home that afternoon.

All she wanted to do was enjoy a cup of tea, change her clothes and then wait for Elsa Zero to make contact. But the counters were cluttered with plates, glasses and bowls; washing-up was piled in the sink. A tower of clothes had been dumped on the floor in front of the washing machine, because neither her husband nor her son had bothered to open it to toss their smelly socks inside, fully expecting that in Zoe's absence the Housework Fairy would do it for them. Cleaning up other people's mess was not how she imagined spies psychologically prepared themselves to bring hunted operatives in from the cold.

'Seriously, Jim?' she said. 'Couldn't you even have managed to fill the dishwasher?'

He looked up from his newspaper as she dumped her bag on the table. 'Everything okay at work?'

'Don't change the subject,' she said, bustling around.

Housework would at least be a distraction from the enormity of what Plowright had told her about Elsa Zero. Zoe didn't condone the agency's plan to liquidate her, but she understood now the reasoning behind the extraordinary decision. If there was even a small chance that Elsa was working with hostile forces, or that a foreign enemy got to her first, the repercussions would be catastrophic. Zoe itched to tell Jim to pack a bag and take Charlie far away, the further the better, but there was no way she could. If Zero's disappearance leaked into the public domain, the consequences would be enormous. It would cause mass panic. And, anyway, if she told him she had offered herself as an intermediary between SIS and a dangerous fugitive, he'd only become anxious.

Plowright had given Zoe strict instructions to carry on with her weekend as usual, and to try to forget that she was about to be contacted by a lethal black ops specialist.

She slumped into a chair. 'Where's Charlie?'

'Playing football in the park.'

'I'm starving.' Despite the mess, there didn't seem to have been much recent activity near the oven. 'What's for dinner?'

'I didn't know what time you were going to be home.' Her husband folded the paper. 'So I thought we'd get a takeaway. How about a cup of tea?'

She gave him the thumbs-up. A takeaway would be perfect after the day she'd had. She watched Jim search a drawer for a flyer from a local pizza house and study it intently, as if he wasn't going to order a deep-pan ham and pineapple, like he always did.

Through the open door to the living room, she eyed the television playing silently on a news channel. A reporter was speaking outside an expensive restaurant on the King's Road where, the rolling yellow ticker at the bottom of the screen suggested, West London gang members had fought a bloody turf battle the night before. Measures had been taken to ensure an alternative version to the truth was presented to the public.

When he had made the tea, Jim reached into the cupboard under the sink, took out a small can of oil and headed for the door.

'Where are you going?'

'To fix that squeaky hinge in the spare room,' he said, just as the front door slammed and their teenage son came in.

'What's for tea?' Charlie asked.

'We're thinking pizza,' said Jim.

Charlie shrugged. 'Sounds good.'

'Welcome home, Mum,' Zoe said sarcastically. 'I really missed you.'

'Oh, yeah.' Her son threw his rucksack on a chair and took a bottle of milk from the fridge. 'Welcome home.'

'How was football?'

'Good.'

'I may have to go back to work later.' Zoe made a sad face. 'I hope you'll manage to cope without me.'

Glugging the last of the milk, he slammed the empty bottle down and wiped away his milk moustache with a sleeve. 'I think I'll manage.'

'Put it in the sink,' Zoe told him, just as a phone started ringing in his rucksack.

Charlie frowned and took his own phone from his pocket. They both looked at his bag. He reached for it.

'Don't touch it!' Zoe screamed.

He stared at her in shock, his hand hesitating at the zip. Charlie didn't know what she did exactly; he knew she worked for British intelligence, but as far as he was concerned his mother did the most boring job imaginable, which wasn't far from the truth.

'Just...' Zoe tried to dial down her panic. It may be Elsa Zero making contact, but it could also be a deadly trap. Nobody knew for sure what the fugitive's intentions were. 'Did anyone go in your bag when you were at the park?'

'No,' he told her, confused. 'Nobody did, but... I bumped into a woman as I was coming down the street. I dropped my bag and she picked it up.'

'What did she look like?'

'Tall, fit.' He blushed. 'Kinda cool.'

'Charlie,' Zoe said, as the ringing continued in the bag. 'Go outside.'

He hesitated. 'Shouldn't you come, too?'

She motioned at him. 'Just go.'

Her son didn't need asking twice and stood outside the door.

'Not in the hallway,' she called. 'Out the front door. And take your father too; I don't want him coming in.'

Zoe unzipped the bag as carefully as she could, not really knowing what she was doing; it wasn't like she was a bomb disposal expert. When it was open, she gingerly looked inside.

Resting on top of the hoodie he'd stuffed in there was a small plastic phone. The screen flashed, but it didn't seem to be attached to anything else. There were no wires Zoe could see, no brick of plastic explosive, or timer with big red numbers counting down. Zoe took it out carefully. It was just a phone, a cheap throwaway thing, and an old model at that. She took a long breath – almost certain she wasn't going to be blown to bits in her own kitchen – and hit the green button.

'Yes,' she said, trying to compose herself.

'Finally,' said a woman's voice angrily.

'Elsa Zero.' Zoe tried to sound as if she was hearing from an old friend out of the blue. 'It's good to hear from you.'

'You know what's happening?'

'Yes.'

'People are trying to kill me.' It seemed to Zoe that Elsa sounded indignant about the fact.

'I believe they are, yes.'

'I don't know why.'

That could be true, or a lie. Someone like Elsa, who had spent a lifetime in black ops, could be playing some kind of elaborate psychological game with her, there was no way of telling.

'The important thing is to bring this whole situation to an end. Let's try and work out together what's going on.'

'Is SIS trying to kill me?'

'I'll be honest with you…' Zoe didn't know how else to put it. 'Right about now, everyone's trying to kill you.'

'Then I'll run.'

'And go where? Even if you do find somewhere safe, Elsa, you'll always be looking over your shoulder. You'll always have to keep moving, and it will never end. And your poor children…' The implication hung in the air between them. 'Let's bring you in. You have my word you will be safe.'

'Why?' Elsa Zero sounded angry. If she was lying, she was a hell of an actor. 'What have I done?'

'You'll get all the answers you need. And we'll find a solution together.'

Zoe held her breath. They both knew Elsa had few options going forward, but she was a mercurial woman used to surviving on her wits, and who had already been almost killed once before in a mission that went very wrong. She could end the call at any moment, and if she did, Zoe knew they would never speak again.

Elsa would run and run – until the inevitable happened. She may manage to disappear off the face of the earth for weeks, months, even years, but with every intelligence agency on the planet looking for her, sooner or later she would run out of road.

If Elsa was going to hang up, it would be… now.

But instead, Elsa Zero said, 'Somewhere outside, somewhere public. Just you and me.'

'Yes.' There was a tense silence. Elsa was far too experienced to believe Zoe would arrive alone. 'Where?'

'Cavendish Square. One hour.'

Elsa killed the call, and with a shaking hand Zoe placed the phone on the table and took a brief moment to steady her nerves.

No time to drink tea, no time for pizza, or to clean the kitchen. She had to call Plowright right away.

17

When someone exited an apartment block on the north side of Cavendish Square, Elsa grabbed the door before it closed. Slipping inside, she made her way to the roof where she could see the entirety of the circular park, nestling behind the shopping mecca of Oxford Circus.

She used Dougie's expensive Celestron binoculars to watch a van as it drove along the south side. The decal on its side stated it was owned by A1 Electricians, a fake name if ever there was one; if Elsa called the accompanying phone number, it wouldn't be in use. The van passed the rear of the John Lewis department store and disappeared onto Henrietta Place.

The roads and pavements jerked sharply in and out of focus as she magnified other potential participants in the imminent events. A car pulled to the kerb directly below her; a helmeted rider on a delivery scooter, its buzz ruining the early evening calm, drove towards Harley Street. A man and a woman walked leisurely past the sculptures in the middle of the square.

Elsa's attention snapped to a car pulling up outside John Lewis. Two men in overalls jumped out and carried cases into an adjacent building: marksmen getting into position on one of the upper floors. She guessed multiple surveillance teams were placed in other buildings too.

Elsa scanned as many windows around the square as she could, half of them reflecting the copper-red sun hanging above the tall buildings of central London, but none revealed any further secrets.

When she heard the low thrum of a helicopter approaching from the north, she went back downstairs and checked her watch. She was due to meet Zoe in less than ten minutes.

Elsa wondered if she should walk away now. Try to find some other way to escape the mess she was in. She was under no illusions that if SIS intended to kill her tonight – the decision would already have been made – they would do it, despite any promises Zoe Castle made to her.

All she could do was hope that Zoe's superiors were as good as their word, and that she would be taken into custody. At least she'd be out of immediate danger; more importantly, her children would be safe.

At 6:59 p.m., Elsa saw Zoe walk the diagonal path to the centre of the square, where she stopped by a bench.

Elsa thought, *here goes nothing*. She was under no illusion that she could be shot dead as soon as she stepped outside. She imagined the tense exchanges between the people watching remotely in Ops at the heart of SIS headquarters and the armed units waiting in the tangle of streets surrounding the square. She may well have been standing in the wings at a packed West End theatre, so many people were waiting for her to make her entrance.

She took a deep breath, opened the door and crossed the road to the square, half expecting each step to be her last.

As Elsa approached, she saw how terrified Zoe Castle was. Where Elsa was all taut muscle and Pilates lithe, Zoe was round-faced and plump in an old blouse and denim skirt. She looked like she should be hosting a supper club with all the other wives, rather than trying to bring in a deadly operative from the dangerous cold.

'Thank you so much for coming.' Zoe looked gratified, as if Elsa was a frosty neighbour she'd finally persuaded to come for coffee. 'I've never done anything like this before.'

Elsa scanned the roofs. 'There are snipers.'

'Don't worry, they're ours.' Zoe clung to the bag hanging from her shoulder. 'And they're here to protect the both of us.'

'Why?' Elsa asked her coldly. 'I don't understand why I've been targeted, what have I done?'

'Come with me,' said Zoe in a nervous sing-song. 'And everything will become clear.'

'Who's trying to kill me?'

Someone was in such a hurry to do it that they had almost dismantled a restaurant to get the job done, so it wasn't a great leap of imagination for Elsa to assume that her head was at that moment in the crosshairs of several telescopic sights, and that professional marksmen were mumbling into throat mics, confirming they had a clear shot and were ready to pull the trigger, just give the order, just say when.

'Before I go anywhere with you,' Elsa said, 'I want to know what's going on.'

Zoe looked stricken. 'I've been given a tiny window of opportunity to bring you in, Elsa, and if I don't do it, they'll kill you. Come with me and you have my word you will not be harmed.' She clearly didn't know how much she was authorized to say. 'You have data, and we need it from you.'

'What data, what do I know?'

Zoe swallowed; she was sweating. '*Please*, Elsa.'

Elsa scowled, but knew she wasn't going to get answers. She nodded, finally.

Relieved, Zoe let out a breath and said to whoever was listening to their conversation, 'She's coming in. I repeat, Elsa Zero is coming in.'

She nodded, receiving affirmation in her ear. Elsa saw an SUV drive into the square and pull up on the east side. Zoe walked briskly to meet it, clinging on to her bag for dear life.

'You're doing very well,' said Elsa, falling into step beside her.

'Thank you.' Zoe looked grateful for the remark. 'You really don't know what's going on?'

'Not a clue. Until midnight, my life was very boring.'

'Everything will be explained to you. You're not going to believe your ears. It's very important we get you to safety.'

'My kids are in hiding,' Elsa said quickly. 'We need to get them to safety.'

They reached the SUV, and the rear doors opened automatically. When Elsa walked to the door on the far side, Zoe placed her hands on the roof.

'I'll make sure it's our first priori—'

Zoe never finished the sentence because in that instant half of her head was blown off, blood and bone bursting into the air directly above her shattered skull. Her body was spun around by the impact of the bullet and she crumpled to the floor.

A moment later, just as Elsa dropped behind the door, the windscreen of the car shattered. Through the back seat, she saw blood spray. The driver's head slammed back into the seat, then fell onto the steering wheel.

More rounds coming from a building ahead of the car slammed against the door, making it judder. Elsa dived into the back of the car and fell across the seat as shots eviscerated the top of the front seats and punched out the rear windscreen. She huddled as gunfire tore into the doors and roof, and through the upholstery; above her, all around her. She dropped into the footwell, pressed as flat as possible on the floor.

Through the open door she saw Cavendish Place, which led to Regent Street. If she could get to the corner she'd be out of the line of fire, but it was twenty or thirty feet away, at least. She'd never make it, she'd be cut down before she managed five steps.

The shots stopped, the last of them echoing off the tall buildings, giving Elsa the opportunity to lift her head and look back into the square. Secret service types raced towards her, drawing weapons from holsters at their belts, but when the shooting started again, they took cover. Then she heard a screech of brakes as a car skidded to a halt on the road directly beside her.

The passenger door flew open, and Elsa stared in shock at the driver.

'The pass!' Camille Archard ducked as the near-side mirror of her car exploded into hundreds of flying bits of plastic and broken glass. The SUV rocked crazily as it was targeted again by relentless automatic gunfire. The rear windscreen shattered, the bonnet and doors shuddered. 'The pass!'

Elsa stared at her in incomprehension.

'Under the wheel!'

Elsa looked to where she was pointing: on the floor beside Zoe Castle's body was her bag, its contents spilled everywhere.

'We've got to go – now!' Camille shouted.

Elsa threw herself into the road, crawling around the back of the vehicle on her hands and knees, praying it would shield her from the gunfire. One of the back wheels was shot out. She heard it pop and hiss. Keeping low, she saw a plastic card had fallen from Zoe's bag, and she snatched it up.

Then she crawled back behind Camille's car and hurled herself into the passenger seat. It accelerated before she even managed to pull the door shut. The windscreen exploding above her head, glass raining down on her shoulders, Elsa hunched low in the seat, as the car skidded out of the square in a hail of gunfire.

18

'Keep your head down,' Camille told her.

They accelerated through a red light on Regent Street, speeding past the wall of traffic shooting across the junction towards them, causing a roar of screeching brakes and horns, and into the tangle of streets north of Oxford Street.

Slamming the car around corners, allowing the steering wheel to spin beneath her lifted fingers, Camille pumped her foot hard on the accelerator, the brake, the accelerator, one after the other, as she swerved between cars, on the inside of the lane, then the outside. Her blonde hair flew around her face as she jerked the car left and right, speeding, then braking.

They slowed in Fitzrovia, the engine purring as they turned slowly down a narrow street and across Tottenham Court Road, slipping into the stream of traffic heading towards Russell Square, then seemingly heading back the way they had come.

Camille nodded at the dash compartment. When Elsa opened it, she saw a baseball cap and dark glasses. 'Put them on.'

Elsa heard sirens; sometimes racing away from them, sometimes towards them.

Gunning the vehicle, Camille swerved onto the wrong side of the road, and straight towards three lanes of oncoming traffic. Elsa clung to the dash with one hand and the seat with the other. Eyes flicking from the rear mirror to the wing mirror, and squinting into the sky – checking for helicopters, for drones – Camille was apparently oblivious they were about to smash into a car that was swerving in panic in front of them.

'Camille!' Elsa braced herself for impact.

Camille jerked the wheel, skidding ninety degrees to perfectly negotiate the narrow entrance to a mews street, and sped up. They were in one of the most built-up city centres in the world, Elsa wanted to tell her, and one of the most heavily surveilled; it was insane to think they could evade capture.

But a garage door opened up halfway along the mews and a Vauxhall Astra pulled out of it ahead of them. Camille slammed on the brakes – Elsa was flung forward – to swing into the garage behind it. Shards of glass fell from Elsa's hair as a brick wall rushed towards them – but the car stopped dead.

Elsa's heart clattered. Zoe Castle's fatal pirouette was still imprinted on her mind's eye; echoes of the automatic gunfire still juddered her bones.

'Get out.' Leaving the engine running, Camille climbed from the car, but leaned back in and pointed to Zoe's pass, which was on the floor. 'Pick it up!'

Elsa snatched it up, and followed Camille to the other car. Two women in baseball caps and dark glasses appeared from nowhere and jumped into the car they had just abandoned in the garage. It pulled out and drove back in the opposite direction. When Camille drove the Astra onto a main road, Elsa tried to get her bearings. They were somewhere in Holborn, or Bloomsbury, maybe Euston.

A helicopter flew above a building. A moment later, a pair of police vehicles sped past in the opposite direction.

Moving into a creeping stream of traffic, Camille rested her elbow on the open window of the driver's side. Her fingers lightly tapped the wheel. They crawled along for several minutes, Elsa's nerves screaming; it seemed to her they were going in circles, continually doubling back towards the square.

'Camille, what's going—'

'Not now.' Camille pulled out of the crawling line of traffic and into a narrow street, where another car sat idling, the doors open.

Camille pulled up beside it, and they changed vehicles again. Two women sitting outside a café jumped up and climbed into the Astra, which roared off.

Now hidden behind tinted windows, driving at a steady speed, they drove for another fifteen minutes, moving steadily in heavy traffic, waiting patiently at lights and junctions, as police vehicles and vans screamed in every direction.

At a red light, Camille pulled up behind an SUV. 'Come on.'

They climbed into the vehicle ahead, swapping with another two women who didn't even glance over as they passed in the road. The lights changed and Camille pulled across the junction, edging to the side of the road to let a police car roar past.

'Where are we going?' Elsa asked, but Camille didn't reply.

She drove once again across Oxford Street, and into the cramped streets of Soho, careful to give plenty of space to the evening crowds who swarmed across the road in search of bars, pubs and restaurants.

Finally, Camille swung into an underground car park. At the entrance a barrier rattled to the floor, and they clumped across a metal ramp, riding the curved band of concrete down into the gloom. When they reached the wide concrete basement, there were only two or three other cars parked in the entire space.

Waiting at the door of a lift at the far end was a group of well-dressed men and women. The car glided to a halt in front of them, and Camille killed the ignition.

Two men walked towards the car. One had a device in his hand, which looked a lot like the dust-buster Elsa kept in her kitchen; the second carried long pieces of coloured fabric.

Camille nodded at the pass in Elsa's hand. 'Give me that.'

Elsa handed her Zoe Castle's ID. When Elsa climbed out, the man with the dust-buster shut the door behind her, and said, 'Raise your arms, please.'

Elsa glanced at Camille, who nodded. Considering she had just saved Elsa's life, it seemed churlish to object, so Elsa raised her arms. The man lifted the device to her head and slowly pulled it all the way down her body. Satisfied, he nodded to Camille. 'She's clear.'

The other man came forward and, like a department store shop assistant, held up two cocktail dresses. One was red and sparkly, the other emerald green. Strappy silver high-heeled sandals dangled from one of his hands.

'Which one?' he asked.

Elsa stared in incomprehension. She had nearly been gunned down, there were probably still bits of a dead woman's brain matter in her hair, and he wanted her to play dress-up.

'Get away from me,' she told him.

'You have to choose one,' he insisted.

'Step. Away.'

Camille came round the side of the car and told him, 'Not now.'

'She can't go upstairs like that,' the man protested. 'I have strict instructions.'

'We don't have time for this.' Camille pushed him away and handed the other man Zoe's pass. 'Get it to our tech guys as quick as you can. We need to use it tonight.'

The man took it and walked off. Behind them, the car was already being driven back up the ramp. Elsa wondered how many decoy cars were being driven around the streets of London, pulling the security services in every direction.

'Come with me.' As the other people in the car park melted away, Camille led Elsa to the lift.

When the doors opened, the deep-red walls and perfumed interior contrasted with the exhaust-blasted concrete car park.

As soon as the doors closed, Camille smiled for the first time. 'Hey, Elsa.'

'Hey, Camille.'

Camille had come back into Elsa's life in her moment of need to save her skin all over again, and she fell into her friend's arms. Elsa almost imagined she could rest there forever – until she felt a sharp sting in her arm. She pushed Camille away with such force that she slammed into the wall.

'Sorry.' Camille quickly held up the stubby needle in her hand. 'It's to neutralize any trackers you may have inside you, it's not going to do you any harm. I come in peace.'

Elsa breathed hard. 'For fuck's sake, Camille.'

Camille laughed. 'How many times do I have to save your life? It's getting embarrassing now.'

Elsa couldn't help but smile. 'You look great.'

Her friend's hair was longer, but she still had the severe fringe that bladed across the top of her forehead, and those amazing cheekbones looked sharper than ever.

'You too, darling.' When Camille came close again, Elsa felt herself tense, wary of more needles. But Camille gently inverted Elsa's hood to let the shards of glass trapped inside it fall to the floor. 'It's good to see you again. I just wish the circumstances were different.'

Once upon a time, Camille had been the nearest thing to a best friend that Elsa ever had. They were comrades, had worked together all over the world, had watched each other's back. But what Camille didn't know was that they had loved the same man, and Elsa felt that familiar surge of guilt.

When Elsa left the business after the Buenos Aires fiasco, when that part of her life was over, it was inevitable that she and Camille would lose contact. Elsa could have made more of an effort, of course – Camille was grieving for the loss of her husband, after all – but the shame she had felt was too much. Camille had saved Elsa's life, and in return she'd had an affair with Steve Carragher, had fallen in love with him, and become pregnant with his children.

'Where are we going?' asked Elsa, as the lift began to slow.

'Someone wants to talk to you,' Camille told her.

Elsa's suspicions had proved correct.

RedQueen.

When the lift doors opened, Elsa stepped out into the middle of a crowded cocktail party.

19

'Wait here,' Camille told Elsa and she walked into the crowd of smartly dressed men and women chatting and laughing over drinks.

Elsa pressed herself against the on-trend bottle-green wallpaper. In her hoodie, leggings and trainers, she stuck out like a sore thumb among all the expensive suits and frocks; almost wished she'd picked one of the dresses.

They were in the top-floor bar of an expensive Soho hotel, the kind of place she only saw reviewed in online magazines these days. A long counter dominated one end of the room and floor-to-ceiling windows ran the entire length, looking out over the West End rooftops. The sun was going down, the sky brushed with wispy pink cloud. The flashing lights of helicopters swept back and forth above the cityscape.

Elsa watched the men and women in designer labels flick their shiny hair in delighted laughter, and wondered how the hell she had ended up here.

Less than an hour ago, Zoe Castle's body had lifted in the air, twisting in a graceful slow-motion pirouette, her feet leaving the ground as the top of her skull blew off.

Elsa shut her eyes and pressed her fingers into the lids to try to dismiss the image. She had seen worse, much worse, in her time. But she had gone out of her way to involve Zoe in this situation. She was an innocent woman who was just trying to do the right thing, and now she was dead.

And yet somehow or other Elsa was still alive; it didn't make sense.

She made a silent vow to make whoever was responsible pay for Zoe's death.

But then her own children flashed again into her mind, and she felt fear surge through her body. Harley and India were all that mattered to her. She had last seen them at the crack of dawn; had left them in the hands of her estranged parents, of all people. What kind of mother was she, anyway? It was *her* job to protect them, nobody else's. She had a very urgent need to know they were safe.

'Oh, you poor thing,' said a voice, and she opened her eyes to see a woman in a glittery ankle-length dress and swept-back hair coming towards her. When the woman grabbed her hands, Elsa's frazzled nerves crackled; she was ready to slam her into the wall. 'I know *everything*! I hope you don't mind me saying, I think you've been very brave. Very *brave*.'

Elsa looked for Camille.

'Considering everything, you still look radiant, a picture of health.' Placing fingers that sparkled with rings to her chest, the woman spoke in an emotional whisper. 'Well done you. Well, *well* done.'

She turned to a man in a dinner jacket who had followed her over. 'Isn't she looking *fabulous*, Melvin?'

Melvin regarded Elsa's scuffed hoodie, torn leggings and dirty trainers, from all the fighting and rolling on the ground in dirt and glass and blood, and said with a lack of enthusiasm, 'We wish you all the best. Come away now.'

'She's so brave,' said the woman to a glamorous senior lady, who hurried over with Camille.

'Isn't she just?' said the older woman. Her sparkling silver hair was worn in a towering bouffant, an alarming helmet of the kind that went out with the Eighties. Her thin figure was crammed into a long white dress that fell to her feet and accentuated her deep mahogany tan. Extravagant jewellery of diamond, gold and other precious metals sparkled in the soft light on her ears, the folds of her neck and on her fingers. The woman's very straight teeth were such a dazzling white they were almost fluorescent.

'Why don't you and Melvin help yourselves to a drink at the bar, Tasmin, and I'll be along in a few minutes?'

When the couple had gone, the older woman flashed her high-voltage smile at Elsa. 'I'm going to give you a big hug for the benefit of the room, so please don't hit me.'

She draped her arms around Elsa's stiff, unyielding body and hung there for a long moment. Her perfume was overwhelming.

'I'm so glad you're here,' she said, leading Elsa into the crowd. 'Do try and smile, darling, you're among friends.'

Elsa looked anxiously over her shoulder at Camille, who stayed by the lift.

'Don't worry, Camille isn't going anywhere,' said the woman. 'I know how busy you are, tonight of all nights, so I promise not to keep you very long.'

Another guest loomed out of the crowd and pumped Elsa's hand. 'God bless, we're all rooting for you!'

'Thank you, Samantha,' said the older woman, and pulled Elsa past her.

Elsa was bewildered by all the attention. 'What's going on?'

'They think you're my drug addict granddaughter just out of rehab,' the woman said in a low voice. 'Forgive me, it was the only way to explain how you're dressed. I do wish you'd worn one of the pretty dresses we hurriedly organized for you; it would have been much more satisfactory if you'd made the effort. A little make-up wouldn't go amiss, either.' The woman smiled sadly. 'Or a shower.'

'Who are you?'

The woman offered a manicured hand tipped with long silver nails. 'I'm Mrs Krystahl, so pleased to meet you.' Her attention was caught by a distinguished-looking man in the crowd.

'Christian!' She lifted herself on her toes to kiss him on both cheeks. 'We must catch up soon!'

She whispered to Elsa, 'That's Dr Christian Vaida, one of the very top cardiothoracic surgeons in the country. If you ever have problems with your ticker, Elsa, he's the consultant to see.' Her eyes twinkled. 'And, my, isn't he handsome?'

'You're from RedQueen,' said Elsa.

'Oh, come now.' Mrs Krystahl spoke in a strained sing-song. 'Wait until we're out of earshot.'

Elsa felt exposed in the glare of the vast windows. The upper storeys of the building on the other side of the narrow street felt oppressively close. Snipers could lurk on the rooftop or behind the blank windows; it wouldn't be the first time tonight.

'Oh, that darned sun is in my eyes.' As if reading Elsa's

mind, Mrs Krystahl lifted a hand to get the attention of someone. Within moments, the windows darkened, dampening the red glare, making it impossible to see inside. They came to a space at the back of the room. 'We can talk here.'

Everyone was middle-aged and well dressed, and seemingly intent on having a good time, but Elsa couldn't shake the feeling there were trained killers in the crowd, maybe several, and scanned the room carefully.

'What am I doing here?'

'I thought we might have a little chat, you and I.' Mrs Krystahl snatched two martini glasses from the tray of a passing waiter. 'About this mess you've found yourself in. It's clear that someone really doesn't want you to give yourself up to British intelligence.'

'I'm lucky to be alive.'

'I'm not sure that's altogether true. If the sniper wanted to kill you, Elsa, I imagine they could have done so easily. And I believe you suspect the same thing. I think the aim was to sow panic and confusion at SIS, and to implicate you further in whatever conspiracy is unfolding. If that's the case, it was mission accomplished.'

'Implicate me in *what*?' asked Elsa.

'Would you like a drink?' Mrs Krystahl handed her one of the martinis. 'I imagine you would.'

'How very convenient that RedQueen swooped in to save me.'

'You're meant to have just come out of rehab so perhaps we shouldn't give you that.' Mrs Krystahl took back the glass and placed it on a table. 'It's bloody lucky, is what it is. We have people embedded in SIS, so we knew of their intention to bring you in. Otherwise, you wouldn't be here now, *not* enjoying cocktails at an exclusive Soho soiree. They'd be torturing you, dragging information out of you in a variety of unsavoury ways.'

Elsa's head spun. 'I don't have information.'

'Well, you know *something*, darling, otherwise the world's intelligence agencies – along with at least one dangerous and as yet unidentified private party – wouldn't be so keen to put you in the ground. All we know is that you went into that apartment with Steve Carragher – and came out alive. Which means while you were inside, you likely saw something you shouldn't.'

'All I saw,' hissed Elsa, 'were men trying to kill me.'

'Well, you must know something, my darling, or you wouldn't be in this pickle.' Mrs Krystahl sipped her martini. 'The best thing you can do right now is *think*. Try to work out what on earth happened during that mission that has made you a target.'

'Why don't you ask Camille?' Elsa nodded towards the lift. 'She was there.'

'Oh, believe me, we've spoken about it in great detail. But nobody's showed the slightest interest in hunting and killing Camille, it's you all the agencies have the hots for. It's quite remarkable, Elsa – the world and his wife wants you dead. It's totally unprecedented, darling, I've never heard the likes of it.'

'RedQueen employees are given the bare minimum of information they need to complete the mission. Besides Carragher, none of us knew anything about the target – that hard drive or whatever it was. You'll know more about it than I do.'

'I wish I did.' Mrs Krystahl played absently with one of the many necklaces that hung on her wrinkled brown chest. 'But Pilot Fish was too classified to even place in the drawer marked Top Secret. The precise objective was known by very few people within SIS. As an outside contractor, RedQueen was told nothing about the target.'

'You sent your people in without knowing what they were destroying?'

'Of course.' Mrs Krystahl frowned. 'It's easy to disavow that way, you understand the game.'

'You must be able to find out.'

'We're trying, darling, but RedQueen has been locked out by the global intelligence community. There's a lot of suspicion, Elsa, and because you were our operative, we've lost a lot of credibility. Our sources inside SIS and the other agencies are coming up with nothing that makes any sense right now. And it may interest you to know that an unusual proportion of the very few people who knew what was on that hard drive are not alive today. They have died of cancers, car accidents, unexpected heart attacks, and so forth.

'With you being hunted by all and sundry, RedQueen stands to lose the reputation it has built carefully over many decades.' Mrs Krystahl raised the glass to her red lips. 'And we cannot allow that to happen.'

'I'm very sorry about your reputation,' said Elsa wearily. 'But they're trying to kill me.'

'Then it's in both our interests to find out what the bloody hell – excuse my language, Elsa – is going on. We scanned you downstairs for any data tag you may unwittingly be carrying under your skin and there's nothing.' Mrs Krystahl turned away to kiss a woman who came over. 'How *are* you, Katherine? So lovely to see you again. We must do lunch.'

Elsa bit her lip, frustrated by all the interruptions.

'If my being hunted for whatever it is I'm supposed to have done, or seen or heard, is such a burden to you, why not just hand me over?'

'Oh, believe me, the back and forth we had about it!' Mrs Krystahl drained her martini. 'The fact is, delivering you dead or alive to one of the agencies will do nothing to exonerate RedQueen of whatever conspiracy is currently unfurling. We have valuable contracts worldwide, Elsa, worth tens of millions of dollars, which are hanging by a thread. RedQueen has built an unparalleled reputation for trust and discretion within the intelligence community. They are the core competencies and values on which our business was founded. And they are being questioned, Elsa, they are being trashed.' Mrs Krystahl spoke with quiet anger. 'This is a state of affairs that cannot be countenanced. RedQueen faces an existential threat. For a hundred and fifty years we have diligently toiled in the shadows of history, and we cannot risk our activities being brought into the light to be prodded and examined. That simply cannot be allowed to happen. Which is why I have been given the authority to provide support to you in your efforts to discover why you have been targeted.'

'I'm going to run,' said Elsa, who didn't see how she had any other choice.

'Nobody would blame you for that in the circumstances. But you know as well as I do, darling, that you can't run forever.' Mrs Krystahl whisked another cocktail off a tray as it went past. 'You don't have the resources or the contacts any more.' Her eyes drifted up and down Elsa. 'And with the greatest respect, you've left it far too late to grab yourself a billionaire Sugar Daddy. I'd suggest it's in your best interests to discover what on earth is happening to you, and why. Aims that naturally align with ours.'

'I don't work for you any more.'

'Yes.' The older woman spun the twizzle stick in the drink. 'And that's a shame. I've looked at your impressive file, and I must say, I would never have let you go.'

Elsa saw Katherine, the woman who had just walked past, glance over; Tasmin and Melvin, too. And it made her wonder again just how many of the men and women in the room were RedQueen. One or two or three – or everyone? Elsa didn't know how many employees and contractors the organization had around the world, but it was entirely possible she was surrounded by assassins.

And if Elsa declined Mrs Krystahl's offer of support, would she get out of here alive? She could take out a few people on the way, perhaps, bloody a few noses, knock out a few bleached teeth, but she suspected she'd never make it to the lift.

'Our actions must be robust, Elsa. We're going to have to take the situation into our own hands and fight back. The only way out is through; that's a quote from someone.'

'We?'

'You have our unequivocal support in your perilous hour of need.'

'I don't even know where to start.'

'Well, that's obvious. You're going to have to break into the SIS headquarters at Vauxhall Cross to steal the files on Pilot Fish.'

Elsa sniggered mirthlessly. The older woman was obviously having a laugh at her expense. 'You're crazy.'

'I understand how you feel about it, but we really have no other choice. And you're an incursion specialist, after all, an expert in getting in and out of places, so it'll be a piece of cake for you. However, it must be tonight – Zoe Castle's regrettable death may not have been totally in vain. Camille will explain to you on the way, but you have to go now.'

Elsa had already been nearly killed once this evening, and didn't fancy chancing her luck again. Breaking into the SIS building, for fuck's sake.

But Mrs Krystahl was right about one thing – what other choice did she have?

There was something she had to do first. 'I have to make a phone call.'

The skin over Mrs Krystahl's face stretched tightly. 'I really don't think you should be making phone calls. They'll be listening across the network – for your name, code phrases. There's probably a whole section of sad little men in GCHQ with voice-recognition software waiting to identify you among the millions of conversations happening across the country tonight.'

Elsa was surprised. 'They can do that?'

'Would you really put it past them, Elsa?' The older lady drained her second glass. 'I certainly wouldn't.'

'Either I make a call,' Elsa said, 'or I catch a plane.'

Mrs Krystahl sighed and nodded to a corner of the room. When Elsa headed there, a man gave her a handset.

Elsa couldn't remember any of her numerous online customer service passwords, but the landline telephone number from her childhood would be forever imprinted on her brain. The local code had changed, but not the main number. She called it, sticking a finger in her other ear to listen over the noise of the room. The phone rang four – five – six times, and then was picked up.

Greta answered. 'Yes.'

'It's me.' When Elsa was met with silence, she added, 'Your daughter.'

Greta said sourly, 'Are you insane, calling here?'

Her mother was right, of course, and Elsa burned with shame and dread that she may have put her children in danger. 'I just need to know they're—'

'They're fine,' said Greta sharply. 'Don't call again.'

And then the line went dead.

Elsa handed back the cordless phone, then returned to the table where Mrs Krystahl had placed the martini; picked it up, intending to neck it. Tonight, of all nights, a fortifying drink wouldn't hurt. But the older woman intercepted the glass before it reached her lips.

'You had better go now, you have a busy evening ahead of you.'

20

The Airbus ACH160 flew over the top of the trees and turned above the manicured lawn, the downdraught from the rotors making a plastic football left on the grass race into a flowerbed.

Sitting in the luxury passenger cabin, Arkady Krupin saw his sprawling Surrey estate for the first time in many months. He and his wife, Natalya, had enjoyed happy times here, but it felt strange to be back; the circumstances bittersweet.

The helicopter hovering as the pilot made final adjustments above the gentle slope of the lawn, Arkady impatiently checked the time on his Patek Philippe Nautilus. He'd intended to arrive hours ago but a business meeting had overrun, which was what happened when you filled a room with expensive lawyers and accountants who all felt obliged to contribute opinions, and he was afraid the party would already be over. On the leather seat beside him in the spacious compartment was a gift box.

'Can we hurry up, please?' he said into his mic.

When the helicopter finally touched down, and Hazlett came in a hunching run across the lawn to open the door, Arkady unbuckled and took off his noise-cancelling headphones. He grabbed the box, but left his Dior overnight bag; someone would pick it up.

The roar of noise beneath the whirling blades was tremendous as they headed towards the veranda at the back of the house. Expensive outdoor furniture ran the length of it. Cushions and folded blankets were placed there every morning, even during the long periods when Arkady wasn't in residence.

With the last of the evening warmth almost gone, outdoor heaters had been turned on. Candles flickered and tea lights guttered. Champagne had been placed in an ice bucket on one of the low tables, as it always was when he arrived. The sight of the two upturned glasses beside it made Arkady's heart clench. He and Natalya loved to sit there of an evening, watching the moon rise behind the tops of the swaying trees beyond the lawn.

Those had been happy days, when they had been in love – or he had been in love with her, at least. Natalya had always craved the life of an English Lady of the Manor, and he had done everything in his power to make her dream come true. But within a year, bored and frustrated by the quiet and isolation of the countryside, she divorced him and moved to a lavish apartment in the city. She still lived there, so his army of detectives told him, partying and spending the tens of millions she won from him in court as if money was going out of fashion.

Arkady had loved this place once, but only because Natalya had loved it – or loved the idea of it – and he spent very little time here now; he found it too painful.

This would be his last visit.

On the lawn, the Airbus powered down, its rotors steadily losing momentum. Three hulking gentlemen, members of his security detail, came to meet him as he headed around the side of the house towards the greenhouse.

'Good to see you, my friends.' Arkady pumped each of their hands in turn. He was their employer, but common courtesy cost nothing.

Anthony Hazlett, his executive assistant, was tall, but even his long legs struggled to match the stride of Arkady – by his own admission, a diminutive, somewhat dumpy man – as they crossed the gravel drive at the front of the house, where a number of expensive vehicles were parked.

Hazlett said anxiously, 'Things have been happening that—'

Arkady stopped to readjust the heavy box under his arm. One of his men had offered to take it, but he insisted on carrying it himself.

'And how are you, Arkady?' he replied in his thick Russian accent. 'Why, I'm fine, thank you, Anthony, it's good of you to *ask*.'

Hazlett blinked. 'It's good to see you, sir. I hope you are well.'

'I'm not sure I like the *sir* bit, but thank you.' Arkady laughed, and clapped his assistant on the shoulder. 'Please tell me I'm not too late!'

'It's still in full swing, sir. But it's important that I update you.'

'There is no update on earth so urgent that it's worth missing a child's party for.'

'The situation with the target is developing in ways we didn't anticipate.'

Arkady waved a dismissive hand. 'It's all under control, I'm sure.'

'The sooner we discuss it, the—'

Arkady wasn't comfortable raising his voice to assert his considerable power and privilege, but he had made himself quite clear.

'I promise I will give you and the situation – which I'm fully aware of, by the way, because you phoned me at least a dozen times this afternoon – my full and undivided attention in approximately…' He glanced at his watch. 'Twelve minutes. But first I must deliver a young man his birthday gift.'

Hazlett breathed hard in an effort to walk and talk. 'But you should know that—'

'Is the situation completely out of control?' Arkady asked. 'Should we be fleeing the country?'

'No, but—'

'Then we will discuss it *after* I deliver this gift.'

'I understand.' Hazlett didn't sound like he understood in the slightest, but he let Arkady continue on his own towards the large Victorian greenhouse that stood a short distance from the house on its western side.

The green-painted structure was derelict when Arkady bought the mansion and its considerable grounds. Natalya had immediately fallen in love with its rusted skeleton and demanded it be renovated. So Arkady had it painstakingly rebuilt to its former glory of wrought iron and glass, a labour of love and outrageously expensive, and it stood now as a fitting monument to another age.

There was plenty of space inside its fifty-foot length to hold events, particularly as large parts of the house were currently out of bounds, and it was the birthday party of the son of his head gardener to which he hurried.

Natalya loved children. She had two of her own from a previous marriage, and he had four, but it was a great disappointment to Arkady that they never had any together; he often wondered whether things would have turned out differently. His own three sons and his daughter were adults now, pursuing careers all over the globe, and it had been weeks since he'd heard from any of them.

Approaching the entrance, he heard laughter and music. Despite the relatively late hour, the birthday party was still in progress. The children must be exhausted!

'Hello, Kieron.' He shook the hand of the huge man standing outside. 'How is that lovely wife of yours?'

'Very good, sir.' The faint tremor around Kieron's mouth suggested he was trying to smile. It never failed to amuse Arkady how these tough bodyguards, these so-called protection specialists, wore permanent scowls. They tried so hard to look menacing, it was almost comical. 'Thanks for asking.'

'And she's being well cared for?'

The man placed a hand on his chest. 'She's very comfortable. Thank you, sir, for everything you've done for us.'

'She'll be well looked after, I promise. In the meantime, there's something I need you to do.'

'Anything, sir.'

Arkady pointed to a nearby shed, and told him to bring some objects from inside and place them at the entrance to the greenhouse. And when he walked inside, everyone was in the party spirit. A trestle table stood near the front with fizzy drinks, snacks, crisps and treats for the children, and beer and wine for the adults.

Arkady made a point of greeting each and every member of his staff – all the housekeepers, maids and gardeners – and asked after their families. He was a good employer to the people who worked at his various properties, and always made a point of memorizing small details about their personal lives. Natalya was often rude to employees, which he had found embarrassing and unnecessary.

Darren was organizing party games for his ten-year-old son, Luke, and the boy's friends, who had come from a village nearby to enjoy his birthday. A dozen kids were running around chairs set out in a line as music played. Arkady's chef was in charge of the music coming from the portable speakers. When she touched the screen of her phone the music stopped, and the kids hurled themselves at the nearest chair.

When Darren saw Arkady, he came over to shake his hand. 'Thank you so much for coming, sir. And thank you for the wonderful party.'

'I wouldn't miss it for the world, Darren! I'm sorry I didn't manage to get here earlier. Work, you understand.'

'It's amazing that you're here.'

'How lovely.' Arkady gave a little bow of gratitude when someone handed him a glass of bubbly. 'And here's the birthday boy!'

With the game finished, Luke came over and his father pushed him gently forward. 'Say thank you to Mr Krupin.'

'Thank you for my party,' said the boy dutifully. It was obvious to Arkady that Luke wanted to get back to his friends, and who could blame him for that?

'This is for you.' Arkady gave the boy the gift one of his staff had purchased at Harrods, and which he had brought with him from London. Luke ripped off the wrapping to reveal a box containing an expensive remote-controlled car.

'Oh my God,' Luke said with excitement as his friends crowded round. 'It's the coolest thing ever!'

Arkady grinned, enjoying the boy's happiness. It had been a long time since his own children had been so young, and back then he had been a distracted parent. He had been busy consolidating his vast fortune in oil, minerals and ore, but he wished now he had been more present as a father.

'But nobody goes home empty-handed,' he told all the boys and girls. 'I have a surprise for all of you. Go and look outside!'

There was a great commotion when the kids rushed out of the greenhouse to discover the brand-new top-of-the-range rally bikes Kieron had placed outside.

Arkady laughed delightedly at the look of disbelief on their faces. 'Enjoy!'

Taking a bike each, Luke and his gang took off across the lawn, intending to race around the grounds together.

'A birthday for Luke to remember, I hope.'

'I don't know how to thank you,' said Darren, as the children darted away between the trees.

'Love your son, my friend, and cherish your time with him.' Arkady squeezed his shoulder. 'Because take it from me, it all flies by very quickly.'

He said goodbye to everyone in the greenhouse and walked back towards the house. In the distance, the boys and girls raced each other around the grounds.

'Be careful!' Arkady called.

When he walked into the large marble reception room of his mansion, Hazlett, who had been sitting morosely in a Louis XIV chair, jumped to his feet.

'Now, my friend.' Arkady clapped his hands together. 'You have my full attention.'

'The target has evaded capture. We managed to keep her out of the hands of British intelligence.'

'That's good, then.'

Arkady and Hazlett strode together down the wide, immaculately renovated corridors of wood, marble and tile to the east wing of the mansion, Kieron following at a discreet distance.

'But she was... spirited away.'

'By whom?'

'RedQueen, we think.'

Arkady shrugged. 'Everything else is on schedule?'

'Yes, of course. But the target—'

'Let's not panic. A train of events has been set in motion, and I promise they will play out as I predicted. More importantly, we're ready at this end.'

Hazlett couldn't let it go. 'But we need Zero to—'

Arkady interrupted. 'Do you trust me, Anthony?'

Hazlett looked offended. 'Of course!'

Arkady reached up to squeeze his shoulder. 'Then please, my friend, you needn't worry.'

None of Arkady's domestic staff were allowed to venture into the sealed east wing, which could only be accessed via a single set of double doors, and which required biometric verification via a palm-reader on the wall.

Arkady lifted his hand to the pad and the doors unlocked. Kieron pulled them open, to allow his employer into the vast room beyond.

Centuries ago, the windowless room they entered had been a giant ballroom where gentlemen and ladies moved with elegance and grace across the floor. Arkady and Natalya had dreamed of holding sumptuous masked balls in this room once again, but it was never to be. Huge chandeliers comprised of hundreds of glittering crystals still hung from the ceiling. Centuries-old portraits of gentlemen in frock coats and ladies in corsets and towering wigs, and innumerable equestrian scenes, adorned the panelled walls. But the room was now filled with desks, tables and monitor screens.

Men and women sat tapping at keyboards and moving their fingers across trackpads, and barely looked up when the three men walked across the room to another door. Arkady once again placed his hand on a scanner.

The door clicked open, and they walked into the room at the far end of the wing. It was just as large, with elegant decorations and cornices that had survived from another age. But the shutters were closed over the windows in this room: they had been nailed shut, so no daylight could get in. Instead, the room was starkly lit by large industrial lamps standing in each corner.

And dominating the space in the centre was a rectangular room-within-a-room, about half the size of the entire space. Transparent plastic walls revealed figures in positive-pressure sealed bodysuits working inside the structure.

A level-4 biolab.

21

Gone midnight, Elsa and Camille opened a heavy steel door, covered with graffiti and torn gig flyers, that was barely visible halfway along a stinking alley in central London, and walked into the cold, damp space inside.

A single caged bulb on the wall above the door threw sallow light on a spiral staircase that twisted steeply into the depths of the earth. A faint rumble came from below, a Tube train running deep underground.

'Have you got the pass?' asked Camille.

Elsa patted the zipped pocket of her hoodie, which contained the small plastic rectangle of Zoe Castle's SIS security ID. She was still incredulous at what she was expected to do. 'That's all I need to get in?'

'Just leave the rest to us.' Camille handed her a Maglite xenon flashlight. 'Good luck.'

When Camille left, the door clanged shut in Elsa's face, sealing her into the dank space. She shone the torchlight against the Victorian tiled wall, its glazed cream surface obscured by a thick layer of grime, and found the top of the staircase.

In her earpiece, she heard Camille's footsteps on the pavement outside. 'Give me a minute to get back to the van.'

Elsa still had so many questions. 'You're sure we'll be able to maintain contact when I'm underground?'

She'd been rushed away from the Soho party in the back of a white van and driven around streets she couldn't see, while people talked *at* her.

Camille had given her a couple of bananas, a bag of chocolate bars and an energy drink. Usually, Elsa wouldn't go near sugary stuff, sugar was *bad*, and she told her clients to avoid it like the plague, but because she was feeling almost dizzy with fatigue she wolfed the chocolate down, dropping the wrappers to the floor, while a couple of geeky-looking people – a young man and woman – gave her instructions she didn't understand as they typed frantically on laptops balanced on their knees.

'You're Zoe,' said the guy.

'But I'm not Zoe,' Elsa told him.

He sighed, as if he was explaining something to a dim child, even though he looked barely old enough to vote. '*Tonight*, you'll be Zoe.'

Elsa clapped her thighs. 'But they'll see I'm not Zoe.'

'Explain it to her again,' Camille told them patiently.

Elsa wanted to punch the geeks in the face. In the last twenty-four hours she'd discovered her fiancé of five seconds was a deep cover agent; she'd been stabbed and shot at and hunted by assassins. All she wanted to do was get back to Harley and India and fly them somewhere safe. She didn't have time to be lectured by these patronizing snowflakes.

'What are your names?' Elsa asked them.

'I'm Simon.' The young man narrowed his eyes. 'But I identify as Flex.'

'And you?'

'Jo.'

Elsa stuffed half a banana into her mouth. 'Say it one more time.'

So they explained it to her all over again as the van moved through the dark streets. It still didn't make much sense to her tired mind, and all the simultaneous laptop activity was giving her a headache in the small, noisy space.

She had to go underground, they said, and into a dead vault, which was an archive deep beneath the headquarters of British intelligence in Vauxhall, where classified data about forgotten intelligence missions, initiatives and strategies was stored. There was a hidden exit, which didn't appear on any map, and she could get in through that.

Then she had to log on to a computer and attach a magic box to the drive that would crack the access credentials. To do that she had to do this thing and that thing, but definitely not the other thing, because 'If the system detects any anomalous behaviour, it will start hacking right back'. Flex and Jo started talking over each other, both trying to explain to her about attack path modelling and generative adversarial networks, and Elsa felt like her brain was going to explode. She could barely manage to file her taxes online every year, let alone be expected to access a highly restricted government computer terminal.

Flex handed her a smooth rectangular box, slightly bigger than a packet of fags, with a wire attached.

'What does this do again?'

Jo lifted her eyes from her laptop screen. 'What do you know about iterative brute force authentication algorithms?'

Elsa, who never liked to admit a lack of knowledge, shrugged vaguely.

'Right, just plug it in and we'll talk you through the rest.'

'Just don't download anything,' said Simon or Flex or whoever. 'If you do that, you'll activate security protocols.'

'Download what exactly, and how?' Elsa must have missed some vital detail among the thousands of confusing instructions they'd given her. 'Am I meant to stick my fingers in the USB port?'

'You don't download anything,' said Jo urgently. 'We just told you that.'

Elsa looked at Camille, *help me out*, but she was doing something on her phone.

'So how am I meant to remember what comes up on the screen?'

Simon/Flex gave her a small digital camera. 'You'll have to go Old Skool Spy. Photograph the screen.'

And then Flex and Jo started arguing with each other in low, tense whispers about what else Elsa should and shouldn't do. It felt very claustrophobic in the back of the van, with everyone's knees and shoulders clashing every time it took a corner, as it rattled around the West End. Elsa didn't understand why they couldn't just go to a Burger King and talk about it over a coffee, but had to admit that would probably be very foolish and dangerous in the circumstances.

'Can you hear me?' she asked Camille now as she clanged down the metal stairs, aiming the torch ahead at the hundreds of narrow, slippery steps circling endlessly into the darkness below.

Despite her fatigue, Elsa tried to find an instinctive

rhythm in her precarious descent, let muscle memory drop one leg in front of the other, let her foot connect to the next step, as she went round and round into the seemingly bottomless depths. On top of everything else, she was getting dizzy.

'We're here,' said a voice in her ear.

'Simon?'

'It's Flex,' he corrected her. 'We're right with you.'

But they weren't physically beside her as she descended into the labyrinth of tunnels beneath the city. They weren't likely to get hopelessly lost, dismembered by a train, or eaten by rats. Even now the rattle of a Tube echoed on the walls around her as it shunted through the darkness somewhere below, taking home the last of the evening's bleary-eyed revellers.

Elsa finally saw the damp outline of a floor in the torchlight: she had reached the bottom. There was no light at all down here. She shone the beam along the sloping, slippery tunnels. Snaking bundles of wires and cables disappeared along the concave walls. Here and there, stalagmites lifted from the floor.

'I have no idea where I'm going.'

All she knew was that she was meant to access a so-called dead vault and, once inside, break into a computer that could provide the information they needed about Carragher's disastrous Buenos Aires incursion, of which Elsa, Camille and Saint were the only survivors.

The deep-level tunnels were supported by circular metal rings, protrusions like the ribs of some prehistoric beast. When Elsa took a step, her feet froze in ankle-deep water, which shone oily black in the torchlight. In their haste, nobody had thought to give her a pair of sturdy boots or waterproof jacket.

'You should see a junction ahead,' said Camille faintly in her ear. 'Turn left and continue walking.'

'I still can't get my head around how I'm going to be able to just walk inside?'

'RedQueen established an undetected presence inside the British intelligence security system years ago, waiting for just this kind of eventuality,' Camille explained. 'We planted a trapdoor in the system that will enable us to bypass all the usual access procedures. All we needed was an active security pass, and Zoe Castle's death gave us that.'

'Good old Zoe,' muttered Elsa.

'Her accreditation hasn't been revoked yet, but it'll only be a matter of hours.'

Elsa approached a metal hatch at the end of the tunnel. Her trainers were soaked through, her feet already numb with cold.

'The dead vault has an emergency exit in case it somehow gets sealed off from the main building. Nobody's used it for years, maybe ever. Very few people even know it exists. Castle's pass will get you inside.'

'But there'll be a camera, yeah?' Elsa pulled open the hatch, as heavy and solid as a door on a submarine, and its hinges screeched with cold. She still couldn't get her head around what they'd told her. 'They're going to see me.'

'They won't see *you*,' interjected Flex.

Elsa moved down another circular tunnel. The floor was dry, at least. The torchlight jerked left and right in her hand, a thin beam tearing through the darkness, illuminating steel beams and ancient wiring that rippled above her head.

'We've created a deepfake version of Zoe Castle, rendered from hundreds of hours of footage of her walking around the SIS building. The image will be mapped around your face and body in real time. The person the night-time security guard will see on the screen will look like Zoe, will be dressed like Zoe, and even walk like Zoe – but it's you.'

Elsa didn't know how she felt about stealing the appearance and biometric data of a woman who'd died only hours ago, even if that identity was solely filtered through the dispassionate eye of a security camera. But if it was the only way to get inside the dead vault, she had no choice.

Elsa came to another junction. Shone the torch along the intersecting tunnels, left then right. Something squeaked in the shaft of light and scurried into the darkness.

'Which way now?'

'Go right,' said Camille. 'If there's anyone in the vault, and there shouldn't be at this time of night, you'll have to take measures.'

Elsa moved carefully, squeezing past junk: rusted filing cabinets and rotting wooden furniture, inexplicably dumped decades ago in this remote place beneath the city. She came to another heavy door, which led into a wider access tunnel where caged bulbs provided dim light above the dirty concrete floor. A ventilation shaft disappeared into one side of the curved wall.

'The computer where the information can be accessed is air-gapped,' said Flex. 'Which means it's disconnected from the internet, and any third-party hardware that could compromise it.'

His statement made Elsa think again of the hard drive in the vault in Apartment 7b all those years ago.

She felt a low rumble in her cold bones. Metal pipes affixed to the side of the tunnel began to sing, as they did whenever a Tube train passed on the other side of the wall. Puddles of water on the ground trembled around Elsa's frozen feet. The roar increased in pitch; for a few moments it was deafening as the carriages cascaded past, and then disappeared into the distance.

Elsa headed up an incline along one final unlit tunnel – and came to a dead end. The usual waist-high bundle of cables continued across the far wall and then back the way she had come.

'I've come the wrong way,' she said.

'Except you haven't.'

When Elsa pointed the torch at the dead end, she saw the faint rectangular shape of a door. The gathered wires that snaked horizontally across the door weren't connected to the bundles on the walls on either side, they just looked like they were; the cables were fake. Even if some unhappy traveller hopelessly lost in the maze of underground tunnels had somehow accidentally arrived at this spot, and even if they had access to better light, they'd never in a million years notice the door unless they knew exactly what to look for. Elsa took out Zoe Castle's pass.

'Here goes nothing.'

'There's a panel to your left,' Camille told Elsa, who pressed the pass against a smooth patch of dull metal embedded in the wall. There was a series of soft clicks, and then the door opened a couple of inches.

'Sooner or later, questions are going to be asked about why someone's walking around in the dead vault in the early hours,' said Camille. 'So be quick.'

'You may have realized already, but I'm not very good with computers,' said Elsa, stepping inside.

'But we are, and we'll guide you every step of the way,' said Flex. 'Let's get to work.'

22

In a room full of surveillance equipment many storeys above the vault, Zoe Castle's entry into the building was automatically registered.

On a small portion of a screen stacked with different CCTV images, the lights in the dead vault flickered into life as Deepfake Zoe – a digital composite of image and biometric data created by a sophisticated AI algorithm – walked down the bunker's central corridor.

Not that any of the overnight security team who were on duty in the early hours of the morning knew who Zoe Castle was; thousands of people worked in the SIS building. But the computer said *yes*, because her biometric details and physical appearance corresponded with the identity of the woman on the screen, and that was good enough.

When one of the night security officers glanced up from his phone to see her walking along the corridor, he thought it unusual that someone was prowling the dead vault after midnight, but perhaps not that unexpected. In the last couple of days there had been some kind of alert happening and staff were working round the clock. He'd seen people running about on the upper floors, supervisors and upper management and suchlike, as if they had the weight of the world on their shoulders.

Gareth, the officer, stood up – he had worked nights for many months, but it was always difficult to stay alert in the stupefying ambience of the early hours – and pulled his jacket from the back of his chair.

'Popping out for a fag,' he said.

23

Elsa moved along the wide, softly illuminated corridor. In this part of the building, far underground, the blank grey walls were bare prestressed concrete, and cold to the touch. Up near the ceiling were what looked like air-conditioning vents, but which introduced security fog into the room in the event that the vault's security was compromised.

At the far end of the wide corridor was a metal sliding door – the lift that connected the building above to this high-security archive. The black bulb of a camera squatted above it on the wall, staring along the corridor, and right at her.

'Get to a terminal,' Camille told her. 'But don't look like you're in a rush.'

Elsa walked into one of the side rooms, a sparsely equipped office. A pair of desks were pushed together, a computer placed on each. Elsa was no expert where computers were concerned, but neither bulky beige terminal looked state of the art. The ceiling lights flickered on automatically as she sat at one of the desks. When Elsa touched the space bar, the computer came to life with a noisy whir. She took out the small box she had been given in the van.

'Now what?' she asked.

'Plug it in,' said Flex.

24

Hours after the fiasco in Cavendish Square, helicopters still flew above the city centre, combing the streets using thermal imaging equipment; surveillance had been increased on the ground. The police were looking for Elsa Zero, too, even if they didn't know the truth of why. Facial recognition override protocols were in place – as soon as she walked in front of any smart camera in a public place, they'd find her.

But the car in which Zero fled in the first chaotic minutes of her violent escape was found abandoned in an alley in Kennington. Her prints were all over the dash, window and handle, but the identity of the driver who sped her away was a mystery. Whoever opened fire in that square had successfully disrupted SIS's attempt to bring her in, had abducted Zero or abetted her escape.

Sitting in his office fourteen floors above the dead vault, Nigel Plowright's concern was that Zero had already been spirited out of the country. He imagined her at that very moment sipping Dom Pérignon as she flew in a luxury jet towards the capital of an unfriendly foreign power. If that was the case, then God help everyone; his own disintegrating career would be the least of his worries.

After the square had been examined, and a suitable cover

story about gangland violence activated for the benefit of the media – nutcase conspiracy theorists and keyboard warriors would kick up a stink, but fabricated evidence would keep the mainstream press running around in circles for the time being – Plowright had spent most of the evening watching footage of the fiasco, trying to piece together the sequence of events.

Situated in a building on the south of the square with easy access to Oxford Circus, the gunman or woman had melted into the evening crowd by the time an assault team managed to pinpoint their position.

One of Plowright's team informed Castle's family of her death and gave them a heavily redacted version of the events of the evening, while he spent a tense couple of hours in a conference room getting shouted at by his superiors via secure video link. He'd been obliged, when he could get a word in edgeways, to explain what he intended to do next, something he barely knew himself. All he could do was say that everything was under control, and assure them that Elsa Zero's trail of chaos and carnage would soon be brought to an end.

He stared at his desk phone now, hoping someone would call to tell him she had been captured by a friendly nation, that she was already en route to a black site, one of those secret supermax silos the Yanks supposedly had embedded beneath the Nevada desert, and would never be seen or heard of again.

But that would just be too good to be true.

Night enveloped the city beyond his window. Plowright felt utterly fatigued. All he wanted to do was get home to his husband and dog, both of whom would probably be sound asleep. He'd grab three or four hours himself, then return to work before dawn.

'Where would she go, I wonder?' he asked Justine Vydelingum when she came in to sit, posture perfect, in the chair on the other side of his desk. To his annoyance, she looked as fresh as a daisy, despite the ridiculous hour. But she was young, full of energy and focus, while he was careening down the wrong side of middle-age; these days, even his aches had aches. 'Give me something, anything.'

'Elsa Zero hasn't stayed in touch with any of her old comrades.' Justine's polished red nail lightly touched the surface of her tablet. 'She's had a fair number of psych evaluations, both in the military and when she was contracted by SIS, but they don't tell us much. Like many in her field, she's been unwilling or unable to form emotional attachments. Her boyfriend tried to kill her moments after reportedly getting on one knee to propose, so you have to respect her thinking on that score.

'She has very few contacts left within the intelligence community that we know of.' She scrolled, trying to summarize. 'The people we've questioned so far, former associates and contractors, say they have no idea where she is, but these people are liars by trade and inclination. She also has, or had, numerous contacts in the criminal underworld – perk of the job – but we don't believe she's reached out to them.'

Plowright stood to stretch his tired limbs. Of an evening, he'd usually not manage to stay awake past the end of the ten o'clock news. *Fuck it*, he thought, *I'm going home*. He needed to get out of his small box of an office, the dark rooms full of headache-inducing glowing screens and humming tech, for just a few hours. He'd wasted too much of his life in this miserable place. His marriage hung by a thread.

Grabbing his jacket off the back of the door, he walked out, and Justine jumped up and followed him.

'Get me a car home, will you?' he said.

'Will do.'

'What about the boyfriend?' he asked as they walked towards the lift. 'What do we have on him?'

'We're going down a rabbit hole where he's concerned. Goes by the name of Joel Harris. Has a furnished rented address in Islington, North London, and supposedly a job at a shipping company, which is registered at Companies House but doesn't otherwise operate. He has a driver's licence, NHS medical card, all that, but very little in the way of any proof of identity stretching back further than a couple of years.'

'Since he met Zero.'

'He's pretty much a ghost.'

'A foreign agent, then. Anyone else?'

'Zero has business clients, and is in semi-regular contact with one or two mums at her kids' school. She's on a parent WhatsApp group, but has only contributed to that once, a discussion about whether it's ever acceptable to attend events wearing pyjamas. All her other relationships appear just as superficial.'

At the end of the corridor, Plowright impatiently stabbed the lift button.

'Who spoke to Castle's family?'

'Holbrook handled it,' Justine told him as the doors opened. 'He has a gentle touch.'

They stepped inside and turned to face the closing doors, ignoring the security officer who stood in the corner with a cigarette tucked behind his ear. 'She had a husband and a teenage son, the poor things.'

'Castle's son encountered Zero on the street,' Plowright said, lowering his voice. Usually, he wouldn't dream of talking about an active situation in a non-secure place, but he needed to give her instructions while he remembered, otherwise he'd end up messaging from the car, or it would pop into his mind just as he was trying to fall asleep in the spare room. 'Get a description of Zero from him first thing in the morning. She might have climbed out of a car, or even dropped a key or address book. Let's leave no stone unturned. We'll need Zoe Castle's husband's permission to speak to him.'

'Why don't you ask Mrs Castle yourself?' said Gareth, the security guard. Plowright turned to tell him to mind his own bloody business, but the man added, 'She's in the building now.'

Plowright frowned. 'What are you talking about?'

'Zoe Castle... she's down in the vault.' When Plowright stared, he blinked. 'Sorry, just trying to be helpful.'

The lift doors opened, and a liquid voice informed the occupants they had arrived at the ground floor, where Gareth intended to smoke outside. But Plowright stabbed the button to close them.

Two minutes later, Plowright and Justine followed Gareth into the security control room.

'Show me,' said Plowright.

The security officer leaned over his work station to click a mouse, transferring the live feed from the vault onto a bigger screen on the wall.

Plowright was stunned to see Zoe Castle sitting at a computer terminal in the lower depths of the building.

'And this is happening right now?' The officer nodded. 'When did she walk in?'

'About ten minutes ago.'

'Show me.'

The guy rewound the footage of Zoe Castle walking along the corridor in the dead vault. Plowright watched, fascinated.

'She's looking sprightly for a woman who died several hours ago,' said Justine.

Members of the security team gawped at her.

'You need to get all your cyber-warrior types in here,' Plowright told Gareth. 'Because the security system is compromised. Where did she come in?'

One of the other officers tapped at his keyboard, squinting at the screen. 'Access Point 457/x/a. It's an underground entrance. I didn't even know we had one there.'

Plowright watched Zoe Castle on the screen, frowning at the computer terminal she was using.

'I want an armed team – right now!'

25

'I'm in,' Elsa confirmed, after the correct authentication credentials had been found and she was able to access the computer. The process had only taken a couple of minutes, but sitting under the watchful eye of the security camera, it had felt like an age.

Despite the chill in the room, she was hot and flustered. In her ear, Flex got frustrated with how long it took her to follow what he considered straightforward instructions, but none of it felt straightforward. Then Jo told her to do something that completely contradicted what Flex said, and Elsa had to lift her trembling fingers from the keyboard while she listened to them argue.

'If she does that,' hissed Flex, 'the system will shut down. Is that what you want to happen?'

'Don't talk to me like that,' Jo told him fiercely. 'That's not what I'm suggesting.'

'I'm just stating simple facts.'

'We'll be back,' Jo told Elsa impatiently. 'Give us two seconds.'

Then Elsa's earpiece went dead. She had to sit there, resting her hands flat on the table in case she accidentally touched the wrong key, until they had worked out their differences and started talking in her ear again.

'Okay,' said Flex with great forbearance. 'Here's what you do...'

She didn't understand any of what they told her to do, but did exactly what she was told, identifying each key and stabbing at it with purpose.

'Now press the tilde key,' Flex told her.

She stared at the keyboard, her eyes swimming. 'I don't know what that is.'

'It's the squiggle beside the enter key. But you must press the shift key. Whatever you do, make sure you press the shift key, or you'll ruin everything.'

'*Ruin everything* is not helpful language,' she said.

She wished he had come down here himself. Let's see how he would have coped with breaking into SIS in the middle of the night. But if he was caught, RedQueen would have difficult questions to answer. If Elsa was captured, however, she'd be dismissed immediately by her former employer as a rogue operative.

Now she had managed to get into the online archive, she was faced with a list of incomprehensible file names cascading down the screen.

'What can you see?' asked Camille.

'I don't know.' Elsa tried to make sense of the random words and numbers.

The operating system was old, and its interface nothing like the one on her kids' tablets, which had helpful shiny icons that allowed them to navigate easily. It didn't matter how long she looked, the list of impenetrable names made no sense to her, and she didn't even know what she was looking for.

It was probably too much to hope for to find a file name that said: Secret_Mission_To_Destroy_Hard_Drive_BuenosAires.

'There are dozens of files here. Hundreds!'

'Okay,' said Flex. 'Are there numbers on the files?'

'Yes.' Elsa traced a finger along the file names. Each ended in six numbers. '310897, 121106, 130609, and so on.'

'So you're looking at dates. Try and find the date of your mission.'

Elsa searched for a file name that ended in numbers 240512. 'Got it!'

'Open it,' said Camille.

Reaching for the mouse, Elsa heard a faint boom above the grinding hum of the ancient computer, and a whirring sound. She stood and walked into the corridor to locate the source of it. The red light on the floor counter at the top of the lift had turned green, displaying an arrow pointed downwards.

'I've got to get out of here,' she said, rushing back to the computer to open the file.

But when the data appeared on the screen, it was gobbledegook. The whole document was a slab of solid text; every line on every paragraph was filled with garbled, jumbled characters, letters, numbers and symbols; there wasn't a single empty space. She desperately tried to locate meaning in the text, as if she was doing a word search in a puzzle book.

'It's gibberish, the document must be corrupted,' she said, scrolling down.

'It could be code,' said Flex, his voice tight with anxiety. 'But we need to see it.'

Scrolling back to the top, Elsa unzipped her pocket, took out the camera. She photographed the screen then scrolled halfway down, took a photograph, scrolled down, took a photo, and scrolled, worrying that the document had no end.

But she made it to the bottom just as she heard the lift approaching.

'Is that the only file?' asked Camille. 'Are there others?'

'I've got to go.'

'We've only got one shot at this,' Camille said. 'You need to make sure.'

'No time, they're on their way.' She grabbed the torch and climbed from the seat.

Elsa reached the wide concrete corridor as the lift machinery sighed – it had arrived at the vault. She could run for the exit, but the doors were going to open in a few short seconds, and she didn't fancy getting shot in the back.

'Drop the deepfake.' Elsa eyed the sinister-looking vents near the ceiling. 'Trigger the security automated system.'

The doors opened and three Kevlar-wearing men edged out of the lift, their M4 carbine assault rifles already aimed.

'Please stay there,' said a voice from behind them, and Elsa glimpsed a thin, sharp-faced man in glasses. 'Keep your hands up. If you move, you will be shot, do you understand?'

'They'll see you,' Camille said in Elsa's ear.

'Oh, I think that horse has bolted,' Elsa muttered.

'Who are you talking to?' The thin man stepped past his team.

'Was it you who killed Zoe Castle?' Elsa said. 'And tried to kill me?'

'My name is Nigel Plowright,' he said. 'Zoe persuaded me to bring you in.'

'And died because of it,' Elsa told him.

'Not too close, she's dangerous,' the man barked at his team, who continued to edge forward. 'This is the last place I expected to find you, Elsa; I thought you'd be long gone. You've saved me a lot of trouble coming here.'

'Just a flying visit.'

'We're turning off the deepfake image now,' Camille told her, and Elsa made a last mental note of where everyone stood.

In the security control room floors above, Justine Vydelingum saw Zoe Castle, with her hands held high, suddenly vanish. Standing in her place was Elsa Zero. A moment later, the screen went blank.

In the vault, thermally generated security fog – glycerine mixed with distilled water – blasted from the wall vents. Smothering the corridor, enveloping everything and everyone in a thick, impenetrable blanket.

The moment she was concealed from view, Elsa began to move. There were three armed men, and she dropped low, spinning on her heels towards the nearest. He lurched out of the fog at her, jerking his weapon in her direction as she thrust her foot into the back of his legs; tipping backwards, he let off a burst of gunfire into the ceiling. She swung the torch backhanded into the helmet of another of the team, the fog billowing crazily as he crashed to the floor.

Elsa was blind, all she could see was a thick soup of white as the fog cannoned from the vents, but nobody else could see a thing either. The fog was designed to disorient intruders and prevent them from gaining access to the computers next door, but she knew that the system would be disabled within seconds.

Moving low between the armed men in a whirl of white gas, she heard the crack of gunfire near her ear; chips of plaster flew off the wall and stung her face.

The man called Plowright barked, 'Stop firing!'

The soft fabric of his jacket brushed her arm as he retreated, trying to reach the safety of the lift, but heading in the wrong direction, and she grabbed him from behind, clamping her forearm around his neck. Plowright felt as light as a feather as she pulled him towards the exit, brushing her shoulder against the wall to keep herself orientated. The exit into the tunnel should only be a couple of feet behind them.

Another gunshot took a chunk of the wall out above their heads, and she told him, 'They're going to shoot you!'

'No more firing,' Plowright spluttered. 'That's an order!'

She dragged him to the door, his heels skidding uselessly on the tiled floor. Watched for disturbances in the fog ahead. She knew the armed men were moving forward, weapons raised.

'You're being ridiculous.' With the crook of her elbow jammed against his throat, Plowright's voice was a petulant croak. 'You won't get out of here alive.'

'You already tried to kill me once and that didn't work out so well.'

'We were trying to bring you in!' His fingers plucked ineffectually against her arm.

Elsa heard the lift doors at the far end of the corridor open again. There was a disturbance in the white wall of fog ahead of her, the downdraught of the lift shaft made the thinning gas swirl, then thin green beams of laser-sights moved left and right out of the fog.

The reinforcements who had arrived wore imaging goggles, which meant they could pick up her heat signature, so she hunched as low as she could behind Plowright. He gasped, too, because the beams of light criss-crossed his chest, shoulders and face as they hungrily searched for a clear shot at Elsa.

'Don't shoot!' he shouted to the invisible soldiers.

'You killed her.' She fumbled for Zoe Castle's pass. 'And tried to kill me!'

'No,' he insisted. 'We were bringing you in, but there are other forces at play.'

'Who?'

'Come on, Elsa, you know what's happening.' Plowright spoke with a sarcasm she felt inadvisable. 'You took us all for fools.'

Elsa slapped the pass against the touch pad beside the door, but nothing happened; the pass had been deactivated.

'Stop this nonsense,' spluttered Plowright. 'It's over for you.'

Elsa didn't fancy her chances with the assault team emerging from the fog like hulking armoured ghosts. Her previous attempt to surrender to SIS had gone spectacularly tits up, and she couldn't visualize any kind of happy ending if she turned herself in now. If she was so bloody dangerous, if the world's intelligence agencies all wanted her dead so badly, then in all likelihood she would disappear. For a long time, maybe, or forever.

Besides, she had done what she came to do. Now she had a chance to figure out what was going on.

Plowright must have sensed what was on her mind because he spluttered, 'If you think we're going to keep highly classified information in this bloody dungeon, you've got another think coming.'

'The door,' she told her team. 'Open it.'

'We can't.' Flex's voice was filled with panic. 'They've changed the permissions.'

The fog had almost entirely dispersed, and the guards, wearing goggles that made them look like malevolent robots, came slowly towards her.

'This is your last chance, don't be a bloody fool!'

Elsa grabbed the pass hanging from the lanyard around Plowright's neck, yanking his head viciously to the side. He let out a strangled yelp as she pressed his pass to the security pad.

'We're not finished, me and you!' she snarled as the door unlocked. As soon as she felt it give against her back, she kicked Plowright into the path of the approaching assault team and flew into the tunnel.

Running blindly, she stumbled back the way she came. Gunfire cracked behind her as she turned into the first junction, causing a flash of angry sparks on the metal tubing along the wall.

'Get me out of here!' she screamed at Camille.

The fog blasted into the vault would have stained her skin and clothes with an invisible substance that'd make her sparkle like Christmas tree decorations in the imaging visors of the pursuing assault team. The only hope she had was to lose them in the tunnels and pray she didn't run into a dead end.

'Where to?' she barked as she splashed through the

puddles at the junction, trying not to bounce off the walls in the dark.

'Where are you?' asked Camille calmly.

Elsa heard Flex and Jo bickering in the background. 'You tell me!'

Heading into a dimly lit access tunnel, water slapping at her ankles, she heard raised voices behind her, the blast of automatic gunfire. A bulb above her head exploded. Another shot must have hit a live cable, because there was an electric crack. Shots boomed like thunder all around her, echoing along the many intersecting tunnels. She was already lost.

'Can you describe what you see?' asked Jo.

It's not like there were street signs, or helpful arrows painted on the walls. All the tunnels looked the same, big and dark, if she could even see them.

'Not helping!' Elsa shouted.

She saw the darker hue of a pipe in the side of the tunnel and slipped into it, pressed herself into the slim channel, crawling on her front to fit inside, fingers sliding on the slimy ground. The space narrowed and the ceiling sloped, until she had to hunch her shoulders in and pull herself along in an inch of freezing water, which rode over her chin and splashed into her mouth. She gagged at the foul, bitter taste.

Elsa was terrified she was going to get trapped. But then the pipe widened again and came out three feet above the floor. She fell to the ground in a wide, domed brick tunnel. She had no time to let her eyes adjust to the blackness, and ran on.

Elsa could hear the barks of the men, but with the weapons they carried, and the bulky armour they wore, they'd not be able to follow through the pipe; she had an opportunity to put some distance between them.

'W – c n't – hel – you,' Camille said, her voice cutting out.

'No shit,' muttered Elsa.

'Goo – luc—'

A faint patina of ambient light came from one end of the tunnel, but the echoing shouts of the men, and their clattering footsteps, came from every direction. Looking down, Elsa saw rail tracks on the floor, perilously close to her feet. She was standing in a Tube tunnel. She couldn't remember which of the four rails was electrified, whether it was one or two, and didn't fancy finding out.

'Camille,' she said. 'Are you there?'

But she'd lost contact. Elsa ran down the middle of the track, careful to avoid the undulating lines of dark metal. And then from far off came a muffled rumble, a Tube train cascading along a track. She froze, trying to place where the noise was coming from.

From somewhere close, she heard the squawk of a radio, and a thin beam of green light swept along the tunnel in the black depths behind her.

Shots reverberated again, and she zigzagged as best she could across the width of the tunnel, jumping left and right across the shiny tracks.

The vague metal lines in the gloom whined. A deep, guttural rumble bounced off the curved tunnel walls. The Tube train she'd heard in the distance was approaching, she just didn't know if she was running away from it or towards it.

The men were getting closer. The green beams jerked along the walls and ceiling. The rumble of the train became a threatening roar. Light climbed one sooty side of the tunnel behind her. The best thing she could do was fling herself against a wall and let it pass, just as her pursuers were doing now, but she wouldn't be able to put distance between herself and the SIS men.

So she ran as fast as she could on the uneven surface between the tracks. Arms pumping, sucking down the damp, foetid air. One touch of the electrified rail and she was toast.

Over her shoulder, Elsa saw the Tube train hurtle into view. Heard the angry cacophony of it, the rhythmic cascade of its wheels on the rails. Its two hundred tonnes would smash her to bits.

Fifty yards ahead was a bright light, and she saw a platform. The roar of the train was deafening; it boomed and echoed in the tunnel, furiously bearing down on her like an enraged monster.

Elsa sprinted hard, trying to ignore her fatigue; thinking of all those early morning runs across the Common, all those punishing hours on the treadmill, all the strength training. But she almost lost her balance in a hole between the tracks and had to readjust her stride in mid-air, only just managing not to land on the live rail.

Twenty yards now.

She kept up her pace, her long arms and legs moving like pistons as she raced towards the station, the tracks at her feet singing their song of electrified death.

It had been a long, exhausting day; she was running on empty.

Ten yards.

The driver of the train must have seen her silhouetted

on the tracks just ahead, in the sallow, muted light of the station. She heard a deafening horn, and the brakes screech.

Seven yards.

People on the platform watched in shock as Elsa raced from the tunnel, the current rails lifting up on either side of her legs on blocks set into concrete. Someone screamed.

And with one last effort, she launched herself, twisting like a high jumper over the raised tracks and onto the four-foot-high platform, rolling clear of the train as it flew into the station in a howling shriek of noise and brakes.

Elsa lay on the platform, trying to stop her heart crashing out of her ribcage.

26

Elsa ran through the station and onto the escalator going up, leaning over the divide to whip a baseball cap off the head of someone on the way down. Rushing onto the concourse, keeping her head low, she vaulted the ticket barrier.

As soon as she reached the pavement, Camille's van pulled up beside her and she climbed in, the vehicle accelerating as the door slid shut. Flex and Jo were still arguing.

'Your way was wrong.' Flex lifted his laptop screen to his colleague's face to show her something. 'The authentication process could have been compromised.'

Jo pushed the laptop away. 'As usual, you're not seeing the whole picture.'

'We could have saved time—'

'Leave it now, please,' Camille commanded. She took the camera from Elsa and handed it to Jo, and the two techs argued quietly about the best way to analyse the information on the photos Elsa had taken.

'We have a secure building we can get you to,' Camille told her.

Elsa shook her head. 'Saint is holed up in the home of one of my clients. I need to make sure he's okay.'

'Tell me where, and we'll bring him in.'

'I'm guessing by now he'll be drunk and paranoid. If your people turn up unexpectedly, there'll be carnage. Take me back there and pick us up at dawn.'

When Elsa told Camille Dougie's address, she realized she could barely look her in the eye. The guilt of her affair with Carragher – the biological father of her children – had gnawed away at her for years. She could just about handle the regret because she'd expected never to see Camille again. But they had been thrown together unexpectedly, and if they were going to work together to find out what the hell was going on, Elsa had to tell her the truth.

Stuck in the back of a van with a couple of bickering techs wasn't the best place to do it, but there was never a good time to make such a confession, and Elsa didn't know if she would even get another opportunity.

She took a deep breath. 'Camille, there's something you should—'

'*Don't,*' said Camille fiercely. 'Not now.'

'You know?'

Camille leaned close to look her in the eye. 'After all these years, you still think I didn't know what was going on?'

Elsa was bewildered. 'But how?'

Arguing on the seats in front, Flex and Jo were oblivious to the intense conversation going on behind them.

'Do it that way and you will corrupt the data.' Flex grabbed the camera from Jo. 'Give it here.'

'When we were in that apartment in Buenos Aires, I could feel the tension every time the pair of you were near each other. I finally knew for sure when Steve took you to find Saint that afternoon. I saw how he looked at you, Elsa, and it was obvious.' Camille's eyes glinted brightly in the gloom of the van. 'So I followed you both.' Camille had seen them on the street, holding and kissing each other. 'That night we... argued.'

Elsa felt wretched. She was tired, stiff with cold, and now finally forced to confront her own terrible betrayal of one of the few people she had ever known as a friend.

'I was furious, I wanted to kill you there and then,' Camille told her in an intense whisper. 'And I think I would have done if he hadn't stopped me. He told me...' Camille took a deep breath. 'He said he was leaving me, to be with you.'

Elsa forced herself not to look away from Camille's intense gaze.

'I was convinced he wouldn't do it, because we'd been there before. There'd been other women before you. Steve lived in the moment, he approached everything he did – work, sex and love – with the same burning intensity, with no thought to the future. Because every moment could be his last.' Elsa sensed the simmering fury behind her words. 'But what I didn't know then was that you were having his children.'

'I'm sorry,' Elsa said quietly. It wasn't much, but she meant it.

'Would you have been as sorry if he was alive, Elsa, and you had stolen him from me?' The anger in Camille's eyes faded and she leaned back against the seat. 'I just wanted to complete the mission, and when it was over and we all got back home, then I'd kill you. But things didn't work out that way.'

The minivan came to a stop. When Elsa looked up, they were outside a building in Soho's Berwick Street. Laptop tucked under his arm, Flex pulled open the side door and said, 'This is me.'

When Jo climbed out with him, Camille said, 'I want to know whatever it is you find on those photos, asap.'

'Got it.' Sliding the door shut, he and Jo walked to a door between one of the many coffee shops shuttered for the night.

The van started moving again, and Elsa told her, 'It was just a stupid fling.'

'No it wasn't,' Camille said acidly. 'You were different from the others, I could tell, and that's what hurt. He loved you.'

'How do you know that?'

Camille's gaze met Elsa's. 'Because he told me.'

Elsa turned away, trying to get her head together. The empty city streets flew past. She thought back to the morning of the mission, but couldn't remember any particular tension between Carragher and Camille. All her memories of that day concerned the catastrophic events in Apartment 7b.

She wasn't in the country for Steve Carragher's funeral, and in the weeks and months following the mission, Elsa made several attempts to contact Camille, maybe with the vague intention of confessing her relationship with him, and to tell her about Harley and India. But Camille didn't respond. She was grieving, Elsa presumed, and up to her neck in espionage matters on a daily basis. In the end Elsa gave up and Camille, like so many of her former associates, and the small handful of friends, drifted from her life.

'Whatever happened between you both,' said Camille, 'I loved him, and I still do.'

'I'm sorry,' Elsa told her.

'So you keep saying.' Camille sighed. 'It was all a long time ago.'

'You saved my life that day,' Elsa said.

'Because I'm a professional,' Camille said. 'And you never leave a colleague behind.'

Camille had held Elsa's hand in the helicopter as she bled out, shouting at her to stay awake, not to fall into unconsciousness; only hours earlier, Camille had apparently vowed to kill her.

Camille lifted a bag off the seat beside her. 'Here I am, trying to keep you alive all over again. Funny how things turn out.'

She took a syringe from the bag and tore a needle out of its packaging.

'What's that for?' said Elsa warily.

'Don't worry, I'm not going to poison you.' Camille held it high so she could see the syringe was empty. 'I need a blood sample.'

'What for?'

'When I'm told to do something, Elsa, I don't ask why. You know what RedQueen is like, it monitors everything. They'll do tests, probably, to make sure you're in good shape for the trials ahead.'

Elsa took off her damp hoodie and let Camille carefully draw blood from her arm. The filled syringe was placed carefully into a Ziploc bag, which was locked in a small box. Seeing the contents stirred memories in Elsa of her hand sliding through the slick of her own blood in the helicopter above Buenos Aires. Whatever bitter feelings she'd harboured against Elsa, Camille had done everything in her power to keep Elsa alive that night.

They sat in silence for the rest of the journey to Dougie's house. The van pulled up at the top of the street.

'Get some sleep and I'll collect you at six.' Camille gave Elsa a burner phone. 'Don't use it for Deliveroo.'

Elsa slid the door open and climbed out. 'I'm worried about my children, Cam.'

'Where are they?'

'With my parents in Buckinghamshire,' Elsa said.

Camille knew enough about her complicated relationship with Howard and Greta to appreciate how difficult a decision it must have been for Elsa to send them there.

'I'll make sure they're safe.'

As the van accelerated away, Elsa made her way to Dougie's house.

Halfway up the path, she heard raised voices coming from inside.

Something was wrong.

27

Too tired to clamber over the tall wooden gate, Elsa kicked it open and ran into the garden.

Standing close to the sliding doors, looking in the thin strip between the lowered blinds, she saw Dougie and his wife, Roberta, gagged and bound to dining table chairs in the living room. Saint paced furiously in his underpants, heating the tip of a bread knife with the flame from a lighter.

Too busy ranting and raving and waving the knife, Saint didn't hear Elsa bang her hand against the pane. But Dougie saw her and wriggled furiously on the chair in a silent plea to be saved from the mad intruder.

Neighbours might already have heard Saint's shouts and Dougie and Roberta's dismal cries; the police could arrive at any moment. Elsa lifted both fists to the glass and smashed as hard as she could.

'Saint!' she called as loud as she dared. Finally, he lumbered to the glass and shifted one of the blinds to look out. His eyes took time to focus on her, he was so drunk.

When he unlocked the door, Elsa slipped inside.

'What the fuck, Saint?'

He jabbed the knife at Dougie and Roberta. Staring up at him in terror, they made panicked noises behind the makeshift gags stuffed in their mouths. 'They just walked in, bold as brass.'

In the hours since she'd left him here – God, it seemed like weeks ago – the pristine home had been reduced to a bomb site. Every surface, the kitchen counter and the coffee table, the sofas and floor, were covered in empty bottles, plates and spilled food. Saint's clothes were all over the floor. He must have been drinking solidly since she left him. It was a wonder he could even stand. At least he had his pants on.

'Because they live here. It's their house!'

'That's what they want you to think.' Saint tried to tap a forefinger to the side of his nose, but it missed his face completely. 'But they could be anybody. *Killers*, Elsie.'

Chubby Dougie, with his belly spilling over his crotch, and Roberta in her flip-flops, didn't look much like elite assassins.

'I know them.' Elsa went around the back of Dougie's chair to untie him. 'Dougie is a client of mine.'

'He's going to kill us!' spluttered Dougie when she pulled the cloth from his mouth.

'Please, take anything you want and go,' wailed Roberta. 'We won't say a word to anybody.'

'Put the knife down,' Elsa commanded Saint. 'These people aren't a threat. And for God's sake, put some clothes on.'

'Then how come I found them sneaking in the door in the middle of the night?'

'Dougie,' Elsa asked as she plucked at the knots behind his back. 'What the hell did you come back for?'

'Someone called us… this morning…' Face purple, eyes rolling up in his head, he gasped for air.

'Breathe, take deep breaths.' Elsa tried to calm him down before he had a heart attack, and when Saint came close, she snapped, 'Back off!'

'Don't die, Dougie,' wept Roberta. 'Don't leave me with these people!'

'They saw... they saw...' Dougie gulped down another breath. 'Strangers.'

'They know our names.' Saint paced manically. 'We're going to have to kill them right now!'

Roberta let out a piercing scream.

'You're not helping!' Picking up his clothes, Elsa shoved them in his chest. 'Go and get dressed.'

'Said they saw someone...' Dougie spluttered. 'Park a car... in a garage.'

Elsa winced. A neighbour had seen her arrive last night. She'd been out of the game for so long that she'd gotten sloppy, and it was going to get her killed.

'Why are you doing this?' Roberta whimpered. 'What do you want?'

'I just needed a place to stay for a night, and knew you were away.'

Freed from the chair, Dougie pointed at Saint, who was hopping about trying to push one leg into his trousers and then the other. 'And that insane *person*?'

'I ain't insane, I've got issues!'

Elsa gestured at him, *stop*. Elsa was of a mind to cut him loose as soon as she could; he was proving a liability.

'He's an associate,' she told Dougie. 'It's... complicated.' She and Saint needed to leave straight away, but she also didn't want them to report her to the police. Putting the fear of God into the couple may be the easiest option. 'Dougie, listen to me, you can't tell anyone we were here. Saint's dangerous, unpredictable, and if you do, he may come back.'

Roberta sobbed. 'He's a criminal?'

'Worse than that, Roberta.' Elsa looked over to where Saint was still fighting with his trousers. 'He's a psychopath with a vengeful personality disorder, and if he believes you've betrayed him, he'll come back and kill you both. Do you understand?'

Eyes bulging in terror, Dougie nodded.

'Tell you what, to make things better...' She'd add a bit of sugar to the pill. 'I'm in a bit of a fix right now, but what about we pick up the personal training sessions again soon? I'll throw in a couple of free workouts, a diet programme, how does that sound?' When Dougie and Roberta stared, she added, 'And I'll help you clear up.'

'Please,' Roberta said in a stricken whisper. 'Just go.'

Elsa didn't need telling twice, and said to Saint, who was still half dressed, 'Come on.'

But when they got to the front door, she stopped. A blue light flashed behind the stained glass; she heard the burble of a police radio.

She pulled Saint back into the living room. 'The police are here.'

'Go out the back,' Roberta said in a shrill voice. 'Just get out!'

But Elsa didn't trust Dougie's wife not to run screaming out the front as soon as they did. There was a door in the kitchen that led to a small utility room, where a freezer, washing machine and dishwasher were plumbed in. She pushed Saint inside, and grabbed Roberta. 'In here.'

'I'm not going in there with him!'

'I promise he won't hurt you.' All the energy had drained from Saint, who leaned heavily against a counter, his head dropped to his chest. 'And if you don't get inside and keep quiet, I'll kill you myself.'

Saint's shaggy head lifted and, opening one eye, he put a finger to his chapped lips, *Sssshhhhh*.

Elsa threw in the dressing-gown cords Saint had used to tie Roberta and Dougie to the chairs and slammed the door shut. The last thing she heard Saint say to Roberta was, 'You've got a very nice house.'

The doorbell rang.

The room was still a complete mess. There was nothing they could do about that now.

Standing at the front door, Dougie sweated with fear.

'We're man and wife,' Elsa said. 'Got it?'

Dougie's eyes lit up. He attempted to take her hand, but she shook him off. When he opened the door, two police officers – a man and a woman – stood looking at them enquiringly.

'How are you folks doing?' asked the male officer.

'Fine, thanks,' Dougie said with unconvincing jollity.

The woman officer frowned. 'Everything okay, sir?'

'Hunky-dory, officer.' Dougie's voice trembled. 'Bit late for a house call, isn't it?'

The male officer stepped forward. 'One of your neighbours heard screaming coming from the house.'

'I'm sorry about that. Roberta and I,' said Dougie, 'were having a… sex game.'

'An argument,' said Elsa quickly.

Dougie put his arm around her and pulled her close, his fingers roaming too far down the curve of her lower spine for her liking. 'But we're fine now, you know what they say…' He winked. 'The best part of an argument is always the making up.'

Elsa kept a smile plastered on her face. The male officer looked at her hoodie and leggings, her dirty trainers, and at the suitcases Dougie and Roberta had wheeled inside when they arrived home.

'Are you going somewhere, sir?'

'Just back from holiday, in fact,' said Dougie. 'We had a lovely time, but we're both a bit frazzled.'

The woman officer's radio burbled on her shoulder and she leaned into it. 'Just checking now, control.'

'If there's something either of you can't tell us…' The male officer lowered his voice. 'Just nod your head.'

Dougie and Elsa both frowned in confusion.

'If there's someone in the house,' said the officer softly. 'If you're being held against your will.'

'There's no one,' Elsa said. 'It's just us.'

The officers gave each other a sceptical glance. 'May we come in?'

'I'm afraid that's not going to be possible,' said Elsa. 'We were just going to bed.'

Dougie looked at her eagerly.

'Just to take a look round, reassure ourselves you're okay,' said the woman officer. 'It won't take a moment.'

'Come in, then.' When Dougie stepped aside, Elsa could have killed him. The two police officers walked past them into the kitchen, where it opened out into the large living room, and looked doubtfully at the mess.

'Had a party before we went away,' said Elsa quickly. 'We'll clear up in the morning.'

The female officer looked at the knife, placed on the counter, that Saint had used to threaten Dougie and Roberta.

'Just about to make a late-night snack,' Elsa explained, walking past her towards the male officer.

He smiled at her pleasantly, but beneath the bright kitchen spotlights her gaze lifted to his cap – she tensed.

The officer's smile vanished.

Dougie screamed. Elsa saw the glint of the knife at the edge of her vision and ducked just as the woman officer stabbed it sideways towards her throat. Elsa grabbed her wrist as it passed above her head, and twisted viciously.

'Стрелять!' the woman shouted, as she and Elsa spun around the kitchen, both grappling to control the knife twirling above their heads. But the ballistic vest the woman wore wasn't enough to stop the bullets fired at point-blank range by the man when Elsa used her as a human shield.

The knife clattered to the floor, followed by the woman, and Elsa flew at the other officer, grabbing his gun hand and propelling him backwards into the living room and over the back of one of the sofas.

His finger trapped against the trigger by her grip, the handgun went off again, making the blinds jump and cracking the glass in the sliding door, as they rolled across the carpet, their torsos coming to rest at a diagonal beneath a low glass coffee table.

Trapped beneath the heavy glass, Elsa's head loomed close to his snarling face as she tried to wrench the gun out of his hands, but the man was strong and she was exhausted. It was only the last of her ebbing strength that kept him from pointing the barrel directly into her face. He thrust his arms up, and with a cry of rage lifted her body, smashing her head and shoulders against the underside of the table, trying to knock her cold.

'Убью тебя!' He jerked her up into the glass again, making the heavy table lurch above them, and giving him enough space to twist the gun towards her head.

She tried to stop it, straining every muscle, but she was trapped. The barrel trembled close to her ear, edging ever closer towards her temple and forehead.

'Отстань от меня!' Elsa hissed, banging her own head and shoulders against the glass now, trying to heave the heavy table off, to find space to move. 'Saint! Help me!'

As she crushed her thumbs over the man's fingers, the gun went off next to her head. The blast was deafening. Her ear shrieked, the sound like a nuclear detonation inside her skull. The world shimmered in her vision, a riot of shape and noise.

She should be dead, but she wasn't; didn't understand why the assassin hadn't taken advantage of her agony. When her eyes began to clear, she saw him blinking furiously and thrashing his head. Thick chunks of glass had fallen onto the back of her head, but also into the assassin's face. A sharp wedge of glass was embedded in the corner of his right eye.

'Saint,' Elsa shouted again, or thought she did, because she couldn't hear her own voice, only the scream of a thousand car alarms.

The man heaved her over so that she lay trapped on the blanket of broken glass beneath him, blood dripping from his face onto hers, using his brute strength to turn the gun towards her again. Elsa resisted, the gun shaking in both their hands, but it came closer. Then he yanked it from her grip and hit it hard into the side of her head, and her perforated eardrum.

Now she'd lost her grip on the weapon, he'd blow her brains out – where the hell was Saint when she needed him? She slammed the heel of her palm into his right eye, hammering the shard of glass deeper. He shuddered as she rotated her thumb, mashing the glass into his eyeball.

It was the assassin's turn to roar in pain and Elsa used that split second of opportunity to flip him over, so that he faced away towards the ceiling. She snapped open her thighs, clamping her adductors around his waist, and squeezed hard. Trapping his gun arm, pulling him tightly to her.

Hunching below him, she locked a forearm around his neck and pulled the wrist with her other hand. Squeezed with all her strength. Unable to hear a thing except for that piercing wail in her head, she strained every muscle, letting all her rage and pain fuel her effort.

The man struggled in her grip, legs thrashing against the floor, his one free hand plucking uselessly at her forearm. Within a minute he lost consciousness, and within two he was dead.

Elsa rolled the guy's body off her and staggered to her feet. She cupped her wailing ear, trying to hear anything. In the corner of the room Dougie was shouting soundlessly, throwing his arms around and pointing at the door. She tensed, expecting more intruders, but realized he was telling her to get out.

Elsa stumbled to the utility room and opened the door. A terrified Roberta peered at her from one corner. Saint was curled up asleep on the counter.

'Saint, get up.' Her own voice sounded like it came from the end of a long tunnel full of noisy machinery. 'We have to go.'

She had introduced carnage into Dougie and Roberta's home. If she stayed any longer, more would follow. As she pulled Saint across his kitchen, Dougie stared in shock at the dead people dressed as police.

'Nothing will happen to you,' Elsa said, conscious that she was shouting. There was no keeping this a secret now. 'Just… tell the police the truth.'

She could hear what he said. 'Who are they?'

'Russian, I think.'

Practically every security agency on the planet was after her, so it was hardly surprising that the SVR, GRU, or whatever state agency employed this pair, had turned up.

'How…' Dougie gawped. 'How did you know?'

Elsa picked up the woman's cap where it had fallen beside the kitchen island.

'The badges on their caps are wrong. Look, they've got the Essex Police crest on it. They should be Metropolitan Police officers.'

When Roberta saw the bodies on the floor and screamed all over again, Elsa left quickly.

28

Elsa called Camille on the phone she'd been given as she pushed Saint through the empty streets.

'We said six,' said Camille in surprise.

'Unexpected visitors. What did you find on the images I took from the computer?'

'I'll tell you when I see you.' Camille directed them to a nearby park. 'Sit tight, and I'll come as soon as I can.'

They headed there, trying to stay out of sight of CCTV cameras atop streetlamps and on shopfronts, and the proliferation of doorbell video cameras that could identify their location. There were probably satellites searching the urban sprawl for her as they moved above the earth in silent low orbit – Elsa didn't know how sophisticated they were, or what kind of image they could pick up at night – but there was nothing she could do about that.

Sirens wailed in the distance, just about discernible among all the other howling sounds assaulting her damaged eardrum, which hurt like hell. The police would already be at Dougie's house. He would be telling incredulous officers what had happened, Roberta would be crying, and someone would be calling SIS about the two dead Russians. Spooks were probably already piling into a car.

The park was a small square of green surrounded by tall

buildings. Saint collapsed on one of the benches, stretching along the length of it. Wrapping her arms around her chest, Elsa tried to make herself comfortable on the other bench, but it was chilly. Her feet were still damp, as were her bum and the backs of her thighs in the thin fabric of her leggings. Saint was awake and looking at something, a piece of paper that had been folded and unfolded so many times it was almost falling apart; the edge of one quarter was shiny with ancient sticky tape.

'What's that?' she asked, and he handed it to her.

It was a faded image of a clapboard shack beside a white beach, a sea of azure blue; his dream home she remembered seeing as they flew into Buenos Aires. Despite everything that had happened to him, he still carried it all these years later.

'Found it yet?' she asked him.

'Don't look likely now,' he said, closing his eyes.

'You'll get there one day. You'll walk down that beach, feel the sand between your toes and lift your head to the sun.'

He blew out his lips. 'I'll be dead first. Ain't no way out for people like us, Elsie. We think we can leave the life behind any time, but we can't. If I ever do get to walk on that beach, all I'll be able to think about is all the bad things I did to get there. It may be paradise, but it'll be the same old hell in my head.

'People like me and you, our lives ain't never going to be all pensions and slippers, quiet days in front of a roaring fire. We're made to be knocked down like skittles. The good ones like you – and me, back in the day – just keep getting up. We keep going, we walk through walls and along the seabed and over mountains, we just keep fighting. We *think* we can let it go, the life, but all we're wired to do is keep fighting. And as soon as we stop, the nightmares start, so we may as well just keep going. Fighting and falling down and getting up again, on and on.'

Elsa flapped her arms, trying to keep warm. She had a home now, a job and a family. 'That's not me any more.'

'Yeah?' His puffy eyes were two pinpricks of light. 'How's that working out for you?'

And, of course, he was right, because the so-called normal life Elsa had magicked out of the air for herself was over, probably for good. All these years later, people still hated her enough to want to kill her, and the only way out of the situation she found herself in was to accelerate into the centre of the shitstorm.

She'd spent much of her life doing the bidding of invisible masters, turning a blind eye to the motives of whatever side RedQueen was working for, and this was where she'd ended up… everyone wanted her dead. And she still had no idea whether it was because she was one of the good guys, or one of the bad.

She held the image of the shack on the beach delicately; she didn't want to be the person who caused it finally to fall to bits.

But Saint shook his head. 'Bin it, I don't want it.'

'Don't be ridiculous.' She folded the paper with meticulous care, as if defusing an unexploded bomb, and placed it in the breast pocket of his puffer jacket. 'When this is over, we'll find your beach.'

A vehicle came slowly around the edge of the park, and its headlights flashed twice.

'She's here,' Elsa said. 'Let's go.'

Saint swung his legs off the bench and shuffled behind her to the car. This time, Camille was driving. Elsa climbed in beside her, and Saint collapsed in the back.

'All right, Camille?' he said, as if he'd last seen her yesterday, and she nodded warily in return, then glanced at Elsa, *the state of him*.

His eyes closed immediately; Elsa had no idea if he was awake or not.

'What's happening?' she asked Camille. 'What did you find on the computer?'

'There's been a change of plan; we're getting you out of here.'

'A change of plan?' Elsa couldn't believe her ears; not that her ears were currently much use. 'What are you talking about?'

'There was nothing in the file we pulled from the vault, no data, no information, so a decision has been made—'

Elsa held up a hand. 'Wait a minute.'

'A *decision* has been made,' Camille told her forcefully, 'to get you out of the country. Somewhere you and your kids will be safe.'

'The only way I'll ever be safe is by finding out what's happening to me.'

'And how long do you think you'll last, racing around trying to put the pieces together? A day, a week? Even if we did have a lead, which we don't, you'll be placing yourself in danger.' Camille didn't take her eyes from the road. 'I'm sorry.'

'And what if I don't want to go?' snapped Elsa.

'Then you're on your own, RedQueen can't help you

any more. If we're found to be harbouring a fugitive, the consequences could be dangerous for every single contractor or freelance we've used.'

'Then let me out,' Elsa snapped. The side of her head throbbed badly. 'Drop me off and I'll do it alone.'

'You're being reckless and unreasonable. Think of your kids!'

Elsa was shocked into silence. Camille had used the one line of attack she had no answer for. She was right, their safety was the most important thing.

Camille sighed and asked gently, 'What happened at the house?'

'Assassins happened.'

'Jesus.' Camille looked at her more closely as she drove. 'You okay?'

'I'll live.'

'It just proves there's nowhere in London we can keep you safe. You must understand the reality of the situation.'

A sudden fierce pain flared in Elsa's eardrum and she lifted a hand to the side of her head.

'You had a lucky escape from the Russians tonight,' continued Camille. 'But tomorrow it could be Mossad, the Bundesnachrichtendienst, or the Ministry of State Security.'

Elsa wanted to cry. Her children's lives were ruined, she was a dead woman walking, and she still had no idea why. 'You survived that mission, Saint survived, so why am I being targeted?'

Camille shook her head. 'I don't know, but you're the only one of us who went into that apartment.'

'SIS interrogated me about that. I was questioned about it time and again. There was a hard drive with a pulsing blue light. We blew it up, Steve was killed, I was nearly killed. That's it, end of story. I'm not suffering from any kind of amnesia, Cam, there's nothing I can't remember about that mission.'

Elsa didn't know where she was, the streets were dark and empty; she was disorientated; they could be heading anywhere.

'Look,' Camille said. 'The plan is to get you out of the country until we can work out what's going on. We're already reaching out to various agencies, I promise you wheels are in motion, and we're confident we can get to the bottom of whatever's going on, find a way out of this mess. In the meantime, we really don't want you getting killed, or God forbid your children harmed. We have a plane ready. You'll be out of the country within the hour, somewhere safe by the crack of dawn. Nobody will know where, not even me.'

'India and Harley...'

'Contact your parents as soon as you're in the air; we'll pick up the kids and arrange for them to join you.' Camille pulled the car to the kerb on a nondescript street and put it into park.

'What's happening?' Elsa asked.

'I can't come with you to the jet, there's too much going on here.'

In the side mirror, Elsa saw a Discovery come up the street behind them, roll past and stop fifty yards ahead. Elsa turned to look at Saint, still asleep in the back.

'What about him?'

'Take him with you, or leave him here. Your choice.'

'He's no good to me,' Elsa told her. 'Not where I'm going, wherever that is.'

'I'll get the guys to dump him somewhere on the way,' Camille said. 'He'll be fine, he's not a target.'

Elsa didn't like running away, it felt like failure, but she couldn't for the life of her work out what else she could do next.

'Where am I going?'

Camille reached over and squeezed her hand. 'Honestly, I don't know, and it's for the best that I don't. It'll be somewhere safe and secure. As soon as the people upstairs find out what's happening, and work out how to solve this situation, we'll bring you back. Everyone at RedQueen is working as hard as they can to open up channels.'

Elsa reached over and hugged her former friend, who reciprocated warmly, despite everything she knew about Elsa and Carragher's relationship. 'I'm sorry again for—'

Camille gently pushed her away so that she could look into her eyes.

'Water under the bridge. The main thing is to make sure you're safe.'

'Thanks for saving my life – that's twice now.'

'There won't be a third time,' Camille said with a smile. 'Goodbye, Elsa.'

Elsa reached over and slapped Saint on the knee.

His eyes snapped open and he sat up sharply. 'Whassup!'

'Come on.' Elsa opened the passenger door. 'We've got a new ride.'

29

Sitting in the back of the Discovery, Elsa couldn't believe that it had ended like this. She was fleeing, and whatever happened next, wherever in the world they hid her away, she would always have to look over her shoulder.

Her supposed crime, whatever it was she was alleged to have seen or done, may be corrected at some point in the future, or it may not. All of that would be out of her hands.

RedQueen had numerous secure facilities around the world, and Camille may have hinted at an endless vacation on a faraway beach of pristine white sand, or a mountain log cabin overlooking a lush forest where she could meditate and learn to whittle wood figures, but Elsa knew better.

She and her kids were more likely to go into hiding in a breeze-block compound in Sierra Leone, surrounded by mercenaries, or bake to death in an underground bunker. She'd be there for weeks, months, most probably years – if she ever came home at all. It may be impossible for RedQueen to even exonerate her; for all Elsa knew, she was in actual fact guilty of whatever she was accused of.

Even if she did return, her former employer would expect to be reimbursed for the effort and resources it had pumped into clearing her name by putting her to work all over again;

to carry out deep cover missions, incursions, extractions; to once again cause merry hell across the world. Maybe Saint was right, she'd been foolish to believe she could ever escape the life. Nine years was as good as it got.

But Elsa couldn't let her children be robbed of their childhood, she would never forgive herself for that. Whatever happened to her, she had to ensure they lived as normal a life as possible, even if that meant she'd never be able to see them again. She felt a sharp ache in her solar plexus at the thought of it.

Saint was slumped beside her, seemingly asleep again. In the close confines of the car the stink of him was overpowering, and she saw the guy in the passenger seat crank up the air conditioning. Neither he nor the driver had bothered to turn when Elsa and Saint climbed in, and their faces were mostly hidden in shadow as they drove.

'You're going to dump me somewhere, yeah?' grunted Saint.

She thought he'd been asleep during her conversation with Camille in the other car.

'You'll be all right, Saint, they're not trying to kill you. I'll arrange money for you, get you back on your feet. We'll get you into rehab. Maybe there'll be enough for you to find that beach home.'

He grunted. 'I'm no good to you.'

'I didn't mean it like that. I've a lot to think about.'

'You're running away,' he said.

'What am I supposed to do?' She turned to him in anger. 'How am I supposed to take on the entire world if I don't even know what I'm fighting for? They didn't find anything on that computer in the dead vault.'

'I heard what she said. Seems to me I heard more than you.'

His red, puffy eyes glinted at her.

'What?' she asked.

'Come on, Elsie. You're losing your touch, love.'

She pointed at her bad ear. 'I could barely hear a thing she said.'

His eyes shifted to the men in the front and he hooked a finger for her to come closer. 'When you told her about the assassins at the house, she said they were Russians.' He made a sad face, as if embarrassed to be the bearer of bad news. 'How did she know?'

Elsa leaned forward between the seats and eyed the GPS, which was blank.

'Which airstrip are we going to?' she asked the men in front.

'I'm sorry, miss.' The guy in the passenger seat didn't turn. 'We're not authorized to tell you that.'

'What's the big secret if you're taking us there anyway?'

He turned finally and gave her a big smile, like an amiable tour guide. 'We'll be there soon enough, I promise.'

'Hey.' Saint prodded the touchscreen on the back of the passenger seat. 'We can play Minecraft.'

Elsa couldn't work out where they were, but if she had to guess they were in or around Putney, heading south. Heathrow was not too far away, but they were hardly going to march her through the crowds there to put her on a plane.

'We'll get out here,' she told the men, and elbowed Saint to get ready. 'Pull over.'

'Our instructions are to make sure you get on a flight.'

'Where?' she asked him again. 'Where are we heading?'

The grey-haired man in the passenger seat looked apologetic. 'Please, Miss Zero, we're just here to take you to the air—'

'Don't engage with her,' the driver told him.

'Charming.' Saint leaned forward, but the grey-haired man's hand lifted over the edge of the seat, to reveal a handgun with a suppressor attached.

'Woah!' Saint lifted his hands. 'Over-reaction!'

The car accelerated. They were definitely in Putney, because Elsa could see the bridge ahead. God knows where they were being taken. Somewhere quiet and out of town.

'They're going to kill us,' she told Saint.

'For fuck's sake.' He scowled. 'What a shitty day.'

The man in the passenger seat readjusted his position to keep the gun on them both, resting his wrist beside the headrest to steady his aim.

'Do you trust me?' Saint asked her, staring with aggressive intent at the guy.

'No, I definitely don't,' Elsa said. 'Let me handle this.'

She'd almost had her head blown off earlier, her ear still throbbed badly, and this gun, a SIG P320, was nearly as close to her face as the previous one had been. The guy in the front couldn't miss.

'I don't feel…' Saint spoke with such feeling that the man jerked the gun in his direction. '…that you're treating me with the respect I deserve. It wasn't just Camille who saved your life in Buenos Aires, Elsie, I did too, and I say we can take him!'

'Not now.' Elsa watched the man tensely.

'We can kill him in a heartbeat,' Saint said. 'Take him by surprise.'

'He can hear every word you're saying, Saint. I think the element of surprise has long gone.'

'I'm going to grab him and rip his head off.' Saint asked the man, 'You didn't hear me say that, did you?'

The man with the gun watched them both carefully. 'Shut up!'

'No.' Saint narrowed his eyes. 'I don't think he heard.'

Elsa watched the man. 'Let me do it.'

Saint leaned towards the window, putting the back of the passenger seat between him and the man. 'Better be quick then.'

The man's gun jerked back in Saint's direction, just as the car sped onto Putney Bridge. And when Elsa edged further from Saint, opening up the space between them, the gun whipped back to her.

'Do. Not. Move!' commanded the grey-haired man.

'Rude!' Saint reached suddenly between the two rods of the passenger headrest and grabbed the guy's wrist, pulling hard so that the gun was forced against the rest just as he pulled the trigger. When the gun went off, the driver's head slammed against the side window in an explosion of blood and bone. His foot jerked, heel first, as the car picked up speed.

Elsa fumbled with her seat belt, trying to get more space to take out the man in the passenger seat, but the vehicle was already veering across the bridge, pulling her into the middle of the back seat. It whipped suddenly to the right when the driver's body slumped across the wheel, into the path of an approaching car at high speed, and onto the pavement. It hit the wall, crashing through it.

Elsa and Saint were thrown forward as the Discovery plummeted towards the Thames.

Elsa's head snapped back – and everything began to slow. The vehicle hit the water, throwing the three survivors in the car against their seat belts. The airbags in the car went off. The windscreen blistered as water crashed against the bonnet and over the roof. Elsa felt the vehicle plunge beneath the river and lift back to the surface in a violent ride, then begin to spin, as it was carried along in the fast-flowing tide in the centre of the river.

Turning her head was painful, but she saw the man in front was unconscious against his airbag. Beside her, Saint's head lolled on his chest. For the second time that night her feet were numb with cold, from the freezing river water that eagerly found a way into the car through fissures and bubbled up from the floor, gushing around her ankles.

The brown murk of the Thames heaved with furious intent against the windows, the heavy mass of it slapping and punching against the fractured windscreen, which was going to give way any second. As soon as it did, the water would pour in and the Land Rover, swept along in the powerful undertow of the river, would sink like a stone.

'Saint!' Elsa released her seat belt and fumbled with his. There was a gash on his temple and his head rolled on his shoulders. He was groaning, at least. 'We have to get out!'

Water was coming into the compartment on all sides. The windscreen shifted ominously under the pounding pressure of the river.

'We have to get—'

And then she heard a faint pop; the windscreen slid from sight and freezing water filled the interior. It poured around her legs and lap, the shock of cold sending her body into crisis, numbing her skin and nerves. The water was so icy Elsa couldn't breathe, and she struggled to stay calm. If she panicked and began to hyperventilate, her body's system would soon shut down.

The front of the car tipped as it dropped. Water frothing at her chest and shoulders, Elsa put her foot to the fractured window in the door beside Saint and kicked. The punishing cold made her ear shriek.

Saint spluttered into life, and Elsa lifted his jaw out of the water swirling around his face, gesturing for him to take a breath in the dwindling pocket of air just below the roof of the car. Dragged down by the fierce current, the vehicle was spiralling into the depths of the river, the still functioning headlight beams cutting through the black water.

Saint thrashed about beside her. The layers of clothing he wore would make it harder for him to swim. Elsa was about to help him climb out of the window when she fell back against the seat. Her face was so numb it took her a moment to realize she had been struck. The man in the passenger seat was climbing between the seats to get to her. He hit her again, she saw his fist in the surge of gushing water, and she was forced underwater, choking on freezing cold. She thought she was going to drown and in a panic arched her back to kiss the roof, gasping for breath in the final, vanishing pocket of air. It would be the last chance she got.

When she submerged again, the man grabbed her, pulling

her down beneath him. His hands went around her throat; he would force the last of her breath out of her and she would drown.

But the man's movements were as sluggish and jerky as hers. Thrashing about, he lifted his own head to the roof. Something hit Elsa's thigh as it flew around in the water. A headrest had been forced off one of the front seats.

Elsa's chest felt like it was going to explode; she couldn't hold her breath for much longer. Her thoughts began to cloud. She didn't know if that pocket of air was still above her, and couldn't reach it anyway.

Sticking out a hand, she instinctively grabbed the headrest when it swirled in front of her again and tried to use it to club the man's head. It glanced off, but she knew he was struggling, even if his hands were still around her neck.

Summoning her last remaining strength, she drove the struts on either side of his head into the back of the driver's seat, using it as a collar to pin him there by the neck. He clawed at the headrest, thrashing in panic, but Elsa lifted herself in the water to kick it against his throat. The man's mouth was jerked opened. In the seconds before he drowned, his eyes rolled up in his head.

Elsa moved towards the black window, a pulsing calm spreading over her. She wanted to stop resisting, stop moving, let the river take her in its icy grip. She yearned to sleep, but knew she couldn't. Slipping out of the car, she used all her last reserves of strength to keep moving away from the dark vehicle and towards a faint undulating light, and not succumb to the stupefying tiredness. She felt herself drift, barely knowing if she was using her limbs at all.

And then she broke the surface of the river. Gasping for air, choking on water. Felt herself go under again and thrashed in a panic. She let out a stricken, noisy cry, and breathed in the numbingly cold night in great, heaving gasps, again and again and again.

'Saint!' she called in a strangled voice when she was finally able to. 'Saint!'

Turning in the choppy water, there was no sign of him, just the river slapping around her face in every direction beneath the moonlight. Shaking from cold and exhaustion, she swam to a slipway she saw nearby, and scrambled out of the water, heaving and spluttering, coughing up water, crawling on her hands and knees as far up the incline as she could, to fall in a shivering heap.

Elsa lay on the slipway, shaking violently, retching with nausea. Teeth chattering, bones icy with cold, body heat steaming off her.

All she did was concentrate on breathing in and out, try to work out if all her organs still functioned. After a few minutes she heard sirens. Lifting her head, she saw figures peering into the water from the top of the bridge, which looked far away. The car had been pulled a long way on the current.

'You took your time,' said a voice.

Saint was lying a foot or so above her on the rough concrete. Of course he was; the guy was indestructible. Elsa laughed, barely a juddering vibration between her chattering teeth.

'I thought they were on our side.'

'Something's changed,' she said. 'RedQueen doesn't need us any more.'

Saint's voice was a garbled quiver. 'What's happened?'

Elsa climbed to her feet. She was freezing, shaking. Her skin was blue, her clothes sodden. 'That's what we have to find out.'

30

Nine years earlier

Camille Archard phoned the home number of the evening receptionist at the target building, claiming to be from the management company that owned it. Speaking in Spanish, she informed her that emergency repairs were due to be carried out that evening, and she shouldn't come into work.

Then Antovic sent a message from the evening receptionist's hacked home mail account to her daytime counterpart, apologizing that she would be ten minutes late to work because of a doctor's appointment, and to go home as usual. It was as simple as that.

As the red sky darkened into dusk, the day receptionist left to catch her usual *colectivo*, the bus home. Dressed as the evening receptionist, in the dark suit jacket, red blouse and black tights she most often wore, her blonde hair hidden beneath an auburn wig, Camille arrived moments later from the opposite direction. Careful to keep her face partially hidden from the camera above, she pressed the entry code at the entrance and the door opened with a harsh buzz.

Beneath the watchful eye of a ceiling camera, she did what the evening receptionist often did before she walked behind the mahogany desk, and pulled her fingers down the long, rigid leaves of a yucca plant in a giant pot inside the door, to check none had come loose.

Then she went behind the desk, moving all the items on it into a particular pleasing pattern, the same way the evening receptionist did at the start of every shift. In the small office behind reception, she boiled the kettle to make a mug of herbal tea. Taking a coaster from a drawer, she placed it on the desk in a particular place.

Then she opened a laptop of the same make, and with the same stickers affixed to the front – the logo of a popular telenovela, Hello Kitty, a cartoon llama – the evening receptionist always brought with her to work. But unlike the usual receptionist, who used the quiet twilight hours to write a steamy romantic novel, Camille used it to hijack the encrypted feed of the security cameras.

'Hola!' she said cheerily to an elderly resident who came in the door, but didn't look up from the keyboard.

Nine minutes later, with a final press of the return button, the numerous cameras inside the building – as well as the ones outside – began to show unremarkable footage recorded at the exact same time – 6:22:56 and counting – from two days ago. If anyone inside the target apartment had also hacked the building's camera feeds for their own security purposes, they would see on their own screens the wannabe romantic novelist standing at the desk with her face bowed to the laptop, a steaming mug of tea beside her, as she wrote of a handsome billionaire's forbidden lust for his pretty chiropodist.

'Synchronized,' Camille said softly into her scalp mic.

Then she let Elsa, Carragher and Antovic into reception. The camera on the opposite side of the street also showed footage from forty-eight hours ago in its live feed, and they stayed close to the wall to ensure they couldn't be seen from the apartments above when they walked around the front of the building.

In the rear office, they opened their bags and kitted up. Put on Kevlar vests and tactical belts, equipped HK416 carbines and ammunition, tanto blades, flash grenades. Carragher checked the final bag, which contained a brick of C4 to blow the contents of the vault in Apartment 7b.

'Saint?' asked Carragher. 'What's our status?'

On the roof of the seven-storey building opposite, lying flat on the hot tarmac, Saint used Steiner tactical binoculars to watch the streets surrounding the building. Whipping his focus to the blocks east and west, he listened to the bustling noise of the city: distant sirens, the throb of traffic, music drifting across Recoleta. 'All clear.'

'Klimt?' Carragher asked the driver, who sat in a van a couple of streets away.

'Ready,' came the terse response.

Seven minutes later, and exactly on time, a car pulled up outside and two men got out: part of the security changeover for Apartment 7b. The two middle-aged men in rumpled suits, one dark-haired, the other with sandy highlights, arrived at exactly the same time every evening. They buzzed to be let into reception.

'Hola!' said Camille with a cheery smile when they came inside. If they saw the receptionist was someone different, they didn't have an opportunity to do anything. The door had barely closed behind them before Antovic shot the dark-haired one in the back of the head, using a Ruger Mk IV with a suppressor.

Before the dead man even toppled into Antovic's arms, Elsa and Carragher appeared from the shadows to train their weapons on Sandy Highlights. Camille and Antovic dragged the dead man into the rear office. Elsa pushed his colleague up the stairs. Carragher followed, carrying the bag of explosives.

'If you don't say exactly, *exactly*, what's expected of you at the door, I'll kill you, do you understand?'

'Sí,' the man replied through gritted teeth.

Elsa and Carragher reached Apartment 7b on the second floor. Carragher placed the bag against the wall, and they both readied their carbines.

There was no surveillance apparatus outside the apartment door, the security team inside was using the building's own network of cameras, which meant they would have seen Dark and Sandy walking up the stairs together, laughing and chatting, just as they had forty-eight hours ago.

Sandy was about to press the doorbell when Carragher saw that they were several seconds too early – their movements had to synchronize exactly with the timestamp on the footage from two days ago. He pressed the barrel of the carbine into the back of Sandy's neck, told him quietly, 'Espere.'

The man's finger trembled at the bell. Carragher checked his watch, waiting for the exact moment. In four seconds. In three. In two, one…

His watch vibrated faintly against his wrist.

'Now,' Carragher said, and the man pressed the doorbell: the ring was loud and shrill.

'What's the weather like this evening?' said a voice from the other side.

The man's mouth snapped open, but if he intended to scream a warning to the men inside, the gun barrel pressed against his lower spine made him think again.

'Intemperate, to say the least.' The man gave the second part of the code phrase. 'But at least it isn't snowing.'

Carragher glanced at Elsa, the ghost of a smile on his face.

Adrenaline rushed around her bloodstream; her heart thumped in her chest, blood surged into muscles; hormones released around her body, increasing focus and concentration; her nervous system spiked, her breathing accelerated.

She lifted the HK416 at the door.

The first lock on the door *snapped* loudly in the quiet hallway.

Elsa made an adjustment to the grip on her weapon.

A second lock *clicked*.

She made a minor adjustment to her balance, ready to move.

And then, the final *scrape* of a chain swinging against painted wood…

The door began to open.

And then everything happened at rapid speed—

Sandy began to shout a warning, but Carragher kicked the man hard, shooting him in the back as he lurched forward. He was already dead when his body slammed into the door, forcing it open. Standing compactly, legs and arms bent to accommodate the recoil of the rifle, Carragher fired twice into the corridor ahead. Two men fell instantly. Another man appeared from a door on the right, and Elsa shot him.

And then they went inside. Covering each side, moving down the corridor quickly, Carragher slightly ahead. Weapons raised, anticipating every door to the left and right, as they had trained to do.

One guy came out of a room directly in front of Elsa and she fired at his chest; he spun, hit the wall and dropped. Carragher kicked open a door on the right, moving inside, staying low. It was empty.

Two men burst from behind a door, letting off short, panicked bursts of gunfire, but aiming too high. Elsa fired, two short bursts; felt the weapon heating up in her hands. Their bodies flew against the wall, blood smearing down the plaster as they slumped to the floor.

Carragher dropped to one knee and aimed when another guy appeared at the far end of the corridor, firing wildly. The man was killed instantly.

Elsa and Carragher entered every room, weapons sweeping in a fluid motion, aiming into every corner. As they approached the door to an en suite, the wood splintered angrily as someone sprayed it with automatic gunfire from the other side; they heard his frenzied shouts of panic. The shots stopped when the man fumbled with a new magazine. Carragher put his foot to the door – it gave way easily – and shot him in the head. The guy fell into an empty bath, bringing a plastic shower curtain down with him.

Stepping over the bodies in the corridor, Carragher said into his mic, 'We're in.'

Elsa stayed alert as he fetched the bag containing the C4 from the landing and brought it inside.

The living room was as massive as the one they had trained in. Like the rest of the apartment, it was furnished ornately, with expensive cabinets, recliners and tables. But there was an additional door in the far wall. When Carragher opened it, another door was revealed, one made of smooth steel.

'Are we going to blow it open?' Elsa asked. That would take time, and make a lot of noise.

He shook his head, then keyed in a code on a pad in the centre of the door. It was twelve characters long, and he didn't hesitate. Elsa heard bolts shunt open. She didn't know how Carragher had the code, but there was so much about the mission she didn't understand.

When the door opened, a small, brightly lit space the size of a wardrobe was revealed. She heard the hum of a cooling system. Inside the vault was a metal table, and placed on that was a rectangular box, the size and shape of a hard drive, with a band of blue light pulsing around the upper edge of it.

'That's it?' she asked. 'That's why we're here?'

Ignoring her, Carragher unzipped the bag and took out the brick of C4. Then he took out a remote detonator, tape, and wire.

'You're sure you've got enough there?' she asked, incredulous. She was no expert but it looked like far more explosive than they needed.

'Got to be sure,' he said tensely.

'Uh, we've got a problem,' Saint said in her ear. 'There are five vehicles, SUVs, moving towards us fast.'

'From which direction?' asked Carragher, without looking up from what he was doing.

'Let me see... every fucking direction.'

'Did everyone hear that?'

In a corner of the room was a table with a monitor on it showing the security feeds for the interior and exterior of the building – the footage from two days ago.

'How do they *know*?' asked Camille urgently.

They could have tripped security sensors, or there could be hidden cameras Carragher didn't know about, in the apartment, in reception, somewhere outside. One of the security men may have hit a panic alarm.

'They're going to be here in two minutes,' Saint said urgently in Elsa's ear.

'How many in the vehicles?' asked Carragher, placing the wireless detonator carefully in the C4.

'I don't know, the windows are tinted. But there are four carloads. We need to leave, guys, like, right now.'

'Stay in position,' Carragher told him irritably. 'Reception, what's your status?'

'Calm here,' said Camille, but there was a tension in her voice.

'I don't think you understand, *Steve*,' interrupted Saint. 'We're going to have company in less than—'

And then Saint's voice cut out.

'Roof, we've lost you,' Elsa said quickly. 'Saint? Camille?'

She couldn't hear Camille or Antovic in reception; Klimt's connection was also dead. Elsa's instincts were screaming. Carragher was in the doorway of the vault, attaching the explosives to the hard drive.

'We have to go,' she told him.

'A few more seconds…'

'We don't have—'

His attention snapped angrily to her. 'We finish what we came to do!'

Then she heard the screech of tyres. Going onto the balcony, she saw three SUVs pull up in front of the building;

men with assault rifles jumped out. She counted a dozen, at least – probably more. Another carload would be heading to the back of the building.

'Camille, Antovic,' Elsa said urgently into her mic, not knowing if anyone could hear her. 'Get out now!'

But she knew it was too late. If they hadn't escaped the building already, they'd be trapped.

Then gunfire started downstairs. Bursts of it drifting up to the second floor from the street as the men rushed towards the entrance. She heard Camille and Antovic return fire from inside. From the window, she saw one of the men fall in the street, and the others take cover behind the vehicles.

'We've got to go,' she shouted at Carragher. 'Right now!'

Carragher didn't turn from what he was doing. 'Just one more sec—'

'Now, Steve!' she told him.

Chips of stone flew off the balcony. Elsa ran inside and threw herself against the wall between the doors as glass and wood shattered on either side of her. She didn't know how they were going to get out, didn't have time to even consider how everything had gone wrong so quickly. Carragher hadn't done his homework properly, or the mission had been fatally compromised.

Carragher kept low as he came over with the detonator in his hand. More shots thwacked against the ceiling from below, sending plaster flying off the cornices. The remaining glass in the balcony windows smashed to the floor, as the gunmen shot up from the street.

They heard the crack of a rifle from high above, Saint returning fire from the roof of the building opposite. The bursts of automatic gunfire on a quiet street in the centre of the city would soon bring the police.

Elsa edged along the wall beside the shattered balcony door to look outside. Two men were face down in the street. More vehicles arrived and men poured out.

'We can jump from the balcony to another, try to get round the far side of the building, or head up the stairs to the roof.'

'Camille!' Carragher rushed towards the central corridor.

But heading downstairs was senseless. Camille and Antovic would be pinned down, maybe even dead already, or heading to the floors above. They had to climb higher, find another way to rendezvous with the van – and they had to do it now.

'Klimt,' she said into her throat mic. 'Are you there? We need you!'

There was a crackle in her earpiece and she heard Saint's faint voice, the thump of his footsteps, automatic gunfire buzzing like static – but it kept cutting out.

'—on – surrou – only chan—'

'Saint?' she shouted, watching Carragher moving steadily along the central corridor towards the closed front door of Apartment 7b, his carbine raised.

'Whatever you're thi—' Elsa heard Saint grunt, and a clang as he jumped across something metal. 'Get it do—'

'Saint, where's Klimt?'

'No id—' The connection stabilized for a moment and Elsa heard him crash through a door into a stairwell, his voice rebounding off the concrete walls, his steps echoing harshly – then cutting out – echoing. 'Heading to the van – stay safe.'

The connection dropped again.

'Bit late for that,' muttered Elsa angrily as she saw Carragher stop in the middle of the corridor. Something was happening outside the apartment.

He turned, raced back into the room and threw himself behind the wall, just as the front door blew off its hinges in a cloud of whirling smoke, and men poured inside.

31

As soon as he had delivered to Camille the data retrieved and decrypted from the photographs taken in the vault, Flex relaxed the only way he knew how, by playing GTA5 online. Screaming into his headset as he took part in heists, robberies, road racing, and made himself a pest on the streets of Los Santos. After a stressful evening, he was wired and on edge, and the only way to wind down was by taking out his anger on hapless NPCs and wolfing down junk food.

Gone five in the morning, and finally needing to sleep, he threw his controller down, telling the other players, 'Bye, losers.'

His home was a tiny flat in Soho, and as convenient as it was to live centrally, the area was full of drunken pillocks who fell out of the late-night bars and clubs at all hours. Flex was finally dropping off in a bedroom the size of a shoebox when he heard shouts from below.

'Flopsy, you up there?' someone was calling. 'Flopsy, mate, I need to talk to you.'

Growling in irritation, Flex covered his head with a pillow, but the voice was insistent.

'Computer guy!' called the man, and that got his

attention. In his T-shirt and underpants, his sagging belly undulating, Flex pulled up the window sash.

A homeless man stood in the street below, among the skeletal frames of the market stalls. There were a lot of people like that in Soho, beggars who followed the cash-rich tourists during the day and spent the night bundled in doorways. Sometimes Flex had to step over them to get to his own door, but they weren't usually such a nuisance.

'What are you doing?' he called down. 'People are trying to sleep!'

'Are you Flopsy?' the homeless guy called up, but then someone out of sight below corrected him. 'Wait… Not Flopsy? Are you Flex?'

He had a bad feeling about this. 'Who's asking?'

The man counted the windows to Flex's floor and told whoever was out of sight, 'He's on the third.' Then he waved. 'We'll be right up.'

'No, wait!'

Flex panicked. Nothing like this had ever happened before. He'd been assured by his employers he'd never be implicated in any wrongdoing, but that if he ever felt threatened he should call a certain number. He raced to find his phone in his small lounge-kitchen.

But he'd had a pizza delivered, and a lot of sides, which he'd scoffed as he played on the PS5, and all the open boxes were spread across the table; his mobile was somewhere under it all. He searched frantically for it, throwing the half-empty boxes into the air – food flew everywhere – but footsteps were approaching quickly up the communal stairs, and along the landing.

The guy downstairs didn't look like police, he looked like a thug sent to kill him. Flex thought of the numerous security breaches he'd been involved in, and his stomach churned. He should never have agreed to hack that camera-phone in Pyongyang! He imagined himself getting waterboarded.

He put on the latch just as someone banged on the door.

'We know you're in there, Simon slash Flex, let us in,' said a woman's voice.

Flex rushed back into the room, opened the window and looked down. Three flights up, he'd never survive the jump, and he was just wearing underpants.

Then the front door flew open – the flimsy chain was as good as useless – and Elsa Zero strode inside.

'Did we wake you?' she asked. The guy from the street came in behind her, closing the door, and his mad eyes immediately fixed on the sole remaining slice of stiffened pizza in the box.

'Are you going to eat that?' he asked.

Terrified, Flex shook his head, and the man folded the slice in two and stuffed it into his mouth, then turned his attention to the last of the garlic bread.

'I need to see what you got from the photos I took tonight.' Elsa added more gently, '*Flex*, I need to see it.'

'Can I use your shower?' The vagrant who had come in with her started taking off layers of clothes. A body-warmer, a puffer jacket, a hoodie. When they slapped to the floor, Flex realized they were soaking wet. She was wet through, too.

'We don't have time for that, Saint,' Elsa told him.

The man called Saint shrugged and headed towards the fridge.

'There was nothing on it,' said Flex.

'There must have been something, otherwise RedQueen wouldn't be trying to kill me all of a sudden.'

Flex gawped. 'I don't know anything about that! I just do computer stuff.'

'I know you do.' She picked up his laptop from a chair and gave it to him, then manoeuvred him by his shoulders to the table. 'So show me.'

'All that information will be on a secure RedQueen server,' he said. 'And protected.'

'Who uploaded it?' she asked.

'I did.'

'Then it shouldn't be much trouble to get to it again.'

'RedQueen will know it's me.'

'You can say we assaulted you. Tell them we threatened to break some of your fingers. We'll break two or three for you, if you want us to make it look realistic.'

Saint slammed the fridge door hard, making Flex jump. He started talking very quickly.

'We analysed the jumble of information you photographed on the screen, and there was hardly anything.' Flex tipped the remaining takeaway boxes onto the floor to make room for the laptop. 'I swear there was nothing about the mission itself, all those files had been deleted or moved at some point previously, maybe years ago. What you found was some kind of auxiliary file that had been left on the drive.' He glanced up at Elsa, who trembled in her damp clothes. 'There are towels, if you want.'

'Please, just get on with it.'

She leaned over his shoulder as he accessed the RedQueen server. Flex's fingers tapped fluidly across the keyboard, circumventing an endless cascade of log-in pages, as Saint put a pie into the microwave.

'Here, look.' Flex finally pointed at JPEG files of the photos she had taken in the vault. 'All that block text you saw, it was just a coded invoice, some kind of requisition order for medical equipment and staff.'

'The hospital facility Carragher set up in the petrochemical plant,' Elsa said to Saint, as he came over, stuffing his face with the pie. 'If it wasn't there, I'd have died. And what else?' she asked Flex.

'It's literally all there is.' He angled the laptop so she could see the data he had extracted from the blocks of text. There was a sequence of letters and numbers in one column, a list of equipment and supplies in another. For an oxygen tent and canisters, a defibrillator, mobile bed, drugs, utensils for surgery; other equipment Elsa couldn't identify.

At the bottom of the page were four names.

Elsa pointed. 'Who are these?'

'The people who worked there.'

She knew they would be military medics, pulled in from British stations in that hemisphere. Their involvement would be secondary and kept top secret. The requisitioned staff would have a strictly limited knowledge of the operation; their role was to provide medical attention to whoever came through the doors of the facility. Once their job was done, they would be flown back to their bases, and the temporary medical station dismantled.

Elsa read the names. Karen Naismith, Timothy Mabey, Nicole Tennant, Aisha Chen. She didn't remember any of these people; had spent most of her time at the facility unconscious.

The file wasn't exactly the bonanza of information she was hoping for. She couldn't see how it could unlock the mystery of what was happening to her. A British military field hospital set up on foreign soil was a classified secret, yes, but the information was at best peripheral to Pilot Fish. It told her nothing.

'It's hopeless!' In a fit of anger, she swiped a mug off the table. 'We keep coming up against one brick wall after another!'

'Sure, it all looks a load of garbage.' Saint wiped crumbs from his beard. 'But if there's one thing I know about you, Elsie, it's that you ain't no quitter.'

The only way out is into the heart of the storm.

This small, stupid pocket of information was all they had. She pointed at the names. 'How do we find these people?'

Flex yawned. 'Search me.'

She spun him round in his chair to face her, leaning so close that their noses almost touched. 'Last time I looked, *Simon*, you were a computer hacker, so get hacking!'

32

'There's something missing,' Tim Mabey told the Artex ceiling in his therapist's office.

Dr Turnham scratched at a stain on the fat end of his tie. 'Can you elaborate?'

Sitting in an armchair in the consulting room of his Pimlico house, the therapist glanced at a clock on the wall.

'I just feel like I'm always on the periphery of things.' Tim clasped his hands over his chest as he lay on a recliner. 'That somehow life has passed me by.'

'You've had an exciting life in many ways, haven't you?' Dr Turnham had heard it all before. 'You've seen the—'

He looked up sharply when he thought he heard a noise inside the house. He listened for a moment, didn't hear anything more, then continued.

'You've seen the world.'

'I've seen the world from behind the fences of various military bases, I suppose, but overall my life has been uneventful... sensible,' Tim said. 'I grew up in a loving, sensible home and fell in love with a kind, sensible woman, and I've got three sensible kids, who all go to good schools. The divorce was amicable and largely without conflict. I've a very sensible job as a doctor. I can't help but think another word for sensible is boring.'

'You were a medic in the RAF.' The therapist was still distracted. 'That must have had its moments of excitement?'

'There was the odd occasion that was exciting, but it was mostly dealing with sprains and—'

To the surprise of them both, the door opened and a woman walked in.

Turnham's notebook fell from his lap as he stood. 'Who are you, and what are you doing in my house?'

Ignoring him, Elsa spoke to the man on the couch. 'Tim Mabey?' Shocked, he nodded. 'Come with me.'

When Dr Turnham demanded, 'What's going on?', Tim held up his hands, *no idea!*

He followed her down the stairs and into the kitchen. Every time he came for his therapy session, Dr Turnham marched him directly from the front door to the consulting room, but the woman walked around like she owned the place.

'My name is Elsa Zero,' she said. 'You won't remember me.'

He stared. 'I dream about you sometimes.'

'Okay, so that's weird.' She gave him an uncomfortable look. 'Do you dream about the people you've operated on?'

'No.' He cleared his throat. 'Just you.'

She went on quickly, 'I need to ask you a few questions. You're a doctor in the RAF Medical Services, right?'

'Not any more.' He'd been in therapy for eighteen months, but didn't go around telling people where he was of a weekend. 'How on earth did you find me here?'

'It's not so hard to find out.' Elsa Zero started opening kitchen cupboards. 'Your diary is in the cloud.'

She found a glass and poured water from the tap, just as Dr Turnham came into the room.

'I don't know who you are.' He stood with his hands on his hips. 'But I demand you leave this instant.'

'I'll be gone in a minute.' She sipped water. 'When I've asked Tim a few questions.'

'You'll go right now.'

She gave him a fierce look. 'Two minutes.'

Dr Turnham whipped a phone out of its cradle on a counter. 'I'm calling the police.'

'Come on, let's get out of here, I know a place nearby we can talk.' Tim smiled at the therapist. 'Same time next week?'

He took her to a café close by. A few hours ago, Elsa wouldn't have dared go to such a public place, but everywhere she went and everything she did was now a dangerous choice, so she thought, *what the hell.*

Tired and aching, damp clothes chafing her cold skin, she could do with some caffeine. Elsa kept her head down and the peak of her baseball cap pulled low, because there were cameras everywhere. Her image could punch up on an image-recognition system at any moment, anywhere in the world, and assassins would mobilize. For all she knew, the AI could be so sophisticated it could identify her by her gait, the swing of her arms, the roll of her shoulders.

She was lucky Tim Mabey even lived in London. The other members of the Pilot Fish medical team were scattered across the world. One worked in Ho Chi Minh, another in Dubrovnik; the third had proved untraceable, even to someone as clever as Flex.

Picking up on her wariness, Tim eyed the shambolic figure who lumbered behind them at a distance.

'There's a man following us.'

'Don't worry,' she said. 'He's with me.'

The café was on the corner of a row of shops. The first thing she did was identify where the rear exit was.

'What would you like?' he asked. 'My shout.'

'Get me a coffee,' she said. 'And as many bananas as they have.'

When he came back from the counter, Tim looked across the table at her in wonder. She was deathly pale, her face covered in angry cuts and contusions, but her eyes blazed with an extraordinary energy and defiance.

'Stuff like this doesn't happen to me every day,' he said. 'Why do you go to a therapist, anyway?'

'I guess I feel like I need to kick-start my life somehow.' He grinned sheepishly. 'It can be... hard, sometimes, can't it?'

Therapy felt like an indulgence to Elsa. There was no better way of learning to appreciate your life, and how to make the most of the present moment, than by being inexplicably targeted for liquidation by the world's most lethal killers.

A waitress placed the drinks and fruit on the table. 'Two coffees and a couple of bananas.'

'All you have is two?' Elsa asked her.

'Looks like it,' the waitress said, eyeing Elsa's muddy clothes and dirty, bruised face.

'So... Elsa Zero,' said Tim cheerfully when she had gone. 'I've often wondered what your name is.'

Elsa stuffed half a banana in her mouth. 'Seriously?'

'Who you are, where you are, whether you were even still...'

She finished the sentence for him. 'Still alive?'

Tim nodded. 'And here you are.'

'I'm sure it'll give you a lot of good material for next week's therapy session, Tim, but I need to ask you about Buenos Aires, when you... saved my life.'

'Am I allowed to talk about that?' The teaspoon tinkled noisily against the side of the mug as he stirred his coffee. 'They said I wasn't allowed to say anything.'

Elsa, whose thoughts had returned anxiously to her kids, looked up sharply when she realized what he'd said. 'Wait, who did?'

'Some people have come to me, several times, actually, and made it clear that my life would be in danger if I ever spoke about that... mission.'

'Let's put it this way, Tim.' Elsa touched his hand to stop the stirring. 'Your life will be in immediate danger if you *don't* talk to me about it.'

'Wow, just... wow.' If she meant to frighten him – it didn't work, because he grinned. 'Who on earth are you?'

She peeled the second banana. 'Just tell me who they were.'

'I don't know, they looked like intelligence agents. You know, spooks. It's always different people. They turn up at the hospital, or at my home, and warn me never to speak to anyone about it. The first time was straight after Buenos Aires when spooks flew to my base, they came a *long* way south, and questioned me for hours.'

'What did they ask?'

'About what happened, and who I met – it was just you,

actually – and whether you were in secret communication with anyone while you were at the facility, that kind of thing.'

'And what did you tell them?'

'That you were unconscious for most of the time, and that only the medical staff went near you. Not that there was anybody else there.'

Sitting opposite him now, Elsa vaguely remembered Tim, and got flashes of the other members of the team who nursed her back to health. She'd been unconscious when she arrived, and rushed straight into theatre, where she was given a massive blood transfusion and underwent a long operation to save her life. Days later, when she finally regained consciousness, Saint and Camille had already flown home. Other than the medical staff, she had been alone inside that temporary facility in the bowels of the abandoned petrochemical plant. Left to recuperate inside a curved structure of inflatable plastic erected inside the vast building's gutted shell.

Organizing the emergency medical facility had been Carragher's final legacy. Without it, she would have died.

'How did you get involved in Pilot Fish?'

'Pilot Fish?'

'It's the code name of the mission.'

'Okay,' Tim said. 'So, I was an RAF doctor, at that time stationed on Ascension Island. Very occasionally I'd be drafted in as medical support on covert operations. Me and the other members of the team would be expected to treat any injured operatives who arrived at the facility. I did half a dozen of those covert missions, the first five times we weren't even needed, we all sat around and were flown back to base without seeing a single person, and the medical tent dismantled. But on the last mission you were brought in. You were in very bad shape, Elsa, it was touch and go in surgery… at one stage I thought you were a goner. You were in haemorrhagic shock, had lost a huge amount of blood, and there were several bullets inside you. We took them out and cleaned you up as best as we could, and gave you a transfusion.'

'The other medical people,' she asked. 'Did you know who they were?'

'I'd worked with them all before, actually stayed in touch with a couple of them over the years. I can assure you, they knew as much about the operation as I did, which was absolutely nothing.'

'And there was no one else there?' she asked.

Maybe a senior spook had turned up, someone in authority who could shed light on the nature of the mission. Someone she'd be able to locate; she'd go to the ends of the earth if she had to.

Tim sipped his coffee. 'Your two colleagues were there briefly, I didn't get to speak to them, but… wait.' Elsa watched him carefully as he replaced the cup on the saucer, looking thoughtful. 'There *was* one other guy.'

She tensed. 'Go on.'

'He was there for a very short time, just before you arrived, in actual fact. He brought the blood. We needed different supplies, obviously, in case any members of your team needed treating. You're AB negative, I remember, which makes you a universal recipient. I barely saw him because you arrived soon after he did and we rushed you straight into theatre. By the time I finished operating, he was already long gone.'

'So you didn't see him interact with anyone?'

Tim thought about it. 'When you came in and we were putting you on a trolley, he spoke briefly to one of your colleagues. The woman who came in on the copter with you.'

Camille.

'Can you describe him, the guy who was there?'

'I can do better than that, I know exactly who he is.' Heart pounding in her chest, Elsa stared at him. 'Back then he was a nobody, but in the years since this gentleman has made quite a name for himself. It doesn't really make sense to me why he was there, but it's not like I could ever tell anyone.'

Elsa leaned forward. 'Who was the guy?'

'Hold on to your hat.' With a dramatic flourish, Tim held his hands out wide. 'It was… Noah Pettifore.'

Elsa scowled in incomprehension. 'I have no idea who that is.'

33

Arkady was chatting to Kieron in the parlour room that contained his full-length bar: a beautiful walnut counter one of his architects had found in a derelict Brooklyn bar, and which he'd had shipped over. Its shelves were stocked with enough alcohol to supply a string of hotels. It was another of Natalya's ideas: she had demanded somewhere to entertain all the VIP guests she dreamed of inviting to this ridiculous house. He was speaking about his stable of thoroughbred horses in the Far East when Hazlett came over and whispered in his ear.

'They're sequencing now.'

Arkady looked up at him with a combination of exasperation and fondness. His executive assistant really had no manners at all.

Still, it was the news he had been waiting for, so he drained the last of his martini and stood. 'Kieron, would you fetch me a coffee from the kitchen? Drinking in the morning is never wise.'

His head of security disappeared to the kitchen as Arkady and Hazlett made their way along the endless corridors of the mansion. The more time Arkady spent in this sprawling place, the more he considered preposterous the vast sums he had spent refurbishing it. In retrospect, his marriage was doomed to fail, and the outlay a colossal waste. As beautiful as it was, he hated the estate now, and would be glad to be free of it.

'Two of our men were found in a car in the Thames.' His assistant's hands fluttered anxiously as he gave the grim news. 'And Zero is on her way to Pettifore's now.'

Arkady wasn't surprised. He had learned a saying over here: to make an omelette, you must break eggs. In an operation as delicate and finely poised as this one, with events always fizzing and twisting in unexpected directions, like firecrackers in the sky, the situation was always going to be fluid.

But it didn't matter any more. The woman was a sideshow now. They had what they needed: it was retrieved in the early hours of the morning and brought here. Zero's role in events was now as negligible as her name. If it was up to Arkady, they'd leave her to her fate, she was now a hunted beast in a world of predators, but he'd made a solemn promise to his absent business partner.

'That's good, then,' said Arkady, and Hazlett looked surprised. 'The situation has changed, Anthony.'

He told Hazlett his intention where Elsa Zero was concerned.

'What?' His assistant's trembling face was a picture. 'Why wasn't I informed?'

'It was only decided a few minutes ago when I took the call. I was going to tell you as soon as I had finished my martini.'

Hazlett frowned. He was a worrier and catastrophizer; adapting his thinking to swiftly changing situations had never been a core strength. But there was no one better at swiftly putting into action Arkady's commands.

'Why would you want to do such a thing?'

'It wasn't my choice, but it's none of our concern.' Arkady shrugged. 'We have enough to worry about, so let's stay out of it.'

'But how will we even make it happen?'

'We have an excellent opportunity coming up.'

Walking into the large reception, with its medieval suits of armour, coats of arms and other accoutrements of country living, all bought at auction by Natalya, they saw a commotion at the entrance. Luke had come in the open doors on his bike and was weaving between the security men, who were trying to grab him. Arkady wagged a finger at the men and laughed. The boy skidded to a stop in front of him.

'Nice turn,' he told Luke.

'Thanks! Why do you have so many guards here?'

'I'm a very wealthy man, Luke, and have many valuable things, so it's always wise to employ people who can protect them.'

'They have guns,' said Luke. 'I've seen them.'

Arkady smiled. 'You can never be too careful.'

'You can't ride the bike in here,' Hazlett snapped at the boy.

There was a crunch of gravel outside and then the boy's father rushed inside.

'I'm sorry, Mr Krupin.' Darren looked embarrassed. 'I'll make sure it doesn't happen again.'

In the great scheme of things, Luke riding his bike down the long, empty corridors – there were parts of the house even Arkady himself had yet to visit – wasn't such a big deal. Let the boy have his fun.

'You have my permission to ride the bike inside, but only on the west side of the house.' He pointed towards the east wing. 'Not in that direction.'

The boy nodded.

'And Luke.' Arkady made a stern face. 'Don't break any of my expensive vases.'

'I'm going to go and get my remote-controlled car!' said the boy and he flew off down a corridor.

'Thank you, sir,' said Darren.

'Boys will be boys. He's not doing any harm.'

When the boy and his father had gone, Arkady frowned. 'Remind me what we were talking about?'

'Zero,' repeated Hazlett tensely.

'Ah, yes. Anthony, my friend, don't worry about her.' Arkady clapped him on the shoulder. 'Everything is in motion now, there's no going back.'

Kieron came across the reception with a paper cup.

'Thank you, Kieron,' said Arkady, taking the steaming coffee.

Walking down the main corridor of the east wing, they arrived at the door with the biometric reader. But when Arkady reached out with his free hand, he clipped the top of the cup, slopping the scalding liquid across his wrist, making him drop it. The liquid spilled everywhere across the tiled floor.

'You see, gentlemen,' Arkady said, shaking his burned hand. 'That's why I never drink before lunchtime!'

Kieron propped open the door. 'I'll clear it up.'

In the ballroom, which Arkady used as his operations

centre, his team were at work. By the end of the day that room, and the rest of the mansion, would be abandoned. If they knew what was good for them, everyone would be racing out of the country.

Hazlett repeated the biometric identification on the inner door that led into the vast room beyond the ballroom and walked inside. Instead of letting it shut, Arkady left it open to allow Kieron to catch up when he finished clearing up the spill.

Within the biolab, which dominated the middle of the room, figures moved about in full-body positive-pressure protective suits. Deep inside the clear plastic walls of the structure, a facility for the handling of the most dangerous organisms on the planet, a bearded man hunched over a biological safety cabinet.

Pressing an intercom button, Arkady said, 'Good morning, Noah.'

Noah Pettifore stabbed a button with a gloved finger and his voice came over the speaker. 'Did you give any thought to what we discussed?'

'I regret it's not going to be possible,' said Arkady. 'Not at this late stage.'

'We need human test subjects.'

'You have mice, you have rats.'

It was difficult to see Noah's face behind his mask, but he grunted with dissatisfaction.

Arkady was distracted by a high-pitched whine behind him. He turned to see a remote-controlled car speed through the door and stop at his feet.

'Mr Krupin!' Luke raced in behind it. 'Look how fast it is!'

The boy looked in astonishment at the giant lamps, generators and the room-within-a-room where men and women in white containment suits moved like ghosts.

Another voice shouted behind the boy, and Luke's father hurried in.

'Come here, Luke! You were told to stay out of...' Darren's gaze lifted in a panic to the alien-looking lab that dominated the space. 'I'm so sorry, we didn't mean to...'

Pulling his son after him, Darren turned to go, but Kieron rushed inside, looking flustered. He'd left the door to the operations room open while he had gone to fetch cleaning materials. Chasing his car, Luke had somehow managed to run through both open doors.

Arkady smiled ruefully. He had also been careless; should have known better than to allow both doors to remain open, even for a short time.

'And I'm sorry, Darren,' he said sadly.

Darren edged away from the handgun Kieron held unobtrusively at his side.

Bewildered, increasingly afraid, he tried not to look again at the biolab. 'We didn't see anything. We... won't say anything.'

Arkady picked up the remote-controlled car and placed it on the table, then pressed the button on the intercom to speak again to the man inside.

'Those human test subjects you wanted, Noah,' he said. 'We have an unexpected opportunity.'

34

According to Flex's research, Noah Pettifore lived in a luxury tower block in Kensington. When Elsa arrived there, she was too exhausted to even contemplate climbing up the outside – if it was even feasible; the building was twenty floors of smooth glass – or find another way to sneak inside.

The lobby was as big and soulless as the foyer of a City bank: all geometric lines, sparkling tiled floor and undulating hanging lights. There wasn't a speck of dust, every polished surface gleamed. An enormous arrangement of flowers was displayed in a giant vase on an incongruous-looking antique table in the middle of the space. An abstract painting with an image as befuddled as the inside of Elsa's head, all custard smears and raspberry swirls across a stormy grey canvas, filled the entirety of one wall.

The lift doors opened and a woman in a fur coat strode towards the entrance, heels clopping noisily. Both she and the vanity dog with bulbous eyes riding in her Chanel bag regarded Elsa with distaste.

'I'm here to see Noah Pettifore,' Elsa told a man sitting behind an enormous desk. He gave her a long look. It had only been a few hours since she'd paddled in the Thames. With her dirty hoodie and leggings, and bloated, sodden trainers, she must have reached Max Saint levels of dishevelment.

'Is he expecting you?'

Elsa eyed the black bulb of the dome camera above the man. With his smooth skin and salt-and-pepper hair, he was of indeterminate age. His name badge identified him as Valentine, a first name or surname, she had no idea.

'Yes,' she lied.

Sitting in front of a monitor, he tapped something on a keyboard. When Elsa leaned over the desk, she saw herself clearly on the reception's CCTV; her image would be bouncing across the planet, but there was nothing she could do about that.

He picked up the internal phone. 'What's your name, please?'

She gave her own name, because out of ideas and energy, she couldn't think of an alternative. 'I'm… a work colleague,' she said by way of explanation.

'Elsa Zero is here to see Mr Pettifore. Work colleague, she says.' He nodded, and put the phone down. 'You can go up.'

'Really?' Elsa smothered her surprise. 'Lovely.'

'He's not here, currently,' said the man. 'But his wife is in.'

He instructed her to take the express lift to the penthouse apartments. As she stepped inside the mirrored box and the door closed, Elsa saw Valentine pick up the phone. Entombed in the confined space, she stood tensely as the lift rose, half expecting it to become trapped between floors – she didn't relish climbing the vertiginous shaft to safety; had done it before and didn't recommend it – or plummet suddenly to the basement, dashing her against the floor. Instead, it rose smoothly to the eighteenth floor to the accompaniment of jazzy muzak.

The door opened to reveal a short corridor of plush carpet, another spectacular flower display in an alcove, and an apartment door ahead. Elsa heard the drone of a vacuum cleaner when she knocked. A young woman opened the door, dragging the machine behind her.

'I was just tidying the place.' She leaned forward to shake Elsa's hand. 'I'm Dani Pettifore, Noah's wife.'

She was perhaps twenty years younger than her husband, with curly auburn hair tied back, and a gaunt, anxious face, and she wore a T-shirt, jeans and boots.

'Let me just get rid of this.' Pressing a square of panelling, a wall cupboard was revealed, and she hid the cleaner away. 'Noah didn't tell me he was expecting visitors. You work with him, you said?'

'Used to,' said Elsa. 'We're more friends these days.'

Dani nodded vaguely. 'Okay, then.'

Elsa followed her into a spacious room with an exceptional view of the city. Two sides of the wall in the corner room were glass, and the other two filled with floating shelves of books, framed photos and awards. A large French desk faced the room on one side, the only item on its surface a MacBook.

Walking out onto the spacious balcony, Elsa looked directly down at the street at the front of the building; the miniscule figure of Saint was sitting on a bench, where she'd told him to wait.

'You have a nice place.'

'Thanks.' Dani rolled her eyes. 'It's all a bit masculine,

but Noah lived here long before I came along. I was about to make a coffee, would you like one?'

Elsa shook her head. 'I'm fine.'

When Dani left the room, Elsa looked at the books, which were mostly scientific, with long, dry titles she didn't understand: *Understanding the Genome*, *A Life in Genetic Medicine*, *Functional Biology*, *Synthesis and Evolution*.

Some of them were written by Noah Pettifore himself. Tim Mabey had described him as a pioneering synthetic biologist. When she'd asked him what that was, he admitted he didn't know, but said Pettifore was a superstar in his scientific field, because of his cutting-edge research in sequencing DNA. Flex had done a thorough search on Pettifore earlier, and had come up with this address for Elsa.

She looked again at the scientist's face on a jacket cover. Pettifore's glowering eyes, furrowed brow, thick beard and thinking man's pout suggested a man who took himself very seriously.

There were obsessively neat stacks of science journals and magazines, *Biology Today*, *Double Helix*, *Genome Editing*; commendations from universities and global think-tanks; certificates awarded by prestigious scientific bodies and institutions she'd never heard of.

And there were plenty of other framed photos of Noah Pettifore. Meeting politicians and business leaders; shaking hands with a UK cabinet minister and a far-right US senator. In one image, Pettifore stood with a diminutive man with a confident smile. Scowling in each and every photo, Pettifore didn't look particularly impressed by any of the encounters.

Several photos were missing on the wall, and there were gaps on the shelf. But Elsa finally found a single image of

Noah and Dani, taken at a function. He wore a tuxedo and she had on a sleeveless dress, which revealed a tattoo snaking down her left bicep.

'Is he going to be back soon?' asked Elsa.

'He just popped to the dry cleaner's,' Dani called from the kitchen. When Elsa went to the doorway, she was tapping something on her phone.

'There! I've told him you're here.' She placed the phone down. 'I was just about to make a coffee, want some?'

'You just asked me.' Elsa smiled flatly. 'But I don't think I'll stay.'

Standing at the central island, almost obscured by the pots and pans hanging above the hob, Dani said, 'Don't be ridiculous, he'll be home soon.'

'I'll be honest, Dani. I'm not getting very good vibes from you, or this whole set-up.'

'Why not?' asked Dani in surprise.

'Let's start with your tattoo in the photo out there, the single one I could find of you and Noah.' Elsa nodded at Dani's bare arm. 'You don't have one now.'

'Oh, that!' Dani said too brightly, as if she was pleased Elsa had noticed. 'I had it removed. Laser treatment!'

'There are other photos missing from the walls, so I'm guessing whoever placed you here didn't get the opportunity to insert your face onto any other images.' Elsa looked around the pristine kitchen. 'I don't think you're his wife, or that anyone's lived here for weeks. No offence, but you're not very good at this.'

Dani moved along the counter slowly. 'Not very good at what?'

'Pretending to be someone else. Is it your first time?' Elsa nodded at the phone. 'I imagine whoever it is you contacted will be here soon, so I had better go.'

'You can't,' said Dani in a strangled voice.

The young woman's responses had taken a funny turn. Dani, or whatever her real name was, was out of her depth. Elsa felt bad for the girl. With a bit of training and preparation, she'd be better equipped to handle the situation.

'I'm guessing you're not a field operative, you're probably a desk-jockey in an agency bureau at whatever embassy and they're short of people on the ground. Your instructions were to come here, wait for me to arrive, then keep me here. You're scared, I understand that.'

'You mustn't leave,' Dani said in a panic as Elsa turned to go.

'Everyone's after me right now, Dani, and there's a reason for that. It's because I'm very, *very* dangerous. Which means you're advised to let me walk out of here, or I'll probably end up having to kill you.' Elsa shrugged. 'And I don't want to do that.'

'You have to stay.' Dani braced her arms against the counter and gasped. 'I'm not allowed to let you go!'

'Take a deep breath,' said Elsa. 'And don't even think about—'

Dani launched herself at a drawer, pulling out a P229 handgun. But Elsa snatched one of the pans hanging over the central island and swung it in a single fluid motion. The metal made a clear *bong* sound when it connected with the woman's head. She dropped to the floor, the weapon skittering across the tile.

Elsa picked it up, checked the thirteen-round magazine,

and left the kitchen. She had just got into the central hallway when the front door flew open and Joel rushed in with the receptionist Valentine, guns pointed at her.

Elsa fired once, twice, and flung herself back into the kitchen. The two men shot back, and retreated out of the door.

'Elsa!' Joel shouted. 'Come on out!'

'I thought you loved me, Joel.' Elsa's heart banged in her chest, all her instincts screamed that she wanted to kill him. 'That's what you told me.'

'Oh man.' He spoke in that unfamiliar American accent. 'I'm still crazy about you, I just wish the feeling was mutual!'

'And yet here you are trying to kill me – again!'

'It's not what I want,' he said.

'I'm all cut up about your feelings.'

'I knew you'd get here sooner or later, Elsa. It's why I love you so much.'

'I can't believe I was taken in by you,' she said bitterly, thinking of her children.

'We were good together, Elsa.' Joel spoke with what sounded like genuine regret, but his voice was getting closer. 'You were the best job I ever had.'

Tired of his treacherous bullshit, she swung back into the corridor and fired again. Joel and Valentine scrambled back the way they came.

'Has anyone done anything to you in the last forty-eight hours, Elsa?'

'Sure, Joel, I'll just answer all your questions,' she called sarcastically. The only way out of the apartment was through the front door. Which gave her two reasons to kill him. 'Fire away.'

'Please, Elsa, it's important. Any tests? Have you been given any injections?'

Elsa thought of Camille coming at her with the stubby needle in the lift of the Soho hotel, and then on the way to Dougie's house...

'Taking my blood,' she said, as much to herself as Joel. 'Is that what you mean?'

She heard Joel whisper to Valentine, and then he called, 'That's not great news, Elsa, but it changes everything. It means we don't have to kill each other. I'm coming in, Elsa, don't shoot!'

Elsa twisted from behind the door and aimed at Joel, trying to contain the rage she felt for him, as he walked steadily along the hallway, hands above his head.

His voice cracked nervously as he said, 'I'm unarmed, baby, don't kill me.'

'I will if you call me baby again.'

'I'm no danger to you,' he insisted.

She aimed at his chest, her finger trembling over the trigger. Joel looked even worse than she did, his right cheek burned to a slippery pink wax where she had mashed it into the hot grill at the restaurant.

'We're back on the same side, Elsa,' Joel told her tensely. 'Killing you now would be pointless.'

'Killing you would be highly satisfying.'

'Hey.' Joel smiled sadly. 'We had some good times, too.'

She would never forget that their whole relationship had been a lie, a monumental betrayal of trust, and a gateway to catastrophe for her family.

'We need to get out of here,' he said. 'I can explain

everything on the way. Everything's changed for you now. Trust me, you're safe.'

Camille had promised her the exact same thing. Elsa had been safe with her former friend right up until the moment she had tried to have her killed.

'You want to know what this is all about, Elsa? I promise you, it's going to blow your mind...' Joel approached slowly, his eyes fixed on hers, hands held high. 'The reason for this whole nightmare.'

Daring to hope, she realized too late she had lost focus; a knife was pressed against her throat from behind.

'Now who's the amateur?' Dani hissed in her ear, and Elsa knew she was dead.

But Joel reached out. 'No, stand down!'

He grabbed the knife from Dani and threw it across the floor.

'She's with us now,' he said, and then told Dani and Valentine to wait outside. 'We'll be out in a moment.'

'Tell me,' Elsa demanded.

Joel walked into the living room, with its magnificent views of the city, and picked up the photo of Noah Pettifore and the small, avuncular man.

'Do you know who this is?' She shook her head. 'His name is Arkady Krupin, he's a Russian businessman, and the main financier of Pettifore's biological research. We believe Krupin and Pettifore are responsible for what happened to you in Buenos Aires nine years ago, and the reason you're currently as popular as a fox in a henhouse.'

'You're CIA,' she said.

'Yeah.' He nodded. 'And as usual we're trying to get you bumbling Brits out of a hole.'

'I don't understand what's happening,' she said angrily. 'Or why you insinuated yourself into my life, and the lives of my kids.'

'Harley and India, are they safe?'

'No,' she hissed. 'They're not safe. I need to go and get them.'

Joel held up his hands. 'The first thing we'll do is get them to safety. This crazy situation has just got a whole lot bigger, Elsa. It's not about you now, it's about the whole goddamn world.'

'Just tell me what it is!'

'You'll be debriefed as soon as we get you all to a CIA safe house.' He sighed. 'I'm so sorry, Elsa. I had hoped, a part of me even believed… I would never be activated.'

'You tried to kill me.'

'The Agency panicked, like all the other agencies panicked, and I was given no choice. But now…' He smiled hopefully. 'Maybe when all this is over, Elsa, there's still a chance we could—'

'Not a chance,' she told him. 'Not in this universe.'

'In another lifetime, then.' Joel nodded sadly. 'We have to go. If we guessed you'd come here, other parties will too.'

When he walked out of the room, Elsa tried to make sense of it. The new information, about Pettifore and Joel and the Russian, Pilot Fish, the constantly shifting sands of trust and betrayal. All of it spun in her throbbing head.

She walked onto the balcony to check on Saint downstairs; they'd pick him up on the way out. But he was gone, when he'd promised her he'd stay put.

'Joel…' she called, getting a bad feeling about everything.

But when she caught up with him at the apartment door, he was backing up. Because Camille was coming in, pointing a gun at them. Stepping over the bodies of Valentine and Dani, she was flanked by two men, who took Joel and Elsa's weapons and then searched them.

'Make sure the rest of the apartment is secure,' Camille told the men and gestured for Joel and Elsa to return to the living room.

'Camille Archard, right?' Joel grinned. 'We haven't met, I'm Joel.'

She ignored him. A ringing sound came from a soundbar below a wall-mounted TV; a telephone icon flashed on the screen. Elsa saw there was a small camera above it.

While her two associates kept their guns aimed, Camille went to the MacBook on the desk and activated the call.

'Krupin,' Joel said, but she already recognized the man who appeared on the screen as the jocular Russian in the photo he had shown her.

'Elsa!' Arkady gave her a happy wave, as if he was Zooming an old friend. 'You gave us a scare with all your frantic running and hiding. Noah sends his regrets that he isn't able to say hello. He's currently doing vital work for me, which he has only been able to complete thanks to you.'

Camille lifted her Glock at Elsa, intending to shoot her.

'It's my sincere hope that we will both be able to thank you in person,' Arkady continued urgently. 'Which is why I want to invite you to my home, as my guest.'

'That was never our agreement.' Camille turned sharply to the TV. 'You said I could kill her, as soon as you got what you needed.'

'Circumstances change, Camille,' Arkady said cheerfully,

his face looming close on the screen. 'And there's been an alteration to the plan.'

'No.' Camille shook her head. 'That's unacceptable.'

'You will still, I am sure, get your wish to kill her at the appropriate time.' He waved his hands in apology. 'I'm sorry, Elsa, this is probably not something you wish to hear.'

'What is this all about?' Elsa asked. 'What do you want?'

Arkady wagged a finger. 'There's a lot of questions to unpack there. When we meet, I'll happily give you the answers you crave. Thank you,' he told someone off-screen when a coffee was placed in front of him. 'That's very kind.'

'Okay,' Joel told him. 'We'll come to you, Arkady, if that's what it takes.'

Peering closely at Joel, Arkady frowned. 'I don't know who you are.'

'My name is Joel Harris, Mr Krupin.' Elsa's former fiancé walked towards the camera. 'I'm CIA.'

'I'm afraid, Mr Harris, that you're an irrelevance here.'

When Arkady gestured to Camille, Joel reminded Elsa quietly, 'Another lifetime, then.'

Camille stepped up and shot Joel in the back of the head. Blood sprayed everywhere as he collapsed to the ground. She stood over him and put another couple of bullets in the body.

When Elsa sprang forward, Camille swung the gun eagerly in her face.

'Easy, Camille,' said Krupin, with a hint of annoyance.

'You promised!' she snarled. 'You said I could kill her!'

'And you'll get your opportunity, but you must be patient. Bring her here.'

He stabbed at a button on his keyboard and the connection dropped.

Handing her gun to one of the men, Camille took out a syringe. She pulled the plastic cap off the hypodermic needle with her teeth and spat it out.

'Fuck him, maybe I'll just kill you anyway.'

'You heard what he wants,' Elsa said tensely as the two men held her still.

'You know what, Elsa?' snarled Camille. 'I'm sick of saving your worthless life.'

Elsa struggled fiercely, but the men held her tight as Camille plunged the needle into her neck.

35

Nine years earlier

As soon as the door blew in, Elsa emptied her magazine into the corridor. One, two, three men fell, but more came inside, moving slowly, inexorably along the corridor. The angry chatter of machine guns filled the room as the intruders returned fire.

Elsa braced herself against the wall on one side of the living-room door, Carragher on the other. They were trapped in the apartment, there was no getting downstairs, no climbing to the roof. The only possibility of escape was along the balcony, but as soon as they went outside, they'd likely be cut to pieces.

'Camille!' Carragher shouted at Elsa. 'She's downstairs!'

If the gunmen had made their way up, it meant Camille was heading to the roof with Antovic or already dead, he must know that.

Moving in and out of the doorway to fire bursts at the figures who moved relentlessly forward, the carbine heating in her hands, she gestured at the hard drive in the vault.

'Blow that thing!'

When the men fired back, Elsa ducked back into the room. Fragments of flying plaster stung her face; the wooden door frame disintegrated by her shoulder. Trying to return fire now would be suicide.

'Do it!' Tipping over the heavy table, making the computer and other apparatus crash to the floor, she and Carragher threw themselves behind it.

He pressed the wireless detonator and the vault exploded in a deafening blast, causing the walls to crack, the door to fly off and cement and plaster to rain from the ceiling. Disintegrating chandeliers flew across the room. Fire poured from the opening, and a dense wall of smoke swept towards them. When Elsa's ears stopped ringing, she realized Carragher was standing in the doorway, obscured by whirls of smoke, angrily firing into the corridor. Screaming, shouting, his face a grimace of fury.

'Get out!' he shouted at her. Elsa ran towards the balcony doors. She didn't understand why he didn't retreat. When the smoke cleared, he'd be a sitting duck.

'Move!' she screamed.

When the magazine on his weapon was empty, Carragher threw it down and turned to follow. But there was a burst of gunfire, and his arms flew up over his head. He fell.

'Steve!' He was sprawled across the floor, not moving. Elsa's instinct was to go to him, but armed men poured from the doorway.

One of them fired a couple of rounds into Carragher's back, just below his Kevlar vest. The body jerked and lay still.

Elsa emptied her rifle at the men, kept her finger on the trigger. Carragher's assailant went down, and another man behind him, and then she ran. She lifted a shoulder, smashing through the shattered balcony doors, stumbled outside.

She was three storeys up. There was no fire escape,

no safe place to climb down. If she jumped, she'd break every bone in her body. Chips of stone flew everywhere, gunmen were firing up at her from the street below as she ran along the balcony. But then one of the men flew into the air, and the others dived out of the way. A van came careening along the road, smashing and scraping against cars parked at the kerb; swerving as the scattering gunmen took aim at the windscreen. Axles crunching, it mounted the pavement.

'Jump!' Saint shouted in her earpiece. At the wheel of the van, he slammed on the brakes.

'Now!' Camille's voice screamed, and Elsa realized she could hear them both again. 'Jump now!'

There was no time to calculate angles or second-guess her desperately narrowing options, all she had left was the instinct that had kept her alive.

Elsa leaped onto the balustrade, but there was another burst of gunfire behind her as men rushed onto the balcony. Elsa felt a shrieking pain in the top of her thigh. Her leg gave way beneath her, and she half jumped, half toppled off the parapet.

Twisting in mid-air, she fell, time slowing as the street hurtled up towards her—

And slammed hard into the roof of the van.

The fall briefly knocked her cold, and when she returned to consciousness seconds later, she barely knew where she was. The vehicle speeding beneath her was swerving wildly, as if trying to shake her off. She rolled across the roof, the onrushing air cooling her damp face, and grabbed at each side, digging the tips of her fingers into the lip above the doors as best she could. She heard gunfire behind her, the screech of tyres.

Her fingers lost their grip on the driver's side, and she instinctively grabbed hold again as the van sped through the streets. The wind rushing in her face as she lay spreadeagled, trying to distribute her mass as evenly as possible, she felt the van swerve. Pressing the side of her face against the warm metal, she heard the gears grind, and Saint's voice shouting below.

'...want it there now... pick us up... emergency...'

Elsa felt a crunching judder as the van clipped the side of a parked car. A sharp corner almost made her lose her grip. Her thoughts became sluggish as the van hurtled through the busy streets, swinging from lane to lane. Unable to feel her left leg, numbness creeping up her side, snaking trails of her own blood shivering and jumping on the roof, she clung on as best she could. Until she couldn't hold on any more, couldn't stay conscious any longer, and she blacked out.

When her eyes opened again, searing bright light burned into her vision. Saint's face loomed close to hers.

'Stay with me,' he screamed, tears running down his cheeks. 'You ain't going anywhere, you got me? You fucking stay with me, Elsie!'

But she couldn't stay with him, didn't have the strength. She wanted to close her eyes and rest, just for a short while, or a long time, or forever.

Just close her eyes. Let her entire life force drain from her, still her indestructible heart. She'd welcome oblivion, leave behind the world and its endless violence. Let it all go.

But somewhere inside of her, she also knew it wasn't just her any more.

Her baby was in her – deep down she maybe sensed it was more than one child. She had to fight, not just for herself, but for the new life forming inside of her. Stay alive for the children.

Camille's face appeared in her blurred vision. 'Steve,' she asked Elsa. 'Steve...'

'Gone,' Elsa said, aloud or in her own head, she didn't know.

Her eyelids fluttered, she was freezing and burning at the same time, everything slowing. Saint was with her, and Camille, too, and the big heavy rotors of the helicopter she was in spun slowly above her; each blade distinct in her tunnel vision, turning with the slow, sluggish swipe of a windmill. She had no idea how this impossible machine could fly.

Life was ebbing from her, but Elsa didn't want to let go because she had her child... her children. And if she lived, if she got another chance, she would take more care of them than she ever did herself.

Her fingers slid in the sticky mess of her own blood on the rough metal floor of the bird. It was everywhere, it seemed to have no end. Blood was draining from her body as fast as it could; soaking the floor, racing for the open cargo door, spilling into the vivid blue sky.

'You fucking stay with me!' Saint shouted, but most of his words were obliterated by the noisy roar of the engine.

Wind brushed against her fevered face. Barely conscious, Elsa watched the sky twist and turn. The sprawling city seemed to recede above her head. She felt a faint pressure on her freezing hand, and when her head lolled to the side, Camille told her softly, 'We've got you.'

But Elsa just couldn't hang on, for herself or the life taking root inside of her, and she fell unconscious.

Her last thought: *I'm going to die.*

36

Elsa opened her eyes to find herself sprawled fully clothed on crisp sheets of Egyptian cotton, her head burrowed in a cool microfibre pillow, in a large room of dazzling white.

She saw a walnut cabinet against one wall, a wardrobe, Eames chair, a woven rug of vibrant colour; a stylish Scandi light hung from the high ceiling. Across the room was a wide door of dark wood.

A tall window looked out over a sweeping lawn and woods beyond, a fragment of gravel drive. She heard car doors slam, crunching footsteps. Somewhere inside the building, someone laughed.

She swung her feet off the bed – her ruined trainers were tucked beneath it, afforded a respect they didn't deserve – and took an audit of all the aches and pains up her legs, body, and on her arms and face. The conclusion she came to was that she hurt in a lot of places. A multitude of swirling bruises covered her torso, every colour of the rainbow, including an angry storm of blue-black clouding her left side. Her left cheek was swollen, her ear throbbed, her shoulder pulsated. But she could still bend her arms, legs, fingers and toes.

Stomping her feet into the trainers, Elsa stood at the

window looking across the sea of flat lawn. The branches of the trees in the woods beyond swayed. If she stood at the extreme left of the window, she could just about see vehicles – four black SUVs and a motorbike – parked on a circular drive at the front of the building.

Elsa didn't hold out much hope when she tried the handle of the door, but was surprised to find it opened, and she stepped out into a corridor.

She was in a large house, a mansion or stately home – Elsa didn't know the difference – because the corridor outside was wide and tall and elegant, with ornamental cornices on the ceiling and a narrow runner carpet revealing edges of shiny floorboard. Paintings of venerable dead people wearing wigs lined the walls.

A man stood to one side of the door, the kind of shaven-headed rent-a-thug who usually flanked Terry outside Panda's club. Elsa tensed, ready to crack his head into the plaster, but he politely said, 'Good afternoon.'

Elsa nodded and walked along the corridor, the guy following at a discreet distance. She heard him murmur into a mic, 'Miss Zero is walking.'

Before she got to the end of the corridor, Arkady Krupin came hurrying around the corner with a pair of champagne glasses.

'Elsa!' he exclaimed, rushing towards her. 'I'm so glad you're awake.' He offered her a flute of bubbling fizz. 'Please, this is for you.'

Elsa had been shot at, sliced, stabbed and nearly drowned, so she eyed it suspiciously. 'What is it?'

'Champagne.' Arkady looked offended. 'Dom Pérignon, naturally.'

She took the glass and threw it against the wall. It shattered and champagne dribbled down the paintwork.

Arkady winced. 'Perhaps later.'

He tipped back his head and downed his own glass, then handed the empty flute to the shaven-headed man.

'You're not going to attack me, are you?' He chopped the air playfully with his outstretched hand. 'Fell me with one blow, snap my neck?'

'That depends,' she said.

'I can assure you, Elsa, you're safe. Nobody here bears you any ill will.' He added in a whisper, 'Except possibly your friend Camille. As you know, she does love to bear a grudge.'

He laughed and told the guard to leave them alone.

Elsa asked Arkady, 'How are you so sure I won't kill you?'

'Because that would be rude, considering how I saved your life this morning, yes?' He grinned. 'And because you're dying to know what this is all about.'

He started walking, and she followed him.

'What is this place?'

'It's my home, one of them, at least. We purchased it nearly two years ago, my wife and I. Every inch of it needed refurbishment, and that work was overseen by Natalya.'

Elsa was no expert on interior decor. 'She's done a good job.'

'She'd love to hear that, but she's gone.'

'She's dead?'

'Sadly no,' he said. 'But we live in hope.'

'Like you hoped to kill me.'

'On the contrary.' Arkady sounded offended. 'We tried

to grab you outside the restaurant, but unfortunately you evaded us.' The fake paramedics in the ambulance, she remembered. 'After that, our best hope was to keep you out of the hands of the intelligence agencies who were so keen to kill you, or spirit you away, until we were able to retrieve what we needed. It was our marksman above the square who ruined your attempt to find refuge with SIS, and who forced you into Camille's orbit.'

'You're RedQueen?' she asked.

Arkady shook his head. 'Camille is RedQueen, but she also works for me. Unfortunately, as soon as we got what we what wanted from you, Camille didn't waste time in arranging for you to be killed. But she, like everyone else, I may add, underestimated you, Elsa, and all she succeeded in doing was to send two of my men to watery graves. Camille of all people should have known better.' He gave her another sweet smile. 'She would have killed you at Pettifore's apartment, for sure. But as well as being tenacious and indestructible, it's also your great fortune to have a guardian angel, which is how you came to be here now.'

They reached a large reception area. 'Pettifore?'

He giggled. 'Noah is a brilliant man, a genius. His work will change the world in so many ways, and it's been a great honour to work with him over the years, but he's nobody's idea of an angel.'

'Where's Saint?' Elsa demanded.

'Saint…' He stared for a moment, until the penny dropped. 'Ah, the gentleman with the questionable hygiene.'

'Did you kill him?'

If Arkady was intimidated by her aggression, he did a good job of hiding it. 'Let me find out.'

The reception was the kind of foyer entrance she had seen in movies about grand hotels, with staircases lifting up both sides of the space, equestrian paintings, suits of medieval armour standing sentry, crests, stag heads on the walls, and hanging dead centre a sparkling chandelier. Packing boxes were stacked beside the open doors, and men were carrying them outside and placing them in a lorry.

'Kieron?' Arkady called over a large man with a cruel face. 'Was Elsa brought here alone?'

'We were instructed to bring the drunk,' the man called Kieron said. 'He's in the bar.'

'Good.' Arkady turned to Elsa. 'Your friend is here, and taking full advantage of my hospitality. You'll have plenty of time to catch up with him, but we must—'

'I want to see him,' Elsa said.

'Later.'

'Now,' she insisted.

Arkady blushed, as if acknowledging a terrible lack of social etiquette. 'Of course you do, it's only natural to want to see your friend. This way.'

He led her down another corridor behind reception.

'You're leaving here?' she said, watching the men carry the boxes outside.

'I'm shipping out a few things for reasons that will soon become obvious, and I won't be returning here again. I'll be honest, this place has never felt like home. Not since Natalya left me.' He smiled ruefully. 'She fell in love with a younger man and took my millions. My advice to you, Elsa, is never get old.'

'Not much chance of that happening,' she said.

'I believed we'd spend our twilight days here, but I hate

this place now.' Arkady got his bearings at the intersection of two corridors. 'This way, I think.'

He led her into another big room with a full-length bar running the length of it, where slumped on a stool, head lowered into his arms, his guttural breath misting the polished surface of the counter, was Saint. A couple of Arkady's security team stood inside the door.

'He's been drinking all my alcohol. It's just as well I'm a rich man.'

'Saint.' When Elsa shook him by the shoulder he grunted, his eyelids fluttering momentarily, but he didn't wake up. 'He needs to lie down somewhere.'

'He was carried to one of the guest bedrooms, but he keeps finding his way back here, according to my men. Your friend is a man of singular purpose. Any injuries he's sustained have been mostly to his liver, and self-inflicted. Now, I want you to see—'

But Arkady's words were drowned out by the sharp sound of footsteps.

Elsa turned just as Camille punched her hard on the side of the face. She fell to the floor, ear shrieking. Expecting another attack, Elsa tried to lift herself, but Camille pulled a gun and pointed it at her chest.

'Did you think I didn't know, Elsa? Did you really think I didn't have a clue?'

Uncertain of what to do, Arkady's men stepped forward. Arkady lifted his hands in a placatory gesture. 'Please, Camille, not this again. I thought we had agreed. Our friend will not be happy. If you kill her, there will be consequences.'

When Elsa tried to get up, Camille brought a heel down

hard on her lower back and she collapsed back onto the parquet floor.

Arkady snapped, 'That's enough!'

Camille smiled nastily, her top lip curling over her straight white teeth, but she stepped back.

'Help her up.' At Arkady's command, the men lifted Elsa to her feet. Hands braced on her knees, she got her breath back. 'Elsa, would you like anything while we're here?'

'I just want to know what all this is about.'

'What a good idea.' Arkady clapped his hands. 'Come, we'll show you.'

Leaving Saint comatose at the bar, Elsa followed Arkady again, conscious of Camille behind her. She felt her former friend's hateful gaze boring into the back of her head; half expected a bullet in the back at any moment.

'He never loved you,' Elsa said quietly without looking around. 'It was me he always wanted.'

'Oh, Elsa,' complained Arkady. 'Please don't antagonize her.'

A tall man in a suit came hurrying along the corridor to whisper in Arkady's ear.

'Thank you, Anthony,' said the Russian, and he rubbed his hands in glee. 'My associate is on their way now!'

At the end of a corridor, Arkady pressed his palm against a biometric reader, unlocking a pair of double doors, and led them into a large wood-panelled room where half a dozen men and women worked at screens. Walking to the far wall and placing his palm on another reader, a second pair of doors clicked open. He pulled one of the bar handles to allow Elsa inside.

The room, complete with chandeliers and wood panelling,

was vast. But the windows had been boarded up, and the harsh illumination in the room came from free-standing industrial lamps in each corner.

'Our biolab,' said Arkady proudly, nodding at the large installation of transparent plastic that dominated the middle of the room. Figures in biohazard suits moved about inside. Generators and humming filtration units surrounded the structure and lined the walls.

In the centre of the lab was an isolation chamber, where a man and a boy lay on cot-beds, their gaunt, feverish faces covered with livid pustules and seeping lesions. Blood had dried around their noses and mouths. The young boy was unconscious, possibly dead, but the man's red eyes bulged in agony, his body arching as he convulsed in pain.

'They're dying, of course.' Arkady smiled gently at Elsa. 'And it's all thanks to you.'

37

Justine Vydelingum found Plowright in his office, kneading his temples between closed fists, a technique he'd used to alleviate stress in the past, but which was doing nothing for him now.

'Don't you ever knock?' he said sharply.

'Everything all right?'

No, everything wasn't all right. He'd been nearly throttled by a trained killer, who had walked into the building, supposedly one of the securest in the country, wearing the face and body of a dead woman, and then escaped into tunnels deep underground by using him as a human shield. This was the very same person he'd been tasked with hunting down and killing.

Plowright felt unbearable tension in the back of his neck, which was very definitely on the block right now.

'I'm alive, so there's that,' he said, trying to look on the bright side. 'What is it?'

'We have two dead Russians in a house in Ealing, and a Land Rover in the Thames. Two unidentified men were found in the car, one shot dead and the other skewered to the back seat with a headrest. A witness saw four passengers in the vehicle and heard a gunshot before it tipped into the river.'

'Bloody hell,' he said.

She handed him a tablet, which he began to read.

'The property in Ealing is owned by a man called Douglas Heston,' Justine said. 'He and his wife, Roberta, returned home early from holiday to discover a deranged man in their house.'

'Max Saint.' Plowright scrolled down the page to a blurred photo – captured on the doorbell video camera of a neighbour's house – of Zero and Saint hurrying along the street.

'Saint was drunk and violent, and tied them up. Accused them of being assassins who had come to kill him. Heston says Zero arrived and saved his life twice, once from Saint, and then when an actual pair of killers, a male and a female, turned up dressed as police.'

'Why Heston?'

'He's on Zero's list of training clients.'

Plowright grimaced. 'She knew his house would be empty.'

His team had pulled Elsa Zero's business contacts from the cloud, but hadn't worked their way through the list. The limited resources he had to work with were a joke, cutbacks had made his job almost intolerable, and the resources he'd been promised were too little too late, even in such exceptional circumstances. He'd pulled in as many staff with the necessary security permissions as he could, but considering the enormity of the crisis, not enough.

He guessed his counterpart in Langley, Virginia, with her tailored suit, glossy hair and dazzling white teeth, had far more people at her disposal, and all the latest surveillance tech, even if they had fewer feet on the ground in London.

The same was probably true for the Vladimirs in Moscow, too.

'We're sure they're Russians?'

Justine sat where Zoe Castle had the previous day, pinching a piece of fluff from the shoulder of her jacket and dropping it on the floor. Plowright's threadbare suit was entirely held together by random bits of lint.

'He said they spoke Russian, so they're either GRU or SVR, take your pick, sent to kill or grab Elsa.'

'How on earth did they find her before us?'

'They probably copied her client list from the cloud, then hacked the home security company Heston uses and saw the alarm was turned off, despite the fact that he and his wife had booked holiday flights and hotels online.' She pointed at the tablet. 'The neighbours directly opposite have a security camera above their garage. If the Russians hacked it, they'd see who was going in and out of the house.'

'Those people,' said Plowright bitterly. 'They know all the angles.'

He glared at his deputy as if it were her fault he hadn't thought of any of it, but she met his gaze impassively. That was the thing about Justine Vydelingum, she never took his bursts of petulance personally, she just got on with the job. Which was why she was going to have a successful career, and why he was likely to have a breakdown and move to a bothy on the Isle of Skye.

And good luck to her, because if he didn't start getting traction in his pursuit of Elsa Zero soon, his career was toast. He felt a headache brewing, and hoped to God it wasn't one of his occasional migraines.

She stood. 'But we do have some good news.'

'Finally.' He slapped the top of his desk, making the flat of his hand sting, and followed her from the office, along the corridor and into another part of the maximum-security area; to the ops room full of screens, where real-time surveillance images of London streets, parks and squares, every kind of public space, covered the walls.

As soon as anyone walked, cycled or drove into view, a grid triangulated across their faces, identifying them and placing their personal details up on the screen. All vehicle registrations were instantly logged. But he knew that the chances of Elsa Zero appearing were slim.

'Play it,' Justine told a man at one of the desks.

On the central screen, which dominated the wall directly opposite the banks of work stations, an image appeared: a field at twilight. Filmed by a satellite two hundred miles in the sky, the resolution was poor, the image in danger of fragmenting into blocks of pixels. But Plowright saw the tops of the heads of two figures running around.

'This was recorded last night at the farm of Zero's parents, Howard and Greta.' She turned to him. 'What do you think?'

'Definitely kids.' He stepped forward. 'Send in a drone to get confirmation it's them, maybe?'

Justine shook her head. 'Zero's old man is retired military, a former Royal Marine. And the mother, well... look in the file.'

She handed him a tablet. On the screen was a digital document, copied from SIS's physical archives, which had been typed, complete with smudged addendums in ink, on a manual typewriter many decades ago. Using his fingers to move and manipulate the image, Plowright found other digitized scraps of information too.

'She's something completely different, by all accounts.'

'So I see,' he murmured as he read.

With parents like that, it was no wonder Elsa Zero was as mad as a box of frogs.

She could have killed him down in the dead vault, could have snapped his neck easily; he was under no illusions about it. But she hadn't. As far as Elsa Zero was concerned, SIS was attempting to kill her, *he* was attempting to kill her. If she was aligned with a hostile foreign power, she wouldn't have thought twice about it.

She meant what she said in the vault; there was only one reason for Zero to sneak into the heart of the very organization hell-bent on killing her, and that was to figure out why.

'Howard and Greta will hear the drone a mile off and they'll disappear,' Justine said. 'If we go in, it has to be hard and sudden.'

Sometimes she spoke to him as if he was a trainee spy, wet behind the ears. But he liked her ambition and drive, her confidence. She reminded him of himself as a young man, back in the day; her clear eyes blazed with passion and focus.

But when Plowright was Justine's age, a good twenty-five years ago, the only way he'd been able to work all night long was by fuelling on coffee and cigarettes. Justine had been working just as long as he had, a good forty-eight hours now, but she sipped peppermint tea and bottled water.

He was shattered, and just wanted to go home, but

reasoned he'd get plenty of rest soon enough. There was no way he was going to survive in his job, not after this fiasco. He'd be kicked out, or obliged to resign. If Zero continued to evade capture, his own compulsory retirement would be small beer compared to the wider consequences.

'How sure are you?'

Images from the edge of space could be spectacular these days – the Yanks reputedly had equipment that could peer up a gnat's bumhole – but the UK's own surveillance satellites were still not good enough to positively identify the little girl and boy on the screen as Zero's kids.

'Howard and Greta are old now, and in ill health,' said Justine. 'They've lived alone on that farm for decades and keep themselves to themselves. We've spoken to their nearest neighbours, and they don't have visitors, full stop. There'd have to be a bloody good reason for children to be there. It's *them,* one hundred per cent.'

'Then send in a team,' Plowright told her. 'Get those kids, we get Elsa Zero.'

38

The children made incessant, infuriating noise.

For all her faults, Elsa had been a withdrawn and sullen child who rarely raised her voice. But her own children were an ill-disciplined and relentlessly cheerful pair who chattered and laughed from the moment they woke to the moment their exhausted heads hit the pillow. They spent the first day running around the field and yard screeching like hyenas.

'They've never seen a chicken, and it's made them giddy,' is how Howard explained it.

He and Greta had been surprised to discover Elsa was a mother, she didn't seem the type, and there didn't appear to be any father in the picture, which was irresponsible in these final, fraught decades of the human race, with societal breakdown on the brink.

They had no idea when Elsa would return for the children, if she even would, so on the second day they put their foot down. Harley and India had to adhere to the busy schedule of the farm. There were animals to care for, horses to feed, cows to milk, chores to be completed.

But removed from the soul-deadening grind that must comprise their London lives, it was gratifying to see the joy on the faces of the children, even if Greta and Howard didn't say it aloud; it was probably the first time they had spent any time in nature. For all their short lives they had been enslaved by the devices they stared at all day, becoming brainwashed by Woke propaganda.

The children were full of questions, the great majority of them idiotic and pointless. But even the Zeros had to admit that they had brought an unexpected energy to their usual routine. Howard and Greta had been self-sufficient for years, had discouraged visitors of any kind, and it was a shock that their home now reverberated with giggles and blather.

There had always been an unspoken understanding between Howard and Greta that they had somehow failed as parents – Elsa's arrival had been unexpected, to say the least – and their estrangement from her was a source of pain they never discussed. The rift was hardly surprising, Elsa had always been wilful and insolent, but they never acknowledged that their daughter was as uncompromising as they were, her stubbornness and disconnection a reflection of their own.

So Greta and Howard never expected for a single moment that she would turn up out of the blue to ask them to babysit. It was obvious that she was in trouble, and despite the long years of separation, she was still their daughter. The Zeros were aware that neither of them was getting any younger – and it could be the only time they would get to see their grandchildren.

But they didn't want to contemplate what would happen if Elsa never came back.

Standing in the kitchen as the children chased chickens in the yard, Howard Zero finished sewing back together Elsa's old rag doll, which he'd found at the back of a cupboard. A flimsy thing, it was barely more than a musty beanbag, with lumpen stitching for a face and button eyes. It had an arm missing, and one of its legs hung by a thread. Howard thought the girl might like it; maybe the boy too, such was the way of the world these days.

Howard wasn't a man prone to self-reflection, but he was surprised to discover that he'd miss the noise when Harley and India were gone, and he knew his wife would too.

'Greta, we should discuss what to do if—'

'Be quiet!' she snapped.

He turned to see her at the sink, where she had been washing up; her head was lifted to the window, her hand suspended over a pot on the draining board.

Their farm was deep in the countryside. There weren't many roads nearby, and few planes flew overhead. It was so quiet you could hear anything approach from far off, particularly at this time of the morning.

Howard felt the noise before he heard it, an ominous flutter in the pit of his stomach. Greta pulled back the grimy curtain and peered out. It was a disagreeable day, and they both hoped they felt the first distant rumbles of an approaching storm.

When they walked into the yard and listened – the kids had run into the field to attack each other with sticks – there was definitely something on the wind, so faint it was barely a change of density in the air.

Howard turned in a circle, trying to locate the source. 'It's coming from the south.'

'Children,' Greta called. 'Come inside.'

They were too busy playing to pay her attention, and

she raised her voice. Harley and India ran inside, followed by the dogs, just as the cracked glass in the windowpane above the sink began to buzz.

Howard and Greta went to either end of the heavy kitchen table and lifted it to one side, pulling away the threadbare rug beneath to reveal a trapdoor.

'This is for you both,' Howard told the children, offering the rag doll.

Harley and India looked at it doubtfully.

'What is it?' India asked.

'It was your mother's favourite doll.' They were wasting time, so he shoved it at the girl. 'Greta will take you downstairs.'

'Don't be ridiculous,' said his wife. 'You take them down.'

'My eyes are better,' he insisted.

'Even with my failing eyesight, I'm still more expert than you, and you know it.'

Howard stared in indignation, but of course Greta was right. Even with her eyes, and the tremor she had in her hands, she would always be the better marksman.

'Fine,' he said shortly.

While Greta swept her arm over the draining board to clear a space, smashing plates in the sink, Howard lifted the trapdoor.

'Down you go, children.'

'It's scary,' said Harley, looking into the darkness.

'Nonsense.' Halfway down the wooden steps, Howard tugged a pull cord, illuminating a long, clean cellar full of shelving units neatly stacked with tins and boxes: enough supplies to ride out an apocalypse for several years. 'Come along now, no more arguments, there's nothing to worry about.'

India crouched at the top of the stairs and peered down at the pair of cot-beds at the far end of the long space. 'What's happening?'

'It's nothing.' Greta tore down the net curtains. 'You won't be down there for long.'

'I'll join you in a minute, but don't worry...' Howard snapped his fingers and the dogs trotted down the stairs. 'Churchill and Montgomery will be with you.'

When the children hesitated, Greta barked with impatience, 'Get down there!'

Reluctantly, the two children went down the stairs, and Howard shut the trapdoor. The dull throb in the distance had coalesced into an ominous rhythm: *thwap thwap thwap*.

'You should go down,' Greta told him.

'And leave you on your own?' said Howard. 'Don't be ridiculous.'

They glanced at each other in brief recognition of their decades of devotion to each other. Howard and Greta had made a solemn promise to Elsa to protect the children, and that's what they intended to do, but they also knew they may not survive the morning.

Greta went into the parlour and unlocked the gun cabinet. She handed her husband a double-barrelled shotgun, and he chambered a pair of rifled slugs, stuffing more into his pocket.

'Give me a hand with this.'

Howard helped her move the cabinet from the wall.

In a hidden recess behind it was a Dragunov SVD semi-automatic sniper rifle. Greta took it out and picked up a magazine loaded with ten rounds of 7.62×54mmR cartridges. Squinting at the weapon, she put her finger to her forehead. 'Where are my glasses?'

'Oh, for goodness' sake.' Howard rolled his eyes. 'You won't be any good to anyone without those.'

'I'm a better shot than you, even without them.' She fluttered her fingers, trying to think. 'I left them in the loo, I think. Go and get them for me, will you?'

When he left, she set up the weapon beside the sink; fitted the curved magazine into it, made adjustments to the bipod. It had been decades since she had fired the Dragunov in a professional capacity, but Greta still took it apart regularly, cleaning and lubricating it, reassembling the component parts with a fluidity and grace that thrilled Howard. They still fired it occasionally, too, in preparation for the end of days.

'They're not in the bathroom,' said Howard, coming back down the stairs.

'проклятие!' Greta cursed. 'Look on the mantelpiece in the parlour!'

As Howard shuffled next door, Greta broke the glass in the window with the stock. Placing the barrel of the rifle through it, she leaned over the draining board, trying to get comfortable behind the PSO-1 telescopic sight; the chevrons were a blur in her vision. A helicopter appeared in the distance, its downdraught making the upper branches of the trees sway angrily.

Howard came back with her glasses. 'You really need to hang them around your neck, I've told you repeatedly.'

'Because you never forget where you put things, do you?' she replied.

Greta took her time placing the glasses on her nose

– Howard stood tensely beside her, rubbing his fingers against his palms – and then made adjustments to the scope.

The weapon was several decades old now, there were many better models available, but it was the rifle that Greta was most comfortable with, and with which she had made the most kills. It wasn't the most ideal weapon in the circumstances – she prayed the helicopter would land at least seven hundred yards away; and the targets would move fast once she made the first shot – but she would do her best.

'Good luck.' Howard moved a stray cup off the draining board and hung it on a mug tree. 'How's your back?'

'Please be quiet.' Greta lowered herself over the rifle. 'I'm trying to concentrate.'

Howard stood behind her with his hands clasped in front of him, peering over her shoulder like a referee watching a snooker player line up a shot. Greta readjusted her position and grip, but it was awkward leaning across the uneven surface of the draining board, so she lifted the back end of the rifle and placed a chopping board beneath it. Squinting into the scope, she adjusted her glasses.

The EC145 came slowly over the field outside in a roar of noise, making the horses scatter. Rotors slapping the air, it tilted towards the ground eight hundred yards away.

The skids were almost touching the grass. As soon as it landed, Greta knew she'd have little room for error. She sensed her husband close behind her and said, 'Don't stand there like a nincompoop, go look after the children.'

He didn't want to leave her, she knew that – together for more than fifty years, she could count on one hand the number of times they had spent even a night apart.

'I'll be down soon enough,' she told him. 'Don't worry about that.'

But Howard lifted the shotgun. 'And I'm not leaving you, don't *you* worry about that.'

And then the helicopter touched down, and Greta didn't have time to worry about the tremor in her hands, or her failing eyesight, or the aches and pains she felt leaning over the draining board. She tried to let her heartbeat settle – at her age, if it ticked over any slower, it was in danger of stopping altogether – as figures jumped from the helicopter.

They were young, fit people who moved with dexterity and speed, who understood the deadly business of killing, and who didn't have arthritic joints.

Three of the figures dropped out of the bird on one side and four on the other. They approached the farmhouse in a hunched run.

The noisy blast of the blades would give Greta a brief window of opportunity. The figures wore Kevlar armour, so she would have to aim for the face. Greta pulled the bolt handle into position and went to work.

Targeting one of the figures at the rear, she lined up the reticules of the scope, and fired. The rifle recoiled in her hands.

The bullet pulled wide. The scope wasn't properly calibrated. There was no paper target she could examine, not this time, so she had to use her instincts as she made adjustments. But the seven intruders, still close to the roaring helicopter, hadn't realized what had happened. They knelt in the grass, semi-automatic weapons lifted, to survey the farmhouse. Greta settled back behind the scope, and fired again.

The head of one of the squad snapped back and he fell. The other two on the left side of the helicopter immediately began to run in opposite directions, zigzagging across the grass.

Greta locked the breech and pulled the trigger again. One of the figures on the right spun and hit the ground.

The pair on the left rushed around the side of the farmhouse, and the two on the right towards the back door, leading directly into the kitchen. Like other sniper rifles, the Dragunov was not designed to hit a fast-moving target at short range.

Ignoring her sciatica, Greta stood stiffly. 'Get downstairs, while there's still time.'

'Don't be ridiculous,' said Howard.

He couldn't hope to kill any of the armoured intruders, but he could slow them down. As the door flew open at the front of the house, he stepped into the hallway to fire the shotgun at the chest of the first figure who came inside. The impact of the slug in his armour sent the man tumbling back out the door, but the recoil also blew Howard back against the wall.

Pain crashed along his spine, stars spun in his vision, but he lifted himself immediately and went back into the kitchen to pull the second trigger, firing at the camouflaged figure at the back door.

The glass in the door exploded as the man ducked away. The recoil caused Howard to topple again and he fell to the floor. Greta had tipped over the kitchen table and Howard crawled over to join her behind it as the man came in the back door and sprayed bullets.

The contents of the shelves, the china cups and jugs

and plates and dishes that had sat there for decades, were obliterated. The glass in the windows shattered and the cupboard doors splintered. Howard hinged the shotgun and pressed in two more cartridges. Bracing himself, he fired again over the top of the table.

'Come on!' The next thing he knew, Greta was tugging at his arm, trying to lift him off the floor. 'Get moving!'

Together they stumbled down the stairs into the basement, Greta snapping in place all the locks on the trapdoor from below.

The children stood at the back of the long, cramped room. The dogs sat whining in front of them.

'We'll not keep them out for long,' Howard told his wife. 'They'll have explosives.'

She nodded grimly in agreement. Footsteps stomped noisily on the floorboards above their heads as the assault team moved about, the murmur of voices drifting down.

'Well,' Howard told the children. 'It's not always as exciting as this around here.'

Greta opened a box on a shelf and took out a pair of Walther handguns, snapped in magazines, and gave one to Howard.

'What's going to happen to us?' Harley asked.

'Nothing is going to happen to you,' said Greta. 'Not if we have anything to do with it.'

But Howard and Greta shared a glance; they knew they wouldn't be able to hold out for long. They were trapped like rats.

'Howard,' said Greta, as they listened to the footsteps of the intruders.

'Yes, Greta?'

'I'm sorry if I've been difficult.'

'Don't be ridiculous,' he snapped again, irritated by the idea she could think such a thing. 'Every single day I have spent with you has been a privilege.'

'We got up to some things, didn't we?' Greta said.

The footsteps above retreated from the trapdoor.

'Oh, yes.' He smiled. 'We certainly did.'

'For the children, then,' said Greta.

'For the children.'

Howard and Greta lifted their weapons, just as the trapdoor disintegrated in an explosion of wood and metal, and smoke grenades bounced down the steps.

39

Elsa walked to the clear plastic wall of the biolab to study the man and the boy in the isolation chamber.

Their ashen faces were covered with oozing sores. Black with gangrene, the man's hands reached for his throat as he retched bile and blood onto his chest.

'My head gardener and his son. The pathogen has been in their bodies for only a few hours, but it has spread at an astonishing speed.' Arkady sounded surprised. 'Replicating, destroying cells, turning the body's immune system against itself. Luke… the poor lad is gone, and his father will die also of massive organ failure soon. It will be a merciful release.'

'You said I did this.' Elsa tried to contain the rage she felt. 'What did you mean?'

'Without you, Elsa, none of what we're doing here would have been possible.'

A man who had been undergoing decontamination procedures let himself out of the airlock of the biolab. With his dark beard and glowering expression, Elsa recognized him immediately as Noah Pettifore, the synthetic biologist.

'Noah.' Arkady gestured at him to come over. 'Let me introduce you to Elsa.'

'We're almost finished,' Noah told Arkady, 'I think the results are pretty conclusive.'

Elsa moved towards Arkady with the intention of beating the truth out of him, but Camille and Kieron stepped in front of her.

'Take one more step.' Camille's grip tightened around her handgun. 'I'd like that.'

'I understand, Elsa.' Arkady lifted a hand in apology. 'You're frustrated and want answers. Twelve years ago I stole a virus, a very deadly biological agent genetically engineered in a secret underground lab by my own government. A synthetic form of *yersinia pestis*, bubonic plague – transmissible by air, and therefore highly virulent.' He nodded at the victims. 'You see what it does to a person in less than a day. Release the pathogen in a crowded public place and the results will be catastrophic – and irreversible. I stole the genome sequence, the instructions, if you will, on how to replicate the genetic structure of the virus, which would allow me to construct a doomsday weapon.'

Elsa couldn't believe her ears. 'And *why* would you do that?'

Arkady wagged a finger, *we'll come to that*. 'I stole the data, Elsa, but then I had a problem. In this day and age, it's impossible to hide such a thing. Anxious about the consequences of such a terrible item becoming available on the open market, the Russian government took the unusual step of revealing its existence to its allies and enemies alike. A number of states, traditionally antagonistic, were even prepared to work together to find it.'

Steve Carragher had led some kind of inter-agency task force to find the data and destroy it, Elsa knew. But the mission had got him killed.

'That put me in an uncomfortable position. If it was proved

I had stolen it, they would have come for me; I certainly wouldn't be standing here now. I needed to find someplace to store the data until everybody got tired of looking for it. But in this world of cyberattacks and hacks, it's so difficult to know where to hide it. Put it in the cloud and it's vulnerable. Place it in a vault and it can still be stolen. The most obvious thing to do was trick the world into thinking the data was destroyed, and then place it somewhere nobody would ever find it... So we hid it in you.'

Elsa couldn't believe what she was hearing. 'SIS did a battery of tests, and so did RedQueen. If you planted any kind of data chip inside me, they'd have found it.'

'There's no capsule or microscopic device.' Arkady grinned, pleased at his own cleverness. 'The genome sequence is written into the cells in your bloodstream, Elsa, like ink on a page. It's encoded into your own DNA.'

It wasn't possible. 'You're lying.'

'Noah can explain the process better than me,' Arkady said.

'The instructions for the genome were encoded directly into memory T-cells in your bloodstream.' Pettifore spoke in a distracted monotone as he tapped at a keyboard. 'Cells in the blood you were given in the medical facility outside Buenos Aires contained the data. Memory cells are only woken up if activated by a particular antigen that causes an immune response. Until those cells are activated, the data is completely hidden. It can't be detected, even if anyone knew what they were looking for.'

Arkady nodded. 'Camille injected you with the antigen, I believe.'

Elsa remembered she was pricked with the stubby needle

at the hotel in Soho. Camille had said she was neutralizing tracking devices.

'And then all we had to do was take a sample of blood. It would have been preferable to have done it before RedQueen sent you down into the vault; there was a danger we may never have seen you again, but we had to ensure the memory cells were properly activated.'

Camille had drawn Elsa's blood in the van later that night, on the way to Dougie's.

'Noah used a genome sequencing device to read the data and recreate the synthetic virus. He's such a clever man, it's been a privilege to finance his work. His technology has opened up a fascinating can of worms, Elsa, which will forever change the way mankind stores information. Human DNA is capable of storing trillions of gigabytes of information, did you know that? That's far more space than on any network of computers. One day, every speck of knowledge will be stored in our own DNA, retrievable at a moment's notice. We'll all be walking encyclopaedias. But you, Elsa – you were the first! That's something to be proud of, no?'

The mission had been a farce. SIS and the other agencies had long suspected the operation was compromised, and were right to be suspicious.

The mission was a sleight of hand; Carragher had walked his team into a trap. Elsa had confirmed that the objective of the incursion had been accomplished and the data on the hard drive destroyed – if it had even been there in the first place. But she had been injured and treated for her catastrophic injuries. Given a life-saving blood transfusion, a small number of the blood cells containing a deadly secret, instructions on how to build a terrifying virus, had replicated in her body.

For all these years, Elsa had been walking about without a care in the world. Working, exercising, watching TV, dating, cooking, sleeping, showering, cleaning, washing, shopping, holidaying, eating, taking the kids to school, collecting the kids from school, paying bills, drinking coffee in the soft play area… and all the time she was going about her business, she'd been the most dangerous woman on Earth.

'You were the best hiding place, Elsa,' said Arkady. 'We couldn't have chosen anyone better to be the vessel for our secret. You were as fit as a fiddle; we already had your excellent physical assessments. Even more perfect, you were pregnant, and had already made the decision to settle for a life of cheerful obscurity, out of harm's way. And if things went wrong in your life, there was an excellent chance you'd be able to survive until the day arrived for us to retrieve the data. As we have seen for ourselves.'

'What if I had been killed on that mission, what then?'

'You certainly gave us a scare. You were meant to get a flesh wound.' Arkady placed thumb and forefinger close together. 'Lose a modicum of blood, enough to justify a small transfusion. But the ammunition my men used had to be real, of course. One of them got carried away, and shot you in an artery.' He shook his head. 'Not a good place, very dangerous and messy. You bled out quickly. If you'd died, we would have had to transfer the data into Camille. But you survived, I'm glad to say. And your critical injury gave even greater credibility to the narrative of the ill-fated but successful mission. Our preference was always for a carrier who had no idea of the strange cargo inside of them, and for many years it made life simpler for us all.'

Elsa looked inside the biolab, where the boy lay dead, his father on the brink.

'Why now, after all these years?'

'A project like this takes careful planning and good timing. It's always been a question of waiting for the right opportunity, for strange times such as these,' Arkady said. 'We're living in a very difficult and unpredictable age, stumbling from one catastrophe to the next. And the situation is only going to get worse. As the climate rapidly collapses, the struggle for control of dwindling resources is only just beginning. The coming years will see a mass movement of people across the planet; violent conflict will increase. Many of the old ways of running things have proved inadequate. There are public figures – connected and influential; a loose affiliation of like-minded people – who believe that our priority is to remodel society into something more resilient and, yes, authoritarian. A system of government that will be able to meet the coming challenges more robustly. Introducing a virulent plague will be the shock cure required to finally put this weak and vacillating world of ours on the right path.'

Arkady joined her in front of the biolab. 'I'll be honest with you, Elsa, we don't quite know for sure what the effects of releasing this virus will be. Millions will die, most probably tens of millions, or more. There will be chaos and civil disorder on a global scale – perhaps years of it. But in order to bring the disaster under control, we simply will not be able to continue the way we have. The world will need to become a completely different place. New laws introduced, long-cherished freedoms curtailed. A deadly plague will be the perfect device to introduce these measures. And then maybe, just maybe, this world will have a chance. You may not believe me a good man, Elsa, but I have the best of intentions.'

'Okay.' Pettifore slammed shut the laptop. 'The pathogen is ready to go.'

'You had better get changed, my friend,' Arkady told Kieron, who stood waiting in his suit and tie. 'Wear something casual, you're going to a concert, after all.'

The man walked out of the room.

'Kieron has agreed to be our vector,' Arkady told Elsa. 'In return for his sacrifice, I've assured him that his terminally ill wife will remain in my care, safe from the biological disaster that's about to engulf the world, and she will receive the best palliative treatment.'

Noah Pettifore asked tensely, 'My ride?'

'You'll leave with me when the helicopter arrives. We'll go as soon as the virus is on its way.'

Watching the man writhe in agony inside the tent, Elsa tried to make sense of Arkady's plan. Years ago her cells had been altered, a deadly sequence encoded into her DNA, her body weaponized without her knowledge, with the intention of causing untold death and devastation. It was vile, insane, beyond comprehension. She was so shocked, and so enraged, she could barely speak.

'Where are you going? Let me guess, far away.'

'Yes, obviously somewhere very safe. Releasing the virus is only the beginning, Elsa. There's plenty to do in the coming months and years, a world to reshape.' Arkady clapped Noah on the shoulder. 'We have been on a long journey, you and I; you too, Elsa. We're all coming to the end of that journey, and stand at the beginning of an exciting new one.'

She didn't understand what he was talking about. 'If Camille took the blood from me, why am I here?'

The tall man came over once again, and told Arkady, 'They're just arriving.'

'Thank you, Anthony.' The oligarch flashed her a big smile. 'You're about to find out. Come with me.'

'Okay, people.' Noah Pettifore placed a finger on an intercom button and told the remaining suited figures in the biolab, 'Wrap it up, quick as you can.'

Arkady led Elsa back towards the reception area. She was conscious of Camille walking behind her the entire time, and of Arkady's security men, who surrounded her as she walked outside onto the circular drive.

Elsa heard a throbbing noise and saw the trees sway furiously in the downdraught of a helicopter as it landed on the lawn.

'I do love a reunion,' Arkady shouted over the noise and the blast of air.

Several men in tactical assault gear jumped out of the vehicle as soon as it touched down. One of them reached back inside and lifted two children from the cabin.

Elsa felt rage and panic in her chest at the sight of India and Harley. Her first instinct was to run to them – maybe she could grab them and escape into the trees – but she felt the barrel of an assault rifle in the small of her back.

Arkady gestured for her to remain calm. 'They have been through enough trauma, I think, without seeing their mother killed.'

She glared at him, but he nodded once again at the

helicopter. Another man had jumped out, taking the hands of her children to pull them beneath the whirling blades.

Even before he took off his visored helmet, she recognized that big, purposeful walk, all these years later.

He dropped the helmet to the ground as he came towards them.

It was Steve Carragher.

40

Nigel Plowright was sitting in the back of a government car, phone clamped to his ear, as it had been for the past three days, the busy London traffic thickening around him.

'Don't think I'm going to take the fall for your incompetence,' a Whitehall mandarin hissed in his ear. This man, along with several others, had called to unload his anxieties and fears onto Plowright's already tense shoulders. 'You're clearly not up to the job, and never have been.'

Plowright couldn't comment on the veracity of the second part of the statement, but the job had been a poisoned chalice from the beginning. As the consequences of failing to find and contain Elsa Zero became increasingly clear, his superiors jostled to distance themselves from the decision to put him in charge of the hunt. He'd just come from a very difficult meeting at the Joint Intelligence Committee, where nobody would look him in the eye. Come the inevitable public inquiry, he'd be the fall guy. Could he be held responsible in the eyes of the law, criminally negligent for the release of an apocalyptic virus in the UK and the deaths of thousands? Was it time to get lawyered up?

'We're chasing a very promising—'

'I don't care what you're chasing,' said the mandarin.

'You'd better get this sorted, Nigel, or we're all fucked. *You*, in particular, do you understand?'

To his relief, the 'call waiting' icon on his phone began to flash. 'Sir, I have a very important call to take, and one that will crack this—'

But the mandarin had already hung up.

'What's the problem here?' The car was stuck in traffic, and Plowright leaned forward to speak to the driver, one of the ancient pool of chauffeurs who had been carrying government officials around since God was a nipper, and who drummed his fingers on the wheel.

'Some kind of diversion,' the man said.

Plowright was going home, finally. He'd take a shower, change his clothes. He was also debating very strongly with himself about whether he should make sure Hugh left the country. *Upstairs* would come down on him like a ton of bricks if he did, but he was reaching the point where he was past caring.

He answered the call. 'Have we got the kids? Tell me we've got them.'

Justine took a deep breath. 'The situation is complicated.'

'Shit, shit, *shit*,' said Plowright with feeling. In the front, the driver didn't bat an eyelid. He was used to hearing hissy fits from the civil servants he shuttled around town. 'What's happened?'

He heard the click of a door as Justine moved through the office. 'Someone got to them before we did. There was an exchange of fire between them and the Zeros, and—'

'Exchange of fire, what are you talking about?'

'Zero's parents attempted to stop the unidentified assault team, but the kids were taken.'

'Are they dead? Howard and Greta Zero, I mean.'

'They're alive and unharmed.' Plowright was surprised. 'We're bringing them in for interrogation.'

'Bloody hell,' said Plowright, with such feeling that even the driver raised an eyebrow. 'All right, I'm coming back in.'

He leaned forward. 'Take me back to Vauxhall Cross.'

The driver nodded and edged out of the crawling line of traffic to do a U-turn. Plowright was so tired he didn't have the energy to keep track of the stream of updates appearing on the secure SIS app on his phone, despite the cascade of notifications. He tried to get comfortable and grab twenty minutes' kip, but opened his eyes to find the driver watching him in the mirror.

'Something I can help you with?' Plowright asked in irritation.

'It's just funny.'

'What's funny?'

If the driver tried to make small talk, he'd report him; he'd take a few seconds off from trying to save the world to send an angry email to someone in Transport, just see if he wouldn't.

'The car behind.' The driver nodded in the mirror, and Plowright realized he'd been looking past him. 'It's been following us for some time, it even turned round at the same time.'

Plowright looked over his shoulder to see a black Daimler with tinted windows a hundred yards or so back.

He cursed himself for not expecting something like this to happen. So many foreign agents had been pouring into the country, the border surveillance algorithm on the SIS mainframe had been pinging like a pinball machine for the last forty-eight hours. And with most of them unlikely to know how to go about finding Zero, it was hardly surprising if one of them decided to cut corners by attempting to intimidate someone who may have critical intel.

Plowright wanted to tell his driver to do everything in his power to lose the tail. But, of course, the old-timer had probably never broken the speed limit in his life. If Plowright worked for the Agency, he'd have been given a dedicated secret service guy to drive him around, a man with a loaded automatic in a holster, tactical defence training and advanced evasive driving skills – good hair, too, probably.

But it was Plowright's guess that the David Jason lookalike in front had never driven over sixty miles an hour, let alone reversed at high speed to complete a perfect, screeching 180-degree turn. A high-speed chase through the busy streets of South London was out of the question; Plowright had little doubt they would end up wrapped around the first lamppost they came to.

He sat bolt upright when they turned down a side street empty of traffic. 'Why are we heading down here?'

The driver pointed to a sign. 'There's a diversion.' But a moment later, the daylight at the end of the narrow street disappeared when a lorry pulled across the junction, blocking their path. 'Now what?'

'Reverse!' Plowright shouted in panic.

The driver pulled the car to a gentle stop, and by the time he'd fiddled with the gearstick, the Daimler had come up behind them, blocking them in.

'Are you fit?' Plowright asked him.

The driver frowned. 'Fit?'

'Can you run?'

'Run, with my knees?' The driver made a face. 'Not going to happen.'

'Get away as fast as you can,' Plowright said. 'And don't look back.'

'I can't leave the car,' the driver protested. 'My boss will have my guts for garters.'

'Do you have grandchildren?'

'Five, as it happens.' The driver perked up a bit. 'The smallest one is only three, and he's a happy fel—'

'If you want to see your happy little grandson again,' Plowright snapped, 'walk away now.'

The driver stared for a moment, then killed the engine, took the keys from the ignition, and opened the door; left it open, too, so that the alarm *ping ping ping*ed.

The old driver moved at a good clip past the lorry – his dodgy knees didn't seem so bad, in the circumstances – and turned the corner. When he had gone, two large men with cruel eyes climbed out of the lorry's cab and walked towards the car. One of them climbed into the driver's seat, and the other into the passenger seat.

Plowright swallowed down the fear he felt and reached for his phone, but one of the men plucked it out of his hands. Plowright knew he should really say something, *who are you* or *how dare you climb into the car*, or even *you'll be in big trouble for this!* But what was the point, really? He'd only be hastening his own death.

A door in the back of the Daimler opened, and he heard footsteps coming along the road. When the door opened beside him, he was surprised to see an older woman wearing a lurid pink jumpsuit.

She gestured with fluttering, bejewelled fingers and long pink nails for him to move. 'Budge up.'

Plowright slid himself over to allow her to climb in. She rubbed her hands together. 'My goodness, it's chilly.'

Plowright looked her up and down. At the tall heels and jumpsuit, the flicky Farrah Fawcett hair still beloved of a certain type of older woman. He hadn't known what to expect, but it wasn't one of the Golden Girls.

'When's Barbie going to want her wardrobe back?' he asked.

'Don't be mean, Mr Plowright,' the woman admonished him. 'It doesn't suit you.'

'You do know you're trespassing on government property?'

'Yes.' Looking around, she frowned. The Ford Sierra was small, and had seen better days. 'I can see it's government.'

She held out a smooth, manicured hand. 'I'm Mrs Krystahl.'

He reluctantly took it. 'Nigel Plowright.'

'Boys, please,' Mrs Krystahl said sweetly, and the two men climbed from the car.

'My phone!' Plowright spluttered. The man who had taken it tossed it back into the car, before heading back to the lorry.

When Mrs Krystahl smiled, the shiny skin on her temples and forehead tightened; but Plowright had seen worse surgery.

'Mr Plowright – Nigel. Please tell me where Elsa Zero is.'

He snorted. 'I don't have the faintest idea.'

'I ask in the spirit of reaching out.'

'Reaching out? There are official channels for that. You don't hijack someone's car and terrorize them.'

'You make it sound very melodramatic,' she said.

'I don't even know who you are.'

'I represent RedQueen, Elsa's former employer. As I understand it, she's currently the unfortunate recipient of a kill order, and it sounds like everybody is trying to get in on the fun.' Mrs Krystahl studied him. 'You people really are out to get her.'

'I suppose it was RedQueen who aided Zero to get into the dead vault?'

She sighed. 'And a fat lot of good it did us.'

'Don't think there won't be repercussions for that. If we find a trace of your organization in our system—'

'Don't threaten me, Mr Plowright.' Mrs Krystahl held an admonishing hand in front of his face. Despite the sweet, girlish voice with which she spoke, there was fierceness behind her eyes. 'RedQueen is the organization the deep state is paranoid about, and rightly so, and I assure you we don't leave our own behind. The elimination of one of our employees—'

'Former employee.'

'Well, yes,' she admitted. 'The elimination of one of our former employees will not be without repercussions.'

'If you've been helping her, you must know where she is.'

'Elsa has unfortunately disappeared.'

'What are you talking about?'

'We lost track of her in the early hours of this morning, along with one of our current employees. Have they been liquidated, Nigel?'

He shifted uncomfortably beside her. 'Please don't call me Nigel.'

'Mr Plowright,' she asked softly, 'are they dead?'

'If they are, it wasn't us. I can't speak for any of the other agencies.'

'The information we obtained from the vault about Pilot Fish was trash.'

She was admitting her company's culpability in the previous night's raid on the vault; the statement, he presumed, intended as a quid pro quo.

'We wouldn't keep information about that mission there. It has a classification too secret to keep even in the drawer marked Top Secret. All Zero would have found were a few crumbs about a medical facility set up by the team leader as an adjunct to the incursion.'

'We both have a desire to bring this situation to an end. There will be a considerable reputational and financial impact on RedQueen if it continues. It's vital that we re-establish our standing within the intelligence community, even if it ultimately means regretfully cutting Elsa Zero loose. Nobody wants a war, Nigel.' She gave him an encouraging smile. 'Tell me what's going on and we could be of mutual assistance.'

Plowright sighed. 'Two nights ago, the US intercepted communications from Steve Carragher, a former SIS intelligence officer.'

If Mrs Krystahl was astonished, it didn't show on her face. 'He's dead.'

'Apparently not. Carragher was presumed killed during the operation called Pilot Fish to destroy the contents of a hard drive that contained data on how to genetically engineer a plague virus. Very contagious, very deadly; very fucking apocalyptic, actually. The Russians engineered this vile thing in an underground lab in Siberia as part of a secret bio-warfare programme. An unknown external threat actor stole the virus, and destroyed the lab to cover their tracks.' Plowright paused briefly, unsure about whether to continue. 'The communication revealed that the data was encoded in Zero's DNA. If the sequence is mapped and the genetic structure of this pathogen replicated in a lab, it could be unleashed anywhere in the world, and there'll be no stopping its spread. We've done the modelling on fatalities,' he told her grimly. 'And it doesn't bear thinking about.'

'I don't believe Elsa knew,' Mrs Krystahl said.

'No, me neither.' After Zero tried to turn herself in, and then broke into Vauxhall Cross, he'd come to the same conclusion. 'Steve Carragher spent two years trying to find the sequence that would be used to replicate the virus, but somewhere along the way he changed sides, and used the operation as a cover to encode it into cells in Elsa Zero's bloodstream, and fake his own death.'

'He knew the intelligence agencies would move heaven and earth to ensure that the genetic sequence for that virus would be wiped out.'

'So he put on a big, bloody show for us. Look, the sequence was destroyed! Mission accomplished! I sacrificed my own life to get it done! When Zero came back from that mission, we looked thoroughly for implants and microchips, anything out of the ordinary.' He shook his head in wonder. 'But we could have put her through three hundred genetic tests and still not found that information whizzing around her bloodstream. All these years, Elsa Zero has been a walking, talking schematic on how to make a biological weapon.'

'And you think Carragher intends to recreate the virus, and release it.'

'The intercepted communication made it clear Carragher intends to release it imminently, and revealed Zero's role in the plot. Where imminent biological attacks are concerned, many agencies share information. As soon as that information came out, just before midnight two days ago, everybody mobilized. Before you know it, London was filled with assassins and snatch teams.'

'If Mr Carragher was so clever as to put this nefarious plot together,' Mrs Krystahl said, 'it doesn't seem like his style to carelessly spill critical information.'

'We believe his intention was always to pit the agencies against each other, and to sow panic and discord. To make a big statement: just imagine the terror when the pathogen reaches Washington, Berlin or Beijing!'

'The agencies must have moved damned fast, because Elsa was attacked on the stroke of midnight.'

'The Yanks had a CIA agent embedded in Zero's life. Like us, they long suspected that Pilot Fish was a farce. The agent, a guy using the name Joel Harris, tried to subdue her, but Elsa got away, and that put her on alert. Lucky for us, because witnesses saw Zero fighting a pair of paramedics at the scene, but the ambulance had gone before the emergency services got there. We think it was Carragher's people.'

'Encoding secret data into DNA, why did we never think of that?' asked Mrs Krystahl.

'The technology is still in its nascency. The only man we know of who has been making any headway on it is a synthetic biologist called Noah Pettifore, and he's missing. We found three dead American agents in his apartment, one of them Joel Harris. The Yanks are livid.' Plowright turned to look at her. 'So now it's your turn. Tell me something I don't know.'

Mrs Krystahl sat with her red lips pursed, absently tapping an enormous gemstone she wore on her finger.

'I'm afraid it's not about Elsa any more,' she told him quietly. 'They'll already have the virus.'

'And how do you know that?'

Mrs Krystahl raised one threaded eyebrow. 'Our employee who disappeared with Elsa is Camille Archard.'

'One of the surviving team members of Pilot Fish.' Plowright sighed. 'Steve Carragher's wife.'

41

Elsa was escorted back to the bedroom and told to wait. An armed man stood outside the door; she wasn't going to be allowed to walk around at her leisure any more.

Head in turmoil, heart pounding, she paced tensely; felt like she had been punched in the solar plexus.

They intended to release a super pathogen in the city – expose innocent people to a highly infectious airborne virus. The Russian spoke some nonsense about forcing governments to their senses and bringing the world back from the brink. But what the project was really about – because what it was always about, in Elsa's experience – was giving people like him yet more power and control.

When the time came for her to make her move, she had to be calm and focused, because it wasn't just about that...

They had Harley and India.

They had her kids.

He had her kids.

He was still alive.

Steve Carragher was back from the dead.

Despite the overwhelming fear she felt for her children, her thoughts kept returning to him. The way he held their hands as they walked beneath the whirling blades of the copter had chilled her to the core. Screaming in fury, she had been dragged away at gunpoint.

Elsa let out a roar of anger and put her leg through the antique hardback chair. Pieces flew across the room. She picked up a broken chair leg. It wouldn't get her far against Krupin's security men, with their assault rifles and handguns; it probably wouldn't even get her out of the door, but it was still more useful than Saint, who was comatose drunk somewhere in the building. Elsa dropped it.

A moment later, the door opened and one of Krupin's goons gestured to her. She walked with him back to the front of the house, a couple of men behind her.

When she got to the lawn, Carragher was there, still dressed in his assault armour, drinking water from a plastic bottle as he spoke to Harley and India. They looked up at him warily.

He smiled at Elsa. 'Hey, look who's here.'

Her children flew into her arms. Elsa held them tight. Kissing their hot heads, drinking in their warmth and smell, feeling the rasp and rhythm of their breathing. Bewildered and terrified by what had happened, they clung to her.

'Leave us alone,' she told Carragher.

He looked surprised, as if he expected congratulations for coming back from the dead, but moved away across the grass.

'I'm sorry,' Elsa told her children quietly again and again, her lips moving across the top of their heads. 'I'm so sorry.'

As if any of this was her fault. The genome sequence of a deadly infectious agent had been encoded into her DNA by people she trusted; by the only man she had ever loved.

'Did they hurt you?' Elsa checked Harley and India for signs of injury. If they had been harmed, she'd kill everyone responsible. But they shook their heads.

'And... your grandparents... are they...'

'Gran and Grandad hid us, there was shooting.' Harley's eyes were wide with fear and confusion, but he understood her unspoken question. 'We don't know what happened to them cos there was smoke, we couldn't see, and the men took us away.'

'I hope they're okay,' said India anxiously.

'They will be,' Elsa told them with a certainty she didn't feel.

'We came in a helicopter,' said Harley, as usual finding a positive to his traumatic experience.

'So I saw.' Elsa smiled. 'How exciting.'

But when he cried, she pulled him close.

India touched her mother's face, tracing a finger along one bruise. 'What's happening?'

'There's been a silly mistake.' Elsa didn't know what to tell her daughter. 'It's going to be over soon.'

But India wasn't fooled. 'The men have guns.'

Elsa, who had lied and lied in her long career, and who was normally very good at it, forced herself to meet her daughter's gaze. 'You don't have to worry about that.'

India looked at her steadily. 'Are we going to die?'

'No!' Elsa pulled her into another hug. 'We're going home.'

'Granny gave me this.' India pulled something from her pocket, a gnarled and ancient piece of fabric. 'It's yours.'

Elsa took the bedraggled-looking thing with one arm, remembered it immediately. This small, ridiculous, patched-up Frankenstein's monster of a rag doll was one of the few good memories from her childhood. As a little girl, she had been inseparable from it; she was amazed Howard and Greta had even kept it. When she lifted it to her nose it smelled damp, musty. Pressing her thumb along the rough cloth, Elsa felt something inside that shouldn't be there, the size of a battery or electronic car fob. She didn't want to rip the toy open in front of Carragher, and gave it back to India. 'Keep it.'

'It's yours,' her daughter said. 'You have it.'

'Granny and Grandad gave it to you,' said Elsa. 'Keep it for them.'

Harley held out his hand. 'I'll have it.'

But Harley would leave it somewhere. If she gave her daughter instructions, India would follow them, so Elsa told her quietly, 'Don't let go of it.'

The girl nodded and took it.

'Will we see them again?' asked Harley, and the question nearly tore her heart in two.

'Of course!' she said, believing that in all likelihood Howard and Greta were dead.

'Can they come and see our house?'

'Sure, I'll phone and invite them.'

'Are we *really* going home?' asked India.

'Hey.' Elsa gave her daughter a surreptitious look that said, *don't upset your brother*. 'I always keep my promises.'

'So you'll get us each a Nintendo Switch, like you promised?'

'And loads of games,' Elsa told Harley, who was looking at Carragher.

'Cool.'

There was something she sensed they wanted to ask.

Carragher threw away the empty plastic bottle and started walking towards them.

'Is that man our dad?' India asked. 'He says he is.'

Of course he did. Another dick move by the man with nine lives. She didn't know what to tell them. She'd rarely mentioned their father; hadn't even given him a name.

'I thought our dad was dead,' said Harley.

You and me both, Elsa wanted to tell him.

Carragher held his arms wide, as if expecting them all to rush to him. 'You guys don't know how long I've waited for us all to be together.'

Harley and India held on to their mother tightly.

'Mum said you were dead,' India told him warily.

'Your mum isn't right about everything, even if she likes to think she is.' Carragher smiled at Elsa. 'Are you guys hungry? I bet you are.'

Carragher told the security men to take the kids to the kitchen to get something to eat. Harley and India looked at their mum. The last thing Elsa wanted was to let them out of her sight again, but she needed to confront Carragher alone, and they needed fuel.

'I'm not going anywhere,' she said. 'I'll come and find you.'

'Hey, guys,' Carragher told the kids as they turned to go. 'It's going to be fun getting to know each other. I understand it's a shock, but I'm here now, and we'll be together.'

Elsa fought the urge to punch him. When they walked away, he didn't take his eyes off the children.

'They're good kids, you've done a great job bringing them up.' Like she gave a flying fuck what he thought. 'And you look great, Elsa. Seriously. It's good to see you again.'

When he reached out, she stepped away. 'Are you for real?'

'You're angry, shocked, I get it.'

'How would you know what I feel, Steve? You've been dead for the last nine years.'

'Let me expla—'

'You betrayed me, you betrayed us all. You nearly got me killed so you could hide data in my DNA, then faked your own death.' Elsa snorted angrily. The only man she ever loved, and their relationship had been a massive clusterfuck of lies. 'It's no wonder I have trust issues.'

'It was a last-minute decision. I had no choice. We had to move fast.'

'But why me?'

'If the agencies ever found out I was alive, suspicion would have fallen on Camille. You were pregnant and getting out of the business – the perfect recipient for the data.'

'So you pretended to love me, slept with me, made me believe we had a future.' All alpha males like Carragher knew how to do was lie and manipulate. He'd probably never had a genuine emotional relationship his entire life. 'And getting every assassin on Earth to hunt me down, was that also your idea?'

'We intended to remove the encoded sequence in the coming weeks. Arrange a routine hospital check-up for you where we would have woken the cells, taken blood, and retrieved the data. You would have been completely unaware of any of it. But forty-eight hours ago, SIS intercepted one of our burst transmissions and we were forced to bring the operation forward. We scrambled to keep up with you, Elsa, same as everybody else.'

'And once you got what you wanted, you were happy for me to die.'

'You're standing here because of me,' he insisted. 'Camille would have killed you otherwise.'

'Where have you been hiding all these years, Steve?' She had so many questions. 'What have you been doing?'

'It's taken a long time to get here.' He turned towards the shuttered wing of the house where the biolab was hidden. 'Years of careful planning to set up the facilities, source dangerous biological materials and get them into the country.'

'To devastate the world.'

'To *save* the world,' he insisted. 'There are like-minded people like me all around the world, embedded in government, the agencies, the military, in all walks of life. We call ourselves The Nexus, and we're going to do what's required to pull the world back from the edge of catastrophe. Many of us have been carefully working towards this point, and we will take control.'

'Careful, Steve,' she told him. 'You're sounding like one of the bad guys.'

'I'm building a better world for the next generation. For my children.'

'Don't you dare talk about them,' she hissed. 'Don't even *think* about them.'

'I know everything there is to know about Harley and India. I've watched them grow up in that shitty little house.' Elsa wondered if there was anyone who hadn't been keeping her home life under close surveillance. 'You've done well to bring them up on your own, Elsa, but I'm back now, and I'll take it from here. I'll give them a proper life.'

There had always been something implacable about Carragher, but anger and resentment poured off him. For nine years, she imagined, he had been forced to watch Harley and India going about their lives from the other side of the world. It must have torn him apart to know that they never gave him a thought, didn't even know he existed.

But now he was back – and he was going to take them from her.

'They don't need a maniac like you in their lives, Steve.' She couldn't help but push his buttons. 'You've been dead and buried for years. As far as I'm concerned, you still are.'

'I could have killed your parents this morning,' Carragher told her softly. 'But I let them live, as a courtesy to you, the biological mother of my children.'

It was a relief to know they were alive, at least.

'We're going somewhere safe, Elsa, where we'll ride things out when the pandemic hits. Come with me, come with *us*. We'll pick up where we left off, Elsa, me and you. The four of us will be a family. Saint can come as well, which is why I had him brought here.'

The idea of spending years stuck in a compound or bunker with Carragher, playing happy families and making plans for the New World Order, didn't appeal.

'Thanks for the offer.' She glared. 'But I don't think so.'

'Okay, then.' He sighed. 'But let's be clear, I came here for Harley and India. They're coming with me.'

She felt her heart thump with fury. 'There is another alternative, of course.'

'Yeah? And what's that?'

'I kill you.'

Carragher smiled, as if she'd just said something funny.

'The kids will miss you, Elsa... but only for a while. You don't have to worry, they'll be safe, they'll have a life of privilege and comfort.'

Her eyes flicked over his shoulder. 'How's Camille going to feel about you taking my kids along for the ride?'

He shook his head. 'It's irrelevant what she thinks.'

'Don't you love her any more? Because she's still crazy about you, Steve. She's been slavishly doing all your dirty work even all these years later.'

'Fuck Camille,' Carragher said with venom. 'She's served her purpose.'

Elsa winced. 'There's something you need to be aware of, Steve.'

'And what's that?'

'She's behind you.'

The smile froze on Carragher's face, but he didn't turn. Elsa had watched Camille approach as she and Carragher argued.

Elsa gave her a little wave. 'Hi, Camille.'

Ignoring Elsa, Camille told her husband, 'Kieron is ready to go.'

Carragher turned to acknowledge his wife's presence for the first time, and then strode off towards reception. 'Bring her.'

'Ouch!' Elsa grimaced. 'That was super awkward. But you've always known it, right, Camille? I mean, there was you doing your master's bidding, putting your cover with RedQueen at risk every single day, while Steve was living a life of luxury, drinking piña coladas as he dished out your orders. And all the time, he didn't care about you; all he could think about was the moment he'd be reunited with his kids... and with me. That's cold, Camille. It must hurt, hearing him say out loud what you've always suspected deep down in that cruel little heart of yours... he doesn't love you. Maybe he never did. Personally, I'd kill him for that.'

'That's not my style, Elsa, you know that. I'll kill his kids instead.' A dead weight of fear dropped into Elsa's gut as Camille pointed her handgun. 'Shall we go?'

42

Greta Zero sat impassively in an interrogation pod, gnarled hands folded in her lap. The pod was a solid steel, soundproof 14×12-foot steel container, which sat in the centre of an empty concrete room in a secure area of the SIS building in Vauxhall Cross. The acoustic foam walls on each of the pod's seven sides were of a distinctive egg-carton waved design. Once the door was closed and sealed it was impossible to hear anything spoken inside, and the space was completely secure from electronic surveillance.

Plowright's original idea had been to let Greta sit alone in the deafening silence for an hour. But you could tell when she was left in the pod – her face was a placid mask – that her will was indefatigable. She would probably enjoy the isolation and use the opportunity to meditate or think about her bloody chickens. As a young woman, Greta had spent many days lying motionless among twisted rubble and broken glass in the ruins of bombed-out buildings, waiting to make a successful shot. Forcing her to wait wasn't going to provide him with any psychological advantage. Besides, it wasn't as if he had the luxury of time himself.

'Open it,' he told one of the guards.

The man turned a handle on the heavy door, which swung open to allow Plowright and Justine Vydelingum inside. Greta barely looked up when he dropped slim green files on the table and fell into a chair opposite. Justine stood at the door.

'Greta, my name is Nigel Plowright.'

'Yes.' She glanced at him. 'You look like one.'

He blinked, unsure of whether he was being insulted. Her polystyrene cup was empty.

'Would you like more water, Greta?'

Her brown eyes, nestled in the criss-cross of lines scratched deeply into the rumpled skin on her face, considered him blankly.

'Very well,' he said, when she didn't answer. 'We saw what happened at your farm this morning, Greta.'

He opened the top cardboard file with the tip of his Bic pen and spread photos of the farm siege, as recorded by satellite, across the table.

'We saw the helicopter come down and... all hell break loose. It was quite remarkable, really. Seven men with automatic weapons climbed out of the bird, but only five climbed back in.' Plowright smiled. 'Someone is rather a good shot.'

'Howard is a skilled marksman,' Greta said tersely. 'He was in the Royal Marines.'

'I have no doubt Howard was a crack shot, Greta, up there with the best the British Army has produced. But as good a marksman as he once was, I don't think Howard has ever been anywhere near as good as Klaudia Romanova Lobkovskaya.'

The old woman watched impassively as he continued.

'As you may know, Klaudia was a celebrated Soviet sniper who mysteriously disappeared in 1972. She won the Hero of the Soviet Union medal *twice*, but is believed to have been killed in a government purge when she fell in love with an enemy combatant. Rumours still swirl about Klaudia, who has become something of a legend in death. There are unsubstantiated stories of a desperate flight to freedom carrying Soviet secrets, of a new identity in the West, even wetwork for British intelligence. Not that I could ever find anything in our files about that, Greta. The cupboard full of classified secrets is very empty where information about Klaudia is concerned.'

Greta's expression didn't change. God, the old woman was hard work. Plowright took out a black-and-white image pinned to the page.

'There are hardly any photos of Klaudia in existence. She was notoriously photo-shy, as many dangerous people are. But this was taken in the early 1960s, when she was a young woman.' Greta didn't look at the photo he pushed in front of her. 'I must say, Klaudia was a bit of a smasher when she was young.'

Taken on a parade ground, the photo showed a young woman wearing a green cotton shirt beneath a dark green Soviet officer's jacket. Her brown hair was worn in tidy buns on either side of her head. An officer's cap trapped beneath one arm, Klaudia contemplated the camera with the same disdain with which Greta regarded him now.

'There'll have to be an investigation, of course, into the deaths of the men on your property, and I imagine some difficult truths will emerge.'

A tremor rippled across Greta's face that may or may not have been a smile. 'Oh, you won't be opening that can of worms.'

Plowright shifted in his seat; because she was right, of course.

She leaned forward and her eyes were hard and cold. 'My arrival in this country was arranged by your government, for whom I did work.'

'You're right, intolerable pressure will be placed on me to stop my probing too deeply into the past, and besides, there won't be any kind of paper trail. But I'm sure someone will do a deal to quietly hand you back, Klaudia.' Plowright winced, *silly me*. 'I mean, Greta. I'm sure you will be given a warm welcome back in Mother Russia. They'll want to talk to you about all the Soviet secrets you stole, and the deaths of certain high-ranking officials, and…' Plowright's voice hardened. 'You will never see your husband again.'

Greta's steady gaze was unpleasant, as if she was imagining him through the magnified crosshairs of a telescopic sight.

'What do you want?' she asked finally.

'Who were the men who attacked you and your husband, and took the children?'

'There was no time to ask.'

'You killed two of them, and yet they didn't kill you in retaliation. Why?'

'Professional courtesy, I suppose,' said Greta. 'I'm not complaining about it.'

Plowright said over his shoulder to Justine, 'Leave us alone.'

'Sir?'

'Go outside.' He gathered up the files. 'And take these.'

She signalled through the window that she wanted to come out. When the door closed, Plowright continued.

'Elsa is being hunted by some very dangerous people, Greta, *the* most dangerous people. Assassins from every major intelligence agency. We have no idea where she is – if she isn't dead already, she soon will be. Do you have any idea where she could be?'

'She wouldn't tell me. She's a wilful and secretive woman.'

For the first time, Plowright sensed tension in her.

'Whoever took Harley and India will not think twice about killing or harming them if it means getting to her.' He watched her carefully. 'Whatever your relationship with Elsa, they're your grandchildren. Even a cold-blooded professional like you must feel some responsibility for letting them fall into enemy hands.'

He clasped his hands on the table and waited. In the total silence of the pod, blood gushed in his ears, his heart thumped in his chest.

'I want to see my husband,' Greta said finally.

Plowright shook his head. 'Give me something I can use, and I'll consider it.'

'Howard and I make our decisions together.'

'Not going to happen,' he said, but a muscle in Greta's jaw tightened, and he knew this was a battle of wills he was destined to lose. He motioned at the window and, when the door opened, told Justine, 'Bring Howard Zero here.'

Unnerved by Greta's unwavering stare, he took out his phone, but realized there was no signal, so they sat in tense silence. To avoid looking at her, he examined the curious undulations on the walls.

Fifteen minutes later, the old man was brought inside. Howard had to stoop to get his tall frame through the hatch.

An additional chair was placed beside his wife. Neither of them so much as glanced at the other, but Plowright sensed their palpable relief at being reunited.

They had wasted enough time. 'Where were the children taken?'

'How are we meant to know that?' said Howard.

'Give me something,' Plowright snapped. 'Or I swear to God this will be the last time you ever see each other.'

Howard glanced at his wife, and Greta nodded.

'The girl has a doll,' Greta told Plowright. 'Or she did when she was taken from the basement. It has a medical alert device hidden inside it.'

'The doctor gave it to me,' said Howard, with a dismissive wave. 'But I've never used it. It has inbuilt GPS with a cellular connection.'

Plowright waggled his fingers to get Justine's attention outside. 'There's a passcode?'

'The whole thing would be pointless if there wasn't.'

When Justine came in, Plowright snatched her notebook and pen, and pushed them in front of the Zeros. 'Write it down.'

Howard picked up the pen, but hesitated over the paper. 'It's escaped me for the moment. Can you remember, Greta?'

'It's quite a long number,' said Greta.

'With several lowercase letters and symbols.'

'The lives of those children and your daughter are at stake, the lives of millions.' Plowright had been as patient as possible, but his voice rose in anger. 'So it would be very, *very* useful if you could remember.'

Howard's chin jutted in the air. He clearly didn't like Plowright's tone, but recognized the urgency of the situation. 'I believe the number is in a cabinet at the farm. Isn't it, Greta?'

His wife shook her head. 'The bottom drawer of the dresser.'

'I'm sure I put it in the living-room cabinet.'

'You moved it,' she insisted. 'When we had that tidy-up.'

'I don't think I—'

'For God's sake!' Plowright jumped out of his seat and told Justine, 'Get a helicopter here, and an armed guard. Howard's popping home.'

43

Except for the two bodies left in the isolation chamber, the biolab was abandoned when Elsa arrived back in the massive room. Noah Pettifore's team were dropping laptops and tablets into bags. All the lab equipment would be left behind.

Arkady Krupin was standing at a table with Kieron, who was now dressed in a hoodie, jeans and trainers, watching Noah carefully handling two sealed glass vials. The slim vials looked empty, except for the slightly fogged glass, but they contained submicroscopic virions that would infect countless people as soon as the deadly contents were released into the atmosphere. The biologist's fingers trembled very slightly as he placed each vial into its own rubber insert in a graphite case the size of a child's lunchbox.

'Don't take any unnecessary risks, Kieron,' Arkady told him. 'Drop one of the vials in Trafalgar Square, then make your way to Euston Station – no need to rush – and drop the other on the concourse. If at any time you feel threatened, smash both vials.'

Watching tensely as Noah closed the clasps on the case, Kieron nodded. 'Understood.'

Arkady squeezed his shoulders. 'You're doing a great thing, my friend. You're helping this complacent, indulgent world come back to its senses. I promise you, your wife will receive the best care available, from the best doctors.'

'You'll be dead as a doornail, though,' Elsa said.

Arkady picked up the case carefully.

'It's perfectly safe,' Noah told him. 'Is the helicopter ready?'

'I want to say goodbye to my staff,' Arkady told him, and Noah gave him a sharp look. 'Don't worry, it will take Kieron fifteen minutes to get to the airstrip, another twenty to fly into London. We have plenty of time.'

'I don't get it,' said Elsa. 'I bet you have a home in London, too.'

'Two. One in Kensington, another in Hampstead.'

'Then why are you doing this? Why release the virus there?'

'Impact,' Arkady told her. 'It has to be a capital of one of the major Western democracies; the West must experience the cataclysm first.' His lips curled in a vicious smile. 'But also, my ex-wife Natalya lives there. Partying, living the good life on my money, without me. I can't think of a better way of ruining her day.'

'Wow,' Elsa said in wonder. 'That all sounds very grown-up.'

'It doesn't matter where it's released,' Carragher told her. 'The virus will spread far and wide. London is only the beginning.'

'And I thought you were going to look after my kids, Steve?'

'We have a safe place. Impenetrable and far away. The virus won't touch us.'

Elsa glanced at Camille. 'You're all going to get on like a house on fire.'

Camille couldn't hold in her anger any longer and stepped in front of him. 'After everything I've done for you, for *us*? All these years I've loved you, and worked for you?'

'Not now.' He spoke in a cold, quiet voice. 'We'll talk about it later.'

'We'll talk about it now.'

'What was it you said, Steve, "fuck Camille"?' said Elsa helpfully. 'He doesn't love you, Cam, if he ever did.'

'You think I'm going to bring up her brats, play mother, knowing that every time you see them you'll think of her?'

'If the situation is not to your satisfaction,' Carragher told her, 'then maybe you need to consider your own future.'

'She said she'd kill Harley and India,' Elsa told him. 'You have to kill her first.'

'Enough!' Arkady clapped his hands angrily at Carragher and Camille. 'I don't care how you two solve your petty squabbles, but you will wait until we've finished here.'

He placed the case containing the vials in a backpack. Kieron knew he was on a suicide mission, he'd be the first person to be infected when he smashed the vial, would die a horrible death within hours, but he picked up the backpack.

'You need to go,' Carragher said, trying to get the conversation back on track. 'To make the rendezvous.'

Kieron nodded, but Camille snatched the backpack.

'I'll see him out,' she said, and walked quickly towards the door.

Arkady shook Kieron's hand. 'Goodbye, my friend.'

When Kieron left, Arkady nodded at Hazlett. 'Get the helicopter ready, we leave in ten minutes.' He glanced at

Elsa. 'Well, most of us. It's a shame you've declined Steve's invitation, Elsa, I think you could have contributed greatly to our cause, and you're an entertaining person. It was lovely to meet you, nevertheless.'

He left the room as Noah continued to direct the clean-up operation.

'I thought you were going to ask Saint to join you?' she asked.

'I did, but he's of no use to anyone these days.'

'It was sweet of you to try to get the old gang back together,' she said drily.

'Say goodbye to him for me.'

'I want to see my children one last time,' Elsa said.

Carragher shook his head. 'You made your choice, Elsa. It's over for you.'

She thought briefly of making her move, but was flanked by a pair of Arkady's armed guards. She'd be dead before she raised a fist.

'*Please…*' The word left a nasty taste in her mouth, especially where Carragher was concerned. 'Don't let Camille hurt them.'

'Harley and India are my future, Camille is the past.'

He intended to kill his wife, Elsa knew. Camille had devoted her life to Steve Carragher, but that didn't matter to him in the slightest.

'Steve…' Elsa would plead with him if she thought there was a chance he wouldn't take her children, but knew it was no good; there was no bargaining with a man like that.

He walked off, telling the men, 'Don't get too close to her.'

44

Bloodyfuckingtittybollocks, Plowright thought. *I'm going to be forced to make the decision, I just know it.*

The medical alert device Howard and Greta hid in the girl's rag doll had pinged in a Surrey mansion owned by the oligarch Arkady Krupin. The man had been implicated in a number of conspiracies, his name had even come up in frantic conversations following the theft of the genomic sequence of the pathogen from the lab in Siberia.

But Krupin had powerful friends within the government of his own country, in the UK and across the world, and somehow he'd always managed to cover his tracks.

But just because Elsa Zero's children had been tracked to his property didn't necessarily mean the virus was being manufactured there. In the ops room at SIS, Plowright gazed at a screen that displayed a high-res image of the massive estate, as seen from the edge of space. Multiple vehicles were parked on the gravel drive; on the vast lawn beside the property was an Airbus helicopter. Since the image was put on the screen, there'd been activity outside, but nobody had left.

Justine Vydelingum stood at his side. 'What do we do?'

'We wait,' he told her.

A pair of Typhoons were taxiing on a runway at RAF Brize Norton, carrying a missile payload with enough firepower to destroy the entire estate. They were waiting to be given the go-ahead, could be in the air within seconds.

The decision on whether to destroy Krupin's mansion had been kicked up to the Cabinet Office Briefing Rooms, which coordinated the government's response to domestic or international crises, and an emergency COBRA meeting had been called. But the pressure on COBRA was unbearable – whatever decision was made had immense consequences.

Blowing the hell out of the home of a Russian citizen, with little evidence of an imminent threat, would cause an international incident – there were at least two children inside that building, God knows how many other people. But a deadly virus could be getting manufactured inside, and sending in ground forces would give the perpetrators more than enough time to release it in a public place. A precision airstrike should completely destroy the lab and its contents, but Plowright had no idea what would happen if the pathogen somehow still managed to get airborne.

'Whatever COBRA decides will be for the best.'

Justine looked at him doubtfully. 'You think?'

What was needed was an immediate response, but there were too many geopolitical consequences, too many ramifications, however they decided to act, and Plowright knew the meeting would be split down the middle.

In the meantime, they had no idea if the infectious agent had been replicated already. Krupin's estate was only thirty-odd miles from London – if the virus was already on its way there, they were well and truly fucked. All of them; the whole bloody world.

'We put our faith in the political process,' he said, not believing for one moment the words that came out of his own mouth.

The military would be there soon, along with the CBRN guys, to cordon off a wide area around the estate. In the meantime, all they could do was move as many spy satellites as possible into position to watch the surrounding area. The Yanks had more sophisticated systems, USA-223 and suchlike, so Plowright's people were talking to their people.

'Do we evacuate London?' someone asked, when his team huddled for a conflab.

'What, an entire city?'

'Cordon it off, then. Stop anyone getting in or out.'

'Even if we had the authorization, how do you intend to lay a ring of steel around a whole city?'

Everyone started debating emergency procedures, flinging out words like *curfew* and *martial law*. The debate became hot-tempered and muddled as all the tension of the long days at work spilled over. Standing at the centre of the group, preoccupied by his thoughts, Nigel Plowright hardly heard what anyone was saying.

Listening to a call coming in over her headset, Justine moved away from the others, then told him quietly, 'Upstairs has said the decision should be made at an operational level. They say it's your call.'

Of course it bloody is, he thought bitterly. *The spineless bastards.*

But he was ready for it, and there was no time to lose. As everyone around him argued, Plowright said, 'Get those fighters in the air.'

45

The guards were going to take her into woods behind the house and kill her. Maybe the last thing she'd glimpse as she toppled to the ground, life draining from her, would be Carragher's helicopter lifting above the trees; her children flying off to a new life and an unknown future without their mum.

Elsa tried not to think about it. Instead, she focused on how close the guards were to her as they led her along the corridors. Annoyingly, they were careful to heed Carragher's instructions and stayed well back.

'Let me see my children,' she asked. 'One last time.'

Neither man answered. Outside, she heard the engine of the helicopter warming up. She knew it would take off in a matter of minutes, taking Harley and India from her forever.

They walked past the room with the bar, where Saint was still slumped on the high stool, and her anger surged.

'Keep moving,' one of the men said, but she ignored him and stormed through the door. Another guy sat at a corner table, assault rifle on his lap, watching Saint. As soon as she came in, he lifted the weapon and stood.

'Are you fucking kidding me?' she shouted. 'I mean, seriously?'

She swiped her foot underneath one of the legs of the

stool, tipping it backwards. Arms outstretched, Saint fell flat on his back. Grunting in surprise, he opened his eyes.

Elsa grabbed two handfuls of his body warmer to haul him to his feet. He tried to focus on her face, which was contorted in rage close to his, blinking one eye and then the other against the light, his head swaying on his neck like seaweed on a tide.

'I came to you because I thought you could *help* me,' Elsa said. 'You said you would help, but you've just been a complete liability. Look at you, you're a mess!'

'That's…' When he finally managed to speak, and she got a blast of his foetid breath, he sounded hurt. 'Maybe I could have… I should have…'

'You're pathetic, Saint!' She shook him roughly. 'He's going to attack London with a biological weapon.'

He grimaced. 'Who is?'

'Steve Carragher!'

'Wait…' His befuddled mind tried to understand her. 'Remind me what year this is?'

'Carragher is alive, he's taking my kids, and all you've done for the last forty-eight hours is get shitfaced.'

Saint reached around her to grab his glass from the bar and gulped down half of the murky contents. 'Sorry, Elsie.'

'They're going to kill us.' She nodded at the three smirking guards, who stood enjoying the entertainment. 'And all you can do is drink.'

He swallowed the rest. 'One for the road, I guess.'

She slapped Saint's cheek hard. It turned crimson.

Swaying on his feet, Saint rubbed it. 'Ouch,' he said, a whole five seconds after she had done it. 'Don't do that ag—'

She slapped him on the other cheek, so hard that his head snapped to the side.

'You've made your point now.' Saint lifted a warning finger, but she slapped him again.

'What's the point of you, Saint?' she said. 'Look what you've done to yourself.'

He nodded sadly. 'I'm sorry.'

'It doesn't matter any more.' Her shoulders slumped. 'It's too late, we're out of time.'

'Come on,' he said, disappointed by her lack of faith. 'We can still—'

'It's over. A lot of people are going to die, Saint. *We're* going to die.'

He picked up a bottle of Scotch from the bar and began to swig. Elsa wrenched it from his mouth. Saint snatched it back, and they grappled over it. Despite his inebriation, he was determined, and the bottle moved back and forth between them. The guards laughed.

'Take your hand off,' he told her, a nasty look on his face.

All it would take was a knee to the bollocks and he'd fold like a pack of cards. 'Yeah, and what'll happen if I don't?'

'If you don't,' Saint hissed quietly, 'I won't be able to throw it, will I?'

Elsa let go as Saint turned and let the bottle fly.

It smashed into the face of the nearest guard, making him stagger. As the other guards began to move, Elsa leaped at him, her momentum swinging his aim to the side. She clamped her hand on his trigger finger so that his SIG MCX erupted in a burst of gunfire that took out the next guard along. She wrestled the weapon from his hands and jerked the butt hard into his forehead. He went limp. Springing to her feet and swinging the weapon at the remaining guard, she saw he was already immobile on the floor, with Saint standing over him.

'We have to go.'

'I need a wee.'

'No time,' she said. 'Got to get my kids.'

'What can I do?' Saint shuffled over as she searched the guard. 'Tell me.'

He could barely walk in a straight line, but he had taken out that man quickly enough.

'They've made a virus, Saint.' She took a phone from the guard's pocket, grabbed his hair to lift his head from the floor and activate facial recognition, opening the device. She looked up at him, torn about what to do next. 'They'll kill millions, but—' Her chest clenched with hurt and helplessness. 'They're taking my kids.'

He staggered from side to side. 'Tell me what you want me to do.'

'The virus is in two vials, which they're taking into central London and releasing at a concert. Trafalgar Square, I think.' She looked stricken. 'The carrier, a guy called Kieron, left five minutes ago.'

'I'll stop him,' Saint said.

He could barely stand. 'You won't.'

'Still got the skills, Elsie.' She heard a battered sense of self-respect in his emotional reply. 'You gotta trust Saint.'

It wasn't like she had any choice, so she activated Google Maps on the phone to find the nearest airstrip.

'He's getting picked up by helicopter. You have to stop him.'

'Got it!' Punching the air, Saint turned to go – and tripped over one of the guards on the floor. Jumping up, he assured her, 'I'm okay!'

Then he staggered off along the corridor in the wrong direction.

'This way!' Elsa picked up a SIG carbine. He turned quickly to follow her towards the reception, which was empty. On the gravel drive outside, she looked at the various SUVs. 'There must be keys in one of these.'

But Saint leaped on the Triumph motorbike. 'This will be quicker.'

He turned the ignition, squeezed the throttle, and the engine roared. A bit of focus seemed to shine in his bloodshot eyes. He revved the machine and it flew off, gravel spurting up behind it.

On the lawn, the helicopter's rotors turned. A pilot sat alone in the front, making final checks. Which meant Carragher was still inside the house – her kids, too.

She made a call.

46

Chewing tensely on his glasses as he watched the progress of the fighter jets on the screen, Nigel Plowright's attention was caught by the live feed of the exterior of Arkady Krupin's mansion.

'Who is that?' He pointed at the two figures who had come outside. One of them roared away at high speed on a motorbike and the other one – who looked familiar, despite how tiny she was on the screen – went back inside. 'Is that who I think it is?'

As a tech scrolled back through the footage, one of Plowright's team came over with a phone. 'Call for you.'

Plowright stared in incredulity. 'Now?'

'It's Elsa Zero.' That got his attention. 'Shall we put her on the speaker?'

'Absolutely not.' The last thing he needed was for everyone in the room to hear their conversation in case this whole episode ended very badly, as was looking increasingly likely, and he took the handset.

'Elsa.' He heard her panting breaths on the other end; she was moving fast. 'Where are you, please?'

'I'm at Arkady Krupin's mansion in Surrey.'

Plowright crossed his arms. 'We're looking at it right now.'

'They're going to release a virus in central London.'

Maybe he needed his team to hear the conversation after all. Gesturing impatiently at everyone to gather round, he put the phone into speaker mode.

'Are you still there?' said Elsa frantically.

'Yes, I'm still here. Can you tell me who *they* are, please?'

'Arkady Krupin and Steve Carragher.'

'Understood. Do you know where the virus is right now, Elsa?'

'It left the building minutes ago,' she told him. 'Wait a moment.'

Plowright winced. 'Elsa, we don't have the time to—'

But then he and his team heard a fusillade of gunfire at Elsa's end. Sustained bursts crackling over the speaker, yells and grunts.

'Where are the ground forces?' he asked one of his team members urgently.

'On their way.'

'Elsa?' Plowright said over all the angry noise. 'Elsa, can you—'

'Please hold, caller!' she shouted.

There was more gunfire, the sound of plaster cracking, something fragile shattering, then silence. He held his breath, expecting the line to go dead, but suddenly she was back, and talking urgently.

'There's an airstrip nearby, the carrier is on his way there with the virus, but Saint is going after him!'

Half of his team peeled off to hunch over a map on a tablet, but Plowright had a sinking feeling in the pit of his stomach. 'The carrier is en route with the virus, and you've sent Max Saint after him?'

'It's going to London,' she confirmed.

'Understood.' He tried to keep his voice steady. 'Do you know where in London, Elsa?'

Her reply was interrupted by more shouting and bursts of automatic gunfire, and then a bang as the phone hit the floor, the sound of a physical struggle; grunts and smacks, a crash; somebody cried out in pain.

'Elsa... Elsa... are you there?' Plowright stood holding the phone, every nerve shrieking, waiting for her to come back onto the line, not knowing if she would.

'Even if we find it, we'll never get to the airstrip in time,' Justine whispered to him. 'The carrier could already be in the air.'

Plowright heard more frantic grunting, and then a sickening crunch: it sounded like a bone, or even a neck.

Elsa came back on, gasping for breath. 'They mentioned a... a concert. In Trafalgar Square.'

Justine and a couple of others left immediately to find out what it was.

'Elsa, do you have—'

'No more questions,' she snapped. 'I was brought here against my will. The genomic sequence of the virus was hidden in my DNA without my knowledge.'

'I know,' said Plowright grimly.

'There's a biolab here that they used to sequence the virus. That's all you need to know. I have to go.'

'Now you listen to me,' he told her urgently before she could end the call. 'You have to get out of there, Elsa. There are fighter jets on the way, we're going to destroy the building.'

'My kids are here!' she shouted. 'Don't attack, there are children here!'

'I'm sorry,' he told her quietly. 'The command has been given already. The most important thing is that the lab is destroyed.'

'How long?' she asked.

'I'd say…' His eyes lifted to the screen where arrow icons representing the RAF jets moved at speed across a digital map. 'You have considerably less than ten minutes.'

The line went dead.

47

Elsa ran from room to room, forcing herself to search the mansion methodically. It was a massive house, she hadn't even been upstairs, and she had less than ten minutes to find her kids.

Whenever someone came into view, Elsa tensed, her finger tightening on the trigger of the MCX carbine – she'd already taken out a handful of Arkady's security men – but mostly she encountered members of the scientific team.

If they weren't armed, if they weren't a threat, she shouted, 'Get out, this place is going to be destroyed.'

Running towards the room containing the biolab, she encountered Arkady and Noah Pettifore on their way to the helicopter. Before the two guards in front of them even lifted their weapons, Elsa fired twice, and they fell dead. Arkady and Noah stared in shock as she rushed towards them.

'Elsa.' The Russian smiled warily. 'Good to see you.'

'Back up!' Frozen to the spot, both men raised their hands. 'I said move!'

'You need to come with us, Elsa,' Arkady told her softly. 'It's not safe here.'

'You're telling me.' She marched them back into the ballroom Arkady used as an operational space.

'Give her whatever she wants,' Noah hissed at the Russian. 'We need to *go*.'

'The pilot will not leave without us,' Arkady told him through gritted teeth.

In the ballroom, Hazlett was putting on a jacket, as if he had just completed a long day in the office. Over the roar of the helicopter's engines, gravel spurted on the drive outside as SUVs accelerated away: Arkady's rats leaving a sinking ship.

'Get out,' she told him.

'We must leave now, Elsa,' Noah complained gently, as if she was making him late for an appointment. 'There's plenty of room for you to join us, my dear.'

'Where are my children?' she demanded.

'I don't know, with Steve, I imagine.' Eyes edging sideways, Arkady screamed suddenly, 'Shoot her!'

She turned to see Hazlett pointing a gun at her across the room. Her weapon snapped up too late, he could have shot her already, but he looked sick to the stomach. She knew immediately that he wouldn't, simply couldn't, kill her.

'I'm sorry,' Hazlett said miserably. Placing the handgun down with a trembling hand, he ran to the door.

'The offer still stands.' Arkady's tone was anxious.

'Shut up,' she told him. 'Get in there.'

She nodded at the room with the biolab and the two men walked inside. As she shut the doors, Noah realized what was happening – 'Wait!' – and rushed at her, but she rammed the rifle between the two bar handles. The doors rattled angrily as Arkady and Noah shoved frantically on the other side, but there was no way out. It was the only entrance to the room, and all the windows were boarded up.

'Elsa!' Arkady's voice rose in panic. 'Let us out, please!'

'Open the door!' screamed Noah, banging his fists.

Elsa registered again the roaring engine of the helicopter outside, the humming thwap of the blades. Heart pounding, she raced out of the room.

She couldn't let her kids be taken away, but had only a few short minutes left.

And when she rushed into reception, she found Steve Carragher heading towards the entrance, pulling Harley and India behind him.

'Leave them alone!' she shouted.

At the sound of Elsa's voice, he turned, pulling out a handgun to shoot her.

'No!' screamed India, and pulled at his arm.

Carragher easily swatted the girl away, but not before Elsa flew at him, knocking the weapon from his hand.

They smashed into the wall.

48

Somehow, Saint managed to stay on the motorbike as it roared across bumpy grass and mud and through hedges; bracken tore at his face; his coccyx juddered painfully on the seat.

He was barely in control of the machine, which slipped and shifted beneath him. Lifting his head to the sky, letting the wind cool his sweaty face, Saint's eyes would drift shut as he felt himself come back to life, and he'd have to remember to open them before he crashed.

Accelerating out of a ditch, the bike's wheels left the ground and landed in the middle of a road, the suspension crunching angrily, to cross in front of a speeding car. Saint heard the stricken blare of a horn, the screech of brakes.

The Triumph flew over fields, bouncing over ridges and ruts, because if he stuck to the roads he'd never make up any time. He just about managed to steer the bike through dense woods. Trees threw themselves in his path; every time he managed to avoid one, another loomed suddenly behind it. He zigzagged crazily, gunning the 865cc engine as hard as he could, mulch and leaves spraying behind the wheels. He rode in a state of amazement that he was still alive, let alone still moving. His hand rolled greedily on the throttle, increasing the speed.

The airstrip had to be close, but Saint couldn't see it. He began to panic; the woods seemed to go on forever. Hurtling down a steep incline onto another narrow country lane, the wheels thudding angrily back to the ground, he saw a smooth ribbon of concrete in the distance where a Land Rover Discovery was pulling up beside a small building.

A figure climbed from the vehicle to watch him approach from a hundred feet away – the guy called Kieron. Saint gunned the bike across the road, accelerated up the incline onto a sea of grass. He'd aim the motorbike right at him, mow him down. Yanking the throttle, bellowing his exhilaration at the top of his lungs; the bike surged. The next thing he knew, he heard a faint crack over the noise of the engine.

The carrier was firing at him. Closing in fast, Saint's concentration wavered. For a split second, he lost control of the bike; it swerved one way and then the other. But he kept going – aiming at Kieron as best he could – and then suddenly the machine tipped beneath him, and he flew off. The bike smashed onto its side, scraping along the ground.

Saint rolled across the concrete behind it, his brain rattling in his skull. The harsh surface of the runway gouged at his clothes. His thigh felt like it was on fire, pain burning up and down his body as friction tore through the fabric. He rolled and rolled, bones and muscles shrieking, until he came to a stop.

Saint groaned, lying on his back; the clouds in the sky spun furiously. If he'd been more sober, he might have felt the pain more, but he was mostly dizzy and nauseous. Later, if he wasn't shot dead, he'd no doubt feel all the rends and cracks and fractures. A symphony of pain would play all over his body; the drum section already banged cheerfully in his skull.

When he lifted his head, he saw Kieron walking towards him, turning like a Catherine wheel in his disorientated vision.

'Wait!' Saint said as the man came over, handgun pointed down at him. When he held up his own bloodied hand, its multiples flew around in front of his face. It was difficult for Saint to know what was up, what was down, just how many Kierons there were, or whether or not he was flying at the speed of light.

He didn't know what to do next, except possibly be sick, until his fingers found a traffic bollard, one of a number placed around a mound of spilled sand at the edge of the runway, and instinctively swung it at the guy. It bumped harmlessly off Kieron's arm, and Kieron waited till Saint climbed unsteadily to his feet, stumbling back and forth to keep his balance, before he raised his gun.

Kieron fired. Saint felt excruciating pain in his shoulder. His vision was obliterated by a blizzard of aggressive dancing shapes. If the guy fired again, he'd be dead for sure, so Saint threw the sand he clutched in his hand. It went straight in Kieron's eyes and when the man's arms flew to his face, Saint lurched forward. Knocking Kieron to the floor, he half jumped, half fell on top of him; slammed the guy's gun arm into the concrete, sending the weapon skittering away.

All the rage Saint felt about his miserable life, all the dreadful feelings he smothered with his addiction; all the poor decisions and wrong turnings; the prison time, the spells in psychiatric wards, the family who had rejected him, all those cold months and years in hostels or on the street; all those times he'd nearly gotten himself killed on behalf of nations, corporations, militias, groups, factions, and obscenely rich men who didn't know who he was, and who didn't care. But, most of all, the shame and guilt he felt at his core about the men he had killed, the families he had broken, the children he'd left orphaned.

All his self-loathing at how he had become a joke, a jester, a fool. His endless, remorseless disgust at what he had done, and what had been done to him, about what he had become, and where he would end up.

And the physical pain too, because his shoulder *really* hurt.

All he wanted to do was punch out all that pain.

He focused it all into the fist on his one good arm, and smashed it again and again into the guy's face. Saint punched and punched and punched, until he was breathless and sobbing, and his hand was numb and bloody. And he only stopped when he realized Kieron had stopped moving, which could have been hours, minutes or moments ago.

Saint stumbled to his feet and roared with triumph.

'Yes!' he screamed, doing a little jig of pleasure on the runway, and somehow not falling over. 'Didn't count on Max Saint, did ya? I did it, I'm back!' He took the flimsy photo of the beach hut from his pocket and smothered it in kisses. 'I'm coming for you, baby, I'm coming home!'

Limping to the Land Rover, he opened the rear door. There was a backpack, and when he unzipped it, he found a small graphite case. Handling it with extreme care, he placed it on the bonnet of the car and undid the clasps. Opening the case, he looked inside.

His good mood evaporated in an instant. 'Shit!'

He had to get back to Elsa, and quick.

There was a sound, a helicopter approaching in the distance. Luckily, Kieron's body was hidden on the other side of the vehicle. Saint watched as the MD 500 came closer.

The pilot thought Saint was Kieron, and he was here to pick him up and take him into London so he could release the infectious agent. Which was fine with Saint, who fancied a ride in a helicopter. It would be just like old times.

Enjoying the draught whipped up by the rotors on his hot face, he waved cheerily at the pilot as the skids touched down.

49

She didn't stand a chance.

Carragher was strong, relentless, his rage fuelled by nine years of resentment. He'd rather kill her in front of her own children than let her take them, and he came at her with all the brute force he had.

Elsa needed all her skill and experience to stand a chance against him; he was a trained killer, one of the best, and she was exhausted, full of aches and pains, her body bruised and battered, reactions slow. In a fair fight, she could have used her natural speed and agility to stay out of his reach, but everywhere she tried to move, Carragher got there first.

His very first punch glanced off her cheek, sending her spinning into a side cabinet; the edge painfully cracked against her hip. He picked her up and threw her to the floor. She landed on her back and the air whipped from her lungs. For a moment she didn't know who or where she was, but the instinct to survive made her scrabble away on her hands and knees. When he followed, she attempted to backheel his shin, but he sidestepped, and grabbed her hood.

She lost time after that. Everything happened in juddering smash cuts of light and dark, of flickering moments and sudden, agonizing pain she was powerless to stop. Somewhere in the back of her mind, she was vaguely aware of the terrified screams of her children coming from a long way off.

Trapped against a wall, Carragher's powerful blows pounded into her flesh; breaking skin, compressing muscle, juddering bone. Cringing from a blow on the left, another arrived on the right. His big fingers dug into her cheeks as he began to crush her head against the wall, the pressure inside her skull reaching intolerable levels, the soft plaster on the wall denting and cracking. Elsa put all her last ounce of energy into a vicious Krav Maga palm strike to his nose. A butterfly of blood exploded across his face and he staggered back.

Baring his bloody teeth, lips curling in fury, Carragher unsnapped the Kevlar, shrugged off the spattered armour, let it fall to the floor, so he could move more freely.

Then he came again with a roar, knuckles as pale as marble across the top of his clenched fists. Maybe his frenzy of anger, his utter confidence, was her only opportunity.

When Carragher swung, Elsa dropped to the floor, rolled and came up onto all fours, skittering backwards like a crab. The patterns of the tiled floor zigzagged crazily between her thighs as she tried to find space, her heels sliding in a slick of blood.

Carragher strode forward and picked her up. Her body left the floor, and she flew through the air; a discordant crash seemed to come from everywhere, and a moment later Elsa vaguely realized she was lying face down on the floor among scattered pieces of medieval armour. When she lifted her head, ear shrieking, vision blurring, she saw the anguished faces of Harley and India across the room, but barely heard their cries of terror.

And she saw one of the staircases.

Carragher walked away, his wide shoulders rolling easily; she didn't know why. But then he took a sword from between the gauntlets of another suit of armour. The steel blade was thirty inches long and he rolled it in his hand, swinging its tip in a wide circular motion, getting a sense of its length and heft, as he strolled back. She was prone on the floor and knew he intended to ram it into her chest until the blunted end cracked the floor tile beneath her.

Elsa tried to get up; she had to get up.

She wanted to tell the kids to run, but they'd only hide somewhere in the house. The fighter planes would be here.

In how many minutes, how many seconds? Typhoons were ripping through the sky towards them at impossible speed, carrying a devastating payload.

Gripping it tightly in both hands, Carragher lifted the sword high above his head and swung it down with huge force, to cleave her in two. Elsa grabbed a fallen axe spear and braced herself beneath the thick wooden shaft. The clashing weapons clanged angrily. Elsa felt a jarring vibration all the way up her arms and into her shoulders. She slid back on the tiles, pushing with her heels, as he lifted the sword and brought it down again and again on the wood, which splintered in two.

She dropped it and frantically crawled towards the staircase. He swung the sword again. Cold steel whistled at the back of her neck to smash into the tile at her shoulder.

'Where are you going?' he said in irritation. 'I expected more of you, Elsa.'

When Elsa reached the bottom step of the curving staircase, he grabbed her by an ankle and pulled. She felt herself slide, blood and perspiration smearing on the smooth tile, the nails of one hand unable to find purchase. Carragher viciously twisted her leg, forcing her onto her back beneath him. Panting, chest heaving, she blinked the blood from her eyes to look up along his massive body in angry defiance.

Carragher lifted the sword above his head two-handed, the tip face down, ready to thrust it into her heart. But she swung up the handgun that had fallen from his hand and spun to the side of the staircase, and which she had desperately scrambled to recover.

Carragher gaped in surprise, his mouth a yawning red mess.

'Try digging this out of your DNA, Steve,' she told him, and emptied the magazine into his chest. He staggered back several steps, bullets punching into his body in rapid succession.

Elsa pulled the trigger until it clicked uselessly. Carragher lay dead on the floor, spreadeagled in the pool of blood unfolding like wings on either side of his body.

The weapon clattered to the floor beside her as Elsa fell into darkness.

'Mum!' She barely felt Harley press himself against her. 'You have to get up!'

Elsa jerked awake. The jets – the fighter planes would be here any second. She had to get them all out, but didn't know if she had any strength left to even move. Lifting her head would be a start.

'I'm okay,' she said, rolling over onto her elbows.

'Mum, please,' he said.

'I'm sorry.' The words didn't seem like enough. Her kids

had just watched their mum and dad fight to the death; Harley and... Elsa squinted around the reception.

'Your sister,' she said. 'Where's India?'

'The lady took her!' Harley was in tears. 'She's got India!'

Elsa could still just about hear the *thwap thwap thwap* of helicopter rotors outside, the roar of the engine, and she staggered to her feet.

Grabbing her son's hand, she stumbled outside, finding a last drop of adrenaline to run onto the lawn. Sitting in the pilot seat of the helicopter was Camille – with India beside her.

Camille grinned at Elsa as the helicopter lifted off the grass. Elsa let go of Harley and raced towards it as fast as she could, but it had already soared twenty feet into the sky. Standing in the downdraught, Elsa screamed in frustration as she watched the vehicle disappear behind the treetops.

But she didn't have time to think about what to do next because she heard a faint ripple of sound, barely a hum.

'Harley!' She ran to her son. 'Quick!'

She pulled him behind her, practically wrenching his arm out of the socket, as the tiny specks of the fighter planes tore almost soundlessly through the distant cloud.

'Run!' They raced towards the trees. 'Keep going!'

As her son raced into the woods, Elsa stopped briefly to look back over her shoulder. Arkady and Noah had managed to prise one of the wooden boards off a window in the biolab room, but it wasn't enough. She saw the panic on their faces as they saw her sprint away and realized what was happening.

She followed her son into the trees, stumbling over the uneven ground, yelling at him to keep running.

'Here!' she shouted.

Elsa pulled Harley to the ground behind a fallen tree trunk, pressed him into the depressed pit below it and fell on top of him as the fighters flew directly overhead. It was only after they had disappeared behind the house that the sonic boom of the jets cracked the sky.

Moments later she heard two – three – four explosions, as the mansion was engulfed in a massive fireball. The temperature at the heart of the inferno reached a thousand degrees in an instant. Concrete and glass and wood shot into the sky and across the lawn as the building was destroyed. The noise was deafening; the carnage total.

Slabs of concrete and glass and steel fell through the trees, which bent against the blast. Elsa spread herself across Harley, trying to keep him safe. She heard branches snap and shatter and fall. Jagged metal and glass thwapped down all around them, spinning fragments of brick and stone, each one a deadly missile, embedding into trunks, smashing into the ground. A solid wall of smoke a hundred feet high pulsed into the woods, drifting through the trees.

Finally, when she was sure no more flying debris was going to slice off the top of her skull, Elsa dared to peer over the top of the trunk. The destroyed mansion, now barely a heap of bricks, was obscured in a thick blanket of smoke and dust. There were fires everywhere, and some of the trees were alight. Masonry and rubble covered the lawn.

The biolab and its contents had been completely consumed in the firestorm. Trapped inside, Arkady and Noah hadn't stood a chance.

She saw, then heard, the jets screech back across the sky, imagined the pilots inside confirming the completion of the mission. They flew off into the distance, returning to whichever RAF base they had come from.

Ground vehicles would be arriving next, from the military and emergency services; CBRN specialists equipped to deal with chemical and biological disaster.

But Elsa was surprised to hear another sound. A helicopter flew over the trees and hovered over the lawn, jerking left and right as the pilot tried to find a space to land among all the devastation. When it finally came down, causing smoke to billow frenziedly this way and that, Elsa was shocked to see Saint at the controls.

She ran over and opened the passenger-side door.

'I didn't know you could fly!'

'Man of many talents, me.' He nodded grimly at the graphite case beside him. 'There's only one vial of the virus, the other is missing.'

'It's not over,' Elsa shouted over the roar of the rotors. She remembered Camille had escorted Kieron out of the biolab room; had somehow got her hands on one of the vials then. 'I think Camille's got it, and she's taken India.'

Saint pulled a hand down his weary face. 'I never took to that woman.'

He was pale and sweating; a bloody stain spread across the top of his bodywarmer. He didn't look like he could even stay conscious, let alone pilot a helicopter.

'You can't fly,' she said.

'Can you?' he asked, and Elsa shook her head. 'Then don't be daft, I've got this.'

Elsa kneeled down in front of Harley. Behind him, emergency vehicles approached the devastated building.

He knew what she was thinking. 'Please don't go.'

'I'm going to get your sister,' she told him. 'The police will keep you safe till...' She felt a lump in her throat. 'I'm bringing India back.'

'I don't want you to go...' His eyes were full of tears. 'But please find her.'

She kissed him on the forehead. 'I promise, now run to the police. You'll be safe with them. I'll watch you all the way.'

He started to go.

'Harley, wait.' She gave him the graphite case. 'Give this to them, tell them to be very careful with it.'

Harley ran around the edge of the lawn, where twisted girders of hot steel weren't likely to slice his leg off. The case banged against his knees, and Elsa shouted anxiously, 'Lift it high!'

As soon as one of the figures in chem-bio suits reached her son, Elsa climbed into the helicopter.

'Where we going?' Saint asked.

She picked up the radio mic on the helicopter's dashboard to call the SIS guy, Plowright.

'India still has the tracker,' she said. 'We can find out.'

50

'There!' Elsa pointed, as the helicopter flew over St James's Park.

In Trafalgar Square, a crowd had gathered. A stage was erected on one side of the space and the area was packed with hundreds of people.

'We can't land there,' Saint said over the headset mic. 'I ain't that drunk!'

'Get as close to the edge of the park as you can.'

She hoped Plowright had organized emergency clearance for them to land so near Downing Street. Other helicopters had escorted them across the city, keeping a distance. Saint did a spot turn behind the Old Admiralty Building, bringing the bird down hard among a collapsing nest of deckchairs.

'Keep your head down,' he shouted as Elsa tore off her headset and flung open the passenger door, the blades spinning at a furious 500 rpm above her head.

He watched her run from the park, killed the ignition, and slumped back in his seat.

Feeling pain flood into his wounded shoulder, he muttered to nobody in particular, 'I might black out now.'

Elsa ran up The Mall towards Trafalgar Square. Groups of people – families and friends, tourists and day trippers – were walking to the event, some kind of gig in aid of an environmental group. The thud of amplified bass got louder as she ran towards it. With public safety a priority at mass events in heightened times, nobody took any notice of the emergency vehicles parked at a discreet distance along Whitehall or the armed officers walking at the edge of the square.

Someone on stage started telling jokes to a roar of happy recognition from the crowd. The comedian's voice carried across the square, with Nelson's Column towering in the middle, its famous lion statues, and the roads that surrounded it to the east and south cleared of traffic and filled with people arriving to join the fun.

Elsa ran towards the top of Whitehall, where Nigel Plowright stood discussing the situation with half a dozen secret service types.

'We shut it down, we have no choice,' said someone, chopping the air for emphasis.

'We'd have to get authorization from a Gold leader,' said a suit from SO15, the Met's Counter-Terrorism Command. 'They'll have to be brought up to date quickly and make the decision.'

Tempers were flaring. 'Fuck the Gold leader, we have to do it now.'

'As soon as we start moving people away, she'll release the virus,' Plowright interjected, as he simultaneously tried to hold a phone conversation. Seeing Elsa approach, he said into his mobile, 'Got to go, Justine, keep the line clear at your end.'

He gestured at the plain-clothes police officer who moved to intercept her. 'She's with me.'

Elsa nodded at the concert. 'What is this?'

'Some kind of benefit gig for a charity, would you believe?'

She could well believe it. Carragher knew what he was doing. Hundreds of people had already gathered in the square; there were thousands more in the surrounding streets. If the pathogen was released, it would spread quickly among the crowd, many of whom were tourists. They'd catch buses and Tubes across the city, drive to different parts of the country; fly home on packed planes across the world. The incubation period of the virus was hours, so thousands of contagious people would already be far away by the time the symptoms began to manifest. They would spread the deadly virus everywhere they went.

'Where are they?' Elsa scanned the crowd anxiously, trying to find Camille and her daughter.

'Over by the fountain,' Plowright pointed. 'At eleven o'clock.'

She saw Camille holding India tightly by one hand. At a cursory glance, you'd think they were just joining the fun.

Elsa walked across the road towards the square. Camille saw her, and their eyes met. She opened the fingers of her free hand to reveal the vial in her palm. The smile on Camille's face was ghastly as she told India that her mother was close. India instinctively tried to go to her, but Camille wrenched her back. Elsa felt a jolt of fright – and rage.

Tears sprang in her eyes, she couldn't breathe, her chest felt like it was going to explode with fury, but there was nothing she could do except dig her nails deep into her own palms. If she tried to rush her, Camille would dash the vial to the pavement before she got close, and India would be infected. Her daughter would die an agonizing death, along with thousands of others.

Trying not to transmit her own terror to her daughter, Elsa smiled with a confidence she didn't feel. *Don't be scared, I'm here. Everything's going to be okay.*

Plowright joined Elsa at the edge of the crowd, which laughed and cheered at the comedian.

'We have to get these people out of here,' Elsa said.

'If we charge in with guns and bullhorns, the crowd will panic and run in every direction. Even if Camille doesn't smash the vial, there's every chance it'll be knocked out of her hand in the surge, and then it'll all be over. Not only that, it's a free charity concert for an environmental cause so there's a lot of politicized people here – we'll have a riot on our hands, too. We're talking to the organizers about getting the concert stopped, we'll blame a gas leak, but goodness knows when that will happen.'

If Camille dropped the vial, it would be impossible to force so many people into quarantine, and there was no way to seal off all the surrounding streets. In any case, the virus would be airborne and could spread in any direction.

'Camille realized very quickly that she's surrounded, and it's made her very jumpy. I managed to get close enough to speak to her, and she made it clear that if we go anywhere near her, or even attempt to evacuate the area, she'll smash the vial. And if we bring her down by sniper…' Plowright's gaze lifted to the tall buildings in his sightline. 'It'll break anyway. She's holding all the aces. What I don't understand is why she hasn't done it already.'

'She'll release the virus soon,' Elsa said.

'How can you be sure?'

'Because she's been waiting for me to arrive. She wants

to see me suffer, and to know that India will be the first to be infected.'

'Why?'

'Because she hates me. The only question is how much time we've got.'

Elsa saw uniforms moving on each side of the square. More marked and unmarked emergency vehicles pulled up along Whitehall to the south. Helicopters flew high above, their powerful cameras trained on Camille and the crowd. The increased presence made a segment of the crowd, antagonistic to the police and the establishment, restless.

There would be marksmen on roofs, more moving into positions in surrounding buildings, trying to find the clearest possible shot of Camille. In the tangle of side streets, inside unmarked vans and lorries, infectious disease specialists were climbing into full PPE.

Less than half a mile away, the prime minister and other high-ranking government officials had already been quietly evacuated from nearby Downing Street, and from Parliament.

Elsa didn't care about any of that. The pain at seeing her daughter so scared and bewildered gnawed at her. But she had to control her rage and fear. The fear was always there, whether she chose to acknowledge it or not; it was the bass note emotion on which all her survival skills and instincts had been built. Elsa had learned to control the thrumming fear inside of her, to harness its energy. If she let it overwhelm her, she was finished.

But this time she felt the fear surge. India was in terrible danger, and Elsa was powerless.

'Let me talk to her.'

'You just said she hates you.' Plowright glanced at a pair of men in deep discussion at the top of Whitehall. 'The professional negotiators have arrived.'

'The only reason she hasn't released the virus already is because she wants to speak to me.'

'I don't recommend it.' Plowright shook his head. 'We have people who—'

The glare she gave him was so contemptuous that he flinched. 'I don't care what you think.'

Plowright contemplated Elsa. By all accounts, she was a blunt instrument, bloody-minded, antagonistic and insensitive, the last person you'd want blundering into a delicate situation such as this, with the world balanced precariously on the edge of an apocalyptic precipice. That wasn't even taking into account the bad blood between her and the embittered party with the deadly infectious agent in a fragile glass vial. But maybe Elsa would be able to distract Camille for a few more minutes, until he could come up with a better plan.

'How long would it take to get here from Vauxhall Cross?' she asked.

'We'd have to get a helicopter there. Maybe...' Plowright thought about it. 'Fifteen or twenty minutes.'

She told him her idea and he looked at her with incredulity. He didn't think it was possible to add any more fuel to the wildfire of insanity currently raging out of control, but Elsa had proved him wrong.

'Absolutely not,' he told her. 'We'll wait for a clear shot. If we time it right—'

'Camille's too clever to allow you to take her down and

you know it,' she said. 'She'll stay hidden in the crowd, and she'll spot any secret service agents who attempt to get near her. The moment she feels threatened, she'll release the virus.'

Plowright exhaled slowly. Up on the stage, the comedian was introducing the next musical act; the jarring chords of an electric guitar jangled across the excited crowd.

'Okay,' he told Elsa. 'Keep her talking for as long as you can.'

'Are you going to kill me, too, is that still the plan?' she asked. 'After all, the data is still inside of me.'

'Let's just cross that bridge *if* we get to it.'

Then he strode back across the road, calling Justine Vydelingum on his phone, to tell her to get a helicopter to Vauxhall Cross straight away.

Elsa tried to locate Camille at the side of the fountain, but her heart leaped when she couldn't see her. She pushed into the crowd, just as the music on stage cut out in the middle of a chord.

'Bear with us, guys,' said the lead singer on stage, using a megaphone someone handed him. 'We're having a few technical difficulties.'

Elsa frantically pushed through the restless crowd, trying to find Camille and India.

Her heart lurched when she saw the rag doll on the floor, where it had fallen out of India's pocket, getting trampled beneath the feet of the crowd. If Camille and India had somehow slipped away from the concert, she'd never find them without the tracker.

'Watch where're you going!' complained one guy as she elbowed past. Turning in circles, looking over the heads of the people surrounding her on every side, she told herself to stay calm – but she couldn't see her daughter, she couldn't find India.

Then she glimpsed familiar blonde hair, a bladed fringe. Elsa forced her way towards it. Camille was threading her way through thick clumps of people, ensuring that marksmen positioned on every side of the square couldn't get a clear shot.

When Elsa got to her, she was standing near one of the lions on the north side. India once again tried to get to her mother, but Camille kept a tight hold on her. Elsa stopped far enough away for people to walk between them, oblivious to the danger they were in.

'We thought you'd never get here,' Camille said, smiling. 'We've come a long way and we're tired.'

'Are you okay?' Elsa asked India. 'Has she hurt you?'

'I wouldn't do that.' Camille looked offended. 'I wouldn't hurt a little girl, not like that. People who don't have kids – not all of us are monsters. Me and Steve talked about having a family. Once upon a time, I really wanted children, but he told me that it was out of the question. He'd say, *do you really want to bring up children in the world we're about to unleash, Camille?* He was adamant about it!'

Camille stroked India's forehead and hair with the clammy hand that held the vial, the glass moving back and forth in front of her face.

'But it was okay for him, Elsa, because he already had kids. Lovable Harley and beautiful India.' Camille pulled India close and spoke into her ear. 'You are such a pretty girl, my darling. He never spoke about them, not to me, but I knew he thought about them *all* the time. I suspected he was watching them, and watching you, Elsa, and that if push came to shove, he'd rather be with them than me. Because with Carragher it's always been about his precious legacy.' Her face twisted in misery. 'I knew deep down he never loved me.'

'He was using you, Camille,' said Elsa gently. 'Just like he used me. But if this is all about getting revenge, you don't have to worry about Steve any more. He's dead.'

'Good for you.' Camille wiped away tears with the back of the hand that held the vial. 'I knew you'd kill him, because you've always been his weak spot.'

When Elsa stepped forward, Camille held the vial over her head. 'Step back!'

'Come on, Camille.' Elsa held out her hands. 'You've had your revenge – he's dead, it's over.'

'But I haven't had my revenge against *you*,' spat Camille. 'Whatever he felt for me, I always loved him, Elsa, and I still do. So I'm going to finish what he started. It's just ironic that his precious little India is going to die along with the both of us.'

'You're going to kill thousands of people to get revenge on me? Kind of OTT, Cam.'

India watched the vial that Camille kept moving about in front of her. Elsa's daughter was a fighter, she was born with the same crazy will of all the Zeros, and Elsa knew that if she got the chance, she'd escape.

But Camille would hurl the vial. India wouldn't make it. None of them would.

'Tell you what, put that thing down and kill me,' Elsa said. 'Just... *please*, let India go.'

'I don't think so.' Camille made a face. 'The moment I put the vial down, they'll shoot me.'

'Don't do this, Camille.' Out of ideas, Elsa felt her chest clench with despair. 'You'll kill tens of thousands.'

'Millions.'

'Tell me what you want.'

Camille spoke with a quiet loathing. 'I want you to know, in the time it takes for you to die, that your daughter is also suffering. That she is dying an agonizing death.' She snarled at Elsa. '*That*'s what I want.'

The crowd in front of the stage was heckling. A number of activists, irritated by the presence of armed police and the helicopters and drones criss-crossing the sky, had started to throw bottles and cans. At the edges of the square, concert-goers confronted police. The commotion rippled across the crowd towards them.

Someone shoved past Camille, jogging her arm, and Elsa's heart leaped into her mouth. It was obvious Camille felt vulnerable in the disintegrating crowd. They were close to the steps on the north side of the square, leading up to the National Gallery, and she pulled India behind her.

'We're going now, Elsa. We won't meet again.'

'Camille,' said Elsa. 'Don't—'

She pointed at the gallery. 'If anybody attempts to follow me inside, if I see any secret service people, I'll drop the vial.'

There was this urgent look Elsa sometimes gave Harley and India when she was in a hurry, when they had to leave for school or get something done, but instead they were pissing around: *be ready*, it said. She gave that same look to India as she was dragged away. Elsa hoped India had seen it, hoped she understood.

Be ready.

By going into the National Galley, Camille was giving them a hideous choice. They could wait till she re-emerged and try to start negotiations – Elsa knew Camille's mind was already made up, she fully intended to release the virus – or they could seal off all the exits, trapping her inside and mitigating the worst effects of the virus.

But they would also be sacrificing the lives of everyone in the gallery. Several hundred men, women and children, India among them.

'I'll be watching,' Camille told Elsa. 'The moment I see anybody come inside, or if the doors close, I will release hell on earth.'

She walked up the steps leading to the National Gallery.

51

Upset at again being separated from her mother, the girl resisted when Camille forced her up the steps. *This must be what it's like to be a parent*, she thought. To get anything done, you had to impose your will on theirs. God knows how anyone put up with it, year in, year out. Camille was tired already of the wretched kid and swung India around to face her.

'You – will – *stop*!' she roared. The girl's eyes filled with tears, but her lips were pressed tightly together in defiance.

Camille dragged India towards the entrance. Armed men at the edge of the square followed as she climbed the steps, careful to stay close to other people.

It took concentration and focus to make sure she wasn't about to get jumped, and with the atmosphere in the square disintegrating, she needed somewhere she could control the situation for just another few minutes… then she would do it, and change history forever.

SIS wouldn't be able to take command of the camera feeds in the National Gallery for a few minutes. Once inside, she'd be able to make sure nobody came in. If she saw any suspicious activity outside the doors, or if any of the entrances and exits were sealed – as soon as they tried to shut down the gallery – she would smash the vial.

If she saw even a glimpse of Elsa fucking Zero, she would smash the vial.

'I'm tired,' whined the girl.

'Me too,' Camille said, as they headed into the foyer. 'Let's sit down.'

They sat on one of the benches in the middle of the large ground-floor space, surrounded by works of art that she barely registered. She pulled the girl closer to her. The thin fogged glass of the vial felt slippery in her sweaty hand. When a woman noted the odd tension between her and the girl, Camille gave her an unfriendly smile. With her pale, perspiring face and haunted expression, she looked like a mother at the end of her tether.

'Mum's going to come and get you in a minute,' India told her. Camille laughed sourly; she had to admit the girl had spirit.

'She isn't going to save you, you're going to die, along with me and all these other people.' When tears fell down the girl's cheeks, Camille felt a bitter satisfaction. 'Cry like a baby, then. Elsa doesn't care about you. If she did, she would never have let me come in here.'

Camille tensed when she glimpsed someone in a peaked cap at one of the main doors. But it was one of the gallery guards giving directions, not a police officer stealthily trying to direct people out of the building.

'You'll see...' India gave her the same disdainful look Camille had seen in her mother.

'I'm not scared of little girls,' Camille sneered.

Camille decided they were just killing time, putting off the inevitable. It was a mistake to come inside, she should have just dashed the vial at Elsa's feet earlier. She'd head outside, stand at the top of the steps overlooking the square and just do it, in full view of the surging crowd and impotent police. Her sacrifice would be a portent of the kind of world – of chaos, conflict and disease – that the virus would herald.

Carragher had wanted the pathogen to create a new world eventually – a better world – but Camille didn't care about that any more. She dragged the girl to her feet, and pulled her back towards the entrance.

'Watch where you're going!' complained one guy when they bumped shoulders. Camille gave him a sick smile. He didn't know how close he was to an agonizing death.

The gallery was packed with people, many of whom had come inside to escape the disturbance outside. Paranoid, suspicious, Camille darted looks everywhere. Watching for a furtive glance in her direction, or someone pushing towards her in the crowd.

She knew exactly the type to look for, because she'd known those people all her life: the SIS agents, the police, special forces and other military men and women. There wasn't a hope in hell any of them would be able to get within six feet of her. But she was careful, and blinking away the sweat from her eyes, she instinctively analysed the people around her: too young, too unfit, too short.

A six-foot man with a buzz cut came striding towards her and she stopped dead, gripping the vial almost to the point where it would shatter, but his eyes were focused on someone behind her; he raised a hand in greeting and headed past her, oblivious.

She glimpsed the crowd trouble escalating outside. She'd throw the vial into the throng, nobody would even see where it landed, or care what it contained, and in a few short hours it would all be over. The contagion would spread inexorably among the population, hospitals would begin to fill with the dying, and the mortality rate would climb...

It seemed somehow fitting that the world would be transformed so close to this place of culture, with its walls of classical art celebrating the beauty of civilization.

Camille walked steadily towards the front doors, which still hadn't closed. The authorities had made their choice. They weren't going to lock down the building, hoping that she would reappear outside and they could begin negotiations.

But Carragher was gone, her treacherous husband was dead, and all that remained for her to do now was to honour his great project – and kill one of his precious fucking kids at the same time.

Camille instinctively stopped in her tracks when a young boy raced in front of her. His flustered mother grabbed him and swept him into her arms.

'I'm so sorry,' she told Camille, and glanced at India. 'You've got the right idea, keeping a tight hold of yours!'

It occurred to Camille that an even better idea would be to drop the vial right there in the foyer and fire her handgun into the crowd, in case armed officers were hidden behind the columns outside the building. People would flee in panic to the exits, and keep running. She'd follow them out, firing more shots, causing even more turmoil and panic in the already turbulent crowd. She'd be shot and killed – which would certainly be a better way to die than succumbing to the coming plague.

It was time. Her journey was over.

Camille unzipped her jacket, ready to take the handgun from her belt.

'Do keep up!' She vaguely heard the voice of an elderly man. 'I want to buy a couple of postcards.'

'I'm coming,' complained his wife. 'There's no hurry. It's always rush, rush, rush with you.'

Heads lowered as they bickered intensely, the pensioners walked slap-bang into Camille.

'Excuse me, can we get past?' the old woman snapped.

'So sorry about my wife.' The man looked mortified. Camille reached for the gun, but was shocked to discover it gone.

Then she felt a sharp stab in the wrist of her hand that held the girl, making her fingers flex.

Camille's immediate reaction was to drop the vial – but it wasn't in her hand.

Greta Zero thrust the bottle into the hands of the little girl and told her, 'Go, child!'

And then India was off and running. Camille roared with shock and rage. Shoving past them, she raced after the little girl, who held the vial in both hands.

Behind her, Howard said into the earpiece disguised as a hearing aid, 'She's got it!'

SIS agents poured into the gallery. Standing hidden to the side of the main entrance, Elsa sprinted in.

India was small and agile and zigzagged around the legs of the visitors in the gallery, but Camille was fast and full of rage and focus, and flew through the crowd, sending people flying to the left and right, bearing down fast on the girl.

India stumbled; the vial jumped out of her grasp – for one long moment she saw it fly in front of her eyes – but she skidded onto her knees, cupping her palms, and it fell back into her hands.

Behind her, Camille screamed in fury. There was noise and commotion as all the agents shouted for everyone to *Get Down! Down on the floor!* so they could get a clear shot at her. But, instead, the panicked crowd ran in front of the raised weapons.

And by the time India managed to get to her feet, Camille was almost on her. Reaching out to grab her. All she had to do was knock the vial from the girl's small hands, and it would all be over.

Camille leaped.

And was knocked sideways when Elsa smashed into her in mid-air. The two women rolled across the ground. Camille landed on her back with Elsa above her. Elsa's forearm clamped down hard into her throat, snapping her head back onto the floor.

Within a moment, Camille was staring up at the barrels of the half-dozen pistols pointed at her.

'Stay down, Camille!' All Elsa's instincts screamed at her to break her neck, kill her then and there, but instead she took a deep breath and whispered gently into her ear. 'Just stay down.'

'May I...' Nigel Plowright walked into the gallery to kneel in front of India, as a protective circle of armed police and SIS agents surrounded them. 'May I take that from you?'

India looked over quickly at Elsa, who nodded, and offered him the vial containing the virus.

'Careful now,' Plowright told her, because her small hands started trembling.

The glass felt damp and slippery when Plowright took it and placed it with the utmost care in a container held by a man wearing neoprene gloves.

Only when the lid was closed and sealed, and the container taken away, did he exhale. His neck and shoulders were drenched in sweat.

'You could have told me you were going to intercept the target,' Howard complained to Greta as she handed Camille Archard's disassembled handgun to an agent. 'Communication is key, Greta.'

'She was about to drop the vial,' Greta said in irritation. 'That was obvious, even with my eyes.'

'I thought we might get some postcards while we're here. You know how I love Titian.'

'You don't think the gift shop will currently be open, do you?' said Greta. 'Honestly, Howard, I wonder about your state of mind sometimes.'

'You're alive, then,' Howard said, when Elsa came over. 'We were beginning to wonder whether we would be stuck with those children forever.'

'I told you to keep them safe,' Elsa snapped, and Greta and Howard bristled.

'We did our best,' said Howard in annoyance. 'And at our age—'

'Thank you.' Elsa's throat clogged with gratitude. Her obvious emotion made her parents uncomfortable. 'For everything.'

'Just don't ask us again,' Howard said. 'The next time will finish us off for good.'

'It was an imposition at first, but I must admit...'

Intrigued, Elsa waited to hear what Greta was going to say. 'It was a pleasure to have the children come and stay.'

'Yes,' agreed Howard. 'Despite glaring lapses of behaviour from time to time, they are mostly nice children.'

'Perhaps...' Greta's eyes lifted to Elsa's. 'If you agree, we could see them again.'

Her parents peered at her steadily, their faces giving nothing away.

'Yeah.' Elsa briskly smudged a tear from her eye. 'I'm sure we can work something out.'

'When is the debrief?' asked Howard, quickly changing the subject. 'I'm sure they'll want to include us.'

'If I disappear,' Elsa told her parents grimly as Nigel Plowright came over, 'tell the world what's happened here, tell everyone.'

'Actually, I was going to suggest a coffee and a bite to eat,' said Plowright. 'It'll only be in the back of a van, I'm afraid. But then we can talk about having you locked away, if you absolutely insist upon it.'

'My gosh, what a day it's been,' Howard said. 'Come on, Greta, let's see if we can get those postcards.'

'Oh, for goodness' sake,' Greta said, and followed him.

Howard and Greta exited via the gift shop.

Camille's eyes blazed with hatred for Elsa as she was marched out of the building.

'What will happen to her?'

Plowright thought about it. 'There'll be due process, of course. In a fashion. And then she'll spend the rest of her days imprisoned somewhere very secure. I don't know where, the decision will be out of my hands.'

'I can't run any more,' Elsa told him.

He nodded. 'We're putting the word out to the other agencies that the threat, in which you were *wrongly* implicated, has been neutralized.'

'But the data encoded in my cells…'

'There are ways and means to deal with that,' he assured her. 'Most probably.'

India had been given an examination by a biological containment team and now she came running over to her mother.

Elsa lifted her into her arms and held her tight. Promised her daughter again and again that she was safe, and told her how much she loved her and Harley, and that nobody would ever harm them again.

Not now, not ever.

52

'Come on, Dougie!' Thumb poised over the stopwatch button, Elsa encouraged him to pick himself up.

Lumbering unsteadily to his feet, he sopped with sweat. It dripped from his nose and chin, and stained the chest and spine of his workout top. Gasping for breath, his face scarlet, you'd think he'd just completed an ultra-marathon, not just completed a second burpee.

It was Elsa's own fault. In the heat of the moment, she'd promised him free lessons, but never imagined he'd take her up on the offer, not after he had almost been killed by Saint and a pair of assassins. But Dougie Heston never looked a gift horse in the mouth.

'Can't...' He dropped to his knees on the garden decking and keeled forward onto his stomach. 'Can't do it!'

'You can!' Elsa barked at the back of his head. 'Just another eight to go!'

He rolled over, his pleading look a mixture of terror and desire. His gaze dropped inevitably to her long Lycra-clad legs.

Sitting inside, Dougie's wife, Roberta, watched sourly over a glass of wine. Refusing the offer of free training sessions, she had done everything in her power to convince

Dougie not to let Elsa visit their new Richmond home; a perfectly reasonable attitude, considering how she had killed two people in their former house.

Dougie groaned. 'Please, no more.'

Months after an apocalyptic plague virus had almost been released in central London, Elsa was back in the routine of her old life; working hard to rebuild her client base. But something inside of her had shifted in ways she couldn't explain.

She was struggling to engage with her business. The drive and focus she had previously poured into it was missing. The enjoyment she got from working with her clients, on training and diet plans, setting fitness levels and chasing goals, just wasn't there.

She couldn't wait to see her kids at the end of the day, of course. But later that evening she had accounts to do, and tomorrow there was a school event to attend; she'd had more than enough of the cliquey, self-important mums who gave her the evil eye across the playground.

Dougie finally stood to lift his arms to the sky, his top rising up over his bulging, hairy stomach. Elsa paused the stopwatch; there was no point in timing his efforts.

'Let's go again, just seven more,' she said with a weary sigh.

Elsa had undergone a gene therapy process which targeted the memory cells in her bloodstream containing the data and caused apoptosis: the cells self-destructed. Her DNA was now clear of the information encoded into it, she'd been assured, although she would continue to have regular checks for the rest of her life.

She couldn't help but wonder what happened to the vials

that contained the virus, or the samples of her blood taken at a military hospital.

'Tell me the data has been destroyed,' Elsa demanded of Nigel Plowright one night on the phone. 'That it hasn't been kept.'

There was a long silence on the line. They both knew that the vials had probably been taken to the MoD's Defence Science and Technology Laboratory at Porton Down, or somewhere even more top secret than that, because there were always more Top Secret places. The UK had announced decades ago that it had destroyed its stock of biological weapons, but Elsa suspected there were wheels within wheels. She couldn't be sure, nobody could.

'I can't assure you of that,' Plowright said finally. 'Because if that's what was intended, the likes of me wouldn't be told.'

There was nothing she could do about it, in any case. The main thing was that her blood cells were clear. If someone tried to kill her again, it wouldn't be because of that.

'Please.' Dropping to his knees, Dougie slapped the exercise mat with an open palm. 'No more!'

'You're going to kill yourself,' Roberta shouted from inside the house. 'If that woman doesn't kill you first.'

Roberta, who was a bag of nerves whenever Elsa was at the house, stood suddenly and went to the front window.

'Dougie...' she called in a voice trembling with worry. 'Someone's pulled up outside.'

Looking for an excuse to stop, Dougie insisted on going to look, and Elsa joined him.

A long limousine with tinted windows was parked on the street.

'You organize a hen night, Roberta?' Elsa tried to joke, but she could see how worried the Hestons were.

'This is you,' Roberta hissed at her. 'It's all your doing!'

'Come away from the window,' Dougie told his wife, and they both stepped back, imagining assassins and murderers rushing up the drive.

Elsa had no idea who was in the car, or why it was parked out front. 'Let me handle this.'

'What did I tell you about letting that woman back into our house?' Roberta told her husband scathingly as Elsa went outside.

Halfway down the front garden, she stopped. As the limo idled at the kerb, the nearside back window lowered smoothly, and a hand with silver nails tapped against the shiny metal of the door.

A voice came from the dark interior. 'A situation has arisen, Elsa, and we're urgently in need of your skills and experience.'

'You're wasting your time.'

'Are you sure?' said Mrs Krystahl. 'I'm a good judge of character, and I really don't I think I am.'

The back door of the limo swung open.

It would be crazy to climb inside. Not long ago, Elsa had been plunged into a storm of life-or-death events: placed in mortal danger, along with her children. She'd been throttled, shot, stabbed, skewered, drowned, and nearly exposed to a deadly virus.

But Elsa Zero had finally left behind her old life, with its constant shadow of violent death. She was a single mother with responsibilities. She had her life back, her own little house, a nine-to-five business; even some semblance of a relationship with her parents.

It would be crazy to get into the back of that vehicle and put it all at risk once again.

Absolutely insane.

Meanwhile, across the city…

Dr Christian Vaida began to reconstruct the aorta of his young patient.

He'd already removed the diseased and dilated aortic root, leaving the valve crumpled in a heap, and now had to replace it with a flexible tube made of woven Dacron, carefully stitch the valve, and plumb in the coronary arteries.

It was a lot of work, and had to be done quickly or the heart, which had already been deprived of blood and oxygen for an hour, may never work again. Speed, concentration and precision were all absolutely essential.

The five-hour heart operation underway in one of the biggest hospitals in the city was notoriously complex, and Vaida was one of the few cardiothoracic surgeons in the country with the necessary skill and experience to steer it to a successful conclusion. The patient suffered from a rare connective tissue disorder called Loeys-Dietz syndrome, in which the aortic root enlarged under relentless blood pressure, threatening to rupture.

But on this occasion Vaida felt under an even more intense pressure, because the patient on the operating table was his nineteen-year-old godson.

Vaida had known Ben since he was born; had held him as a tiny baby, gone to his birthday parties, and encouraged the clever young man in his ambition to study medicine. Ben was as dear to Vaida as if he were his own son.

The boy's father was one of Vaida's oldest friends, and when his condition was diagnosed, the family insisted immediately that Vaida perform the operation; they would trust nobody else to do it.

Vaida tried to clear his mind and do what he did best. He'd made countless life-or-death decisions in circumstances just like this, but would never forgive himself if something happened to the boy.

He began the delicate work of re-implanting Ben's aortic valve. There was no room for error: the slightest misalignment and the valve would not function, leading to catastrophic heart failure.

Working with a rock-steady hand, anticipating every subsequent step of the operation and clearly communicating with his team, Vaida was in total control. The boy was in the safest hands possible.

Ben had holidayed with the surgeon's own family numerous times – Vaida remembered one memorable trip to the Pyrenees – and he made a vow to himself that when his godson was back on his feet, they would go again.

Vaida and his team worked in absolute silence. Because Ben's heart had stopped, there was no intrusive beeping monitor, and no hissing ventilator sound because his lungs had been switched off.

Nearly halfway to completing the valve procedure, Vaida told the scrub nurse, 'We'll need a couple of 5/0 prolene sutures for the next stage.'

But as he spoke, Vaida was shocked to feel a faint buzz from the back pocket of his scrub trousers. It caused his hand to do something it hadn't done in twenty years of surgery – it trembled.

The phone he'd carried with him everywhere, and which always remained hidden in a pocket, and in a drawer at his bedside when he slept, had finally rung.

After all these years, Vaida had almost convinced himself, had fervently hoped, that it never would. But it had – and it couldn't have happened at a worse moment.

His breathing became heavy, laboured. He felt sick, because he knew what he had to do.

'Christian?' asked one of his ten-strong operating team, and he looked up to see everyone in the theatre staring at him. They all heard the phone now, buzzing in his pocket; surprisingly loud in the shocked silence.

Vaida's instructions had been clear: he must answer it immediately. And as soon as he did, his life as he knew it – his marriage, his career, his happy life with his family – would come to an end.

The surgeon took one last brief look at the unconscious body of his godson, fighting for life on the operating table, critical parts of his heart not yet reassembled, and stepped away.

To everyone's horror, Vaida walked out of the theatre, leaving Ben suspended precariously between life and death.

Ignoring the clamour and alarm behind him, he pushed through the swing doors into the corridor of the theatre suite. Lowering his surgical mask, Vaida took out the phone, which buzzed patiently.

The screen display showed 'unknown caller'. Vaida connected the call, placed the phone to his ear.

'Zero Day is here,' he was told.

'Yes,' he said, in a voice barely a whisper.

'You know what you have to do.'

The caller disconnected.

Vaida dropped the phone in a yellow box of used sharps that he knew would end up in the incinerator, and made his way to his office, stripping off his theatre cap and mask and dropping his gloves and gown as he walked.

Locking the office door behind him, he opened the bottom drawer of his desk, took out the many files and papers he had dumped there, and lifted the false bottom to reveal the secret compartment beneath.

Hidden there was a black P365X SIG Sauer handgun, a slim suppressor, and a fifteen-round magazine, all of which he put in his briefcase.

He hadn't even changed out of his scrubs when he left the hospital minutes later, never to return.

One life was over...

His devoted wife of ten years, the three children he loved so much, his beautiful house and holiday home on the Algarve, the brilliant career he'd carved out for himself...

All of it gone for good.

Already, Vaida felt like he had woken from a dream. His new life had begun.

How long he had left, he had no idea.

Acknowledgements

I'm so pleased you read *Zero Kill*. If you enjoyed it, please consider leaving a rating or review; it really does help people find the book.

As usual, there are plenty of lovely and talented people who helped in the writing of it. My thanks to virologist Sir John Skehel, bioengineers Dr Jagroop Pandhal and Prof Ben Almquist, Liz Waterman, Caroline Maston, Cameron Hough, pilot Rory Auskerry, computer guys Graham Beale and Adrian Scottow, the mighty John Rickards for editorial advice, and his knowledge of a whole range of useful shit, and cardiac surgeon and author Samer Nashef. Michael Gradwell, Kevin Horn and Jason Eddings have patiently allowed me to plunder their emergency services expertise for six books now – time flies!

Thanks as usual to my agent at the Ampersand Agency, Jamie Cowen, who joined me on a rollercoaster ride of highs and lows during the unusual writing experience of *Zero Kill*, and I'm grateful to Book-To-Screen Agent Hannah Weatherill, at Northbank Talent Management.

They're a hugely talented and dedicated bunch at my publisher, Head of Zeus. I'm talking about editor Bethan Jones, and Laura Palmer, Peyton Stableford, Polly Grice, Ben

Prior, Andrew Knowles, Christian Duck, Dan Groenewald, Jenni Davis, Nicola Bigwood, and Nikky Ward.

Much love as always to Fiona and Archie, who put up with me on a daily basis. And big cuddles to my four-legged work associates Jason and Gracie, who kept me company and ate all the treats, every last one.

About the Author

M.K. HILL was a journalist and an award-winning music radio producer before becoming a full-time writer. He's written the Sasha Dawson series, Ray Drake series and the highly acclaimed psychological thriller *One Bad Thing*. He lives in London. Visit him at www.mkhill.uk.